Cherokee Rock

DRT&O'iSOⅣYAJE₺ϷAⱶⲄꝀWↄⲄGMⱯↄOIH૩ⲨⱰ₺ⲊⱠhZꝯOᵛ

JAMES A. HUMPHREY

ᎠᎡᎢᎣᎤᎥᎦᎧᎨᎩᎪᎫᎬᎭᎮᎯᎰᎱᎲᎳᎴᎵᎶᎷᎸᎹᎺᎻᎼᎽᎾᎿᏀᏁᏂᏃᏄᏅ

CONTENTS

DEDICATION

To the memory of my paternal grandmother Ella Waters,
great grandfather Andrew Waters (Dawes Roll Signees,)
and my ancestor Aney King who survived the Trail of Tears.

Grandmother Ella inspires my stories.

PREFACE

Public knowledge of Cherokee history, culture, and language is sparse. A partial reason for that limitation may be awareness.

The author, a citizen of the Cherokee Nation, inspired by his paternal grandmother, presents these story elements through fiction as an entertaining learning experience. He attempts to explore her world with dignity, appreciation, and respect. Cherokee is his "in progress" second language and while not having been raised in the culture, the author's intention is to present information and events from the Cherokee worldview.

Readers may determine their own opinions about his success.

Please be aware:
Cherokee Rock unfolds during violent years of Indigenous history. Those sensitive to turmoil may be offended by the events portrayed in this narrative.

ᏣᎳᎩ ᎧᏃᎮᏓ

ᎠᏎᏍᏗᏍᎩᏂᎦᎵᏍᏙᏗᏴᎠᏗᎴᎯᏇᏏᎨᎢᏛᏯᎳᏍᏛᎢᎦᏯᏍᎦᎮᏯᏛᎢᎾᎯᏴᏯᎾᎲᏙᎾᏟᎭᏃᎤᎠᏗ

JAMES A. HUMPHREY

CHEROKEE ROCK

CHAPTER ONE — Enoli

ᎠᏰᎸᏐᎢᏍᏚᏉᏫᏯᎠᏎᏆᏅᏋᎭᎢᎦᏍᏫᏓᎴᏫᎹᏝᏩᏐᎥᎭᏃᏯᏴᎬᏴᏁᎭᏃᎹᏚᎤ

Ten-year-old Enoli (ᏎᏃᏟ e-no-li, Black Fox) sits with his legs crossed beside his mother, Ahyoka (ᎠᎮᎤ ah-yo-ka, She Brought Happiness.)

On the second circumference of a double circle, they hold their places in a ring behind Paint Clan's men. Their family's space sits empty in the front row.

The mother smiles at her son and nudges him into the primary ring.

He moves with apprehension and eyes the men, who do not notice the intrusion.

She pats her son's back and leans closer to his ear. "You are the man of our lodge, Enoli. It's time to replace your father."

A tall, older woman with traditional male tattoos from her hairline over face, neck, and shoulders stands and addresses the gathering, "Our warriors fight with loyalist rangers against the colonists. We have no protection. Old Tassel, my friend and First Beloved Man, urges us to make peace with these Whites who move into our lands. We must listen. He is wise and loves our people."

It is July 1780. This council deliberates in a central clearing of a warm weather encampment in the northwest corner of what will become the state of Georgia.

Prominent in dress and attitude, the gathering's war woman presides.

Many open-air lodgings surround the council circle. Young tree saplings, crossbeams strapped together with sinew, form their roofs of bark and animal hides. Underneath, families store possessions on platforms.

Other rough-hewn log cabins in the village feature wide doorless entries covered by suspended deer hides.

This night, lodge ground levels for sleeping sit empty as their inhabitants surround a central community bonfire that releases sparks, embers, and smoke into the sky.

Mohi (ꮙꭿ mo-hi,) the Paint Clan's shaman across the circle from the war woman, leaps to his feet. "Joseph Martin, indian agent for the Americans at Chota, sent word to the colonial's Governor Patrick Henry. My friend Dragging Canoe warns that Virginia and North Carolina send an expedition. A thousand over-mountain men in a fleet of dugout canoes under Shelby and Montgomery invade on the Tennessee!"

The older war woman with the face markings motions for the medicine man to return to his seat. "Years past, my son died in battle with British and White loyalists! The colonies fought their war with Britain and now against us. They faced the strongest army in the world! I say it's time to lay war clubs aside. We must seek peace."

The group's shaman stands for a second time.

He surveys the circle of men warmed by the fire.

For display, he nods respect to his tattooed adversary. "I listen. These words I heard before. Yes, we fear the White settlers, for they are a few that represent many. They take our earth, kill our animals, and have modern weapons. Let us control our own lives and destiny! I understand we cannot fight alone. So, join Dragging Canoe and scalp Whites before they drive us from our homes!"

"Shaman Mohi." The old woman sits and stares directly at the medicine man. "The spirits of the animals, of our world, of this fire and that moon above walked with you healers for generations. Stories of the great Stone Cloud are still told around our fires."

Enoli sits near Mohi, and the healer's physical presence and powerful demeanor captivate his attention.

The old war leader's voice weakens, "Since settlers came with their weapons, tools, and the black holy book, your shaman's powers weaken. They say the son of Stone Cloud still summons spirits from Cherokee Rock, but the Paint Clan watches our holy man's talents drift away as the smoke from this council fire."

"Do as you wish, old woman." The Paint Clan's spiritual leader brushes a hand across his mouth and nose against the smell and mist from the fire. "But Dragging Canoe returns soon."

"He is a war leader and does not understand the ways of peace as a shaman should," the leader points at Mohi.

The shaman notices Enoli, the newest young man at the fire.

He stares at the boy. "Old men and the mothers of youngsters long for peace, but many of our young and strong will join our cause."

War woman rises to her feet. "Dragging Canoe is also young. Yes, he is a brave fighter." She points at Ahyoka and Enoli. "Let our mothers and our young and strong make this decision for themselves."

Mohi stomps a foot and spits into the council fire's edge. He bends and grasps warm black ash dampened by saliva between his fingers.

The shaman smears black in two lines across the boy's cheeks.

His protective mother pulls her son into her arms.

The warrior mutters with disgust and stalks from the meeting into the darkness.

Enoli watches the shaman's exit, touches the ash on his cheeks, and his chest swells with the pride of new adult responsibility.

***

The next afternoon, adulthood status reverts to play as the young man skips along a trail beside his mother.

She carries a basket. "I was proud of you last night. You sat in the council with men."

"I did not feel like a man, Mother. I felt like a captive wolf cub."

"It reminded me of when I was your age." She grasps her boy's hand. "One evening, around our campfire, my grandfather told me of a battle that goes on inside grownups."

"A battle?"

"When cubs become wolves, Enoli. He said two wolves fight inside us. One is evil. It is anger, and its cubs are envy, jealousy, sorrow, regret, and greed. They feed on arrogance, self-pity, guilt, and resentment." She looks at her son to assure herself that he pays attention. "Also inferiority, lies, false pride, superiority, and ego."

"Evil wolves eat bad things. Do you think I am a bad wolf?" Enoli stares into his mother's eyes.

"No Son. The other wolf is good and what I pray to the Unetlanvhi (ᎤᏁᏢᎠᏅᎯ u-ne-tla-nv-hi, Creator God) you become. Its cubs are joy, peace, love, hope, serenity, humility, and kindness. They feed on benevolence, generosity, empathy, truth, compassion, and faith."

Enoli thinks for a minute. "How do you know which wolf wins?"

His mother looks at her boy. "The wolf that wins is the one you feed."

Enoli smiles, and she releases his hand. "But now, enjoy boyhood. It is a beautiful day, and you will grow up soon. I have berries to pick."

Enoli runs ahead and plays.

She sings an ancient lyric in the hills and gathers blueberries. "I am of the Unetlanvhi (ᎤᏁᏢᎠᏅᎯ u-ne-tla-nv-hi, Creator God), Ho! I am of the Unetlanvhi, Ho! Ho! It is so. It is so. Ho! It is so, it is so."

Her son sneaks through the brush, and his imagination scouts for White colonists on behalf of the British.

Around the two, summer heat colors the brush a parched green.

The Indian woman spots berries and stoops to gather the delicacies into a double shell basket of woven reeds. "I am of the Unetlanvhi, Ho! I am of the Unetlanvhi, Ho! Ho! It is so. It is so. Ho! It is so, it is so."

***

With a head full of recent fireside stories where warriors battle White settlement encroachment onto native lands, the youngster imagines the British and their Indian allies staged against colonial settlers.

Enoli scouts for a detachment of soldiers and scans the terrain ahead for white-trimmed blue coats and shiny brass buttons. He ranges forward before the column and looks back.

Ahyoka hums her tune and adds more fruit to her basket.

The boy hears movement in the brush and ducks behind a tree.

Enoli peeks.

Two farmers, colonialists with muskets, wait in ambush between two trees and a huckleberry bush.

The boy scrambles from the foliage to behind rocks and peers over their tops.

Two figures wait, not armed men, but a man and a woman.

The female, a ripe chestnut burr hue and covered with fine prickles, crouches in the brush. The male behind her looms as a chokeberry-colored shadow.

Ahyoka joins her son in concealment. "Wait," the mother touches his shoulder. "I see them."

"Those are not British or settlers." The lad seeks comfort. "I am afraid." He grips a small knife in a beaded sheath at his belt.

"No, Enoli. They are Kosvkvskini (Evil Ones.)" The woman's voice trembles in fear. "Run, bring Shaman Mohi, and don't look back."

The mother grasps her son's shoulders and shakes. "Promise me you won't."

The boy disobeys.

At the top of the hill, Enoli stops and looks along the slope.

***

Enoli's mother drops her basket of blueberries, and they spill. She sings a song to the mountain spirit. "I am of the

Unetlanvhi (ᎤᏁᏟᎠᏫᎭ, u-ne-tla-nv-hi, Creator God), Ho! I am of the Unetlanvhi, Ho! Ho! It is so. It is so. Ho! It is so, it is so."

The covered-with-prickles woman approaches.

With hands upraised and eyes on the sky, Ahyoka stands and faces the threat.

She opens and spreads her arms, the universal symbol of greeting or capture.

The evil shadow draws close and, porcupine aggressive, expels pricks.

Spines pierce Ahyoka's skin and stimulate red pimples.

The Kosvkvskini cackles as she circles Enoli's mother, arms outstretched.

Her prickly cactus skin erupts into a spinal barrage that speckles the air thick as fire ash.

The male sings as he follows his mate and sweeps into a sickly dance around the boy's mother. "I am of the Great Pox, Ho! I am of the Great Pox, Ho! Ho! It is so. It is so. Ho! It is so, it is so." As he touches or shadows Ahyoka's skin, lesions fester and become black pustules.

***

Enoli flees, and his lungs ache with each breath. Brush and branches whip his face and shoulders as he crashes through the bramble.

After an hour of effort, he bursts into the clan's encampment and stops the first adult, an older man.

"A Kosvkvskini attacked my mother! I must find Mohi!"

Color drains from the elder's face as he cowers away from the name of the evil spirit.

The gentleman stumbles but points at an open-air structure.

Several people, an extended family, live in the dwelling owned by their family matriarch.

Enoli runs to the indicated lodge. "Mohi!"

The shaman steps from his home. "Enoli. What do you want? You took your place at the council fire last night. You must wish to fight with Dragging Canoe."

"No! My mother sent me." The boy gasps for breath from running. "She picks berries but… but…"

"What's the matter? You're old enough to go to war, so speak!"

"A Kosvkvskini attacks mother!" He points over the ridges that surround the village. "She needs a shaman."

The medicine man laughs, "They are legends, Son. Only White settlers attack our people. Times have changed."

"You don't believe me?" Enoli looks at the shaman. "My mother is of the Paint Clan. You want to be the medicine man of our clan. Protect us. I saw them!"

"You say." Mohi preens before others who, disrupted by the noise, step out of their cabins and lodges to investigate. "Describe the Kosvkvskini."

Enoli glances at the onlookers. "A woman and a man, she first, with burning eyes and skin the color of ripe chestnuts. Her skin is burr hue and covered with fine prickles. The man is more of a shadow and follows with yellow eyes. His long arms open to embrace you. They were Kosvkvskini. My mother said so and sent me for help."

Mohi and the onlookers stare in stunned silence.

One bystander breaks the frozen reaction. "Mohi, protect us from this evil!"

"Silence! You don't control me, and I'm not afraid of old

evil spirit legends." The medicine man reenters his lodge and withdraws a medicine bag. "Lead me to your mother, Enoli."

Bystanders applaud and shout as the youth and the shaman jog from the village. "The Unetlanvhi (Creator God) protect Mohi, the Paint Clan's beloved shaman!"

The boy and the healer trot into the hills.

***

They retrace the young man's steps as clouds gather over distant ridges. At a run, the two eye distant lightening. Darkness sweeps above the horizon.

"The signs are not good." The shaman follows through bramble, and thorns tear leggings and moccasins. "What did you see?"

Without breathing hard from the running, the younger Enoli sweeps his hand across the sky. "Two spirits, a man and a woman. They came from behind a bush. My mother sent me for you. I ran but looked back. The woman cast spines which the man turned to black sores."

Mohi stops. "The White man's smallpox!"

The boy spins to face the medicine man. "Why do you stop? She's over the next hill."

"We must bring help to carry her body." The healer turns to retrace his steps.

"No!" Enoli rips his knife from his belt and brandishes it toward Mohi. "Coward! You fear the pox! We help my mother now!"

The older man stares at the knife and into the boy's eyes.

He whips a fist against the youngster's wrist and knocks the weapon loose.

Enoli lunges to retrieve the blade. His ribs suffer the thump of his opponent's foot, and the boy rolls in pain.

The older picks up the blade. "I am the shaman leader of the Paint Clan, you little nothing! Your mother has the pox. She could give it to us. For the sake of the clan, I will not take that risk. We do this my way. Do you understand?"

Enoli squirms on the ground with both hands pressing sore bones. "I understand you are a coward and hide behind your medicine bag while my mother needs help!"

Mohi slams a second foot into Enoli's stomach, and the boy expels air.

His last vision of consciousness frames the Paint Clan's shaman silhouetted against deep clouds split by distant lightning.

CHAPTER TWO — Squirrel

DRTᏠᎤᎥᏍᎤᏗᏁᎩᎯᎫᎬᏇᏆᎮᏛ⏞ᎳᎳᎾᏛᏓᎬᎷᎱᎣᎥᎤᎯᎻᏣᎩᎾᏖᎷᎿᏥᏂᏃᎤ

Three days later, one open to the air lodge of the Paint Clan's village stands totally enclosed by bark and animal skins. Loaded with extra pelts and rough hemp blankets, its small top opening puffs smoke and steam from a stoked fire within, dampened by water.

The sweat lodge encloses Ahyoka, on a ground mat smothered by coverings.

Enoli, on knees beside his mother, holds herbs and oils and stares at Mohi, who beats a drum and shakes rattles over the mother's head.

The medicine man's shaven skull sweats from a hemp tie that encloses a top knot. It resembles a hair geyser. In long deerskin boots, the healer's symbolic tunic falls to their tops.

The son's gaze shifts to the patient's face, which pokes from covers.

The woman's skin displays smallpox pustules.

Flesh, white from dehydration and wrinkles, salty and moist, drips.

An assistant enters the lodge with a pottery basin of spring water.

The senior medicine man whips the coverings from his patient and douses her body with cold liquid.

Ahyoka convulses from shock into a fetal curl, and the caregiver replaces the blankets.

Sweat repops from facial pores, and the woman's eyes roll under half-open eyelids.

The boy leaps to his feet and hands the bowl of medicines to Mohi. "Your ways murder mother!"

He lunges out of the heated lodge into the fresh air and sucks oxygen into starved lungs.

***

The young man stomps from the small cabin up an incline and sits in the shade under a tree.

He stares at the shelter.

Family members come and go throughout the afternoon.

They enter the dwelling, stay for extended periods, and traditionally crowd the ill relative.

As the sun sinks near the horizon, Enoli withdraws a pouch of corn and munches. He watches the movement around his sick mother's lodge.

A rustle in the foliage nearby attracts the boy's attention.

A tree squirrel, Saloli (ᎤᏌᎶᎵ Sa-lo-li, squirrel), with a distinctive flash of white fur on the underside of its tail, sits on hind legs and rubs forepaws.

The boy flips a grain kernel near the animal. "Why do you have five toes and only four fingers?"

The small furry head engulfs the food but takes offense. "Why do you have thumbs, Tsalagi (ᏣᎳᎩ Tsa-la-gi, Cherokee?) Don't mock. Think you are the favored people? Not true; I climb trees much better."

The young man tosses another welcomed morsel.

"Who do you watch?" The rodent wrinkles a nose. "You

mope under this tree since midday."

"Mother dies from smallpox," the corn feeder peers at the sweat lodge.

"You share food, so, welcome or not, I give wisdom." The furry animal shakes a bushy tail with enthusiasm. "Real people travel little. Because squirrels are much better in trees, we move around and see the world. To the north atop a great rock, the son of Stone Cloud teaches apprentices how to heal humans. He treats those sick by the pox differently. No family crowds, no cramped and hot lodges, no ice-water baths, rattles or shamans who spout chants the spirits forgot long ago."

"The medicine man that cares for my mother is Mohi, the Paint Clan's shaman." Enoli flips another kernel.

"A nobody," the animal scoots its belly on a tree branch, "but most have heard of Stone Cloud and his son."

"Stories around the campfire told by old folks." The young man throws another tidbit.

"Your caretaker is human and does what humans do best. He murders your loved one to prove a point. The healer chooses not to follow reason," the squirrel's whiskers shake. "His brain rejects new ways as radical or experimental. Perhaps he doesn't even want to help, which my experience and wisdom prefers. He only cares about his professional standing in the Paint Clan."

Mohi's assistant steps out of the sweat lodge below and swings his arm, a motion to come for Enoli.

"They summon. Go be an accomplice in your mother's murder." The squirrel scurries up the tree. "But I wait for your return, with corn."

***

The boy jogs from the ridge's tree and enters.

His mother lies motionless.

"Did she die?" He looks at Mohi.

"No. I have done what I know." The healer drops to his knees beside Ahyoka. "She does not improve. I watched a White doctor treat in this manner. That patient recovered."

"What are you doing?" The youngster turns to the older fellow.

"They call it bloodletting. It cannot make her worse. She dies unless I do something." Mohi stares at the boy. "The colonial doctors say blood becomes stale as water in salt flats when someone lies still and ill. Remove the pollutant and the patient freshens."

"Freshen? I am ten years old. She is my world. You must provide a cure. My life is useless without her."

"We have little choice. Do nothing, she dies. I heard a Raven Mocker beat its giant wings above this sweat lodge. So, I do the bloodletting." Mohi waves a knife in front of the boy's face. "If she meets death from the treatment, the White doctors killed her, not I. Do you hear me?"

Enoli trembles and nods yes. "Mother told me stories of those black raven fliers."

The shaman opens an artery which spurts blood from Ahyoka's left arm.

The son stares as a red stain grows on the floor of the sweat lodge.

With each splat, the pool enlarges, and the boy grits his teeth.

He fixates on the puddle and rocks back and forth in rhythm with the splashes. "When do you stop it?"

Mohi looks at Ahyoka. "When she faints."

The boy's hands shake. "She's gone now."

The healer feels for a pulse in his patient's neck. "No. She still lives. That is good." With sinew, the shaman tightens a makeshift tourniquet above the woman's elbow. He presses deer skin to his knife's bloodletting slice, and the flow lessens.

***

Later, with the bleeding completed, Ahyoka shows no evidence of life.

The boy checks her pulse at the neck's vein and feels slight movement.

Alone, the son sits and stares at his mother's lips, hoping for a whisper.

The sweat from the lodge's heat no longer dampens the woman's brow.

An assistant hauls a pottery jug of icy creek water into the lodge.

He yanks Ahyoka's coverings and douses the body.

The shock causes no reaction, and Enoli leaps to his feet. "You're an ignorant apprentice!" The boy screams as he lunges at the midsection of the attendant. "You are not helping!"

The two scuffle and attract Mohi, who enters the hut and pulls the combatants apart.

"Get out! Leave my help alone. You interfere."

The battling boys separate, and the older man slings the concerned son out the lodge's door. "Wait outside. We will call if she dies!"

The youth stumbles backward. "Not if, when!"

"She needs more bloodletting," the healer looks in at his patient, "without your interference."

Enoli charges.

Mohi steps aside. With a moccasin-clad foot, he trips and upends his attacker.

The ten-year-old rolls.

"You murder my mother! You're an ignorant phony!"

The healer stares hatred and starts a retort, "I told you the White…" He notices others that watch the turmoil and closes the lodge's entrance.

***

The boy struggles to his feet, lurches up the hill and drops against the tree to recapture breath.

In the tree's branches, Saloli waits for more corn.

Enoli spies the small furry pest and shoos it away. "I have no food. Find another place to mooch."

"I've been listening. The medicine man treats your mother with the White man's bloodletting?"

The youth nods recognition.

"With leeches or by blade?" Saloli's whiskers vibrate.

"Does it matter?" He looks up at the animal.

"Yes, Human. I can't fathom what you don't know. The suckers take little blood and cause less damage," the furry one curls a lip with disdain. "Son of Stone Clouds says a good medicine man does the least harm."

"You said Mohi only cares how things appear to the Paint Clan?" The boy stares at the sweat lodge. "Now, I believe that."

"That's the result of shaman involved in politics." The squirrel attempts to sit on its tail. "We bury nuts and make babies. Keep life simple, I say."

"Smart. You animals never become political." Enoli watches the furry companion.

It descends the tree headfirst.

"We do, sometimes, when it interferes with meals or children, but it doesn't do any good. Humans stay busy killing each other, and that makes you hungry. Squirrels pay the price. Many of my kin end life on roasting sticks without skin."

"Then why are you talking to me?" The boy stares at the little animal.

"You are of the Paint Clan, with the birthright of medicine men. I spent years at the place called Cherokee Rock. Son of the great Stone Cloud teaches the shaman's arts and does no harm there. I sense you are shaman material and think you should go to his school. You can help the favored ones stay well and in peace."

"How does that reflect on you?" The boy stares at the animal.

"Healthy and happy Tsalagi eat venison, buffalo and the White man's cows. Those meats taste better than squirrel."

"Leave me alone. I am only interested in saving mother."

"Afraid you are too late." The fuzzy one sits on his tail and blinks.

Wails rise from within the sweat lodge, and several extended family members exit the entry flap as puffs of steam and smoke escape.

Enoli watches Ahyoka's sisters weep. "Ahyoka, Ahyoka, Ahyoka," they sing their loved one's name repeatedly with each breath.

Brothers and uncles smear ashes from the tribe's fire on faces, in hair, and on shoulders.

Under the tree on the slope above, the little fluffy animal looks at his new friend. "Go to your people. I sense you offer more comfort than the Paint Clan's medicine man. You have many responsibilities."

Enoli's eyes tear as he stares at the cabin.

The squirrel rubs paws together before its rib cage. "You begin a journey to adulthood without parents. I am sorry, but step boldly into the future, for I see promise."

Enoli nods at his new mentor, then turns and walks from the hill.

***

An Uncle meets the boy. "You are in worn clothing." The man hands his nephew a pottery jar of liquid. "As the nearest relative, close her eyelids. This is willow root water. Mohi rests. We will call him when you have prepared Ahyoka."

The young son mumbles thank you and slips into the room.

He stands alone with the body.

Smoke and steam from the sweat treatment no longer engulf the interior.

The fire lays extinguished by dirt and sand. Wispy tendrils rise from coals and escape through the hole in the roof.

Ahyoka lies upon blankets, and her blank open eyes point at the vent.

Her son drops to his knees and cries. He smothers the sounds of pain with both palms.

The squirrel pads into the lodge, unseen by the boy or anyone.

It sits on haunches and watches Enoli's grief flow.

When the young man's tears subside, the little tree rodent shakes a long tail and speaks, "I see you have willow root water. That is an old way. Son of Stone Cloud teaches not to touch the body of one with the pox, even your own mother."

"Why do you watch?" The young man realizes another life is in the hut. "I don't want a father, and sure not a pet. Go away."

"I follow because your spirit calls. I do not hear most humans, and they are deaf to my words. Listen to wisdom. Son of Stone Cloud burns sweat lodges with clothes, possessions, and garments. Boil everything to kill the smallpox."

"I do not know your exalted medicine man. His father, they speak of as the greatest shaman, but you visited only a son. Did you talk to him as we do?"

"Yes, that is how I realized you are healer material." Saloli rolls an upper lip over large front teeth.

"Who appointed you to serve as his recruiter?" The youth turns to his mother. "I will respect the old way."

"And bathe the body in willow root water?" Whiskers on the animal's nose vibrate. "You take significant risk."

Enoli looks at Ahyoka.

Black, ugly pustules cover once radiant skin, and many ooze pus.

The boy shivers, bends, and with both hands slip eyelids over pupils.

He unstraps her buckskin jacket and lays one collar aside, which exposes more lesions.

With a rough hemp woven cloth, the son dampens a corner in willow root water and cleans his mother's neck.

"I see my newest friend is the same as the favored ones. You have a death wish," the rodent chit-chits.

"No, Saloli. I believe the Unetlanvhi will protect while I cleanse my parent's body."

"Then, you do not listen to the teachings of Son of Stone Cloud." Saloli's whiskers quicken.

"You quote the man's words, and they sound reasonable. But, the entire time of Mom's life, she believed in the old ways. I cannot change that path at the end." The devoted youngster continues to wash his mother's pustules in sacred water.

The rodent watches in silence.

"Little one, wait outside while I do this." The boy waves a cloth as an instruction to exit.

His friend complies. "I wait in the trees. If you do not die of the smallpox, I know you are most favored by the Unetlanvhi Creator, another reason that I watch over you. While I am gone, I shall ask the animals to intercede, and sometimes He listens." The rodent pads out of the sweat lodge.

Enoli's grief overwhelms youthful adulthood, and with head in hands, he weeps.

Ahyoka's sweet song lyrically fills the boy's brain and memory.

The voice calms loneliness. "I give you love thoughts for you to keep. I am with you still; I do not sleep. I am a thousand winds that blow, I am the light flash that glints on snow. I am the spring warmth on ripened grain, I am the gentle touch of autumn rain."

Enoli opens his eyes and stares at his mother.

The woman's pustule defaced face lies on her mat and its smallpox ravaged visage palls the lodge.

However, her soul sings in the boy's ears, "When you awaken in the morning hush, I am the swift uplifting rush of birds in circled flight. I am the soft stars that shine at night. Do not think of me as gone. I am with you still, in each new dawn."

CHAPTER THREE — Burial

DRTᏠᏅᎶꞋᏕᎠᏐᎩᏳ AJEᏒᎮᎪᏗᎡᎷᎳᏔᏫᎡᎶᎷᏗᏲᏴᎣᎮᎻᎶᏴᏋᏴᏁᎻᏃᏈᎣᵛ

The following day, Enoli wakens to traditional Cherokee grieving.

He rolls on his sleeping pallet and discovers Mohi.

"Youngster, on your feet. We practice seven days of mourning." The shaman's tone rings forceful and commandeering. "Each rise of the sun follows Paint Clan custom."

The boy struggles to a seated position. "She was my mother. I grieve my own way."

"Tradition says bury the dead as soon as possible. She had the pox, so we don't dig under your hearth. We'll build a place." The healer grabs an arm and pulls the youth to his feet.

Outside, Enoli points at a hilltop. "Under that tree, the one that stands alone and whispers in the wind."

"Not proper." The older man shakes his head.

The boy, with moist eyes, turns to the healer. "I know of a stream near blueberry vines. We went often, and she sang songs to the water."

Near the dwelling, the healer indicates a waist-high sandstone abutment. "There, close. Far enough for protection from the illness, with plenty of rock. It offers a perfect and traditional burial site."

"But is nothing like my mother."

"She won't sing to streams ever again." Mohi turns and walks toward the cabin where Ahyoka's body waits. "Come with me. Face duty as a grown person."

Enoli watches Saloli scurry from the trees and join his breakfast source. "Have any corn this morning?"

The boy jerks his head at the village. "I'll get you some."

The medicine man hears, "What?"

"I said I'm coming to help you."

At the place where he slept, the young man retrieves a pouch of corn. He munches kernels as he follows Mohi and pitches several to the furry eater that follows.

"Feed that squirrel." The healer opens the flap of the sweat lodge. "Fatten him for somebody's dinner."

The little animal stops. "I dislike this man."

Trailed by Saloli, the youngster and the adult carry Ahyoka, encased in blankets, to the rock outcrop.

With more slabs of sediment, the two labor in silence and encase the deceased within an eighteen-inch layered wall.

A rocky cover prevents human or animal disturbance.

The medicine man places the last stone on top of the entombment. "Gather her things. With a pox death, they are unclean. Burn them at this gravesite. After seven days, I return and build a new fire in your lodge to purify your home. Then we go to the river and cleanse our bodies."

"Mohi, I must thank you for what you have done, but I question your…" the pre-teen squints at the older man who stands in front of the sun "… qualifications."

The shaman tolerates the boy's impudence but shifts his body language. "What are you implying?"

Saloli hustles along the sandstone abutment's top and

sits upon its haunches several yards from his young friend. "Careful. Your words anger."

"I remember the years that I have been alive." Enoli hoists a last rock to the pile. "The animals and the birds walk and talk to me. I hear the trees as they support each other. The clouds tell me stories of when our people owned this earth."

"They don't communicate with me, and I am a shaman." Mohi kicks at Saloli. "I notice this rodent follows you."

"Who's he calling rodent?" Quick paws on the ground avoid the attack. "Did I call him Injun or Quack?"

"I believe the Unetlanvhi has chosen me to be a Dideyohvsgi (ᏗᏕᏲᎲᏍᎩ di-de-yo-huh-ss-gi, medicine man teacher.) My mother bore me to bring new worlds to my people. She knew of my talents and told me. I think training is necessary, perhaps an apprenticeship with you?"

The flattering proposal pacifies Mohi, and he drops to heels. "I will consider your thoughts."

"Thank you."

"I have known you since you fed at your mother's breast. Never have I seen any inclination or interest in my profession."

"Ahyoka loved me and believed my heart was a healer's."

"Your mother is not here to champion you. How do I believe you?"

The little animal hisses as he paws his front teeth, "This ego-centric charlatan is only interested in control."

The boy stands before the medicine man. "Did you hear what Saloli said?"

"You speak to rodents?" The shaman jumps and flays his hands. "Disgusting!"

The fuzzy one retreats several paces, and its fur bristles.

"Yes. And they to me." Enoli surrenders no ground.

"Those who talk to lowly animals are not apprentice material."

"Why not?"

"I want apprentices that communicate with wolves or bears. Now that your mother lies under those stones, who's going to suckle you and tell you to listen to squirrels?" Mohi spits at the boy's feet and stalks away.

"That hazelnut talks to snakes, maybe buzzards?" Saloli watches the exit and turns to Enoli. "Got more fresh corn?"

***

The following days blend in a subdued blur of grief and ceremony that parade across Enoli's mind.

By Cherokee tradition, no family voice raises in anger, and relatives speak lightly as they eat and drink less in memory of the deceased.

The morning of the fifth day after Ahyoka's death, the relatives gather around Mohi as they continue traditions.

The boy lurks behind uncles and avoids contact with the Paint Clan's shaman, who directs the rituals.

"I shot this bird with an arrow." The hunter holds a carcass above his head for the group to see. He plucks feathers from the right breast and withdraws a knife from his belt. The man slices a small meat chunk.

Several of the women family members chant the deceased's name, "Ahyoka, Ahyoka, Ahyoka, Ahyoka."

The shaman steps to the fire inside Enoli's mother's open-sided log home. "We have purified this lodge and placed iron it its medicine pot. We have prepared willow root tea, and you have drunk and are pure. This woman died of the pox. We now roast this ceremonial food. If it pops and throws pieces onto the family, her sons and theirs will soon die of the sickness. If it does not pop, we are safe."

The man pitches the breast slice into the flames.

The members crowd closer as the meat heats.

Several adults hold their breath in anticipation.

The bird chunk splatters and small bits sprinkle near feet.

The family stands frozen and silent, but stare at a smoking morsel on Enoli's moccasin.

Everyone steps away from the boy.

"The Unetlanvhi speaks." Mohi presses his palms against each other.

***

Mourning continues for two more days.

Enoli takes part in a mental fog, quarantined by his relatives and included in his mother's ceremonies only on the periphery.

Each daybreak of the remaining mornings, mourners immerse themselves in water for purification before they visit the grave site.

Ahyoka's sisters, supported by tribal women, wail and gnash their teeth in grief but eye her son and keep distance.

On the seventh and final grieving night, family and relatives prepare food for a feast in the council lodge.

That evening, Enoli skips the festivities and escapes with chills to a pallet in his mother's cabin.

High fever, headache, back pain and tremors rack his body as he rolls off his mat to vomit. Daylight and darkness blend in the young man's eyes as he battles the onset of smallpox.

The heat within his head, ratcheted higher by Mohi's sweat treatment, rages.

The boy's consciousness walks in other worlds.

Unaware the medicine man dances with rattles, chants, and splatters sacred potions, his youthful mind explores adventurous things.

The shaman's apprentice douses spring water over a shivering body, unnoticed and without dream disruption.

***

Enoli and Saloli sit upon clouds and view the world. "Where do you go after you die, my furry friend?"

"Depends on who or what you believe and the power who created and rules." The little one wags his tail. "Sun worshipers assume a soul lingers where the person died. The essence moves to the distant and miserable west."

"That sounds too lonely for me. Our kind retreated over the mountains from the French, the British, and now the White colonists. We go no farther."

The squirrel cleans his whiskers. "Many believe when you die you become part of a larger or smaller form. You grow tiny with time and vanish. A soul ceases. You shrink in proportion to how well you endured."

"My life is only ten years. I have not lived poorly." The boy rubs sweat off his brow.

"Other Cherokees pray to three souls who rule distinct but connected levels." The little rodent spreads four paws on the coolness of the cloud. "One reigns over the predictable upper world of the past represented by fire, another an underworld of changes in the future symbolized by water."

Enoli wipes sweat from his eyes.

The fuzzy preacher whizzes for consideration. "Pay attention. The third domain is the present, where humans mediate between the other two. Those who die free of specific sins and vices dwell with the spirits forever. People with grievous transgressions leave with evil hosts and scream in torment."

"That sounds written in the White man's black book." The youngster rolls in physical discomfort, unmitigated by the words.

"That God had a Son who rescued the dying." The little animal struggles to his feet. "We must talk later. Your family is here."

"How do you know, Saloli?" The youth peers at the clouds.

"Because I am not ill. I watch them look at your skin rashes in their world."

"I am self-conscious. Are they ugly?" The youngster reaches for his pet.

"You reach out, and your aunts and uncles touch. Many shall suffer from your pox."

"Don't let them!" Enoli pleads with his companion.

"They are human. I am only a squirrel."

***

The ill boy tosses and thrashes on his mat, and his body, racked with fever, commands his mind. His spirit travels in the mists and searches the puffy white tops for his furry friend.

***

The small wiggler rides the next cloud. "The Great One asked me to offer you company and wise counsel."

As the two soar in the heavens toward distant mountains, night darkens, and clouds gather to cover the stars.

They fill the boy's dreams.

Ominous threat rumbles, and an occasional strike of lightning punctuates the horizon.

The young man opens his eyes.

Wind from the approaching storm sways the grasses' crowns, and they bend in the unison of waves that sweep the land. The boy sits and gazes across the grass sea.

"Where are we Saloli?" Enoli looks at his friend.

"Still west of the mountains, but they approach." The small one jumps from his cloud to join the youth.

A darkness ahead erupts, and light with thunder shatters the youngster's ears.

Two figures stalk in narrowing circles. The female form glows a ripe chestnut burr hue covered with fine prickles. The male creeps behind her, a shadow of chokeberry color.

"I am afraid." Saloli seeks comfort and presses closer.

"They are Kosvkvskini. I have seen them." The boy's voice trembles with intimidation.

The spiny woman approaches, and her circle tightens. This evil draws close, and in a porcupine move, she brandishes pricks. Her male follows, and his red, feverish eyes glow in the night.

"They appear because we violate the old laws and ignore traditional treatment for the pox." The furry one scrambles to the boy's neck and peeps over his shoulder.

"Kosvkvskini! I have your evil curse, and my friend is a squirrel. He is not your prey! Why do you come with the storm?"

The woman, half-wraith and part pustule-scarred abomination, extends skeletal fingers and points an extended nail. "You abandon the ways of old and follow paths forged by false teachers. For sins such as these, we visit you and your clans."

Enoli stands his ground. "My shaman is Mohi of the Paint Clan."

"Is he the Unetlanvhi (Creator God's) child?" The woman drops her hand.

"No, his father was a warrior."

"You real people are not the only ones we attack." The pustule person watches the storm on the horizon. "We hit the White man who follows the Son of his God. The settlers ignore their gods from before and worship that deity."

"I am interested in the real people." The boy clutches his animal near his chest.

"Kosvkvskini come from before those days. Real people and others lived over the oceans. The Cherokee existed by favor of the water beetle. Others, by the serpent."

"Leave us. Take your diseased creeper with you. Times change. I no longer believe in you. This must be a dream." The boy attempts to vanquish the wraith with a wave of his hand.

"I have the power to hurt you," the woman crosses her prickled wrists, "and many of your people, along with the White settlers, have not experienced my embrace. I have much to do."

"Go! Do your work, and leave me and my animal alone." Enoli grasps his furry friend.

The threat opens her arms, wide bat wings, and rises to find and engulf new victims.

The gusts of air from massive uplifts dislodge Ahyoka's son from the safety of his cloud.

With Saloli, he plummets toward the earth.

"Boy! This is unsafe! I have a cousin that flies. I do not!" The little one flaps its tail for lift.

Enoli, twisted in mind by fever, watches the darkness of the Kosvkvskini recede above him and braces his body for impact.

With a massive whoosh, a giant eagle snatches the two from their death fall.

With wind whipping through twenty-foot feathers and huge talons gripped around the youth and squirrel, the majestic bird soars above the Appalachian Mountains. "I am the Creator God's wings. It has designs for you, young man."

The boy looks under their flight and watches mountain crests flow as ocean waves. "What plans are those, Great One?"

"Without black pustule death. I return you to your sweat lodge."

CHAPTER FOUR — Defenseless

ᎠᎡᎢᎣᎤᎥᎦᎧᎨᎩᎪᎫᎬᎭᎮᎯᎰᎱᎲᎳᎴᎵᎶᎷᎸᎹᎺᎻᎼᎽᎾᎿᏀᏁᏂᏃᏄᏅ

Three weeks later, before the sun breaks the horizon, family and shaman no longer stand vigil over Enoli's mat and the village sleeps.

The patient on the mat sits cross-legged and inspects a few remaining dried arm pustules.

Saloli sits on its haunches in the lodges' opening. "Mohi takes credit for your recovery. He bragged of healing prowess at council fire last night." The squirrel's whiskers vibrate.

"Don't even remember him being here," the boy shakes his head.

"He was. Your memory suffers from delirium, but his methods did not cure. They nearly killed with those ridiculous sweat lodge ice baths." The furry one chuckles and rubs both paws together. "At least there was no bloodletting."

"You do not catch smallpox twice. For that, I am indebted to the Unetlanvhi. In the fever, I swore to teach and treat our people."

"A human listened and prayed?" Saloli rolls lips, and his eyes sparkle. "That's new."

"I pledged to become a medicine man and lead a revival of spiritual greatness."

"Pompous, even for a real person."

The boy stands and stretches. "No. Grateful to get through the pox."

"Enoli promises much for ten years old. Squirrels are smarter. Work hard but never promise much. You do not know how many acorns we bury to survive the winter."

The youngster imitates the motion. "You dig often, but forget."

"True," Saloli rests upon his tail, "but not this year. You have corn, so I don't need to hoard."

"Then watch me. I am weak. If I fall, get help." He steadies on two feet for the first time in weeks.

The little animal on haunches, darts eyes and scrambles to safety space. "You're teetering."

"I have been on this sick mat too long. Dizzy." Enoli locks knees and firms. "I think I can walk."

"Then come! I hear danger." Alarmed, the furry one leaps out of the lodge. "Follow me!"

The boy staggers after his companion out of the village, up a hill and into a pile of rocks that overlook the Cherokee community.

"Too weak. This is it. No further." Lungs heave.

"Stay low." The little scout peeks around a rock.

The Paint Clan sleeps in peace below the ridge.

Enoli notices movement in the woods on the opposite side of the camp.

Several dozen White men dressed in deer skin but most in rough woven cotton colonial uniforms sneak into the encampment.

A dog barks, and the intruders freeze. They wait for surprise until the animal settles and then creep further.

"What's this?" Enoli hugs the rocks for concealment.

"Dragging Canoe's message warned us that Shelby's over-mountain men and continentals under Montgomery come." Saloli shakes his tail and thumps the ground. "The Whites hunt favored people and not squirrels for a change."

"I need to warn the families." The boy rises to knees.

"You do and we're both dead." The small sentry backs closer to the rocks. "They will scalp you and skin me for dinner."

A Cherokee man swings open the door of a lean-to cabin and investigates the dog bark.

A huge puff of black smoke hangs on the end of a White man's musket as the blast echoes through Enoli's ears, a moment delayed by the distance, and the suspicious bark checker falls dead.

Pandemonium erupts as men burst from other cabins and lodges.

One of the first into the open, an older peace proponent from the circle council, drops to knees. "No. Don't resist. They will kill everyone. Surrender!" A musket ball rips the chin off her face.

White men aim muskets and find targets but hold fire as screams of passionate submission vibrate in the dawn's fresh air.

"What do we do?" Enoli stares at the carnage.

"Run and hide. Come on." Saloli retreats from the rocky concealment.

With fear along his spine, the young man watches Mohi leap from a lodge and dash for a horse tethered nearby.

The shaman slices the tether with a knife and lunges atop the animal.

Militia whip their weapons toward the escapee and two fire, but the medicine man slides to the opposite side of his horse.

He whips the mount with the side of his blade, heels his horse's flanks, and pounds through the militia into the woods.

Warriors dash for weapons and horses.

Women gather children and run for shelter.

The over-mountain militia discharge their firearms, and many targets fall. As a few reload, others attack with knives and hatchets.

Enoli freezes in concealment and fixates on a White settler that grabs a six-year-old boy from a home and impales the child with a massive knife. With one whisk, the volunteer soldier scalps his defenseless victim.

The child's hair falls to the ground and seeps blood.

"Come! What are you staring at?" Saloli paws the earth. "We need to hide."

Enoli crawls backward from the rocks, stands and follows the little scout into the woods. It moves fast from dirt to tree limb to bush and returns to higher traction.

The boy runs on the surface and crashes through the bramble with deep, oxygen-starved breaths.

"Quieter! Not so much crashing!" The furry pathfinder stops for a moment. "You leave a trail a blind mole could follow."

Enoli tails the scout into the woods and rocky foothills and away from the annihilation.

The weak boy struggles through the abutments and up the runoff crevices. He shadows the small animal.

Saloli stops at a cave's entrance. "Hide in here. You are too tired to run. They will discover our tracks but won't trail us this high."

"Good. I can't go farther." Enoli slides on his stomach through the rock opening into concealment, and the fuzzy one sits at the entrance on his tail as a lookout.

"I was lucky you sensed the White men before the attack." The boy settles shoulders on the cave's floor.

"My nose works better than yours, but this time that wasn't necessary. Favored people smell, but over-mountain soldiers stink. They spend their days with hogs."

"Cherokee resemble them. We only want to live, hunt, and tend pigs. Why do they hate us?" The young man rubs his nose and stretches to see out of the cave opening.

"My ancestors have always been afraid of the Whites and their appetites." The lookout settles to a stomach. "Long before gun powder and muskets, my uncles told stories of new humans, not the actual ones that lived in our mountains and hunted with arrows, those that came from the East with sticks that smoked. They killed us with hard black balls that tore into flesh as those weapons boomed. Most of my relatives in the East got eaten."

"Only for food." Enoli scans the brush and trees. "Whites do not eat the true people. They shoot us from hate."

Saloli scratches one side with a hind claw. "Colonials detest everybody. They spit at the British and French who resemble them but sound different."

"Then why murder my folk?" The boy settles into his cave concealment.

"Because humankind is violent. The settlers clean the land of weeds. You are a weed in the way of farms and food. And not of their kind. To Whites, real people are not human."

"They think of us as smallpox, as Kosvkvskini."

Saloli snorts agreement. "Quiet. Rest. I will watch. Let's hope it's safe to move after the moon rises."

An exhausted Enoli settles and soon dreams.

***

The youngster's mind joins the British and their Indian allies staged against colonials and settlers.

The boy scouts for a detachment of soldiers and scans the terrain ahead for white-trimmed red coats and brass buttons. He ranges before the column.

The youth hears movement in the brush and ducks behind a sapling. Enoli peers forward along the trail.

Two immigrants, colonialists with muskets, wait in ambush between trees and a huckleberry bush.

The boy jumps from the tree to rocks and peeks over their tops.

Figures lurk, not armed men, but a man and a woman.

The female crouches in the brush, a ripe chestnut burr hue covered with fine prickles.

A male looms in the rear as a shadow of chokeberry color.

The woman closes, and gnarled fingers reach and shake Enoli's shoulder.

***

"Wake up," Saloli thumps Enoli with his tail. "You're snoring and making too much noise. The White settlers are close."

The boy draws breath and rolls to one side. He slips a knife from its sheaf and lifts his head to view outside the cave's entrance.

Nothing moves in the darkness, and the trees loom as oppressive sentinel guards.

Clouds drift across the moon, and dim light cast shadows that blink in the night. Every shape becomes a settler to the boy as he scans the terrain.

One shadow speaks, "Trail's old. And I dislike hunting Injuns after dark. Good way to lose a scalp."

Another voice penetrates the blackness. "You're right. Head back."

A Southern Devil Scorpion, an inch long, crawls across Enoli's hand onto the earth. He panic stabs the menace with his blade.

"Hear that, Jebediah?" Threat floats in the air.

His little friend looks at Enoli, wrinkles his nose, and dashes through the cave's entrance. Fast paws propel the animal through rocks and brush.

"Just a tree squirrel. We're getting jumpy." One shadow lowers his musket.

The boy hugs low in the cave and waits, holds breath and then takes air through a hand. He peeks out the entrance.

Nothing moves, and he settles into hiding.

Movement rustles leaves outside the cave's entrance, and Enoli's hands tremble as he looks.

The round hole at the end of a cylinder of iron, to the terrified boy, looms as large as the moon inches from his face.

The White settler cocks the musket, and his blue eyes peer behind the barrel past the weapon's hammer.

Not much older than Enoli, the young man's whiskers bristle his chin in the moonlight. Blond, dirty hair thrusts under a battered hat, and freckles appear as cool spots across his nose.

Enoli squeezes his eyelids shut and awaits an explosion. Nothing.

He opens one eye, and the militiaman continues to stare. The White settler uncocks his weapon and raises the barrel.

He sits in silence and studies the Cherokee boy.

"Jedediah! You coming? You all right?" The other's voice floats among the dark tree shapes.

The settler boy stands and disappears into the darkness.

***

Each unfamiliar shadow and sound outside the cavern amplifies and threatens.

Enoli wipes sweat from forehead and slumps into concealment as he searches the terrain for militia.

The normal night's breeze rustles foliage and, to the youth, the peaceful cacophony becomes onrushing demons, intent upon murder.

Each demon pauses, and for an inexplicable reason deep in the mind, dissolves outside the cave's entrance.

Fear and dread swell the boy's eyes and ears, and he recoils with Saloli's reentrance.

The animal eyes shine wide in the dim light. "I followed for a while." Its whiskers stand out stiff and straight. "I sensed more. We stay here. Many hunt the real people."

"We're not creatures to be hunted." Enoli's words tremble in the night.

"But its fine to stalk squirrels?" The little scout's tone tightens. "Animals are your life. We die to feed you. Don't humans think concerning that?"

"You're the first wild one I spent time with, and you talk."

"That avoids my question."

"The answer changes me," the boy smiles. "You teach to be an ally, not an enemy."

"This day, a squirrel saved your scalp by distracting those settlers. Remember that."

"Yes. Thanks."

The little one nestles next to the boy's knees and squirms into the leaves on the cave's floor for comfort. "You're welcome. Get some sleep."

After a moment of silence, the boy turns to his side. "Whites are not total evil."

"Think so?" The furry one squiggles its nose.

"Yes. The soldier called Jedediah had me in his musket's sight but didn't shoot."

"I saw." With wide eyes, the animal wiggles his tail. "Why?"

"Don't know. Maybe he viewed you as a boy, his age. Or even humans become tired of killing. Get comfortable. Sleep." Saloli squirms into the leaves of the cave's bed. "But if you snore, Human, I'm going to wake you." After moments of silence, the fuzzy one crowds closer to Enoli's warmth. "Or, the White boy's Unetlanvhi (ᎤᏁᏓᏅᏫ u-ne-tla-nv-hi, Creator God) protects him for bigger plans."

***

The next day, after furry scout checks that White settlers no longer prowl, the boy and his friend descend through the timber to the village.

The cabins and lodges of his childhood home smoke and lay silent in the valley below the hill.

Enoli and Saloli inspect the ruins.

39

Many scalped Cherokee bodies, both children and adults, lie among the smoldering debris.

"I am helpless." The youth spreads both hands.

"Then recognize the plight of my kind." The fuzzy one sits on haunches.

"The pox takes mother and murderers kill the rest. There is nothing I can do in my power to prevent more of this. I cannot carry my people's problems." Enoli drops head into palms and releases months of suppressed tears.

"What are you going to do?" Saloli's boy-side eye blinks.

"What real humans do. Bury my folk and kin. Bury their promise, and their dreams."

CHAPTER FIVE — Dragging Canoe

ᎠᎡᏔᏍᎣᎢᏍᎤᎭᏴᎠᏎᎬᏆᎦᎳᏢᎳᏪᏓᎶᎹᎧᏍᎣᎯᎲᎷᏴᎮᏏᎮᏁᎲᏃᏀᎣᵛ

The next morning, Enoli sleeps on the ground near his burned-out lodge as early mists float above the cooled piles of the Paint Clan encampment's debris.

The semi-permanent village's remains rest between two protective sandstone abutments and a small creek bed that flows along one overhang through the settlement.

Horsemen move into the death-captured collection of charred Cherokee shelters.

A clay bowl near Enoli's nose vibrates from the impact of nearby hooves. The boy wakens and one eye flutters open.

Saloli sits on back legs at the burned lodge's entrance. "Riders come. Not militia. They don't clink iron shoes."

Mounted warriors armed with muskets dismount in the center of the village.

Mostly young men, in loincloths and leggings, individuals display heavy body and facial tattoos in traditional designs and survey the destruction.

The fighters wear soft-soled moccasins, and those with or without firearms carry bows and arrow quivers.

Enoli rubs sleep from his mind. He rises and steps out of the charred log frame of Ahyoka's cabin, and his furry companion jumps upon a shoulder.

The warrior nearest the boy rides a feisty mount that twists and turns as it stomps. His hair bunches backward, stiff with a band holder that supports three eagle feathers. A black stripe encircles his eyes and nose, and to his shoulders, red mud stains his skin.

Bear claws and large dark beads adorn the man's neck, and rings hang from his ears. He lifts his musket above his head and blasts powder skyward.

The boom reverberates around the valley.

"Revenge the Paint Clan! If you hide in the rocks and caves, Dragging Canoe calls for warriors to fight the White settlers!" The leader turns his horse and eyes the surrounding outcrops and timber.

Enoli steps near the warrior, and he spins his animal to face the boy.

"You are too young! The Whites eat children." The mount's hooves pound away. "I demand the healer, Mohi! Around campfires, taletellers speak of a person who cures the disease that kills my fighters. Bring me the medicine man."

"I am here," the healer's voice echoes over the group from the hill.

"You cure Unudakwala (smallpox)?" The warrior kicks his horse and lunges to the face the source.

"Yes, I serve as healer of the Paint Clan." The shaman stands in the abutments above the village and looks at the fighter.

The war leader slides off his animal and hands its reins to an assistant. "I am of the Wolf Clan, but I know your people's history of healing. Come where I can see you."

Saloli noses Enoli's ear. "I think it is wise not to annoy this warrior."

Others surface from hiding in the trees and rocks. They return with the medicine man into the burned camp.

As Mohi walks into the village center, Dragging Canoe's men stop and hold the healer before he meets the war leader.

"You speak the words of a braggart. Show me proof you heal, Medicine Man." The fighter withdraws a club from his belt and jerks his head. His protectors release the shaman.

"Look around you, Dragging Canoe. Most of these, I cured." Mohi sweeps one hand toward those alive that remain from the defeated village.

The leader points at several corpses. "These scalped ones too? The White man is deadlier than the pox. Why are they not buried?"

"We now realize the murderers no longer hunt. My people will bury our own." The healer points at Enoli. "This boy suffered the illness, and I brought him to health. He is part of my proof."

Saloli curls his body around the boy's neck. "Do we want this attention?"

Mohi stares at his recovered patient. "Look, he still wears a few dried marks of a Kosvkvskini."

Dragging Canoe peers at the youth and turns to the medicine man. "Let others grieve. Gather your herbal pouch and supplies you need. Ride with me against the Whites!"

"Wait!" Enoli holds his arms in the air for attention. "The shaman did not bring me thru the pox. The Unetlanvhi saved me when I promised to serve our people."

"Did you say that?" Nose whiskers vibrate.

"How old are you, Boy?" The leader steps closer. "Eight?"

"No. I am ten, almost eleven."

The warrior laughs, jumps and mounts his horse in one smooth motion. He rides close as the sun breaks the horizon and morning light flashes across his eyes. "You should thank your healer, not criticize his success."

"Mohi did what he could. His knowledge is primitive. He used the ancient ways, the sweat lodge, ice baths, rattles, and chants."

"This one uses his ways." Furry friend abandons the boy's neck and clings to his back opposite the warrior. "Make him angry, and he'll split your skull."

"You are better than the old methods?" Dragging Canoe fingers the war club at his waist.

"He drained blood as the settler's doctors do and brought death to my mother."

War leader stops his mount. "As the Whites?"

Saloli's friend stands before a hater of settlers and their government. "Yes. But in my fever, I spoke to the Unetlanvhi who saved me."

"You talked to the Creator God?" The man leans from his horse and peers into bright eyes.

"Yes."

"Is that why you didn't bury these brothers?" The warrior whips the back of his hand across young lips and face, "Show respect for your elders, your kin and the old ways!"

Enoli grimaces and licks blood from his burst lip.

The mounted rider kicks his horse and, as it turns its flank, knocks the youngster to the ground. "Come with us. You are an inexperienced fighter but too favored to starve with these leftover hide-in-the-hills cowards."

As the fighting men mount in the council clearing, Mohi

steps closer. "I go with Dragging Canoe but remember your dishonor."

Saloli jumps to the ground away from the medicine man.

"One day, you will regret your words." The shaman knees the young man in the crotch, and he collapses with pain. "When you are a fly-infested corpse!"

The mounted warriors pound out of the valley, followed by those on foot.

Enoli struggles to his feet and follows the footmen.

Saloli pads along but jumps to ride upon his shoulder.

"You may leave if you wish. I am with my people and can take care of myself." The boy shifts the furry one to a more comfortable perch.

"Maybe so? But not so well against Mohi."

The youngster spits. "He sees me as a threat. That's the last time he will surprise me."

"Threat or mortal enemy," whiskers vibrate, "he doesn't tolerate opposition."

"I like you, Saloli, but don't think this is your cause." The boy shifts the little one to his arm. "A war party doesn't welcome peace advocates."

"Might be dangerous," the animal clings, "but the corn supply I steal has dried up in this village."

***

Dragging Canoe's warriors travel through the foothills of the Appalachian Mountains.

The mounted fighters lead, and those on foot trail. The walkers straggle, and the column breaks into smaller groups. Scouts range the woods to alert the main body if danger threatens.

45

Walkers arrive for the night as the sun sets. The camp, semi-permanent, appears larger than the Paint Clan's village with groups on both sides of a freshwater creek.

To Enoli, the number of sweat lodges for active treatment of smallpox warn of disease.

"So, they came to us not to save lives from the militia. They needed Mohi to treat their sick." The boy nods his head.

"Think you're right. I leave you for the night. Too many real people need dinner." Saloli jumps to the ground and scampers to a nearby tree.

Enoli walks through the encampment and familiarizes himself with the new surroundings. He pauses at a sweat lodge and listens to suffering.

No camper pays attention to a ten-year-old unattached kid except one warrior. "Paint Clan boy! You, we just saved. Come to our fire. We share our supper with those that have no families." The man includes Enoli in his group. They roast venison on a spit over an open-air campfire.

The youngster settles into the warm circle of allies and listens to the men talk. Their meat smells and pops with scent and flavor.

"Dragging Canoe promises to make our people great again. He remembers when our lands stretched on both sides of the mountains and leads us in return to that day." One warrior shakes his war hatchet at the fire.

"The Whites are weak. They are farmers. Their weapons sit at their sides as they dig the earth and create holes for seeds. smallpox is our strongest enemy."

Another man rises. "After Mohi stops the pox, we strike the White settlers!"

"Others say live in friendship with colonists. They are traitors who lose." Hatchet-holder struts before the fire. "Dragging Canoe always wins. Those peacemakers promise but cannot deliver our lands and our way of life." Warrior with the war club chops a chunk off the venison roast and hands it to Enoli. "Eat Dragging Canoe's food and warm your body. You must be strong to kill settlers."

The group settles into dinner, and the youth pockets corn kernels for Saloli from the group's clay serving bowl.

***

Days pass, and the boy's world moves in slow motion.

Sunrise brings his fuzzy friend and walks in the woods.

Midday, the two hunt for venison or rabbit; the furry one prohibits squirrels. Evenings bring more war talk around campfires.

Only descriptions of smallpox deaths interrupt.

As the time flows, fewer reports of pox restrict the militancy of Dragging Canoe's followers.

During a middle morning, Enoli wanders through the camp with little purpose other than curiosity.

His surroundings bustle with preparation.

"Here, wrap this extra pemmican in your blanket." A woman stuffs provisions in her husband's pack.

Men prepare horses and backpacks for travel and conflict.

Warriors emerge from their cabins and lodges, bid their families goodbye, and move to the council circle in the center of the encampment.

Enoli, with Saloli on his shoulder, joins the tide.

"Why the excitement?" The little furry wags its tail and flashes its white fur tail slash.

"I think the talk around here turns to action." The boy watches a warrior color his forehead.

Fighters gather around the central council circle.

A Cherokee, most beloved, war-woman parades before the men. With red paint over the side of her face, she brandishes a musket. "Warriors!"

The crowd cheers.

"We have camped too long. Over-mountain militia and the continentals raided our villages while we nursed our sick." The firebrand fires her rifle into the air and powder smoke engulfs the group. As it clears, she reloads. "We can wait no more. Blood law demands revenge. It is the Cherokee way!"

Dragging Canoe guides his horse into the melee and pulls the militant woman onto his mount with him. "Warriors! Mohi has won our battle with the sickness!"

The medicine man walks behind his leader.

"With smallpox gone, as our war women call, we turn to those that invade!" The warrior dismounts. "Drive the Whites out of our lives!"

The congregation of fighters cheers and screams with enthusiasm.

On horseback, the war-woman rides behind Dragging Canoe out of the encampment.

Enoli stands in the council clearing and watches the spectacle.

"They refused to let me go with them." The boy shades his eyes from the morning sun. "They said I was too young."

"Good thing, boy of the real people." The animal clutches the youth's shoulder near his ear. "Their leaders lie."

"Not so loud." Enoli grasps his friend and pulls it from his neck into the crook of an elbow. "Don't forget where we get your corn."

"The settlers are stronger than your tribe and the other tribes." Saloli shivers. "I have seen them move west over our mountains, and they will not stop."

"The Whites," he scratches the fuzzy one, "are smallpox. Both are unstoppable."

50

CHAPTER SIX — Son of Stone Cloud

DRᏠᎣᎥᏏᏍᎠᎸᏯAJEᏍᏘᎠᏲᎦᎾWᏓᏞGMᎣᏑᎤᏲᎯᎯᏚᏣᏲᎦᎠᏄᎯᏂZᏔᎣᏽ

Days out of Dragging Canoe's encampment, Enoli trudges through the brush of Georgia with Saloli scampering in the lead. The boy wears a loincloth with deerskin leggings and moccasins. His small knife in a decorated sheath hangs at the waist, and he totes a shoulder pack.

"My heart feels free since we left. Those were not my people. The warriors' wives and relatives saw me as a coward, or a traitor."

"My stomach grumbles for their corn." The boy's companion scurries up a tree trunk.

"Last time I wandered, my mother and I met a Kosvkvskini." Enoli's eyes dart through the landscape.

"The spirits punish your tribe for breaking tribal codes and not performing religious ceremonies correctly," Saloli cracks an acorn. "Not you and your mom."

"Laws mean little with the pox." The young man drops to his knees for a rest break.

"Your people drift from the old beliefs! They don't practice traditions." Furry one chomps the fruit of the nut. "This is not sweet corn," the squirrel spits, "and chewy. Sure we can't go back?"

"They die from the Kosvkvskini's oozing pustules."

"Not you." The animal licks long whiskers. "You will never catch the disease again."

"That is true. It spared me." The youth stands and lifts his pack. "Lead on, friend. This is far from home."

Enoli shifts his load as the guide scurries ahead along an obscure trail.

That afternoon, the little scout stops atop a ridge. They look along the slope.

In the valley, two dozen Cherokee lodges cluster beside a creek, which bubbles through the encampment.

Several structures support added hides and blankets, but no smoke billows from these unused sweat houses.

Others stand open with sides removed for air circulation.

In each, a person lies on an elevated mat and families gather vigil-distanced from the patient.

In the center of the town, a bonfire burns clothing and possessions. Family members carry items to the flames with long branches.

"They fight the pox, Saloli. I can help." Enoli strides toward the camp with his friend at heels.

***

The boy nears the encampment. An imposing figure steps out of the first lodge. The middle-aged man stands before the young one and extends a hand palm out. "Stop. Who are you?"

"I am of the Anowodi (ᎠᏃᏬᏗ ah-no-wo-di, Paint Clan)." His little companion collides with an ankle. The furry animal shakes a head and staggers from the abrupt collision.

"This is an Aniawe (ᎠᏂᎠᏪ ah-ni-ah-we, Deer Clan) village. I am Anowodi but have not lived with my people for many years." The man's tattoos cross mouth and chin and stretch pustule scars that deface traditional facial art. "I am a medicine man, and this camp battles Unudakwala (ᎤᏅᏓᏆᎳ oo-nu-da-qua-la, smallpox)."

"My mother and I encountered a Kosvkvskini. She died, but I survived with only these small marks." The boy touches his neck and lower jaw.

"Are you deranged? Kosvkvskini do not bring the pox!" The healer laughs. "Only in dreams."

Saloli clears his brain and eyes.

Upon haunches, the boy's companion evaluates the man's tattoos.

The familiar marks spread across mouth and chin. "Enoli, this medicine man knows evil spirits!"

The shaman jerks and stares at the fuzzy escort. "You speak to the youngster? I thought I was the only person who communicates with animals outside a dream."

"You understood?" The boy stares in amazement.

"What is your name?" He rests a hand on the younger's shoulders.

Saloli expels air in a primitive expletive, "I told you of him, Enoli!"

"No one besides me hears you." The amazed youngster lowers his pack with a jaw open. "You must be an important healer."

"It's him, the great healer." The boy's little friend stares at the man's tattoos.

"No. But I am the son of greatness. My father was Stone Cloud."

Furry tail pads forward, "Remember me from Cherokee Rock?"

"The shaman lifts the squirrel.

"I lived in the woods near your school for years, but please put me on the ground."

"Of course." The great man pats the animal on firm ground. "There were many around Cherokee Rock. We fed corn. Sorry, I don't recall you and that white slash tail."

The little one sits on haunches. "But I remember. This is my friend Enoli. I was leading him to you."

"I am of the medicine tribe." The youngster extends a hand. The two grasp wrists. "I survived the pox and promised the Unetlanvhi to help my people."

"Did your squirrel promise?" Son of Stone Cloud laughs, and the warmth of humor softens his content. "Most I know of are self-centered."

The youth glances at his companion.

The fuzzy one shivers through fur and speaks for himself. "I am not only this boy's friend. I am his family. We work together. Where Enoli goes, I go."

Son of Stone Cloud laughs with pleasure. "You had the pox. Squirrels do not catch the disease. Come, walk with me into the village."

The shaman and the boy pass a lodge where a child suffers from fever. Its skin and bark walls sit open to the air, and the patient sweats on a mat above the ground on branches that form a second floor.

"Circulation allows the sickness to flee, and in warm months it cools. A sick person feels body comfort. The old sweat lodges stand empty since I arrived." The medicine man points at an unused encased room.

"You do not live here?" Enoli walks closer to a male patient.

"No, this clan sent for help," Son of Stone Cloud follows the boy. "When we contain the disease, we will return to the school at Cherokee Rock."

"This man's pustules seep." The youngster dips a cloth into a clay pot of creek water and swabs salty drops from the patient's forehead.

"Yes, in a contagious period. Notice that we allow no relatives or visitors." The shaman sweeps an arm at the surroundings. "For the next six to eight days, this man spreads the pox."

"The Paint Clan's healer kept mother in a lodge while he danced with rattles to entertain the kin." The young man's thoughts relive the treatment.

"And she perished from the heavy cough, not the causative illness. The old way doused the sweaty with ice water." The older gentleman thumps his chest with a fist in protest. "As many died attempting to breathe as from high temperatures."

"This man may die of fever," Saloli hops up to the second level of the lodge, "but his breath sounds normal."

"I do not believe he will succumb to suffocation. But we can use the fluids from his pustules." The healer examines the bumps and swells on the patient's face.

"I don't understand." The boy looks at the teacher.

"Last year, a slave escaped the British occupation of Charleston. He told of a practice in Africa. They take a dab of fluid from a scab and apply it to a minor cut in another person's skin. A few of these patients died but most only suffered mild fever and became well." The older healer slips a bundle of eagle feathers from a pouch.

The shaman dabs the end of a quill into puss on the patient's jaw.

Enoli watches, and Saloli's whiskers vibrate faster than a tuning fork.

With the feather, followed by the boy and his furry friend, the healer exits and stops a woman. "Your turn." He nicks her shoulder with a knife and presses the sticky quill onto the wound. "Go to your lodge and rest. You will be sick soon."

She smiles, nods understanding without fear, and continues her walk.

"An easy treatment. As a first duty, Son of Stone Cloud's assistant, help with the rest of the village."

"And you are sure that won't kill them?" The boy watches the treated one walk away.

"Yes. Since the slave shared his family's practice, I heard of a White man named Cotton Mather who sixty years ago controlled a massive outbreak of the disease in the town of Boston. Dozens died but most became immune."

"I have a small knife," the volunteer pats a belt sheaf, "but I will need eagle feathers."

***

For the rest of daylight, the boy and the great shaman inoculate villagers.

The evening of the tenth day after inoculations, Enoli and Son of Stone Cloud sit cross-legged at a campfire in the encampment. The light from the flames speckles Saloli's nose as he nestles beside his friend.

"None are sick with the pox. You are truly a successful medicine man." The youngster nods at his mentor.

"One of the prime rules for a healer is not to judge before he knows the facts." The shaman looks at the sleeping semi-permanent camp. "The disease takes time to infect. Today is too soon to expect fever."

"When should we look for dying?" Saloli sits back on haunches.

"Tomorrow is the eleventh day. The fever flares in the morning." The man turns from his companions at the fire.

"How many will die?" Enoli wipes perspiration from his forehead.

"You sweat. Fever?" Fuzzy little fellow at his knees jumps into the boy's lap.

"No, the night is warm."

"One or two," the shaman shakes his head, "better than no inoculations."

"I dread the sun." The boy lies shoulders on a sleeping mat. "Deaths remind me of my mother."

"We make the sick comfortable. Open their lodges for air circulation and insist the families burn clothing and possessions the fever touched. This will be over in fourteen days, and we return to Cherokee Rock. Now sleep. You need the rest." Son of Stone Cloud rolls his back to the fire.

Saloli settles next to the boy as Enoli slips into a night world.

***

Dark storm clouds gather, cover the stars, and fill the sky in the boy's dream.

Ominous rumbles follow an occasional strike of distant lightening. They punctuate the horizon.

The young man opens his eyes.

A Deer Clan village no longer surrounds. No fire burns near his sleeping mat, which now rests in a vast plain of long grass.

The wind from the approaching storm sways the blade crowns, and they bend in unison as waves on the land.

Enoli feels at his waist and grasps his furry friend who awakens. "You do not sleep, real people. What bothers you?"

The boy sits up and gazes across the sea of green.

A man and a woman stalk. The female, a ripe chestnut burr hue covered with fine prickles, creeps with the other behind, a shadow of chokeberry color.

"I am afraid." The squirrel presses closer.

"They are Kosvkvskini." The boy trembles.

Evil woman approaches and draws close. Imitating a porcupine, she brandishes pricks. The male follows with red feverish eyes that glow in the night.

"We violate the old laws and ignore traditional treatment for the pox." The furry friend scrambles to the boy's neck and peeps over a shoulder. "That's why they come."

"Kosvkvskini! I am an apprentice to the Son of Stone Cloud! Why do you threaten?" The boy stands with Saloli on his back.

The woman, half-wraith and part pustule-scarred Cherokee, extends a skeletal hand and points a forefinger's extended nail, "You abandon the ways of the Unetlanvhi and follow paths forged by false mentors. For sins such as these, we visit."

"Teachers are often incorrect. Son of Stone Cloud learns from nature by trial and error. He is not a hoax. His soul searches for answers from the Creator God." Enoli confronts the wraiths.

"Is he the Unetlanvhi's Son?" The woman drops the pointed finger.

"No, he is the offspring of a great shaman."

"Your people are not the only ones we call." The pustuled person observes the storm boil on the horizon. *"We visit the White men. They follow another god's child. The settlers ignore their gods from before the adoption of One God. We Kosvkvskini come from those times. The Cherokee lived by favor of the water beetle and the far land's fair skin people at the will of Zeus."*

"The evil ones eat too many acorns," Saloli nips at the boy's ear. *"She rambles through history as fast as I bury nuts."*

"Leave." The boy waves a hand. *"Take the diseased creeper with you. We change. I no longer believe. This is a dream."*

"I do not have the power to hurt you." The vision crosses her arms in resignation. *"But many of your people and the White settlers have not experienced my embrace. I still have much to share."*

Enoli wakens with his furry friend asleep at the waist. He rolls and hears the first feverish groan from a Deer Clan lodge nearby.

***

For the next two weeks, the boy, Son of Stone Cloud, and Saloli work to create conditions within the encampment that foster wellness from smallpox.

An enormous bonfire of clothing and other items blazes constantly in the center of the village instead of a council fire.

Family members tote water from the creek and swab sweaty foreheads. With the remaining jugs, they slosh vomit from lodges.

Near the end of the recovery, Saloli rushes to Enoli and

59

Son of Stone Cloud, "Warriors come on horseback. I counted twelve."

The boy and the shaman twist to the south where Dragging Canoe, followed by Mohi, rides with young Cherokee fighters into the Deer Clan village.

"That's only eight." His friend jumps to the boy's shoulder. "When I spotted them, the warriors pulled three White captives, two militia and a woman. Four or more guard the prisoners."

Son of Stone Cloud steps to meet the visitors. "We have the pox in this village. I am a shaman and tell you to bypass this illness."

Dragging Canoe reins his horse to a stop and looks at the village. "I see no sweat lodges?"

"Air cools their fever," the medicine man confronts the warrior.

"How many have died?" The leader dismounts.

"Three. One more may not make morning."

"Then you do not have the pox. Do you have the illness of chickens?" The red-eye-painted and black-chinned horseman dismisses the shaman by body language. "People of the Deer Clan! Listen to the words of Dragging Canoe. Come! Gather! I have news."

As the villagers exit lodges and approach, the warrior nods to his medicine man. "Tell this apprentice his patients have the egg's pox."

Mohi dismounts and steps in front of his professional colleague. "I am Mohi, shaman of the Paint Clan. I serve the liberators of Cherokee lands, led by Dragging Canoe. When we succeed, I will return to my work."

The greater medicine man spreads his arms. "I have no loyalty to any group. I only strive for the real people. You know me as Son of Stone Cloud."

Mohi twists to his colleague, stunned and flabbergasted by recognition. "Then they don't have the chicken's pox?"

The great practitioner, with his fingers clasped, smiles and shakes his head negatively.

Ignoring the conversation, Dragging Canoe struts his horse in front of the crowd. "We fight White settlers who take our lands! They are many, and we are twelve. Four of my men guard three of our enemies who will roast on my campfire tonight. Come. Watch! Militia burn, but their smoke smells different. Attend, but if you are of the age to resist the settlers, your presence joins this war party. Understood?"

Mohi grasps the leader's elbow and speaks into an ear.

The warrior eyes and considers the greater shaman.

He turns to the crowd. "Talk says this village suffers from the pox. I know you have only three dead. That is not a Kosvkvskini visit! Some of your heroes spend too much time clucking like chickens and spreads their sickness!"

The leader leaps upon his horse, laughs at his pox joke, and circles the animal. "Come! Watch me burn a White settler tonight! Then ride with Dragging Canoe!" He heels his mount and leads the band out of the Deer Clan village.

"Mohi did not see us." Saloli rubs front paws together.

"Good." Enoli smiles agreement.

CHAPTER SEVEN — Acceptance

DRTꭶOꞋiꮝꭽYᴧJEꮙꭾᏗᎻᎢꮪWꭷᏒGMᏀꭶOᎻᏃᎽᎾᏛᎾᏁhᏃꝯOᴠ

Through the woods that night, Enoli walks toward the glow of Dragging Canoe's campfire, and Saloli prances before him on the ground.

The animal stops a few feet forward and sits on his haunches. "You know I am the best thing you have, a father figure. You're an eleven-year-old kid with no family, no prospects, and no path to grow. If you do find your way by luck, I expect your future is death from a settler's musket ball."

"For you, my friend, I'm better than corn." The boy laughs. "You have a human to boss. But it sounds like you don't think I'm worth the effort?"

"You view this wrong." The animal follows Enoli. "Listen to me. You apprentice with Son of Stone Cloud. You were born of the Paint Clan, with the birthright of shamans. An apprentice-ship is a possible destiny. Yours. What an opportunity!"

"So, I am worthy of your time?"

"If they offered me a permanent nest in the world's most acorn-covered oak tree, would I accept?"

"No. You would search for one in a cornfield."

"Poor example I chose." Whiskers droop. "I advise you to apprentice with Son of Stone Cloud."

"First problem, he hasn't asked me." The boy stops and looks at his friend. "Second issue is why?"

"You want a better life?"

"It is more complicated than that."

"You humans make everything complex."

"Smallpox is only one thing that kills my people. We don't care about shaman talk that doesn't help cure the disease. Most just die. The land, crops, family are more important."

"You reject my fatherly advice?" Saloli's whiskers vibrate.

"You mean well, but it makes no sense. Reality forces a choice between Dragging Canoe and Son of Stone Cloud. The shaman's a better man. Smallpox holds us, but not the land. My people need warriors to save our home." The youngster continues into Dragging Canoe's camp.

Furry one stops. "Go ahead. Join the fighters. That kid at the cave might have shot you. With you defending me, I'm safer in a tree."

"Hunters like targets on branches. Someday, one's going to blast you off a limb." Enoli shudders as a frigid chill tickles his backbone.

Musket blasts from the celebration ahead echo through the woods.

"Not today. Unless those shooters get lucky." Saloli scurries up the bark of an oak.

***

The boy walks into the light of Dragging Canoe's council fire, which burns in the center of his warriors' temporary lodges.

At an end of the pit, an entire venison roasts on a spit. Attendants turn its pike for even cooking.

Warriors surround a split barrel's top and dip clay cups.

"Dragging Canoe shares the White man's molasses rum!" The drinker staggers as he dips another cup.

Enoli joins the drinkers, and a fighter shoves a full vessel into his hand. "Drink! Our war party captured good stuff from the militia." The server waits for a response.

The young man drinks alcohol for the first experience and expels his mouthful. "That is terrible! It burns!"

The warriors at the keg laugh and clap the boy on his back, which encourages his gag reflex.

Enoli throws the liquid in his cup into the grass and wipes his lips. He looks to see who watches.

Near the opposite edge of the recruitment party, three Whites, two men and a woman, hang upside down tied to chopped tree limbs that suspend across low-hanging branches.

The boy walks from the rum keg to the cooking fire and admires the roasting meat. Dozens of corn cobs and fresh squash cook over coals and flood the air with delicious smells.

Other young fellows from the Deer Clan's village, older and of prime recruitment age, drift into Dragging Canoe's camp.

Several join the group at the rum keg and relish drinks from their hosts.

Enoli turns toward a commotion.

Mohi beats a drum. "The noble warrior, captor of these settlers, he who of stops their invasion, Dragging Canoe!"

The medicine man steps aside, and the leader walks into the light around the fire pit. "Men of the Deer Clan, we welcome you to our camp. Eat our food! Drink the White man's molasses rum! Celebrate our victory!"

Enoli moves behind a group of older men to avoid Mohi's sight.

Dragging Canoe struts to the three bound captives.

"Settlers are weak! These terrified worms dig in our tribal earth." The war leader reaches and grabs a wad of the woman prisoner's hair.

He yanks her head upward, whips his knife from his belt, and slices her open mouth across the juncture of top and bottom lips.

Upside down, the woman's skull hangs with a limp jaw and blood spurts onto the ground. Her throat gurgles air as she bleeds.

The two suspended men's legs spasm as they watch with eyes bulged wide.

"These others are militia." The war leader in red paint points his bloody knife.

Enoli focuses on the youngest's captive's face.

His mind revisits the cave hiding place and the youth White settler who peered at his forehead along a musket barrel.

Jedidiah, not much older but enough that whiskers bristle his chin, blubbers tears of fear, and blood drips from one ear. The boy's blond dirty hair frames freckles that dot orange spots in the firelight across his nose.

Dragging Canoe parades before the woman as she gurgles. He gestures toward the other prisoners, "These are captured militia cockroaches. They will no longer steal our lands."

Warriors grasp the limb where the older militiaman hangs and lift.

They check with the leader, who nods.

One on each side of the fire pit, they suspend the settler over the flames like a spit of venison.

Screams penetrate the night.

When his noises stop, they drop the body into the burning logs and coals.

It crackles and pops.

Enoli bursts through the cluster of young Deer Clan recruits and strides to the blond head of Jedediah as the White boy hangs upside down. "This one, I claim. No one harm him!"

Dragging Canoe turns to the two boys and laughs, "He would take your scalp!"

"No! His musket barrel pointed at my forehead, and he didn't fire!"

The warrior leader twists to his audience. "Should I release him?"

His eyes focus on Mohi.

"Yes!" Enoli drops to his knees and begs, "Don't kill him."

The leader's medicine man whips out his war hatchet and lunges.

The boy jumps between the weapon and the prisoner with his hunting knife drawn.

Boom!" A round hole spots the White settler Jedediah's forehead. Blood spurts from the opening as a musket's retort explodes from across the firepit.

A horizontal plume of black powder smoke hangs over the fire and traces to Son of Stone Cloud, who lowers his firearm.

Mohi turns away from Enoli and glares at the shaman.

Dragging Canoe glances at his audience before spreading his arms in welcome. "Healer! Do you join our war against the White settlers?"

"No. I battle the pox."

The boy Jedediah hangs without life, and a pool of blood grows below his head.

"That man I shot spreads the sickness," Son of Stone Cloud leans on his rifle. "Burn him. He sickens our people no more."

Dragging Canoe considers the shaman's words for a moment and points at Mohi, "Our shaman cured our fighters of the disease." He turns to the shooter who reloads his musket. "We thank you for preventing more."

The healer motions to Enoli. "Come. We have no more business here."

With jealous hatred in his eyes, Mohi watches the skilled physician and his charge walk away from the war camp.

***

Out of hearing by the Dragging Canoe warriors, the youngster looks up at his savior. "That militia boy was not sick. Why did you shoot him?"

The older man smiles. "Saloli saw him from the trees and remembered the boy spared you. He came for me. Your friend knew you would act. You and the little one make an excellent team."

"Animals live in the old way," Enoli returns the shaman's grin, "from ancient days of peace and equanimity. We real people are savage beasts who live by blood law and spew hatred. The White settlers are only guests within our lands."

"Or usurpers? I return to Cherokee Rock. You have no parents and no plans. Travel with me. You are of the Paint Clan. Train to be a healer."

The two walk through the dark woods in silence for a moment.

"Thank you, but no. I detest the world's hostility and how we attack each other. It must stop. If I hide from the world, I cannot face life, smallpox, or the settlers."

"Don't answer quick like a mockingbird." Saloli drops to the boy's shoulder from a tree. "Consider what the great one offers."

Son of Stone Cloud understands the fuzzy animal. "I hear what your companion tells you. But I do not want you to commit against your wish. It is a lifetime choice."

Furry one pops the white of its tail against his friend's neck. "You are eleven years old. Think of adulthood without skills."

The shaman slips an arm about the young man's shoulder. "My offer remains. You and I are the only ones of the Paint Clan that understand your little friend. Saloli tells me you struggle with questions and search for a path. The Unetlanvhi (Creator God) will guide."

***

That night, Enoli tosses in his sleep and dreams.

Through dense undergrowth, the boy follows his mother over moon-lit hills under low clouds. The wind and the terrain resist progress as Ahyoka waves from one hundred yards ahead. Her face glows, and she beckons him to follow.

"Wait!" his voice floats under the sky.

She moves forward to the next ridge where another glow lights the horizon.

In the finest ceremonial headdress and deerskin vest, a vision stands, whom she embraces.

Mother turns to her son, and he lip-reads her words, "Enoli, your father, a great fighter who died in a battle with the British before you were born."

The youngster stops in awe of the figure that shines before him.

The warrior peers at his offspring for the first time. "You are a black fox. Your soul is dark and disturbed. You slink around wary of life and imitate your namesake. I did not give you courage to cower in a den under a log and fear the world."

"Then why did you create me?" The boy drops to his knees.

"To extend my deeds through you. I no longer fight the White man and his ways. I left that duty for you. Your mother called you Enoli (Black Fox,) and I was not with you to object."

"What would you have named me?"

"It was your mother's choice. To change, you must earn the right. Only you may create a new identity under the Unetlanvhi. The manner that you live your life will decide a name."

Enoli hangs his head with humility and indecision.

His father's voice rises above the hills, the clouds, and echoes off the moon. "Black Fox you are. An appropriate name. Your soul wanders, and your intentions stumble. Follow my lead. Find your way."

"And how do I do that, Father?"

"Stand as a man, not a child. Discover direction from the Unetlanvhi. Examine yourself and listen to the quiet words within you. Eleven years old is a wonderful time. Your mother and I cannot guide you further, but you do not need our thoughts. Search inward and then step outward. That is the path from Black Fox to whomever you become. Go. Find your way."

Enoli tosses in his sleep and his dream seeps behind his eyes, out of focus.

The following morning, the boy accepts Son of Stone Cloud's offer.

72

CHAPTER EIGHT — Apprenticeship

ᎠᎡᎢᎣᎤᎥᎦᎧᎨᎩᎪᎫᎬᎭᎮᎯᎰᎱᎲᎳᎴᎵᎶᎷᎸᎹᎺᎻᎼᎽᎾᎿᏀᏁᏂᏃᏄᏅ

The fall of 1780 changes the colors of the landscape.

The tutelage of the Son of Stone Cloud grows and educates Enoli into adulthood.

From his base under Cherokee Rock, a lime deposit abutment that extends over the mix of two rivers deep within tribal lands, the great medicine man apprentices many boys from ten to fifteen years of age.

An enormous cave under the outcrop, accessible only by a concealed passageway, provides a home and an educational laboratory.

From the rock's viewpoint, the landscape for many miles lays open, security monitored.

The dispersal of his Paint Clan, thoughts of warriors and White settlers, the French and Indian War's residual tribal alliance with the British during the colonies' fight for independence, and other distractions fade from the boy's mind as he works through his apprenticeship.

He concentrates on lessons and daily duties.

The Son of Stone Cloud, with an ability in dream interpretation, often instructs through night's sleeping thoughts.

In one lesson, the shaman induces his apprentice with a mixture of herbs boiled in owl pellets. As the boy settles onto his night's mat, he hugs his constant companion and pulls its furry body to his chest.

Blessed by the ability to understand squirrel chitter, Enoli's thoughts and mind drift into thoughts of the ancient days when animals, birds, fish and insects communicate with the real people.

***

Those musings transfer to reality.

Wildlife lives with the Tsalagi (ᏣᎳᎩ ja-la-gi, Cherokee) in peace and friendship, but their population and lodges spread and crowd the originals from their homes.

Real people invent hooks, knives, bows, and arrows and harvest life for flesh or skin.

Smaller beetles and frogs die from carelessness or under Indian heels.

For safety, the majority calls for a council.

Enoli hears of these meetings and sends Saloli to observe and report on their agenda.

Bears meet first.

A leader with white hair from the North presides.

"The Aniyuwiya (ᎠᏂᏳᏫᏯ ah-ni-yoo-wi-yah, principal people) shot my older brother with arrows. When he was too weak to fight back, they pierced his ribs with spears." The bear stands on his hind legs and displays his chest. "They ate his flesh and wore his skin for warmth in the winter."

"They cover their lodges with my cousin's fur," a second dark one jumps to his claws, "and wears her teeth as a necklace!"

Unnoticed, Enoli's spy settles on the branch of a tree that overhangs the meeting.

First bear calls for war, "We are strong! The Aniyuwiya are many, but we are bigger! Death to the murderers!"

White hair from the north gestures for order. "What weapons do they have to hurt us?"

"Bows and arrows!" Several in attendance respond by clapping paws and clattering claws.

"What are they made of?" The older moderator directs his question to the applause.

"The bow is wood and the string, my cousin's entrails." The accolades become clenched fists.

"Then I say," the speaker pauses for audience attention, "use their weapons against them. Let us make our own and reconvene tomorrow."

Saloli stays still and hides upon his limb until the council disperses.

Overnight and the following day, one animal searches and finds ideal locust wood for bows, and a martyr sacrifices himself for the greater good to donate entrails for cord.

Enoli's little spy, from the same branch as before, watches the gathering collect that afternoon.

A young brown bear, ready for war, demonstrates the first bow. He steps forward in front of the moderator and members. He flies an arrow after drawing its string.

The youth snorts as a long claw catches the draw and the shaft's point, misfires, and buries into the earth inches from the moderator's paw.

The white hair leader jerks his leg away from the quivering shaft, "You aim at me?"

"No. I must trim my nails," the warrior looks at his lengthy appendages.

"Then you become unable to get up trees," the moderator grasps another attendee's foot. "One of our kind died for bow string. But if we cut our claws, we cannot hunt for food. We will starve together. We use our teeth and feet as our weapons. Aniyuwiya's bows and arrows are not for us."

Deer conducts the next council in a clearing in the forest where Saloli hides in the brush at its edge.

After discussion, females resolve that every real person that kills their kind asks for permission in advance.

They choose a small fast buck, quick to avoid danger, and gifts it with the power to inflict rheumatism on stalkers if they cannot ask for its prey's pardon.

During the talk, Enoli's spy creeps closer to the gathering through the grass to better hear. More alert than bear, these animals notice its brown fur.

The leader, with twelve-point horns, thumps to its feet. "We see you in the brush. Step forward. Join us as we decide how to handle the Aniyuwiya."

The squirrel sits on its haunches. "I listened. The Cherokee eat my kind's flesh and use our pelts for warmth and decoration. But I have befriended Enoli, a young student of the great shaman, Son of Stone Cloud, and cannot embrace your cause."

"Then, why are you here?" The buck lowers its rack to the ground.

"My friend knows wildlife meets and no longer wants to live in peace and mutual respect. He sent me to listen and watch your councils."

"And report back?" The leader paws the earth with a hoof. "Yes."

"Instruct your master and the great shaman teacher with

him that they cannot slaughter deer without repercussions. Inform the other Aniyuwiya, they must ask pardon first or rheumatism cripples the hunter. When they kill one of us, Fast As The Wind runs to the blood stains. He listens to the deceased spirit. If it heard the prayer of the killer, fine. If not, he follows the blood drops to the traitor's lodge. He enters unseen and strikes with the infliction. Go tell that to your friends."

Saloli hurries through the grass to deliver the message to Enoli and Son of Stone Cloud. His path leads over a creek tributary into a large lake where fish and reptiles air their own grievances in joint council.

As the furry ally of the Aniyuwiya pauses, he hears those that slide upon scaly stomachs decide to make their Cherokee assassins dream of snakes in slime that blow vile smells on their faces.

Those that breath water vow to give Indian anglers raw and decaying meat so they lose appetite, sicken, and die.

Saloli recognizes the threat to his friend Enoli and takes to the trees where he travels faster, only to stumble upon a gathering of the birds, insects, and smaller animals who council together.

The Grubworm presides over the deliberations.

They decide seven votes condemn humankind.

The moderator recognizes Frog (ᎬᎶᏏ wa-lo-si), who jumps to speak, "We must check the increase of people! They crowd us off the earth. Man has kicked me because I'm ugly until my back shows sores."

Bird (ᏥᏒᏩ tsi-su-wa) condemns humans, "They burn my toes."

Grubworm requests clarification.

"They cook our bodies on a stick over the fire, so our feathers and tender feet roast first!" The flier extends his wings so attendees may admire his plumage.

Saloli steps from concealment. "We share our land with Cherokee. I coexist with one by the name of Enoli. We must live together despite our differences. My friend never hunts for reasons other than food and clothing. He is not more guilty than you who eat smaller animals or each other. I say only those that have never harmed can vote to harm!"

Saloli's words enrage the council, and they strike with stingers and bites. He curls in defense and suffers back wounds from head to tail.

The assembly abandons their attack as Grubworm refocuses the meeting, "We must devise and name new diseases, so humans cannot survive!"

As the group invents plagues to inflict upon the Cherokee, injured Saloli sneaks away and through supreme effort rejoins Enoli.

***

"You bleed. What's happened?" the boy leaps from his cot to help his friend.

"There is much danger." The small animal collapses. "Humanity has broken its treaty with the birds, fish, insects, and snakes. You kill for food and clothing. Others you destroy without thought and my types are angry. They meet in great councils to rid their earth of you. There is nothing to do. I fear our friendship and my loyalty ends. Man cannot survive." Saloli surrenders to exhaustion and sleep.

Enoli lifts the small, injured messenger to his sleeping mat and turns to his medicine pouch.

The apprentice spreads a paste on its wounds. "Good work, my faithful scout. This heals your body, but forever you carry the stripe on your tail and know your attackers remember inflicting these wounds."

The young shaman replaces the Goldenseal into his bag and pauses.

He stares at the sparse contents available for use.

The youngster assures himself the squirrel rests and then surveys the cavern. Son of Stone Cloud and the others sleep.

Enoli steps into the night.

Moonlight sparkles reflections off the rivers below Cherokee Rock, but the apprentice moves away into surrounding scrub and timbers.

He shifts his medicine bag's strap for more comfort over his shoulder and follows the path of the moon through the brush.

As the young man walks, the breeze strengthens. Limbs of trees brush together, and their music drifts. Grass rustles and adds more tenor to the natural symphony.

"Enoli, son of She Brought Happiness, can you heed our call?"

"Mother, is that you?" the boy stops. He concentrates on the subtleties of the wind through plants, large and small.

"No, but we are as friendly to you," the breeze returns across the grasses. "You and your people face danger as you walk this night. The animals have evil designs. They invent sickness and diseases that place your people in great peril."

"Why do you warn me?"

"Because we believe in peace," a hickory tree rumbles its roots deeper into the soil.

"We are man's friends and can prevent what the beasts invent," a small bush rustles. "Deer created a fever that cooks the brain and kills. Crush my berries for a remedy. Use me in your need."

Enoli picks its fruit and collects more in his medicine bag.

Moss on a nearby rock calls so soft the young shaman cannot recognize the sound. "Scrape me from this host. Use me in the nose of those who catch the frog's limp that causes loss of legs. I live on many stones. Use me."

The youngster scrapes blue-gray growth from granite into his collection and turns to another voice in the breeze.

"And me."

The apprentice moves from plant to grass to tree throughout the night, then to herbs and berries, each with its individual remedy.

***

Next morning, Enoli returns to the cave under Cherokee Rock as dawn spreads color on the rivers.

Saloli sleeps on the mat and his back heals, but the young medicine man applies an added Goldenseal treatment.

"Every plant has its use," Son of Stone Cloud stands over his apprentice, "if we know of it. That was your dream walk's purpose."

"And I communed with the plants," the youngster rises to his feet.

"We forget as our people desert the old ways." The great shaman's voice cracks with sorrow. "Few have your gift.

Always remember in the search for the relief for your patient, the spirit of the plant suggests a proper remedy."

"And I must listen, Sir, because I now know they talk low."

"To most, they don't speak," Son of Stone Cloud raises his arms to the cave's ceiling in blessing. "Revengeful animals create new evils such as the pox. That is their right, for we have wronged them. The plants give the antidote to you that listens."

"Talented teacher, I believe it is my life to search and find the cure for the disease that killed my mother," Enoli falls to his knees.

"Her death delivered you to me for such a mission. No Paint Clan son, including me, hears as you. Heal your pet as your child, and your talent may save our people."

The boy takes the shaman's extended hands as he pulls his apprentice to his feet.

"Many years ago, I encountered an enormous bear who sent me to search for one of seven eagle eggs. Each represented a clan. The mighty spirit told me to bring him the Paint Clan's. I traveled far and struggled to discover the eagle's nest, and when I did, the noble bird tricked me with another substitute egg. Bear grew angry and killed the bird. He gave me its powerful feathers." The great medicine man withdraws an adornment from his own head. "This is of those plumes."

Enoli feels the quill as the teacher inserts it into his hair. "I am not worthy of such an honor, sir."

"It is a symbol, a potent talisman that anoints you to your noble cause. Wear the feather as you explore a new world. One day, you will find your own."

CHAPTER NINE — Benjamin

ᎠᎡᏘᏚᎤᎢᏍᏚᏈᏯᎠᎫᎬᏉᏢᎲᎾᎦᏕᏯᏈᏒᏣᏕᎦᎷᎬᎹᎠᏕᏬᏌᏐᎫᏕᎩᏎᏍᎻᏃᏊᎣ

Five years of study and apprenticeship passes as Enoli, under the tutelage of Son of Stone Cloud, transitions from a talented orphan to a promising young shaman.

Secluded at Cherokee Rock with his teacher and fellow students, he immerses his mind in a world of discovery.

Beyond sequestration and isolation, humankind changes.

A year earlier, on September 3, 1783, the Treaty of Paris formally ends the American Revolution. Hostilities cease unilaterally in America.

The British and their Cherokee allies lose the colonies, a significant development in young Enoli's life.

With the loss of English support, Dragging Canoe turns to the Spanish for help in the war against Whites. His medicine man, Mohi, coordinates the alliance.

A fresh wave of White settler families flood Native American lands, and the influx redirects Son of Stone Cloud's attention from the safety of Cherokee Rock.

He assembles the apprentices within the cave below the outcrop.

"We have enjoyed years of peace and study." The great shaman looks at the boys and young adults that surround the cave's council fire. "We cannot isolate from our tribe and the world that encroaches upon our pursuit of knowledge. The Appalachians stood as a barrier between our people and those who fought against our English brothers. That war ended, and we lost."

"Do we have to leave Cherokee Rock?" A young apprentice stands.

"No. Warriors led by Dragging Canoe and many from the middle towns east of the mountains attack Whites who settle on the Appalachian's west side. But more settlers still come. Late last year, Major Peter Fine's militia burned Cowee, and Whites continue to take our land. They declare a New State of Franklin. Their goal is to become part of the United States of America."

Enoli stands, the first of the senior apprentices to question. "What right have they to tribal lands?"

"Our Chickasaw allies signed the Treaty of French Lick. Lower Cherokee were signers. That agreement stopped attacks, so White settlements grow." Son of Stone Cloud stabs a clenched fist into the air. "These few signatures do not represent the majority. Those farmers have no rights to the soil!"

"I know one who fights!" An adult voice calls from the cave's entrance.

The apprentices spin to identify the interrupter.

Another medicine man strides into the council circle, "I am Mohi, shaman to Dragging Canoe."

The boy's pet whips its tail.

"The Spanish hold East and West Florida," the warrior pauses, "and Louisiana, Texas, Nuevo Mexico, and Nueva California."

Saloli jumps upon Enoli's shoulders, "Enoli, that is the

shaman from your Paint Clan village. Beware."

The speaker continues, "Our new allies provide arms and supplies to attack the invaders."

"I was young, little one, but remember."

"Dragging Canoe recruits all who resist settlements in our native woods," Mohi steps to the center of the council.

Son of Stone Cloud crosses both arms and steps aside.

"Near the mouth of Coldwater Creek below Muscle Shoals, the French founded Coldwater Town," Mohi points beyond the cavern, "but now the Lower Cherokee and the Upper Creeks use that base to trade arms for the defense of our territory."

Students applaud but maintain focus on the warrior's words.

"Spain signed two new treaties with Coldwater Town to provide additional firearms." The warrior draws a war hatchet and stabs the tool into the air. "With those weapons, he attacks the over-mountain farms! Who among you intends to defend sacred lands?"

The boys and young men of Cherokee Rock rise in unison, "We pledge our lives to Dragging Canoe!"

As the clamor and excitement subsides, Son of Stone Cloud raises his hands, "You do not comit to Dragging Canoe. I will go with you! But we vow our lives to the freedom of the Cherokee Nation and our homelands!"

All but Mohi jump and yell. They proclaim a shaman medicine school's recruitment.

The recruiter nods satisfaction without enthusiasm. His eyes search for loyalty in the soul of Son of Stone Cloud and this crowd's potential warriors.

***

As enthusiastic young men praise an emotional decision, the White settlers of the over-mountain region of western North Carolina petition the Congress of the Confederation, the governing body of the United States of America.

They ask recognition as a new state, the State of Franklin.

The request fails a required two-thirds vote for passage.

Angered, the settlements organize a secessionist government, the Free Republic of Franklin. Their goal becomes a permanent foothold in the Cumberland Basin.

Separated by native territory, dual settlements comprise the new state, both almost autonomous.

***

As the encampment in the cave under Cherokee Rock prepares to uproot and join the war leader, Mohi receives an emissary.

After moments of consultation, the shaman instructs the messenger and turns to Son of Stone Cloud. "Our task has changed. The White over-mountain settlers declare a new free state. A wise leader, Old Tassel, and others negotiate a treaty of peace. Dragging Canoe directs we join the old man and provide security."

"My apprentices trained for healing, not war." The teacher surveys the shamans that surround and listen. "I am unsure if we are ready for immediate wartime responsibility."

"Leave your young ones with caregivers. You, senior students, and I travel. The rest stay here or go home. Old Tassel and Abraham of Chilhowee expect to sign a new treaty. Dragging Canoe instructs us to plead with them not to give more soil to the settlements."

"We expect to cede more?" Son of Stone Cloud stares at the messenger.

"Yes, all land south of the French Broad and Holston Rivers and west of the Big Pigeon east of the ridge between Little River and the Tennessee," Mohi nods and straightens his back.

"I know these leaders." The great medicine man shakes his head in amazement. "Why would they do that?"

"They love peace and want to see no more Cherokee die." The man clinches both fists. "Pacificists have little courage!"

Son of Stone Cloud places one hand on Enoli's shoulder. "Old Tassel is right but has chosen the wrong method. Dragging Canoe respects the old man and wants him protected. Come."

"Do we defend against settlers," the apprentice extends both hands palms up, "or warriors?"

The teacher glances at the war advocate recruiter and places one hand on the youngster's shoulder, "Both, perhaps."

***

Several days later, June 10, 1785, Son of Stone Cloud, Enoli, and Mohi sit in a council circle outside Hugh Henry's fort, built to protect the White over-mountain settlements.

Free State of Franklin's representative, Governor John Sevier, and his adjutant, Major James Hubbard, occupy chairs in the clearing on the bank of Dumpling Creek.

First Beloved Man Old Tassel, Hanging Maw, Abraham of Chilhowee and Sturgeon of Tallahassee settle cross-legged with their contingents in a circle with the White men centered at its apex.

The old pacifist stands and waits for silence.

He extends arms and hands in a gesture of welcome and acceptance, "The warriors, leaders and representatives of the Cherokee Nation, agree that all the lands lying on the south side of the Holston and French Broad Rivers, as far as the ridge that divides the waters of Little River from those of the Tennessee, are open to peaceable habitation and cultivation."

Mumbles of disagreement ripple through the gathering.

"Our land may be lived upon, enjoyed, and inhabited by our brothers, the White people," the speaker raises his voice above the dissent, "from this time forward."

The representatives of Franklin nod in unison with Governor Seiver.

"We also agree to not molest or interrupt those settlers," the peace leader looks at the group, "because they settle or inhabit the said tract of land."

Mohi leans in front of Enoli and muffles his voice, "Dragging Canoe won't accept this."

"Then he breaks the agreement established here," Son of Stone Cloud covers his mouth for privacy.

John Sevier stands, "The state or government of the Free State of Franklin and the new American nation will pay a reasonable and liberal compensation to the peace leaders for the soil they grant."

The crowd stands silent and unimpressed.

"The states that possess and enjoy those lands agree in good faith." Governor Sevier spreads arms wide. "The engagement now made and entered between our governments and the Cherokee may never break or dissolve."

* * *

Days later, with Saloli on a shoulder, Enoli follows Son of Stone Cloud and Mohi as they travel away from the west slopes of the Appalachian Mountains. The young fellow and pet listen to the leaders a few steps ahead.

"In respect for the treaty, Dragging Canoe sends three warriors to protect Old Tassel. We will support them." The shaman-turned-warrior leads the group as they jog through the brush and trees.

"That old man is not a fighter, he's friendly with all. The settler's government gave him a red and white cloth with bright stars on a night sky. Their famous symbol maker, Betsy Ross, sewed the banner." Son of Stone Cloud maintains the pace without heavy breathing. "He exhibits it at home. Why does such a man need Dragging Canoe's protection?"

"You sequestered at Cherokee Rock too long. They forced Old Tassel and Hanging Maw to sign the Treaty of Dumpling Creek. The agreement allows Whites to punish all that shelter warriors against the settlers." Mohi stops and signals for silence.

Enoli drops to knees with the other apprentices.

The leader calls like an eagle into the trees, and the announcement floats a return as three armed fighters and a boy join the travelers.

"Greetings. I am Dragging Canoe's shaman," the medicine man indicates his followers, "and this is Son of Stone Cloud. The boys are his."

A tattooed warrior, dressed in a white man's britches and a broadcloth shirt, steps forward. "I know you. I am John Watts. Dragging Canoe sends us to protect Old Tassel from any reprisals."

Enoli eyes the warrior's leather, thick-soled, White man's boots, but his focus shifts to the different appearing boy that accompanies.

The young fellow stands shorter and younger, wears settler's clothing that shows considerable wear but carries a knife the length of a forearm belted to his waist. He rests a hand on the hilt of the weapon with relaxed comfort.

The apprentice medicine man continues to stare at one of the few people of African descent that he has ever seen.

"I was expecting fighters, not children," John Watts surveys the pupils, "but I have heard of the Son of Stone Cloud."

"Dragging Canoe sent me," Mohi turns Watts' attention. "I recruited these others."

"We delay and waste time. There're many hours of daylight left to travel." John Watts leads the group through the brush.

***

That evening, Enoli rests with friends around a small campfire. The older men circle a flame several yards away.

"John Watts is Old Tassel's nephew. Some call him Young Tassel." A younger shaman apprentice postures superior awareness.

"Yes. That is why Dragging Canoe sent us to protect his uncle," the arrived fighter with the huge blade in his belt confirms the boy's speculation.

"Us?" Enoli inspects the new arrival. "You are part of a fresh *us* and unknown. I am Enoli, senior assistant to Son of Stone Clad. I am a shaman in training. And who are you?"

"The name is Benjamin Waters, a freedman. I have papers." He sits cross legged.

An older boy eyes Benjamin. "We do not know that name?"

"A freedman is what he wants to be. John Watts does not own me. We became friends after my freedom. My mother and father were slaves."

"Some Cherokees have those," another apprentice shares his knowledge of the world beyond Cherokee Rock. "But I think only the rich ones. I have never seen a slave but hear you can buy one."

Benjamin whips the long knife from his belt and lunges at the speaker. The blade stops inches from the other boy's throat. "You want to purchase your own?"

Enoli intercedes, "Put that sticker away. This boy doesn't know what he speaks about. The students of Son of Stone Cloud believe all are free like you, freedman."

Benjamin's hand trembles with indecision and the knife quivers.

"He meant no insult. Lower that blade, Waters." The student leader's voice steels.

The new arrival considers the words for a moment, then slips back to his position around the fire. He slides the weapon into its sheath. "We are friends in the fight against White men. Call me Ben. My mother gave the big name. I like it short."

"That's right. We are on the same side, Ben," Enoli relaxes. "Where are your parents?"

"Don't know. After I won freedom, their owner sold both and shipped them somewhere on a wagon. That night, I took my paper and ran away."

"Your paper? Did that keep you from being sent?" A young offending apprentice's voice cracks. "I cannot imagine staying without your mother?"

Benjamin pauses and observes the orphans that stare into their fire. "None of you have mothers and fathers?"

"Son of Stone Cloud teaches like a parent," the boy's cracking solidifies.

"The paperwork saved me from being sold. That previous winter, Mr. Waters gave his child a sled and told me to pull the kid. Because I was a slave with no choice, I did."

The apprentices focus on the newcomer's story.

"The White boy did not think I pulled fast enough. Instead, he slid down a hill without me and could not stop. He left the snow onto the ice of a lake. It cracked and broke." The story-teller pauses.

His audience draws a collective breath.

"My owner's son was drowning, but I rescued him. For that, the father offered my freedom. When they filled out the document, it identified me by my owner's name, Waters." Benjamin smiles at his new colleagues.

All the fellows around the fire stare at the freedman.

"We have no slaves and never will." Enoli breaks the silence. "We and Son of Stone Cloud would not have it otherwise."

"I like you," Ben nods positively. "I believe as you do."

"Let us be friends." The apprentice shaman pulls his own knife. "Bring blood on your palm so we may become brothers in war and peace."

Benjamin Waters withdraws his blade a second time and pokes the tip into his skin. He reaches across the fire.

Two friends lean together, and bloodstained hands join.

CHAPTER TEN — Parley

ᎠᎡᏘᏐᏪᎢᏐᏲᏫᎩᎠᏤᏫᏣᏘᏞᏂᏪᏐᎷᏥᎹᏛᎦᎣᏲᎲᏐᏲᏲᏤᏸᎾᏁᏂᏃᏨᎧ

Enoli and Ben jog behind their leaders several days into Dragging Canoe's ordered protective mission for the Cherokee beloved man and peacemaker, Old Tassel.

Without horses, the party progresses through woods. Unlike the plain's tribes, boys from birth travel their mountains and foothills by foot.

Saloli rides upon the back of the first shaman apprentice's neck and spends his time with eyes on Ben. "This new partner of yours runs faster than a deer chased by wolves."

"He does."

"What did you say?" Benjamin looks.

"Nothing. I was talking to my little friend."

"Were you?"

"Yes. He complimented your running."

"Why did I not hear him?"

"It's a gift I have. Sometimes animals and plants talk to me. Only when they want. Not my choice."

"Days ago," Ben glances at his new companion to gauge his reaction, "I thought you crazy, but John Watts told me of Son of Stone Cloud. He said you were the great shaman's successor, his chosen one."

Neither young man speaks for a distance as they jog.

The freedman breaks the silence, "He says Mohi hates you and your teacher."

"I know. Why does he detest us? He is my clan's healer."

"John Watts thinks he's jealous."

"I can't stand him. He is a sham," Enoli judges his friend's reaction.

"Nor can I." Ben looks at the young shaman. "What bothers you?"

"His arrogance, ignorance, and incompetence killed my mother."

"That's real." The freedman chuckles. "My issue is trust."

***

Later, Mohi and John Watts discover a homestead on the Little River. Above the farm, late in the day, they crouch with their party.

Below, a small cabin in the valley smokes from its stack, and seven White settler children play tag around its walls. A young man plows straight furrows in the earth with an ox. His young wife follows her husband and plants seeds in the soil.

Near the home, a grandmother hangs wet clothing on a makeshift line.

"Settlers!" Mohi's hatred spits the words.

"We can bypass them. Won't lose more than an hour of travel time," John Watts slips away from their concealed observation.

"A peaceful family," Son of Stone Cloud pulls back and agrees with the new leader, "of no threat to us or our people. Let them live in peace."

"No!" Mohi disagrees with the other two. "Settlers come as locusts through our woods. One first, and then many. Dragging

Canoe taught me well. We kill them where we find pestilence."

"A man, a couple of women, and seven children? There is no victory in causing them harm," the great shaman shakes his head.

John Watts' two warriors listen, and Mohi turns to them, "Dragging Canoe demands we stop White colonists. Are you with me?"

They glance at their leader, but blood law hatred in their eyes stimulates an allegiance shift.

Both nod in agreement.

"My task is to reach and protect my uncle, Old Tassel, not murder unarmed settlers," Watts stands firm. "I will not help you."

"Nor I or my apprentices," Son of Stone Cloud crosses his arms with determination.

"Cowards!" Mohi and the two warriors check their tomahawks, knives, and flintlock muskets. "I'll report your traitorous cowardice to Dragging Canoe."

The three, now a war group, hurry away along a tree line, out of view by the settlers.

John Watts looks a Son of Stone Cloud, "Should we stop them?"

He watches the fighters scramble from the hill. "Blood lust is an evil thing that cannot end without spilling some. Boys, stay here. Enoli, come with us."

"And I go with my friend," Ben steps close.

The two men and the younger ones slip to the crest of the bluff, a concealed observation position.

Below in the valley, children's play continues in peace. The laughter of peace drifts in the fresh country air, and their voices reach the ridge observers.

"Nathan! John Kirk returns Friday. You have a week to finish that planting," the grandmother calls to the young man in the field, and his wife waves in return.

From their viewing point, Enoli and Ben watch the three Cherokee warriors circle the brush behind the cabin.

A child screams. Mohi bludgeons her forehead with his battle ax.

With knives drawn, the attackers chase and slit the other children's throats.

Petrified, the grandmother stands with her wash, trembles and convulses as Mohi, with his bloody tomahawk, steps closer.

She shrieks in fear for help. "John Kirk! Husband, I need you. God, save me!"

The attacker smashes her jaw into her spine with one swift swing.

From plowing, the young farmer runs to support his mother-in-law as her daughter flees for protection in the brush across the field.

A warrior aims his musket and blows a bloody part of the man's skull from his head, then drops his firearm and catches the wife, who stumbles in the plowed rows.

With the screaming woman, he joins Mohi and shoves her into the cabin. Both warriors follow to dominate the soon lifeless female.

***

Atop the ridge, Son of Stone Cloud abandons their observation and, with John Watts, gathers his apprentices. "My sons, the Whites invade our lands as ants. Kill the queen, which eliminates their beds, and they migrate elsewhere. Not so with the White settlers. Their children and mothers are not our enemies. Their men and governments are." The shaman looks at John Watts for reinforcement, and the leader nods agreement.

"These warriors shame our people in that valley below," Watts points at their abandoned viewpoint. "I do not endorse useless slaughter of helpless women and children. Old Tassel, whom we travel to protect, agrees."

"I want you to remember this day," the great shaman picks his pack from the ground and removes eagle feathers. "At Cherokee Rock, I gave each of you an apprentice feather. The time for your training ends with this lesson."

He slips a second quill into each boy's hair. "To each of you I now assign a shaman's mark."

The teacher turns to John Watts. "And to the nephew of the wise Old Tassel," he slides a quill onto the man's head, "who I will call Young Tassel for the wisdom he shows, I award the first feather beyond Cherokee Rock. These recognize men who bring pride to our people."

Enoli and Ben, along with their fellow students, applaud the award as Mohi and his warriors approach.

"Hi-yee! No more settlers in our valley!" Mohi's eyes flash, and he jabs his musket into the air.

Young Tassel stares at the shaman warrior. "I will travel to my uncle. Take your men and report your victory to Dragging Canoe. He needs fighters."

"I will go. I do not tolerate slackers." The murderer spits on the ground near Watt's boot.

"Son of Stone Cloud doesn't celebrate victories over women

and children," the great medicine man confronts the lesser shaman.

Mohi grips his musket, and his knuckles turn red from the pressure. He stares, and his eyes betray his true thoughts; distrust, envy, and disgust.

The warrior jerks his chin, and with the signal, his warriors follow their leader and jog to the southwest toward Dragging Canoe's headquarters.

***

Weeks later, Saloli rides Enoli's shoulder as the party nears Old Tassel's home in the Tennessee Valley at the base of the Smokey Mountains.

"Ben did not receive a Son of Stone Cloud feather." The furry animal shifts to the side, away from Benjamin, and licks the new medicine man's earlobe. "Is that because he is not Cherokee? Or because he is not worthy? Perhaps because he looks different from the genuine people?"

"No, he has not received our training." the young shaman twists to get a glimpse of his friend and pet.

"But John Watts did? Is it only a Tsalagi honor?"

"You are right. Maybe? It was not my choice."

"You talking to that squirrel again?" Ben jogs, several yards behind Son of Stone Cloud, through the trees.

"I am. He's questioning my prejudices." The pet's owner sweeps the animal off his shoulders as he runs and cuddles it in his arm.

"Does he? Smart squirrel."

John Watts holds a hand in the air and the party stops.

Below them, an Over-hill town of a dozen permanent structures lays in a valley.

One cabin displays an American flag, which flaps in the breeze above its entrance.

Several Cherokee move around the village.

Enoli and Ben follow Son of Stone Cloud and John Watts into the settlement.

Old Tassel meets his nephew. "We heard travelers' approach. I am pleased to see family! And who are these with you?"

"Sir, I present the great shaman, Son of Stone Cloud. You know Ben, and his friend Enoli is a novice. The young men are apprentices."

"Welcome! Friends of John Watts, come into my home and share my comfort. I am honored by Son of Stone Cloud's presence." The old man opens his door.

"It is I that am privileged to be a guest of Old Tassel, First Beloved of the over-hill Cherokee." The great shaman follows his nephew into the cabin, and the others trail.

The worn travelers settle into the comforts of Old Tassel's home.

The host lights his pipe, draws and exhales tobacco smoke into the room.

A rich smell assaults Enoli's senses as he tucks Saloli into his tunic out of sight.

The over-hill leader passes the pipe to Son of Stone Clad as honored visitor. His guest follows the host's lead.

"Nephew, you are not here to stroke your family favor?" The old man smiles with Son of Stone Cloud's positive reaction to his best tobacco.

"No, Dragging Canoe of the Chickamauga fears White reprisal for his raids and sent me. He tasked us to protect you," John Watts winks at his uncle.

Old Tassel accepts his pipe and passes the smoke to his nephew. "You have traveled for several weeks and are not aware of news. A war party of Dragging Canoe's murdered eleven members of a settler named John Kirk's family on Little River. The man was not there, just his women and children."

John takes the pipe. "We were part of that but did not do the killing. Dragging Canoe's shaman Mohi and his warriors committed the act."

"I am pleased that you did not participate. Smoke, enjoy," Old Tassel watches his nephew draw on the pipe. "Colonel John Sevier retaliated against several Cherokee towns in the Little Tennessee Valley. They took their revenge."

The leader offers the smoke to Enoli.

The young novice looks to Son of Stone Cloud, who nods approval.

He inhales and smoke spills out of his nostrils.

A rush of excitement and pleasure sweeps his brain moments before seizures cramp his lungs. As he fights to not cough, the new smoker passes to Ben.

Benjamin sucks a draw in and blows a stream from his lips.

To his young medicine man friend, the action indicates that it is not a first pipe.

Enoli's eyes redden and tear. He stuffs both hands over a coughing fit.

The door to Old Tassel's cabin swings open, and a young warrior distracts the group's attention from the gagging young shaman. "An unarmed wagon visits with a Major, and a white cloth on a stick, at the reins. Nothing hidden."

"Bring him to me." Old Tassel takes his pipe from Benjamin Waters, empties its bowl into his fireplace, and smiles at Enoli.

"You appear to recover. If you had not, we do not lack qualified medicine men."

He places the long smoke on his hearth, and it leans against the mud brick.

A young warrior reopens the cabin's entrance and escorts a uniformed Major into the home.

The man looks at the individuals, and his gaze lingers on Benjamin.

The aged host gentleman steps forward, "I am Old Tassel."

"I am Major James Hubbard. It is an honor to greet you. I was most relieved to see the American flag above your door."

"Your government gave me your banner when I signed the Treaty of Chotey," the leader surveys his enemy. "They told me your Betsy Ross made it."

"Which means you are a human controlled by reason, not sentiment." Hubbard eyes the muskets held by John Watts and Son of Stone Cloud. "I came unarmed to prove that we are reasonable."

"I think you carry no weapons to show me you will not shoot me," Old Tassel chuckles.

"Dragging Canoe leads, and he is a man of passion. Abraham of Chilhowee tells me you lead the over-hill Towns. He and I believe we have too much killing, and it's time to parley."

"You have spoken to Abraham?" Old Tassel cocks an eyebrow.

"Yes. He invites you to travel with me under a flag of truce to find a path to peace. He offers the security of his home," the Major stands and waits.

John Watts breaks the silence. "I am a representative of Dragging Canoe. If Old Tassel travels for a parley, these warriors and I must attend for his safety."

The Major nods approval.

"We leave at daylight." Old Tassel crosses his arms across his chest.

"How was your first smoke?" Benjamin whispers to his young, sick, shaman friend.

CHAPTER ELEVEN — Commitment

ᎠᏣᎢᏏᏬᎥᎢᏎᎣᏂᎧᎠᏤᏕᏈᏓᏂᎦᏎᏫᏗᎢᏩᏥᎩ

The following morning, Major James Hubbard waits on the wooden seat of a U.S. Army escort wagon. Resembling a Conestoga but smaller with large rear wheels, four mules pull its weight. The wagon's back half supports a gray canvas cover, unlike the traditional cream-colored arch. From a front corner, a pole rises with a white truce banner attached.

Old Tassel steps out of his cabin, turns, and admires the American flag above his door. "Major, my people fought with the British during your revolution. Before that, the French, which I regret. We lost many brave heroes that did not listen to me. Your battle was different, for freedom. We, as you, wish for a free land."

John Watts and Son of Stone Cloud, with muskets, follow the elderly man. Enoli and Ben, without firearms but with Saloli, trail the warriors.

"I bring your red, white and blue banner with us as a sign of peace with your settlers." The peacemaker turns to the youngsters, "Take our new symbol from their flag-maker woman off my door. Attach it to the pole under the white flag."

"Sir," Major Hubbard clears his throat, "Our customs dictate no pennant flies higher than that of the United States, even the truce sign."

Old Tassel eyes the soldier. "Your ways do not bode well for the cause we seek. You come with power and might. It is wise that I negotiate." The venerable peacemaker climbs onto the wagon's front seat next to the officer.

The others load supplies and gear into the rear of the transport and climb into its covered enclosure.

Enoli enters last with the folded American flag.

Saloli jumps from the ground and lands on the young shaman's lap.

"I have never ridden in a White man's cart. I wonder if the mules that pull mind the extra weight?" The furry animal's whiskers vibrate as he looks around the wagon's interior.

"Those are army animals, my friend. They pull loads so heavy and long they no longer even understand your question." The young shaman strokes his friend's ears against its soft fur.

"Yes, they have suffered long," Benjamin grips his hands together. "Mules are slaves. My parents toiled for their masters. The animals do the same but don't realize it."

"They know, but as your mother and father were aware, they have no choice," Enoli peers at the freedman.

"You were talking to your pet, not me, right?" Ben chuckles as he reaches for and pets the little animal's coat.

The furry one wiggles his nose with pleasure, and Enoli nods agreement.

Son of Stone Cloud and John Watts sit together near the front of the wagon's interior and talk, unconcerned the young men and the animal overhear.

"Your uncle is a brother of peace," the great healer cocks his head toward Old Tassel on the seat, "and strength. My Over-hill brothers are wise to choose him to parley with the White colonists and their army."

"He is. Too much," John Watts leans closer to the medicine man, "and beyond comprehension, if you ask Dragging Canoe."

"Many of our people believe we can drive invaders and their soldiers over the mountains." Son of Stone Cloud sits straighter. "I am realistic. It is time to parley. The settlers' numbers and muskets press from the East. The Spanish want the South. North and West belong to the Sioux and the Comanche. This is the last section of homeland to discuss."

"Nothing promises victory," John Watts grits his teeth. "I am the son of a British trader. Half my blood runs White. But my soul is Cherokee, so we find a path, bloodshed or bonding."

Enoli looks at Ben and jerks his head toward the rear of the wagon.

His companion nods "yes," and both young men scramble out and walk.

Saloli jumps from the new medicine man's shoulders and scrambles into the surrounding trees and brush.

Benjamin watches his friend's pet disappear into the foliage. "That little thing has enthusiasm. How do you keep pace?"

Enoli looks his friend directly in the eye. "Diet. You are what you eat, and he eats nuts."

Ben stares at the youthful shaman, who jabs his shoulder. "That was funny. Don't you know how to laugh?"

In silence, the two walk together.

Enoli breaks the mood. "What's significant to you, Ben?"

"My free paper, commitment and trust are a few," the young freedman smiles at his new companion. "And you?"

"Commitment is important. I committed to something when I lost my mother," Enoli glances at his blood brother. "You may not believe me, but I intend to find a cure or a prevention for the White man's smallpox."

"I support you," Benjamin looks his friend in the face. "You studied under the greatest shaman of our time. John Watts told me several times if anyone can, it's you."

"Son of Stone Cloud taught me to inoculate with cowpox. It is not the solution, only a step in the right direction."

"Inoculation?" Ben cocks an eyebrow.

"Yes, give a person a slight case of the disease, and his body will learn to fight the sickness. Have you had the disease?"

"No."

"Then you need my treatment," Enoli nods a vigorous affirmative as Ben recoils.

"Not me! I'm not nuts like your squirrel!"

***

Later that day, as the wagon pushes into the early evening, wolf howls and barks intrude upon the caravan's journey.

"I hear. Just over this rise is a village. We will camp there overnight," John Watts leans from the wagon's side, and the two young men climb into the rear.

As the mules pull over the hill, below in a valley, packs range through Cherokee wattle and daub houses. A small settlement clusters around a creek. Several animals eat corpses' human flesh drug from mats.

Moans of a few Indians underlie the pack's hunting growls as the hungry attack the weak.

John Watts stands and fires his musket.

The wolves scatter to escape the village.

"Smallpox," Son of Stone Cloud glances at Old Tassel, and he nods agreement.

"Pull out of here. Move up-creek where we can camp," the leader moves uphill.

"Hold," Son of Stone Cloud climbs from the wagon as John Watts stops the team. "Help them."

The younger shaman points at his friend Benjamin. "You stay with the caravan. I've had the sickness. You haven't."

Ben understands, and the great man and his apprentice enter the village.

The others turn uphill.

"Enoli!" Ben hands a musket. "Take this. The wolves may come back."

The younger waves, "No. We will be fine."

***

With Son of Stone Cloud, Enoli walks among the cabins and surveys the pestilence.

Every house includes dead smallpox victims. Three contain terminal patients who moan with fever.

"The sickness never kills everyone. Where are the survivors?" Enoli pulls a mat with a moaning woman out of her lodge into the fresh air.

"No supplies, animals, medicine men, they left these to die," Son of Stone Cloud shakes his head. "I wait with these three until they pass. Go with the wagon. I expect to catch up after I bury them."

"I think I should stay," the younger shaman looks around, "because wolves might come back tonight."

"No, protect Old Tassel. These wild dogs are not a problem," the great medicine man winks at his graduate apprentice. "Remember, I talk to animals. They are wary. I will tell them their meal is diseased."

***

The following morning, Enoli and Ben walk behind the wagon, which John Watts drives. Major Hubbard sits beside him, and Old Tassel naps.

"That village changed my mind." Ben looks at his friend. "How's that?"

"Fix me, make me like you and the great medicine man."

"That takes years of training, but it's an idea. You might become the first freed shaman."

"Not what I mean," the freedman stops. "Inoculate me, so I won't die."

"Oh! I do that by giving you the cowpox. Problem is, we have no patient for a sample. But I will, next I find."

"What if I catch it before then?" Ben resumes walking.

"You succumb or survive. Many live and never sicken again."

"I'll take the second choice." Ben's attention flips to focus on the trees as the wagon passes. "Isn't little one up there?"

Saloli scampers from a tree trunk and scrambles onto the medicine man's shoulder.

"Welcome back," Enoli scratches its neck. "You went missing for two days?"

"I trailed White men with muskets. They ride horses a half-day to the north," the furry friend wiggles his nose near an ear. "One they called John Kirk, but he was not the leader. Their commander wore a Major Hubbard uniform."

The young shaman recoils. "John Kirk?"

Benjamin looks at Enoli, "I heard John Watts say Kirk was the name of the people Mohi massacred."

"Saloli told me he leads a party, armed," the youngster peers to the north as if he hears the invaders. "Come."

They climb into the rear of the wagon and scramble forward to their leaders.

John Watts pays attention.

"Men with John Kirk ride north of us," Enoli notices Major Hubbard pays interest.

"How do you know, young man?" The Major stops the wagon's team.

"My squirrel told me."

"That one?"

"Yes."

"It talks to you?" John Watts looks at Benjamin. "Is your friend ill?"

"This shaman speaks to animals, as I do," Son of Stone Cloud turns the conversation.

"Did you understand the animal?" John Watts twists to the older healer.

"No. I wasn't there. It selects who can communicate, and only those with the gift," Son of Stone Cloud reassures the others. "What did it tell you, Enoli."

"It's fine that you share my news," the furry body wiggles his nose at his friend.

"Saloli trailed White men with muskets. They ride horses a half-day to the north," the young medicine man warns John Watts, "One rider they called John Kirk, but he was not in charge. Their leader wore a uniform."

Watts stares at the White officer. "What do you know?"

"Nothing. We travel under a flag of truce. There is no danger," Hubbard points at the banner on the wagon.

Old Tassel leans forward. "The White man, John Kirk, should ride armed. Our warriors murdered his family. Abraham of Chilhowee invites us to parley. Major Hubbard traveled with that invitation under our Nation's protection. I trust Abraham and the major. But we should not ignore this threat. John, with Son of Stone Cloud and your two young apprentices, intercept these people. Avoid violence, if possible, but prevent them from disrupting our conference."

The younger men jump from the wagon to the ground.

"Safe travel, Uncle," Watts holds a musket above his head.

Old Tassel smiles. "It is you, my nephew, who faces danger. May the Unetlanvhi look over you."

The caravan moves along its route.

Enoli and Ben watch it leave.

***

Watts and Son of Stone Cloud strike a fresh path through the brush, but the two friends linger.

"There goes a tired peacemaker. What do you think?" Benjamin elbows his friend.

"I assume the old man brings harmony to our lives."

"He chose his way early in life." Ben watches the wagon disappear into the woods. "I admire him for that."

"Yes, he did. And I choose a trail right for me," Enoli opens his future.

"What's that, Blood Brother?"

"My days as a child, my apprenticeship, my formative time finishes. I walk now upon a truce mission for Tsalagi families.

That is my path as a shaman, a life commitment to the good of my people."

Ben smiles, "A dangerous path."

CHAPTER TWELVE — Retribution

DRTᏮꞳᎥᏕᏬᎥᏏYᎯJEᏇᏘᎯᏝᏜWᏚᏁᏩMᎯᏕᎣᎥᎯᏏᏙᎾᏆᎾᏁᎲZᎯᏫ

Saloli joins his young shaman friend with news as they break camp the following morning, "The Whites move eastward. They have a several hour lead. Hurry or we will lose them."

Son of Stone Cloud pays attention to the animal. "Our scout speaks only for you."

"Those we seek travel east." Enoli points toward the sun.

The great medicine man looks at John Watts, and both leaders with the younger men trailing shift packs and muskets upon their backs and jog into the underbrush.

***

The following afternoon, the group pauses in the concealment on a ridge to view the aftermath of violence in a valley.

Several crude cabins below, reduced to black piles of rubble, smoke.

One remains, the only untorched residence in the Cherokee village of Chilhowee.

Beside that lodge, without a team, the wagon driven by Major James Hubbard's transport sits unoccupied.

Many corpses surround different dwellings, and no movement disturbs the death pall.

John Watts stands, "I don't think any survived."

Son of Stone Cloud leads the group into the valley, "I fear we are too late."

Enoli and Ben follow their elders, and Saloli scampers with them.

At the unburned Abraham of Chilhowie's residence, on the roof from one corner, a pole holds a white flag of truce.

The young shaman and freedman trail their leaders into the cabin.

Inside, dead and tied to chairs, Old Tassel, Hanging Maw, Abraham, Sturgeon of Tallahassee, and three others droop forward with skulls smashed or embedded by tomahawk.

Son of Stone Cloud steps outside and looks at the white banner as his companions join him. "The flag of truce is a protection inviolable even among the most barbarous people. It is sacred by law and custom. These murders are atrocities."

"There is no time for that." James Watts looks to the surrounding hillsides. "We follow."

"Their trail leads east," Saloli wiggles his whiskers at his young shaman friend. "At least eight White men. The tracks are boots, not moccasins."

Enoli points into the hills. "He says they fled into the woods, maybe ten of them."

John Watts and Son of Stone Cloud scan the eastern horizon.

"Against two of us?" The nephew of Old Tassel stares a Son of Stone Cloud.

"Four," Benjamin Waters smiles at his young shaman friend, and Enoli nods agreement.

"They flee for Jonesborough," a fifteen-year-old Cherokee girl steps out of the brush.

"Who are you?" Watts with musket ready spins to the voice.

"I am Walela (ᎤᏓᏪ wa-le-la, Hummingbird,) grand-daughter of Abraham. They killed him. No, murdered them." The young woman drops to her knees in tears.

Watts pulls her arms to stand, "You must be strong for you grandfather. He was a most beloved man, and we will avenge him."

"Paw Paw was not for vengeance. He lived for peace." Walela turns from the war leader, takes two steps, and faints.

She falls toward Benjamin, who catches the girl and lifts her into his arms.

"Take her into the village. There must be other survivors. Find someone to care for her and catch up when we camp tonight," Watts looks at the murderers trail into the brush.

The blood law vengeance party of Enoli, John Watts, and Son of Stone Cloud lift their packs and weapons and follow Saloli as the furry scout leaves the village and scurries along the heeled track trail of boots.

***

Benjamin carries his ward into Chilhowie's smoking ruins.

A few Cherokee survivors sift through the rubble for items of use and value.

Walela wakens and looks up at her caretaker. "Who are you?"

"Benjamin. John Watts told me to carry you to your people," the freedman smiles.

"Put me down. I can walk." The young woman's eyes flash fortitude, and Ben lowers her to the ground.

Walela glances at the other survivors, then back at her escort. "I know these families. I will be all right. Thank you, for carrying me so far."

115

"Call me Ben," the freedman's brow wrinkles with concern. "I can't leave you here alone."

"I am fine, Ben. These people are my clan." She sweeps a hand toward the others. "I am the granddaughter of Abraham and care for his cows. They pasture over the ridge. With them, I make my way."

He nods understanding and turns.

"Ben."

He twists back to the young Cherokee woman.

"I hope we meet again," Walela smiles.

"And I," Benjamin grins, "but I must catch up with the others." He jogs away.

***

Late the following day, as the avengers of Old Tassel's death converge upon their targets, the party of murderers camps for the night.

John Kirk paces at the campfire around Major James Hubbard, who sits with a musket across his knees and gazes into the flames. Several armed men rest at a fire while others gather firewood.

"Them filthy Injuns got it good." Kirk spits his words in the major's direction. "I saw my wife and kids dead in my house when I tomahawked every one of them!"

"Those old fellows didn't massacre your family, Kirk." Hubbard looks up from the flames. "Younger ones, I expect a war party did. Those were men who hoped for reconciliation."

"Ain't going to be no peace for any Injun near the Free State of Franklin unless it's a buried one." The angry White man punches the air with his musket.

116

"You executed those Cherokee for vengeance," Major Hubbard stands and faces the pacer. "Governor Seiver knows Dragging Canoe's the threat, not those old men."

"We'll kill him and his warriors!" John Kirk spits into the fire.

"Maybe? But, that's not easy. They are not old and fight back. The governor wants an agreement. Push them away from Franklin, and when the time is right, you can use your tomahawk. First, tie them to chairs with a peace treaty."

"Is that why you're expecting a visitor from Dragging Canoe?"

"How did you know?" Major Hubbard faces John Kirk.

"Bring him in!" Kirk looks at his other men.

Two subordinates drag Mohi into the fire circle and thrust him to his knees before their leader.

The shaman struggles against his captors, and his eyes flash hatred and disgust toward Major Hubbard.

"Is this what Governor Seiver calls a flag of truce?" Mohi glares at the Major before John Kirk backhands the captive across the mouth.

"Stop, Kirk!" Hubbard grabs the assailant's hand.

The White man's eyes flash vengeful blood lust.

"This is Dragging Canoe's representative." The Major throws the man's wrist downward. "He works under the protection of the governor. Untie him!"

"Your reception shows your genuine sentiments. But I promise a report to Dragging Canoe how you honor your word," One of Kirk's men cuts his bondage, and Mohi rubs red chaffed wrists.

"Not if you're a dead spy," John Kirk draws his tomahawk.

"Wait!" the major puts his hand upon his weapon. "You harm this emissary, and the governor punishes. The Free State of Franklin does not tolerate insurrection!"

The vengeful White man returns the hatchet into his belt.

"That's better." The major sits by the fire and sweeps a palm in welcome. "I talk for Governor Seiver as you speak for Dragging Canoe. Let us find a path forward together that benefits both."

"My leader instructs me to tell you he agrees your settlers may occupy the upper towns. He is from Chickamauga now, and you must remain in the north. If you stay, we won't attack," Mohi nods personal approval of his offer.

"Rest with us tonight," Major Hubbard smiles, "and return to Dragging Canoe tomorrow."

The emissary nods agreement.

"Tell him Governor Seiver considers the offer generous. He will ban settlement outside the Free State of Franklin."

***

In the darkness of that night, Enoli, Benjamin, and Saloli jog after Son of Stone Cloud and John Watts as they approach the Whites' encampment.

Watts holds a hand in the air for stealth.

In a clearing before the observers, Major Hubbard, and John Kirk sleep in blankets near an extinguished campfire.

Mohi sleeps nearby with several other blanketed forms.

One White man stands sentry with both hands gripped together on the barrel of his musket and his hat tipped low over his face. The guard rocks. He teeters between awareness and dreams.

"Eight to four? Not good odds," John Watts surveys the camp.

"Enoli and Benjamin have never made war," Son of Stone Cloud glances at the younger men.

From his pack, the shaman removes eagle feathers and hands one to each of his companions, "For courage, victory, and a reminder of your heritage."

"We'll spread out and take them from each direction," Old Tassel's nephew slips his feather into his hair and checks his two flintlock muskets. He withdraws his war hatchet, "No noise until I silence the sentry."

The younger men follow his lead, and the four slip away to surround the campground.

Enoli walks through the underbrush with Saloli. "I'm a medicine man, not a fighter. We heal better than hurt."

"If the camp awakens, I will warn you." Saloli wags his tail with nervous excitement and scampers up a tree trunk to an overhead route.

The healer-turned-warrior creeps closer to the camp but stops behind a bush.

The half-asleep sentry grunts and falls with a hatchet embedded in his skull.

A musket discharges from the other side of the sleeping men, followed by other blasts, and black powder smoke obscures the view.

The closest sleeper leaps to his feet with a flintlock.

Enoli aims and fires. His discharged ball impacts the target mid-chest. Blood splatters the ground.

The young medicine man drops his empty firearm and lifts a second.

Out of the powdery discharge before him, a Cherokee waves his palms. "Don't shoot! I'm their prisoner!"

Enoli stares over his barrel with his musket's sights centered on Mohi's forehead.

He lowers the rifle, and Mohi yanks it away.

Dragging Canoe's shaman spins and blasts a White man that charges from the smoke.

The attacker falls and lands atop the first corpse.

"Give me your tomahawk, boy!" Mohi extends one hand.

Enoli swallows and surrenders his weapon.

The older fighter screams and attacks the encampment through the powder smoke as other long guns flash fireworks in fog.

Saloli joins his human, and both move forward through the dissipating smog.

Benjamin steps beside his allies, "I got two!" The freed-man's adrenaline-enhanced voice shakes with tension.

"Anybody shot?" the younger shaman lifts his musket as a form emerges out of the smoke.

"Son of Stone Cloud." Watts's face drips blood. "A chest wound. I'm fine. This blood's from the sentry."

The apprentice rushes through the camp and stops. Before him, dead on the ground with Enoli's tomahawk in his body, Major Hubbard lies. Mohi stands over the body.

A few steps further, Son of Stone Cloud sprawls near John Kirk, who stares skyward with a wet red-rimmed hole in his forehead above one eye.

Enoli drops to his knees beside his unconscious mentor. From a wound below the ribs, blood drips.

Benjamin lunges alongside. "Is he alive?"

"Yes, get water boiling, and I'll need clean cloth for bandages. The ball's still in him and I must remove it," the young medicine healer swallows at the thought.

He touches Ben's hand. "Help me, Ben. He is the only father I have ever known."

CHAPTER THIRTEEN — Massacre

DRꭶꝹꙐꭲꮝꙌꮅꮿAJEꝥꝓꭷꮺꭶꭹꮃWꮂꭰGMꭱꝺꝍIH5ꮿꭼꭲꭹꮅhZꭰꝹꮻ

Weeks later, Enoli sits with his mentor in John Watts' encampment. Son of Stone Cloud, with his chest bandaged, leans with his back against a tree trunk. Saloli chatters from a limb above, and Ben crouches on the great shaman's other side.

They watch hundreds of Cherokee warriors with families bustle through their daily lives.

"Old Tassel's murder brings many supporters to his nephew's camp," Son of Stone Cloud watches the crowds.

"Dragging Canoe brought in his party this morning, I hear," Benjamin notices Saloli jump in the tree.

"Watts met with the governor of West Florida," Enoli informs Ben. "The Spanish, the French and English, they want Cherokee land."

"You're right." The shaman strains onto his feet but groans from the effort. "We need guns and supplies to resist the colonists. The treaty equips and feeds our warriors."

"Rumor is we're to attack White's Fort and the Holston River settlements, drive the White settlers across the mountains." Enoli checks Son of Stone Cloud's bandages, and the man grimaces.

"The Southwest Territory is strong, stronger than the State of Franklin, and consider themselves part of the United States of America. To force them over the mountains is impossible." The greatest shaman shifts his stance for comfort from the pain.

"Younger voices gather with John Watts. One young warrior has many followers. His name is James Vann. He believes change is necessary. Says Whites are too powerful and grow each day. He fights for a Cherokee Nation where we can live in peace and co-exist with the White settlers." Enoli looks at his patient for approval.

"This new fighter aligns with Old Tassel. That is good. What do you know of him," Son of Stone Cloud breathes and his lips curl from the painful effort?

"He's from the mouth of Little River. His mother was of the Anigategawi (ᎠᏂᎦᏔᎦᏫ ah-ni-ga-da-ga-hwi, Wild Potato People) clan, but his father was a White trader. Talk says his mother's uncles raised him in the Cherokee ways." The younger shaman offers his arm as the older shifts his weight and groans.

"He rose to be a leader in resistance to the invasion of Whites in the lower towns, as Dragging Canoe did," Ben looks and smiles. "But the two are very different, I hear."

Son of Stone Cloud nods understanding and approval. "This is too much. I need to sit down." The two help the wounded man, and his eyes close for rest.

Saloli drops to the ground next to his companion. "I dislike humans. They look at me as breakfast."

The young shaman laughs. "You should join your own kind for a while."

Benjamin jerks his head to attention. "What? I'm a freedman. I do as I please, remember?"

"Calm, my friend," Enoli places his hand on Ben's shoulder.

"I was talking to Saloli. He's afraid these fighters want him for breakfast."

"Oh! Sorry. No offense meant. I never understand his gibberish," Ben settles against the tree for his own nap.

***

Days later, John Watts leads a thousand Cherokee, including contingents brought by Dragging Canoe and Mohi, plus their Creek allies and a large group led by James Vann.

Enoli and Benjamin Waters march with the contingent.

They travel without Son of Stone Cloud, who rests and recovers at base camp.

Saloli ranges the tree branches above the war party and stays near his friend.

At night, warriors dance around bonfires and stoke their resentment and hatred of settlers.

Dragging Canoe dances and chants death oaths. "Scalp the colonial men, women and children!"

"No! We fight brave and tall against soldiers, not the weak and small!" Young James Vann fires his musket in the air.

The settler-hater halts his prance and spins toward the speaker. "Whites slay our wives. They murder our babies. Scalps that hang from our belts replace our families!"

"Yes, kill the militia," the new leader faces the Muscogee warrior. "We push Whites over the mountains to their homes. Women and children cannot travel without protection. Our warriors stand against men. Women and youngsters, we allow to return to their homelands across the mountains!"

"When we attack White's Fort," Dragging Canoe lifts his war hatchet, "I scalp anyone who fights me!"

"They defend behind walls," the younger leader thrusts a fist in the night air, "worthy opponents that protect their families. We drive them from our lands because we fight and defeat their soldiers!"

The crowd of dancing Cherokee and Creek acclaim both men's words with chants and oaths of vengeance, a murderous frenzy.

Early afternoon of the following day, the blood brothers, with the many fighters who travel on foot, catch up to the band's commanders who ride mounts.

The leaders cluster below a rim that conceals them from a small White settlement called Cavett's Station.

"Why do we rest?" Enoli grabs the knee of a mounted warrior.

"There's a town over the ridge. James Vann wants to bypass them. Dragging Canoe says no fighters to our rear when we attack White's Fort." The leader leans from his horse.

"What did John Watts order?" Ben glances at the man.

"He sent Mohi to tell the settlers to surrender and promise no harm to captives." The fighter turns to the bustle as Mohi returns.

Watts meets the healer. "Did they agree?"

"Yes, most of them have gone to defend White's Fort." The medicine man hands his leader a settler-carved peace pipe. "They knew we were coming, but a few stayed to pack families for transport."

"Good. We will leave a few to guard these Whites and move past. We arrive by midday tomorrow."

Enoli twists to view Dragging Canoe, mounted with a musket in his clenched fist, as he jabs the weapon at the ridge of concealment, "Those are settlers! Death! Muscogee and Cherokee, attack!"

The lower settlement's warrior leads a spontaneous unplanned charge of his followers and allied Creeks into Cavett's Station.

***

John Watts sits his mount, stunned at the insurrection.

Musket fire and war whoops reverberate and mix with the screams of dying women and children.

Young Tassel's jaw trembles in anger.

Ben leans to Enoli's ear. "Is he going to let them massacre those families?"

The new shaman grits his teeth, "He has no choice."

Childish voices scream in terror from beyond the ridge.

Watts resumes command and directs the remainder of his force, "Save the mothers and their children!"

Watts' loyal followers ride and run to join the conflict in defense of White children.

Enoli and Ben approach as a Cherokee attacker slits the throat of a settler woman, one of a few alive.

Blood stains and surrounds the killing, with bodies strewn through the collection of cabins.

Muscogee warriors and their Creek allies scavenge wood bins, horse shelters, and haystacks for more victims.

James Vann grabs a small White boy from the ground and pulls him onto his saddle.

Nearby, Dragging Canoe kicks heels into his horse's flank and charges. As the warrior thunders past, he hatchets the child's skull.

As the murderer's mount slides to turn, the defender lifts and aims his musket.

"Shoot me! Let your poisonous White half's blood pull that trigger!" Dragging Canoe shakes his war ax in the air.

The son of settler's finger trembles before he lowers his weapon. "Listen to me!" Vann points as Enoli, Ben and other fighters watch. "There rides a baby killer!"

Dragging Canoe whips his tomahawk from his belt, pauses, and glances at the warriors who observe the encounter.

In disgust, the leader spits onto the ground, jumps from his horse, and scalps a dead White settler with one slash of his ax.

The warrior jabs the scalp into the air and howls a victory scream.

***

Many of James Vann's fighters gather for commands as Dragging Canoe's men and the Muscogee Creeks pillage the settlement.

"Anyone that slays another woman or child answers to me!" Vann walks his horse among a few survivors. "Collect them as prisoners!"

The upper town's Cherokee spread through the town and try to stop further slaughter.

The blood brothers walk together around the corner of a cabin.

A three-year-old cries for his mother as he toddles out of an overturned corn crib.

Enoli sweeps the boy into his arms for protection and turns to Benjamin. "Come. Let's get away from here. I want to save this one."

Ben nods agreement and leads, with his musket at the ready, away from the melee.

A few minutes later, separate from the massacre and in the relative safety and concealment of brush, the two friends catch their breaths.

"What are we going to do? This child learns to walk." The freedman leans to look at the youngster in his friend's arms.

"I don't know. I won't let the Muscogee warriors murder him," the young medicine man smiles at the toddler.

"Dragging Canoe will, if you give him the chance," Ben looks at the thicket for movement or physical threat.

***

Hours later, as evening approaches, the friends walk upon a path through the brush and woods along a deer hunter's trail worn by moccasins over decades.

The sound of horses behind them causes the two to turn.

John Watts leads several mounted warriors and more on foot. "I feared you died. Son of Stone Cloud can welcome you home. What's that you carry?"

Enoli extends the White toddler, and the horseman stops.

"Another prisoner. We have his mother, I expect. Let us join them." The leader nods to one of his men. "We'll take the child to Vann's group. I instructed him to deliver the women and children to White's Fort."

The mounted warrior lifts the toddler from Enoli's arms, turns his mount, and trots back along the trail.

"Saloli, follow. I want him to find his mother," the young medicine man drops his furry friend to the ground.

The animal shakes its tail and flashes up the nearest tree.

"Come. I am sure Son of Stone Cloud worries," Watts nudges his horse into movement, and those on foot move behind the horses.

***

As the main party of Cherokee returns to their headquarters, Saloli jumps from sapling to brush along the hunting path.

Often, moving fast, the animal pauses and waits for the warrior with the toddler.

Impatient, the limb climber extends his lead until stopped.

Below him, on the road, Mohi rides alone. The tracker eyes the earth.

Trail sign lays obvious from a previous large party. Multiple sets of hoof prints and pressed flat grass by moccasins extend the trail's width on each side by several feet.

As Saloli observes, the warrior with the toddler approaches, sees Mohi, and stops. "What news?" The man extends a hand, palm upward.

"Watts distrusts the men at White's Fort. He orders White women and children to die. Turn over that child."

"I just left our leader. He told me to take this boy to James Vann." The escort's statement hangs in the air as Mohi's thrown tomahawk embeds his chest. The body coughs, drops the toddler, and rolls from his horse.

On the ground, blood gushes from his mouth as he sputters, "You fight for Dragging Canoe?"

Mohi smiles as he dismounts.

He walks to the fallen escort, draws his knife, and slices the victims throat.

The medicine man turns to the crying infant, on his back nearby, and smashes its skull.

130

As dead prey, he drags the caretaker and child off the pathway into concealment by brush.

Saloli watches with whiskers twitching as Mohi checks to ensure no one observed the murder.

The shaman mounts and continues along the obvious trail.

In the trees, the small furry scout follows but pauses above the healer-turned-fighter.

Mohi looks to the rustle in the tree.

The animal and killer meet alone, and the medicine man remembers.

He whips his musket to his shoulder and fires.

A lead ball smashes through Saloli's chest. With a last whisker twitch, Enoli's friend loses his grip and falls from the tree.

The assassin dismounts, withdraws his knife, and cuts off the rodent's tail.

He admires the white slash in its fur and stuffs the distinctive appendage into a saddle pouch.

CHAPTER FOURTEEN — Hopewell

DRᎪᎤᎤᎣᎥᏍᎤᎭᏫᎩᎠᎫᎬᎬᏭᏣᎠᏴᎳᎤᏫᎤᏀᏍᎷᏭᎣᎭᏐᏹᎾᎧᏅᎭᏃᎶᎤᎤ

Months later, near James Vann's headquarters, Enoli and Ben hunt deer with bows and arrows. The two young men talk and check their surroundings for game signs as they walk.

"We have attacked no settlements since Cavett's Station. Do you think Vann influenced Watts?" Benjamin watches a clump of brush suitable for doe. "He thinks we should adapt to the Whites."

"After the massacre, Young Tassel changed." Enoli studies the hideaway. "Saloli could find us a buck."

"I miss that little corn cob," Ben smiles.

"Something happened to him." The shaman pauses.

"Yes. Not much corn in the woods, and he's not returned."

"John Watts evolved and also Son of Stone Cloud. They become more Vann and Old Tassel." Enoli watches the treetops that blow in the wind. "Winter's coming. More change blows from the north. People say the government of the White settlers proposes a new peace treaty."

"What do you think happened to your squirrel?" Ben looks at his companion.

The young medicine man's voice resonates sadness. "The little thing had enemies. A vulture or a fox ate him, I expect."

As the hunter speaks, his physical bearing changes to suspicion. "Someone's coming."

The hunters conceal themselves in the brush and watch for movement.

A wagon clears the bramble and moves into the clearing.

Pulled by two mules, the four-wheeled transport lumbers with a load of blankets escorted by Dragging Canoe's warriors.

Mohi walks yards behind and supervises the band.

The concealed friends, press closer to the earth and maintain silence.

The blanket shipment clears the opposite end of the clearing, and its guards disappear into the woods.

Enoli stands, "Why is he escorting a load of blankets?"

"Because of Dragging Canoe's orders, I suspect," Ben joins his erect friend.

***

Several hours later, upper town Cherokees convene their council within the encampment.

John Watts presides, with Vann and Dragging Canoe separated on opposite sides of the circle.

Enoli and Benjamin, with Son of Stone Cloud's arms over their shoulders, carry the famous shaman to his seat.

The great medicine man sweats with fever. He grimaces with side pain from his infected wound.

John Watts stands, and the group settles. "Mohi arrived this afternoon with a proposal of peace from representatives of the United States. That offer comes with a goodwill gesture, a wagon load of blankets to warm our families this coming winter."

Dragging Canoe rises, "My great shaman deserves the gratitude of our people!"

134

The delegates of the council circle thump the ground with fists, pipes, knife handles, and muskets.

"They offer peace to our Nation with favor and protection. Their words come with conditions," Watts pauses and glances around the circle. "We must restore our prisoners, including slaves and property."

Benjamin leans closer to Enoli. "No worry. I have papers."

"No citizen of theirs shall settle on our lands, and if anyone violates the agreement, we may punish that violator." The leader looks to the lower town representatives.

Dragging Canoe rises, "The State of Franklin steals my land so I will kill those settlers."

James Vann stands on the opposite side of the circle. "No. Not with this agreement. The Franklin immigrants are citizens of the United States who have declared their independence. But they are protected."

"Then their scalps hang cleaner!" Dragging Canoe laughs.

"We concede lands with this treaty but firm our boundaries," Watts interrupts the competing warrior. "You take no fresh scalps!"

The group settles and responds to the leader's demand for full attention. "And we accept conditions. Restrain retaliation. Whites regulate trade. We tell the United States of any design against them by any warrior or tribe."

Someone in the group's dissatisfaction surfaces, "Betray our friends?"

The leader clears his throat, "The Cherokee sends a deputy representative to the national Congress to speak for us. And the United States guarantees peace and perpetual friendship."

James Vann stands across the council circle. "What do we call this concession?"

Son of Stone Cloud nudges Enoli. "Help me to my feet. I wish to speak."

John Watts holds a formal carved pipe above his head, glances at James Vann but extends the smoke symbolically around the circle. "The Whites name it the Treaty of Hopewell. If we agree, our representatives sign at the time of the first snow."

Enoli and Ben steady Son of Stone Cloud as he stands to speak to the council.

John Watts notices the great man rise, "Our greatest teacher of peace and healing rises."

The younger men feel the sick man's arms shake with his effort to stand.

His medicine voice rings strong, "Friends, you know I love harmony and practice the medicinal arts. This Treaty of Hopewell allows us to rebuild. Yes, it lays a western boundary for White settlement further into our lands. As the Spanish now, and the British and French before, they promise to favor and protect the Cherokee Nation. I fear, when this no longer suits, their words on this paper are talking leaves and blow away in the wind."

The phrase, "talking leaves," reverberates around the assemblage and many nod and repeat.

"Let me sit, boys," Son of Stone Cloud's knees partially collapse, and Enoli and Ben lower him to the ground.

"You tire," the younger medicine man leans close. "Should we take you back to your sleeping mat?"

"Not before I apologize. I called you a boy. Today you are twenty-one, past a youth. May this momentous treaty mark your birthday and allow you to work for our people. I know you. Your words will never be talking leaves."

***

As Enoli and Ben help Son of Stone Cloud to his bed, they pass families who gather extra warmth for the approaching winter.

Blankets no longer pile high but fill half Mohi's wagon.

"Those White man's comforts go fast." The freedman watches the distribution.

"I'll get Son of Stone Cloud several if you can help him to his lodge?" The junior medicine man accepts his friend's nod of approval.

Enoli examines the varying weights of coverings. He notices stains of blood and body fluids on the cloth.

"Where did these come from?" The young healer turns to a lower town attendant.

The man shifts the inventory for easier access. "Mohi brought them from the settlers at White Fort," the worker drops a pile onto the wagon's rear for easier access.

"No, I mean where within the place?" He examines the stack on the tail rest.

"He said they used them where they cared for their wounded and sick." The attendant walks to the front for another load.

The new shaman leaves the wagon and its blankets and hurries to the lodge of his leader.

He stops at its entrance and takes a deep breath. "It is Enoli. May I speak to you for a moment?"

From within, Watts' voice invites the young man into his temporary home and the shaman enters.

Around a small fire, Dragging Canoe and Mohi share a pipe with the upper town's leader.

"Come, smoke with us," the host indicates a spot near the fire.

"I bring unwelcome words."

"So do many that enjoy my hearth these days. Dragging Canoe tells me of White free staters who push out of Franklin to massacre and kill. Mohi warns the Unetlanvhi (Creator God) dislikes our treaty. What could you tell me worse?" The northern Cherokee leader drags on his pipe.

"I saw much smallpox sign in my youth and time assisting Son of Stone Cloud." The young shaman glances at the leader's two guests. "Those who bled and drained pustules used the gifts from White's Fort. The pox stains the entire load."

Mohi twists and stares. "Of course, Whites used them. Do you think the settlers give us items unused in quantity?"

"Son of Stone Cloud and I believe items discarded by those with smallpox pass the infection to others."

Dragging Canoe's medicine man leans backward and laughs, "Son of Stone Cloud believes, or is it you, apprentice shaman, that pushes your opinion because your mother died of the disease?"

Enoli lunges at his enemy, but Dragging Canoe grasps his shoulders. "You are not the quality healer of Son of Stone Cloud. And I know you are not the fighter my Mohi is. I suggest you control your temper and watch your words."

John Watts lays his pipe beside the fire and rises to his feet. "The opinion of Son of Stone Cloud and his apprentice counts. He is qualified as a medicine man. Some call him Talks to Squirrels. We follow advice from honored sources. Pause the blanket handout."

"Thank you, Sir. That name is old. My little furry friend disappeared months ago."

"The squirrel with the white fur on the bottom of its tail that used to follow you around?" Mohi's voice resonates over the fire.

"Yes, the same one from our Paint Clan encampment," the younger shaman stares at his enemy.

Mohi chuckles, and the confrontational mood breaks. "That was six or seven years ago. That animal died of old age."

"I saw your teacher still suffers from his wounds." Dragging Canoe's tone remains unwelcoming. "You should attend to your master's health, young apprentice, and let us tend to the encampment's."

***

The following morning, James Vann interrupts Son of Stone Cloud's breakfast with his two caretakers.

He steps into their lodge unannounced. "I understand Enoli found signs of pox on those blankets from Fort White."

Son of Stone Cloud swallows his mouthful of venison and grimaces with pain.

He looks up at the early visitor, "Yes, we were talking about that fact."

"Even with the new treaty, I cannot afford to lose my fighting men."

"Nor our people's women and children." The great shaman eyes the hickory tea that bubbles on his fire. "Enoli, a drink for me and our guest, please."

Vann relaxes. "Don't you teach that blankets contaminated by pox pass the sickness?"

"I do. I expect an outbreak from those gifts."

"That I cannot allow." Vann studies the wounded healer. "How can I prevent this?"

Son of Stone Cloud sips, "You cannot stop it at this point, but variolation saves many of your warriors."

Vann accepts a small pottery bowl of drink. "And what is variolation?"

"We give your men the pox. One or two out of a hundred die, the others recover after light illness." The great shaman peers over his tea at the warrior. "If we do nothing, thirty or more."

James Vann sips his tea for a moment. "With my warriors, make it happen."

"No, I cannot." Son of Stone Cloud shrugs. "I am no longer powerful enough. My wounds still fester, my flesh rots. Enoli, my senior shaman, must administer the variolations."

"Which I can do." The new medicine man motions for Benjamin to stand. "My friend can assist."

James Vann frowns and stares at the sick and weak old man.

"Your fighters must know the risk," he returns the stare. "Tell them if they live, they never fear the pox again."

***

Later that day, early reports of smallpox infection appear on two of Dragging Canoe's blanket wagon's escorts.

Enoli and Ben rush to the ill Indians, one of which displays pustules.

"He has it," the inexperienced shaman bends over his first patient.

"Give it to me," Benjamin lays his hand on his buddy's shoulder. "This is the time. I do not want to fear this my entire life."

"Are you sure?" The new medicine man studies his friend's eyes.

Benjamin nods yes and extends his palm. He withdraws his knife from his belt and slices a minor cut into the flesh below his thumb.

Enoli leans over the sick patient and swabs a pustule with a small stick.

Wet with slime, the swab shakes in his grip as he rubs the sickness into his friend's hand. "I don't fear this, but you should. I had the disease when I was a boy, and my mom died of it."

"I barely remember my mother. Her face, I do when they sold her. She cried and threw me a kiss as they took her away." Ben looks at his blood brother. "If I die, I do as a variolated freedman."

CHAPTER FIFTEEN — Determination

ᎠᎡᎢᎣᎤᎥᎦᎧᎨᎩᎪᎫᎬᎭᎮᎯᎰᎱᎲᎳᎴᎵᎶᎷᎸᎹᎺᎻᎼᎽᎾᎿᏀᏁᏂᏃᏄᏅ

Several days after Benjamin's variolation, the disease attacks, and Enoli divides his time between care of Son of Stone Cloud and his friend.

Of the two patients, the old gentleman declines while his apprentice fights the infection that consumes his superficial hand wound.

Both sleep for extended periods.

When awake, the great medicine man and his young caretaker bond beyond even the father and child relationship.

"When I am not asleep, Enoli, I hear a noise in my ears. It is my mother calling for me to join her and our clan."

"We can fight this, Sir. I have used every herb and chant you ever taught me. The red flames around your wound become larger. For months, they don't improve." The young shaman examines his elder. "What do I do wrong?"

"When the plants teach healing, they never promise a cure for everything." The great healer groans as he attempts to shift his weight. "How is Benjamin?"

"The same. The pox shows on his neck, but only a few sores. He sleeps." The caregiver glances at Ben's blanketed form asleep on the opposite side of the lodge. "I am sure he recovers soon."

"That is good. You need his friendship. My dreams tell me you face issues as my successor that I only dreamed of fighting." Son of Stone Cloud's eyes show concern. "I know I cannot be with you, but I am pleased Ben replaces me."

"What are you speaking of, Great One?" Enoli leans closer.

"My night stories. Kituwa (ᎩᏡᎦ ki-tu-wa, Real People) dress in their death clothes, simple cloth to join our ancestors. Our lands become smaller with each treaty, our numbers fall with each battle against Whites and disease." The famous shaman struggles for the strength to continue, "Children grow without education of the old ways and most of their parents ignore the plants and animals."

"The Absolute Spirit will lead the Kituwa to a new dawn." The ex-apprentice wipes fever's sweat from the great shaman's brow.

"I pray so, but I place my faith in you," Son of Stone Cloud smiles at his pupil.

"What more can I do?" Enoli swallows and draws a deep breath.

"We stumble in confusion. My father showed the path, and I followed his trail through the wood's darkness. Now, my mother calls for me to join her. I have no heir to lead my people. When I'm gone, you must wear my moccasins."

"They are too large," the young healer smiles at his patient.

"Your day comes, my son." The patient's eyelids droop with exhaustion. "As you walk with the Kituwa, your feet will grow. You are a dideyohvsgi (ᏗᎮᏲᎲᏍᎩ di-de-yo-hv-ss-gi, teacher.) My dreams describe your future. True to my visions, Dideyohvsgi is your new name."

***

The great shaman slips into slumber, and Enoli stands over him for a time.

He checks Benjamin.

Several pustules on the freedman's neck no longer ooze, and crusts form on other sores. The ill patient tosses and turns on his sleep mat.

His friend covers this second patient's shoulders and stares across the lodge at Son of Stone Cloud.

After a moment, Enoli looks skyward. "Unetlanvhi, a special person soon walks with his ancestors. Grow my feet to fill his moccasins and my new name." The young medicine man steps away through the lodge's entrance into fresh air.

The wind chills from the north as an early November snap sweeps drifting light snowflakes over a gray encampment.

Semi-permanent lodges and primitive cabin structures house a thousand Cherokee and Creek warriors with their families.

***

The alliance between the lower towns of Dragging Canoe and the upper settlements of John Watts frays as a fresh treaty with the government of the White settlers belittles its importance.

Enoli, Son of Stone Cloud's newest shaman with an anointed new name, Dideyohvsgi, looks at the settlement.

Several structures serve as sweat lodges. They shine bright from fires within and host families who stand vigil.

The disease comes with the snow, but many, as Benjamin did, endure Watts' and James Vann's ordered variolations.

They suffer mild symptoms and now, against Son of Stone Cloud's guidance, defy Dideyohvsgi and attend the sweat ceremonies.

Mohi and other Dragging Canoe shamans conduct the ritualistic ice-water douses of pox sufferers and chant-dance in heated lodges for their patient's pleased relatives.

These aunts and uncles support the practice and ignore the safety of variolation.

Dideyohvsgi watches several families load their possessions and leave the settlement to return to their upper and lower town homes.

The fighting force assembled to resist Whites melts as new snowflakes.

The days become shorter, and temperatures continue to fall.

Benjamin recovers from his bout with the pox and rejoins the Dideyohvsgi variolation effort.

As the population of the headquarters' temporary settlement falls, their workload becomes less.

Summoned to the lodge of John Watts, he and Ben sit with the leader who passes a smoke pipe. "Soon, we travel to endorse the treaty. James Vann, Dragging Canoe, and I sign for our groups. Son of Stone Cloud should. Can he consent and is he able?"

"The great shaman wants to represent his people. He is very weak. We could bring him in a wagon, but the risks are high. He will decide." Without coughing, the young medicine man passes the smoke pipe to his freedman friend.

"I hope he can sign." Watts looks to the lodge entry as James Vann interrupts. "Welcome, you are better. That is good."

The host smiles, "Son of Stone Cloud's shaman tortured me, and I have the scars to prove it." The leader rubs pock marks on his chin. "But now, thanks to his medicine, I do not fear the sickness. My warriors no longer die."

John Watts turns to Dideyohvsgi, "Did Dragging Canoe and his men accept your treatment?"

Vann steps to the fire. "That is why I am here. He and his fighters packed and left this morning for the lower towns."

"Without variolation?" Watts' wrinkles his forehead.

Dideyohvsgi stands, "Dragging Canoe's shaman, Mohi, does not recognize variolation."

"Then they carry the illness as the blankets did," Watts passes the smoke to James Vann.

"I am not sure." He looks at both the leaders, "Mohi traveled with those blankets for days."

"No matter, the harm's done," John Watts studies the fire. "The Creek Cherokee alliance dissolves. We no longer are strong enough to fight the settlers. This peace treaty is crucial. I know war dominates Dragging Canoe's heart. He may attack the settlements near the lower towns?"

James Vann watches his leader, "Baby killer said this morning he will be at the signing."

***

Later, on November 28, 1785, Benjamin drives a two-mule team as it pulls Son of Stone Cloud along a road on the banks of the Seneca River in northwestern South Carolina.

Blustery winds from the north flap the canvas cover, invade its interior, and dry the fever sweat on the shaman's brow.

Dideyohvsgi holds the exceptional man's head in his lap and attempts to cushion each bounce from wheels as they clunk over ruts.

Ben leans through the front flaps. "Won't be long now. Hopewell Plantation's just up the way." He turns from the river as Hopewell Road twists through oak woods that stand in the winter without foliage.

Past the trees, groups of Cherokee camp below the log main house of the plantation near much smaller individual rooms for slaves.

Ben stops the mules at the Indian campsites and sticks his head inside the warmth of the enclosed bed. "We're here. Our people stay by the slave quarters. Brings memories and makes me nervous."

Dideyohvsgi turns to the wagon's rear.

John Watts opens the canvas. "He made it. That is good. How is he?"

"Asleep, feverish, but he wanted to come." The young shaman shifts his weight.

"Benjamin Hawkins is here. and we endorse the treaty this afternoon." The leader peers at Son of Stone Cloud.

"Benjamin Hawkins?" Dideyohvsgi's Ben holds the entry behind him closed against the wind.

"Representative of the United States." The warrior looks at Ben, "Right now, he rests in Andrew Pickens's cabin."

"I heard of Benjamin Hawkins. He is a slave trader." The freedman clears his throat.

"Could we move our patient indoors?" Dideyohvsgi distracts Watts' attention.

"No. Pickens requires our Cherokee representatives to camp with his slaves," Watts grits his teeth and his eyes flash in anger. "His plantation only allows Whites to sleep in the main cabin."

***

That afternoon, as the wind whips from the north, at the appointed time, John Watts waits in a White man's clothes, a dark coat over a ruffle shirt, knee pants, and black calf socks with leather shoes. He pulls a tri-corner hat tight over his unpowdered natural hair.

The leader stands by a hewn table under a massive oak tree near the plantation's main cabin.

Dragging Canoe, James Vann, and other Cherokee dignitaries, dressed in their finest symbols of power and authority, stand and stamp their feet against the chill.

Dideyohvsgi and Ben sit beside Son of Stone Cloud, who rests on canvas strapped to two poles.

Families of the Indian representatives cluster nearby with local slaves who watch the proceedings.

The Cherokee wait.

***

New flakes of snow add to the chill and drifts near the treaty oak and the patient men below its limbs.

"Dideyohvsgi, should you take Son of Stone Cloud to the wagon?" John Watts looks at the young medicine man.

The great shaman coughs and grimaces in pain but wags a finger.

The families grow restless, and Dragging Canoe turns to face the main house. "Where is their delegation? Does the United States want actual war? This warrior tires of waiting. I say burn that cabin and return home!"

"Patience, Dragging Canoe. Hawkins is their government." John Watts raps his knuckles on the table.

The Hopewell Plantation's front entrance swings open.

An army uniformed Major steps out and clicks his boot heels together. He snaps to attention with a formal salute.

A stout man in a black frock coat and powdered hair follows

and looks to his host, Andrew Pickens, who, with a contingent of armed soldiers, enters the yard.

Benjamin Hawkins and his squad march across the frozen ground to the treaty oak.

He stops at the table and surveys the Cherokee delegates.

His eyes linger on Son of Stone Cloud for a moment.

The imposing United States representative clicks his heels together. "We gather here to sign the Treaty of Hopewell and its addendum. The principal business comprises the following points."

Dideyohvsgi and Ben look at each other.

Hawkins unrolls the document in his hands, "Governor Blount agrees to a higher annual compensation for lands relinquished by agreement."

Murmurs ripple through the attendees.

"Second, he removes White people settled to the southward of the hill which divides the waters of the Tenassee, and Little River. That ridge becomes the border. Third, no further settlement."

Dragging Canoe looks at John Watts and nods affirmative.

"We offer an annual allowance of plows and other implements." Knox lays the parchment on the table.

One of his soldiers provides a quill pen and ink, "If agreed, Cherokee representatives now sign."

John Watts steps forward and pauses.

He looks at Dideyohvsgi and Ben.

The leader nods for them to endorse first.

With the young shaman and his friend at each end of poles, they carry Son of Stone Cloud to the table.

They lower the weak man, and he signs. His thin fingers shake, and his scribble smears unintelligible.

"You two as well. Witness the old man's signature." A soldier extends the quill pen.

As they lift the gentleman and carry him to rest in his wagon, John Watts and the other leaders sign the document.

***

In the wagon's warmth, the shaman grasps Dideyohvsgi's hand. "In my twilight days, I bring peace and a period of prosperity to my people. Please, get me back to Cherokee Rock where I may die in my spiritual nest."

Dideyohvsgi looks at Benjamin and returns to his mentor, "Father, I swear to take you home."

"Do you hear that?" The weak man's eyes glance at the wagon's flap.

He turns and follows the patient's look. "What?"

"Then you are not listening, Shaman. Do you sense the hummingbird wings?"

The younger healer listens, "Yes. Soft. Far away."

"That is a Raven Mocker that searches for me. It knows I near my end."

"The sound is closer but still distant," Dideyohvsgi returns his attention to Son of Stone Cloud. "More than taking you to Cherokee Rock, I swear to devote my soul to the peace and prosperity you spent your life to earn."

"Our people need more than guidance," the sickly shaman's eyes flutter. "They need to be free of smallpox."

"The Unetlanvhi and your teachings will help me defeat the disease. Sleep now. Ben and I take you home."

"I failed. The Raven Mocker comes." The old man relaxes. Dideyohvsgi tucks a blanket under his head.

"They feared the strength of Cherokee Rock." The weak voice struggles. "It may visit me sooner."

CHAPTER SIXTEEN — Burial

ᎠᏕᏘᏍᎣᎢᏍᏩᎶᏴᎠᎫᎬᏇᏜᎠᎸᎦᏏᎤᏪᏛᏁᏫᏥᎤᏗᏅᎦᏺᎤᎲᏗᏴᎮᏉᎾᏁᎻᏃᏇᏅ

Spring warms Cherokee Rock as Dideyohvsgi and Benjamin carry Son of Stone Cloud to his final rest.

The early rising sun sparkles off the river's confluence near the outcrop's base, and the night's feeding Whippoorwills repeat rhythmic calls.

The young men lie the body aligned north and south in the center of the rock's top.

They stand for a moment and soak the reflections from the rivers into their souls.

"Why do this, Ben?"

"Because I care, my friend. You are the only person who has ever cared in return. This fellow was your father, maybe the people's. I don't remember mine, so I share yours."

"There was enough of him for both." The medicine man stands and stares at the waters below for a moment, then collects rocks to cover the body.

Benjamin totes stones and helps his friend.

As the pile increases and buries the great shaman, Ben notices movement on the estuaries. He points, "There. Someone comes to visit."

Dideyohvsgi shoves the last rock into place and stands. He shields his view against the glare and looks for movement.

Two small dark shapes in a distant canoe trail a wake on the river.

"Think they are paying respects?" Ben shades his eyes.

"No. They are the Kosvkvskini."

"The what?"

"Evil spirits that spread smallpox among the Cherokee," the medicine man pats the last rock on Son of Stone Cloud's grave.

"We both survived the disease. What could they crave?" Ben peers across the vastness at the river.

"They murdered my mother. But the pestilence senses their greatest enemy lies under these stones. He is gone. Now they want my people." The shaman hurries and climbs off the top of Cherokee Rock.

"Then you need an ally," the freedman follows.

The two scramble from the rock's roof and into the cavern's underneath entrance. A pile of cut timber for winter fires inside the opening provides a first line of defense. Beyond, a cooking fire burns.

The young men supplement the wood with burnable lodges, blankets, canvas, tables, and extend a small wall of dry combustibles across the cave's entry.

Outside, daylight's brightness dims and a murky fog gathers.

"The Kosvkvskini come! Burn the wall!" The two rush and light their defense with burning cooking timbers.

The two watch the defensive wall.

Dideyohvsgi looks through heat fumes for movement. "smallpox cannot survive flames!"

"Why do these things come?" Ben spreads coals under fresh wood on one end.

"Evil carriers sent by the Unetlanvhi punish us for not following the laws," the shaman yells back.

The heat vapors and distorts the Kosvkvskini as they step from the mists outside the cave into the entrance opening.

The woman leads.

Benjamin watches the apparition move toward the flames.

His medicine man friend sees the threat.

Walela, the young Cherokee girl saved and carried to her village but now dressed in a fine scraped deerskin dress with an ornate belt, walks through heat in dainty beaded moccasins. She opens both arms and invites. Her eyes sparkle, and lips moisten.

Ben steps forward, able to walk on coals.

The freedman feels a hand on an elbow, which jerks him away from the flames.

"Benjamin! Look here!" Someone is in the mists that surrounds Walela calls.

Dideyohvsgi slaps his ally, which shocks the glaze from the freedman's eyes. "Listen! Do you hear? Do what I do." He begins a chant with ritualistic footwork, and continues to grasp the freedman's arm. "Dance!"

The two do the Itohvnv (ᏔᎥꞶᎣꞷ i-to-hv-nv, smallpox Stomp.) The shaman moves with trained perfection, and the partner stumbles as he imitates the ritual.

Benjamin's head clears. He looks across the fire line for Walela.

A pockmarked old wraith with long gray hair in shoulder strings wears pustule-stained blankets. Soulless eyes follow Ben's dance.

Miniature porcupine pricks poke through cloth and bristle from her arms.

The male spirit follows and hovers on the opposite side.

His infested features flash hatred and sickness at the young shaman. The figure floats along the fire wall in search of an opening.

As Dideyohvsgi and Ben chant and dance for survival, the evil and disease-ridden death wraiths slobber and thrash to attack fresh prey.

With a high-pitched starvation howl, the prickly demon launches her body into the heat.

Flames consume pestilence.

The male uses her body remnants as a foot bridge and bounds over the hot barrier.

"This is it, Ben!" The medicine man twists toward his friend.

"Not this time!" Benjamin lunges at the vision, which engulfs the freedman in powdery blackness.

Muck sweeps over the fire line and fills the cave. Disease and death capture Cherokee Rock and the decades of healing the cave represents.

Dideyohvsgi falls to knees before his attacker and spreads both arms wide.

From the entrance, a beam of light pierces the grotto and slices the murk. Brightness floods the cave's floor and creeps up walls.

"You are my disciple, and I am well pleased." The thunder of the Unetlanvhi (ᎤᏁᏢᎥᎯ u-ne-tla-nv-hi, Creator God) reverberates through the space.

Mist and darkness within the cave return to health and normality.

The defensive wall of fire extinguishes, as if the north wind blows its embers cool.

Dideyohvsgi stands over the evaporation moisture of the smallpox carrier.

Its weak echoing voice trembles with defeatism, "You are a loyal son of Stone Cloud. My powers die, but my legacy spread over the earth. I remain victorious."

"No. You melt and walk in darkness forever." He looks at the black puddle's eyes near Benjamin's body. "Remove this pestilence! Tell us how to prevent the pox."

"You burned my wife. Go milk a cow." The puddle fizzles over one eye.

"What?"

"Suck an udder, ignorant Shaman." A last eyeball melts in the tar.

The victor watches putrid life forces extinguish. "No curses will save you. The Greatest Power has spoken."

Benjamin stirs, reincarnated, and sits. He rubs both eyes. "What happened?"

"You charged the dark sprits and won," Dideyohvsgi helps his friend to stand. "As they melted, it was trying to tell something about a milk cow."

"I'm all right. Are you?" Ben feels his chest.

"Think so, but this place feels dirty. It's worth cleaning. Cherokee Rock is where the Kosvkvskini perished. It births the people into a future free from the pox."

***

Weeks after the confrontation, far from Cherokee Rock, the two blood brothers walk through the woods that protect and surround the lower towns.

"John Watts lives in the next village," Dideyohvsgi directs forward.

"I thought he and Old Tassel were from the upper villages." Ben looks at his friend.

"The Treaty of Hopewell conceded those lands to the Whites, and he moved south," the shaman pushes through brush off trail. "James Vann as well. But Dragging Canoe's the lower town's accepted leader."

"Divided government." Benjamin pushes bushes aside.

"Nothing gets decided in the turmoil. Mohi speaks loudest and is more in touch with those people. He talks so much there's no choice but to listen." Dideyohvsgi breaks out of the brush onto a foot trail.

"If someone claims you are a slave long and often, in the mind, you become one, another's property. Learned that on a plantation," Ben chuckles with his story.

"Mohi speaks for Dragging Canoe. Says the old ways died. Of course, he and the people that agree are the new way. They kill White settlers." The shaman strides faster on the free-of-brush foot trail.

"That violates the treaty." Ben increases his pace.

"Blowing leaves, isn't that what Son of Stone Cloud called treaties?" Dideyohvsgi looks at his travel mate.

"The old medicine man knew. Colonists move south past the upper towns." The freedman smiles.

"Invisible promises, ignored and forgotten." The healer stops. He surveys the trail. "I hear something."

The two travelers hide in brush and check their muskets. Armed, they wait in silence.

A black and white animal with an enormous udder saunters into the clearing, accompanied by another.

Dideyohvsgi stands and laughs. "A milk cow! Looks dangerous."

Ben watches it round the curve into the meadow, followed by a young woman.

He steps from concealment, "Walela!"

The Cherokee milkmaid turns to flee and then recognizes the freedman. "Benjamin! Is that you?"

Her earlier savior jogs toward the girl. "What are you doing here?" Near the herder, Ben stops an urge to hug.

She halts as well. "These are my cows, remember? When the treaty took our homes, I moved with Watts' followers to the lower towns."

"Fine animals. You are a rich young lady!" Ben laughs as his buddy joins the two.

"With perfect skin," the shaman admires Walela's chin, throat and neck.

"Don't forget you are a disciple of the Unetlanvhi, Friend," Ben's voice rumbles a warning, and Dideyohvsgi catches himself.

"Your skin is perfect," he walks around the girl, "from a professional point of view."

He smiles at Ben. "I am a shaman trained by Son of Stone Cloud and am most interested in the pox. Obviously, you have never had the illness. Ever been near the pustules?"

Walela looks at Benjamin and the young freedman nods endorsement of his friend's inquiry.

"Yes. Mother died of it. I nurse many who fall sick. Most believe I cannot get the sickness." She slaps the haunches of one cow and turns the animal to the trail from which it entered the clearing.

"Interesting. A few do not catch the disease." The shaman rubs a chin and studies the girl. "Most unusual."

"We are going into this village. Your town?" Ben steps near the young woman.

"Yes. Come. The cows are fat with food, and it will be time to milk soon. Protect me and the livestock." She slips a hand into the crook of Ben's elbow and leads him into her village.

Dideyohvsgi watches the two for a moment and follows into the lower town of Crock.

***

The next day, the men wait in the shade of an oak near John Watts' lodge.

With backs against an oak's bark, they bask in leaf-speckled sunshine.

"Life is good, medicine man." Ben pats his full stomach.

"It is, but I miss Saloli. Expect to see the little fellow scurry from this tree trunk at any time to share the local gossip." Dideyohvsgi looks up into the tree's foliage.

"I'm sure the talk centers on two men sleeping outside Walela's lodge last night. But what a meal! I still taste the venison and corn."

"You ate enough," the shaman chuckles. "Should I prepare a stomach potion?"

"No, I'll recover."

"Dideyohvsgi!" John Watts' voice breaks the men's stuffed stupor.

160

The leader strides to the shade. "Sorry. I was hunting deer this morning. I didn't know you were visiting."

"We surprised you." Ben smiles and the warrior friend shakes his head in agreement.

"Good! I am sure you did not travel this far just to enjoy my new town's hospitality. What brings you?"

"I have news you will find hard to believe," Dideyohvsgi looks at the leader.

"By nature, unwelcome?" John Watts sits cross legged in the shade. "Or lies, spread by Dragging Canoe and Mohi for their own purposes?"

"Such as?" The young medicine man leans forward with interest.

"Usual things. White attacks on settlements that didn't happen, denial the pox plagues our people, rumors the United States wants land for a new state, and George Washington is king. James Vann calls Dragging Canoe Baby Killer. He should call him False Talker."

"We came a distance to make you aware that something most significant happened at Cherokee Rock." Dideyohvsgi revives the leader's attention. "Kosvkvskini attacked to destroy Son of Stone Cloud's legacy. Ben and I fought but lost. The Unetlanvhi saved us, and the evil ones perished. They are dead and gone forever. Never will the sickness plague the people again. Smallpox died. There is no source for new infections."

James Watts sits and studies the two young men for a lengthy time.

He picks at the grass near his feet with suspicious fingers.

"You see this battle, freedman?" The leader stares at Ben.

"You do not believe?" Dideyohvsgi straightens.

"Wait. Do not jump to conclusions." The warrior glances to check who can hear and then leans forward. "You both know that I am only half-Cherokee. White blood makes me question our ways sometimes. There are things mother spoke of that threaten if I did not eat fresh turnips. To me, those stories discipline my tastes for vegetables."

"I am not Cherokee," Ben's voice steels as he confronts the other man, "and did not even realize what a Kosvkvskini was."

Watts listens to the freedman.

"Something not invited came, yes, evil and corrupt. Its presence spread fear and illness miles ahead on their journey to Cherokee Rock."

The war leader swallows as the words sound earnest and true.

"I was there and fought the attack. Dideyohvsgi battled for our lives and soul. That is what I know. Listen to your shaman."

John Watts sits in silence for a moment with eyes that evaluate the two young men. "I am sorry for thinking White. Please, how can I help?"

"Smallpox is your enemy," the medicine man glances at Ben before he returns attention to the leader. "It is more powerful than settlers, stronger than their United States, amuck in our lives and the greatest threat to our way of life. The recent development is the source dies and the disease no longer spreads. Now, with the support of the plant and animal spirits, a chance exists to defeat the left-over illness."

The war leader fixates on Dideyohvsgi's words.

"My mother died of the pox, and I promised Son of Stone Cloud salvation. I cannot win without help. I must save families. Stand and back my quest to cure the sickness and wipe it from Cherokee land."

"Both sides of me, Unetlanvhi and the White God, support such a mission," John Watts extends a hand that Dideyohvsgi grasps. "You have my commitment and that of my followers."

CHAPTER SEVENTEEN — Lies

ᎠᏔᏍᎣᎢᏍᏬᏛᏴᎠᏎᎾᏈᎠᏢᎯᎦᏎᏫᏛᎾᏕᎷᏏᎦᏐᏁᎪᎯᎲᏗᏴᎮᏬᎮᏁᎯᏂᏃᏛᎤ

Several days later, John Watts disperses runners and riders to spread a call for a gathering of the lower town's leaders to be convened under the same oak where he greeted and met with the young men from Cherokee Rock.

He plans for the council on one evening of the full moon.

Dideyohvsgi and Benjamin sleep and eat at Walela's lodge, as if she is her family's matriarch.

Each day, the friends go with the woman as she herds her milk cows on the surrounding lands and searches for fresh grass.

The shaman wanders on the trips and looks for medicinal solutions in berries, roots, and seeds to aid the prevention or maintenance of people with pox.

Benjamin spends his time with Walela.

He helps the unselfish girl guide her herd, find fresh grazing, and milk the animals each day.

The medicine man, as he focuses on his profession, ignores the milkmaid and the freedman.

"Your friend is only interested in his medicines?" the owner supervises her cows.

"Dideyohvsgi promised Son of Stone Cloud to save your people from the pox. His mother died of it. I think that's more of a reason than his promise." Ben chews a grass blade and watches his friend. "But he does what he says."

"Did you know her?" The young woman looks at her companion.

"His mother? No. I only knew his squirrel," Benjamin smiles.

"Tell me." she moves closer, interested.

"Long story, for another time." The freedman's attention focuses on her closeness. "Your parents and family died. What do you plan for your life?"

"My cows give me a present occupation. But I want children, a husband, and a real future, as everyone else. And you?"

Benjamin turns on his elbows, "The same. Someday a cotton plantation. But no slaves. Only Freedmen work my crops."

"You are an ambitious man, Mister Waters," Walela leans closer and kisses the freedman. She withdraws and sits on her heels.

The two sit in silence for long moments and enjoy each other's company.

Ben breaks the mood. "Today in this pasture, with the clean air in our hair, you have my attention. That is wonderful, but a dark sickness and war shades the Cherokee. Dideyohvsgi offers hope and light. I am committed to helping him. The one you want; I cannot be soon."

"You underestimate me, Benjamin," she clasps her hands together in her lap. "But you should accept that others say your friend is weak and a false shaman. They claim he seeks a cure for the pox that is not an actual threat. Mohi says that your medicine man wants the Whites to invade our lands, so he discovers new worlds. Invents a culture where you, I, and the people return to the plants and animals as in the stories of olden times."

"That man is a liar." Ben's voice hardens.

"And Dragging Canoe?" Walela looks at the freedman. "Take care, Benjamin. I fear what waits in your future."

***

Several days later as they follow a smallpox report, Dideyohvsgi and Ben approach Ustanali, a lower town's village.

The place is one of sixteen communities east of the Blue Ridge Mountains across the Piedmont plains.

Lesser settlements surround the larger ones.

The communities divide into three groups, the lower, what is now Georgia and western South Carolina, the middle towns eastward from the Appalachians, and the Over-hill on their slopes.

The groups share culture but govern autonomously.

Uneasy peace in the lower section since the murder of Old Tassel and violence in the upper and middle sections drive most Cherokee allegiance to Dragging Canoe and his followers.

Dideyohvsgi enters the warrior's heartland.

Its Uku (ᎤᎫ, u-ku, First Beloved Man) meets the shaman. "Greetings! We welcome the emissary from John Watts!"

"Osiyo, (ᎣᏏᏲ, o-si-yo, Greetings) Uku!" He nears the resident. "I draw thorns from your feet. We walk the white path of life together. As a brother of my blood, we greet you."

The Uku turns toward his village with the two men at his sides.

"John Watts sends me to variolate your people."

"And many die. Is that correct?" The villager stares at Dideyohvsgi.

"A few," the visitor assures the emissary. "The others recover. And they never fear the pox again."

"Our leaders tell us differently." The friendship stops. "The great shaman Mohi teaches smallpox is no more. He says in a terrible battle of determination and spirit, our Dragging Canoe defeated and killed the Kosvkvskini. No longer does their sickness stalk our villages."

Dideyohvsgi glances at Benjamin, who stands with a frozen face.

The medicine man shakes his head, "John Watts believes we should take precautions."

"That kills my people?" The villager opens his palms with concern.

"You do not believe Watts?" Dideyohvsgi looks past the village's representative.

"John Watts is a fighter. Dragging Canoe is a greater warrior, and Mohi is his healer. John Watts variolates his own, but the families of Ustanali are Dragging Canoe's." The leader's voice raises with frustration. "I withdraw our welcome."

***

That evening, Dideyohvsgi and Ben pitch camp in a clearing near Ustanali along a hunting trail that leads to the next town.

The two cook a rabbit.

"You talk to animals, but you also eat them." The freedman smiles at his friend across the fire.

Dideyohvsgi flips the meat.

"Consider slaves. Your lower towns have them. Did the favored people bargain with us?"

"You're in a good mood. What got you riled?" The medicine man resumes his seat.

"Answer my question."

"No, we have no legend for that. But Cherokee believe in free humans. Only a few who trade with the Whites own slaves."

"From the numbers I see, looks as if you trade a lot," Benjamin kicks a coal closer to the flames.

"Many adopt the White man's ways. My people listen to the loudest, such as Mohi and Dragging Canoe," Dideyohvsgi stirs coals with a stick. "And to slave owners."

"Lies repeated become facts," Ben spits into the fire, and the moisture hits an ember and sizzles.

Both men fall silent as the smell of cooking rabbit and ember smoke sweeps upward in rising heat.

A rustle in the darkness attracts their attention. Both lunge for muskets that lean against a nearby tree.

"Don't shoot! We mean no harm," a woman's voice penetrates the night.

"Then show yourselves! Step forward," Dideyohvsgi holds his weapon at ready.

A Cherokee woman, with an infant and two youngsters, moves into the campfire's circle of light.

The children grip their mother's dress for security.

"I am from Ustanali. The Uku does not know. I heard you visited today, and my baby is sick. Can you help?"

Dideyohvsgi steps closer and removes a blanket from the infant.

A feverish face peers from the bundle, and sweat moistens the child's forehead.

"The boy has the pox." The medicine man watches the woman.

She trembles in fear at the words. "The Uku does not allow smallpox. Our shaman says the sickness is no more. I can't go back."

Dideyohvsgi looks at Ben, who smiles as he glances at toddlers who clings to their mother's skirt.

"Stay here with us, but you must let me variolate you and your children." The medicine man grasps the woman's elbow. "It makes you sick with the pox, but most recover and never catch it again. The baby, I'm afraid, may die because he has the fever."

***

Four days later, the clearing along the hunting trail serves as a field hospital.

Primitive lodges built of local material house patients.

Benjamin cools feverish brows with water from a nearby creek.

The mother who stumbled into camp lies on a mat with her two children, recovering from variolation.

Other more ill, newer arrivals, lie in other temporary spaces.

Dideyohvsgi pokes newcomer's palms with his knife and rubs pustule seepage from the original sick baby into those wounds.

A boy grasps his variolation to stop blood. "You know, medicine man, that we cannot return to our village until we are well?"

"Yes," the shaman pats the boy's shoulder, "and I won't let you go back. We can't spread the smallpox."

"There is no pox," the youngster shakes his head. "Mohi

says it's from chickens. Dragging Canoe killed the Kosvkvskini and banished the disease."

"Son, this has nothing to do with that minor illness," Dideyohvsgi laughs. "The name of it came because when you suffer the sickness, you look pecked by hens."

"That's not what Mohi preaches," the boy's body language shifts to confrontational. "He is Dragging Canoe's chosen one. He is a greater shaman than you are."

"Variolation makes you sicker than chicken pox. By the next full moon, you recover. Go rest with your family. I have others to variolate."

***

For days, Dideyohvsgi and Benjamin treat refugees from Ustanali. They require smallpox variolation of the non-infected.

The people in their clearing lie on mats in makeshift lean-tos and battle symptoms.

Most fight, aware of their affliction, but a few choose to deny reality and pretend otherwise.

In the middle of an afternoon, a commotion approaches from the south.

The Uku of Ustanali parades before several tribal leaders with Mohi at his side and stomps the hunting trail wider.

Ben hears the approach. "Dideyohvsgi, hear them?"

The healer nods, "Please, greet our visitors."

Benjamin trots toward the noise and confronts the small group, "Hold here, if you recognize what's best for you."

The Uku and Mohi stop.

"I told you we did not welcome you in Ustanali!" The leader puffs his chest with self-importance.

"And we know your message. This is not Ustanali," Ben does not carry his musket.

Dragging Canoe's representative recognizes the freedman.

"Waters," Mohi steps ahead of the others. "Does John Watts send you?"

"He did. We battle an infestation of smallpox." The freedman stands in the path.

"The pox from chickens?" The medicine man laughs and pokes the Uku.

"No. The pustule disease! Up this trail. Dideyohvsgi and I care for many from Ustanali."

Mohi pushes past, and Ben follows Dragging Canoe's rep into the encampment.

"I expected you!" Mohi spies Dideyohvsgi as he cools a patient.

"What do you want?" The younger healer stands.

"I want to show the Uku his people you murder with incompetence," the older shaman steps closer and looks at a woman with smallpox. "A few will die of the chicken's pox! This upper-town apprentice to a dead and forgotten prophet spreads pestilence. They want you to think John Watts knows everthing. No! Dragging Canoe killed the Kosvkvskini! John Watts and his deception kills loyal followers of Dragging Canoe. Make our hero First Beloved Man!"

Dideyohvsgi stands over his patient and stares at the hysterics for a moment.

He steps to a mat nearby and lifts the cover from a small body.

The baby brought to the encampment by its mother lies dead and covered with the pustules of smallpox.

The Uku with Mohi gasps for breath and reacts several paces backward.

"Leave us," Dideyohvsgi grits his teeth together and re-drapes the child, "to care for our people in peace."

***

Weeks later, after most of the recovered patients return to their lodges, Dideyohvsgi and Benjamin burn the encampment's lean-tos and temporary care spaces.

Along with mats, bedding, and other items, the materials create an impressive bonfire.

Smoke from the heat rises into the air, a giant black column of defeated sickness and despair.

Both men stand and watch the flames, hypnotized by the dance.

"Thank you," a voice interrupts.

Dideyohvsgi and Ben turn to view the woman who lost her baby. Her two smiling children hang one to each hand.

"I am sorry we did not save your child," the young medicine man nods.

"You saved these. And others. We will always remember you and Benjamin," she clasps her hands below her chin. "You lead your people."

"The Unetlanvhi guides. Stay healthy."

"You as well. But I have a warning. Where you walk, lies prepare the path. Do not go into the village. The Uku devotes himself to Dragging Canoe. You are in danger there."

"Thank you. We travel home. John Watts, sent a message to return as soon as we are able."

CHAPTER EIGHTEEN — Council

DRTᏖᎤᎣꞌᎢᏚᎣᏆᎩYAJEⳠᏜᏗᎯᏨᏔᎳᏔᎶᏒᏨMᎯᏖᎡᏬᎯHᏙᎩᎾᏓᎾᏁhᏃᏋᎤⱳ

In 1788, John Watts meets with Dideyohvsgi and Benjamin in his lodge in a remote location west of the Appalachian Mountains.

The command post hosts a large war party of remaining upper-town warriors who gather near North Carolina's Washington District in what is now Tennessee.

"Our fighters demand vengeance for Old Tassel's murder, an attack on the White settlements despite the Treaty of Hopewell. My uncle was not violent. I cannot urge peace any longer. They call me Young Tassel with derision," the leader laughs.

"You do not take this direction without thought," Dideyohvsgi nods.

"Dragging Canoe says kill Whites until they vanish from this earth. That is impossible. Our towns and people are autonomous. But politics moves to unite the Cherokee under a single government and one head, a supreme First Beloved Man."

"That should be you, Sir," Benjamin glances at his shaman friend for approval.

"Dragging Canoe has many votes and gathers more. His popular voice, Mohi, beats his drum." Watts stares at the healer. "You may have heard that liar claims the warrior even destroyed the Kosvkvskini?"

"Not as stupid as the claim smallpox resembles chicken pecks," Dideyohvsgi smiles at his leader.

"Their followers believe the lies." John Watts shakes his head and falls silent.

After a moment of reflection, he snaps full attention back to the guests. "Delegates to elect a leader must be familiar to the people." He pauses and considers the medicine man. "Most in the upper-towns know you represent the memory of Son of Stone Cloud."

"I consider it an honor to be a representative," Dideyohvsgi nods.

"Good. But first, we plan an attack on the White settlement at Gillespie's Station. I lead with upper-town warriors without Dragging Canoe's help or any from the lower towns."

***

Eighteen days after meeting, Dideyohvsgi and Ben, concealed by trees, survey Gillespie's Station, which guards the road to White's Fort in the old State of Franklin.

A log one-story cabin borders the trail. This trading post, inn, and guard station supports a crude sign with the name of its operator.

A large war group led by John Watts, on foot but well-armed, surround the two and wait for commands.

The site sits in silence. Windows in front stand shuttered tight. Long gun ports dot the shutters.

A stone fireplace emits a trail of smoke that floats away in the day's breeze.

"They know we were coming." Benjamin watches the station near Dideyohvsgi's elbow.

"We have no surprise. There's a musket behind each of those

gun ports." The shaman looks through the trees for John Watts.

"Watts isn't Dragging Canoe." Ben glances at his friend. "He won't attack."

"Look." The medicine man points.

The clearing around the station slopes up to a tree line behind the cabin. Smoke drifts from within the trees.

With whoops and war calls, warriors push a wagon piled high with brush flaming onto the incline and retreat into the woods.

The cart rolls true and impacts the rear of the cabin. Its flames dump against logs.

The fire licks the cabin's roof and the structure smokes.

Minutes later, the station's door flings open and members of the Jones Company of volunteer riflemen dive out of the inferno for protection behind water barrels and stumps.

The Cherokee warriors in the surrounding trees attack.

Black powder smoke floats in the clearing before the cabin as the White militia company resists.

Overwhelmed by numbers and firepower, three men, two women, and several children cower together near the station's entrance among their dead.

"Enough!" John Watts screams as he reaches the survivors. "We take these as prisoners! White's Fort is not far. Come! Follow me! We drive the Whites across the mountains to their own lands!" The leader trots from the burning cabin down the trail toward a larger settlement.

Dideyohvsgi and Ben follow with the war party and its prisoners.

"If these knew, so will the defenders ahead," Ben warns his friend.

"Maybe John Watts has a bigger surprise than a burning cart for them?" The shaman shrugs his shoulders.

"Where you go, I go," Ben follows.

***

Arrival at White's Fort presents a more fortified settlement.

Three two-story log buildings and a dozen smaller structures cluster together with a surrounding and connected six-foot post fence, with every rail planted in the soil.

Inside the enclosure, a corral contains fifty horses.

An entire company of volunteer mounted riflemen man the fence, and others poke muskets from firing ports in shuttered windows and doors.

"We're outnumbered." Dideyohvsgi lowers his head behind a fallen log.

"Yes. What do you think Watts' surprise is?" Ben with his friend crowds the earth behind their protection and concealment.

"Maybe he's going to pass out eagle feathers like Son of Stone Cloud," the shaman smiles at his companion.

"No eagle feather's going to make me attack that fort." Ben's sense of humor dulls with the thought.

Without direction or leadership, undisciplined warriors who hate Whites break concealment and charge the stockade.

Without mercy, militia musket balls rip through the courageous but exposed flesh of hate-filled warriors.

John Watts, forced to choose between attack and slaughter, screams above the melee, "Attack the fort!"

Benjamin leaps to his feet from behind his log with Dideyohvsgi beside him.

The shaman trips his friend with the barrel of his musket, and both fall.

A mounted volunteer's ball rips the trunk of a tree near Ben's face, and a splinter of wood tears across the freedman's skull.

Moments later, Ben's fuzzy vision focuses on Dideyohvsgi as the medicine man shakes him. "Come on, Ben! On your feet!" the shaman's lips move, and the freedman lip reads.

Sounds, screams of pain, and musket discharges flood his senses along with the shaman's voice. "Too many died! Watts ordered a retreat!"

Dideyohvsgi flops one of Ben's arms over his own shoulder and drags his friend from the clearing around White's Fort.

They struggle off the trail and into the brush and trees. Thorns and bramble tear at the two as they push for safety. The medicine man loses footing, and both fall.

They roll down an embankment into a gully.

The fall and roll returns Ben's concussion to unconsciousness.

Dideyohvsgi grabs several fallen limbs and debris. He pulls the forest trash over their bodies for concealment and lies in silence.

Shortly, two horsemen cross the ridge nearby but do not notice the spots of blood and surface disruptions where the two tripped and began their roll.

"We sure whupped them savages." The lead mounted volunteer looks at his trailing companion on horseback.

"Keep your eyes on the woods, Sam. We killed a bunch, but it only takes one to get your scalp." The second volunteer moves past the decline to the concealment gully.

As silence returns, Dideyohvsgi examines Ben's bloody skull.

The wood chunk's path across the rear of his friend's head seeps blood but does not spurt, a good sign.

The medicine man opens his water pouch and washes the wound. He looks about.

Nearby, a green moss grows on a tree root.

With a handful of the moss, the shaman treats his friend's injury. He wraps a portion of his tunic about the head, which holds the moss in place.

Satisfied, the healer lies beside the freedman and waits for darkness.

Several sounds of volunteer horseman threaten their security, but none come close.

***

After dark, Benjamin returns to consciousness, "Where are we. Oh! My head hurts."

"Go back to sleep. You are fine but need rest." Dideyohvsgi checks the moss. "Sleep a couple of hours, and then we'll find Watts and our warriors."

After midnight, the medicine man wakens his patient. "Come on, Ben. Let's get out of this gully."

Ben stands, smiles at his friend, and unsteady upon his feet follows Dideyohvsgi up the incline.

***

Several weeks after the disastrous attempt to capture White's Fort, delegates from both the upper and lower towns gather at the first attempt to form a Cherokee unified tribal council.

They meet at Oostanaula, Georgia, east of New Echota.

The purpose of the council is a union of Cherokee clans and election of a First Beloved Man.

Dideyohvsgi and Benjamin sit under a northwest Georgia tree with a group of delegates and listen to Little Turkey.

"My brothers, many of you support Dragging Canoe." The candidate for the highest office struts with the aura of a politician. "Let me remind you Dragging Canoe represents the clans of the Chickamauga and is a baby killer. Others support John Watts. He lost his upper town villages to the settlers after the defeat at White's Fort and now brings his people to crowd our land."

Dideyohvsgi leans closer to his freedman friend. "I hear this candidate's qualification is he knows many, talks much, and does little."

"He better calm the oratory about Dragging Canoe or feel Mohi's knife in his sleep," Ben chuckles.

The speech increases volume, "Dragging Canoe or John Watts fights the White settlers in a futile effort. Our tribal lands shrink with their warfare."

Little Turkey pauses, and his eyes fix upon Dideyohvsgi. "To make war upon the Whites requires warriors. Our mothers grieve for their sons taken by the pox. Our clans shrink daily because of the sickness. Dragging Canoe swears he killed and banished the Kosvkvskini. John Watts claims to sponsor variolation, which makes all ill. Neither candidate knows the path of the disease, but I say make peace with the settlements! Shed no more blood. Bury no more of our sons! Then we can live in peace and cure our people!"

The delegate crowd nods heads in approval and clap.

"Watts lost favor at White's Fort." Ben looks from under his eyebrows at his friend.

"And Dragging Canoe's hands drip baby blood," Dideyohvsgi winks and turns to stare at Little Turkey. "This loudmouth may win after all."

***

The following day, the Cherokee meet in council.

Delegates take places in a large circle around a basket of peach pits, stained red by river mud, white by the sun, or black from campfire ash.

Talk and gestures support individual candidates, and the clamor amuses Benjamin, "They sound like clacking hens."

Dideyohvsgi surveys the attendees, "And act like spoiled children."

A moderator steps into the center of the council circle with a smaller empty basket. He thumps a walking stick on the ground for attention.

The circle calms.

"I am proud to announce three candidates for First Beloved Man. Vote by their clans proposes each. From the upper towns, nephew of Old Tassel and warrior, John Watts."

Near Dideyohvsgi and Ben, the leader stands and waves his right hand in greeting.

"From the middle towns, newly elected representative, Little Turkey," the moderator points at the orator from the day prior, and he stands to applaud the crowd.

Ben leans close to his friend. "Outstanding qualifications always win, don't you think?"

Dideyohvsgi chuckles and puts a finger to his lips.

"The lower towns and the Chickamauga nominate their war leader and enemy of the White man, Dragging Canoe!" The moderator spins and point across the circle.

Dragging Canoe jumps to his feet and punches a clenched fist in the air.

The moderator waits for order and holds his empty basket in the air. "Before you, in the basket, you have vote tokens of three colors, selected by lot. Black for John Watts, white for Little Turkey, and red for Dragging Canoe. Delegates! File past. Select your candidate and place your token in the basket that I hold upon my head."

In solemn progression, the delegates of the circle reach for the tokens, select, and vote for their candidate.

Dideyohvsgi, without Ben, selects a black peach pit and drops it into the voting basket.

Upon completion of the vote, monitors for each candidate, which include Mohi for Dragging Canoe, sit with the moderator and count peach pits.

The council sits and waits.

After counting, Mohi stands in disgust and stomps to Dragging Canoe. He whispers in the warrior's ear, and the two leave the council circle.

"Looks like Dragging Canoe lost," Dideyohvsgi fist pumps his friend's shoulder.

The moderator rises and returns to the circle's center, "It is my honor to introduce the unified Cherokee Nation's First Beloved Man, Little Turkey!"

Ben looks squarely into the shaman's eyes, "Your people have problems, not solutions, my friend."

Dideyohvsgi notices John Watts rise from his seat in the circle. The leader locks eyes with the medicine man and shakes his head with resignation.

With Ben, the shaman steps close to his leader. "Sorry. I voted for you. But not enough did."

"That tragedy at White's Fort cost me. I will support Little Turkey, but I do not believe he is a powerful leader for our people."

"I wasn't a delegate but would have voted for you as well." Ben nods at the leader.

"Thank you. Not much has changed. Cherokee lands only become smaller." The warrior turns to Dideyohvsgi. "No matter the lies Dragging Canoe repeats, smallpox is a more vicious enemy for our people than the Whites. Go back to Crock. Work on that. I'll summon you if I need you."

CHAPTER NINETEEN — Crock

ᎠᎡᎢᎣᎤᎥᎦᎧᎨᎩᎪᎫᎬᎭᎮᎯᎰᎱᎲᎳᎴᎵᎶᎷᎸᎹᎺᎻᎼᎽᎾᎿᏀᏁᏂᏃᏄᏅ

Walela spots Dideyohvsgi and Benjamin as the men approach her lodge in Crock. She runs to greet one of the travelers.

The Cherokee woman with spotless skin flies into Benjamin's arms and hugs. "I am so happy! You return!"

The shaman watches the greeting, "Have I missed something? Two of us left."

Walela blushes, "Good you returned too."

Ben shrugs at his friend, slips an arm around the woman's waist, and leads the medicine man toward her lodge. "They sent us back for a time. Don't know how long, but not as guests. Got paid for our service with White man's coin, so we are not beggars."

"Benjamin! You know you stay free! But I'll take the healer's cash."

Days flow into weeks without a return request from John Watts.

Idyllic romps in the flower-covered meadows of northeast Georgia by Ben and Walela, as they roam cows, become one person-too-many events.

Dideyohvsgi seeks stimulation elsewhere.

***

The healer day trips to surrounding pockets of population and the larger settlements of the lower towns.

Often, these trips extend for a week or more, but Benjamin concentrates on his milkmaid and ignores the absence.

With medicine bag and musket on a shoulder, the young teacher walks a hunting trail. It leads to a group of families two days from Crock.

Above, a squirrel jumps, and the shaman stops to watch the flurry and remembers.

The animal pauses and wiggles whiskers with curiosity, but neither speak.

After a moment, the little furry fellow loses interest and scrambles away.

"Go, have a good life. If you meet my buddy, I say hello and miss him," the soft words drift in the breeze toward a vanishing bushy tail.

Dideyohvsgi follows a trail worn by deer and moccasins.

A sound from the brush ahead distracts, and for safety, he hides behind a tree.

A boy, fourteen years of age, trots along the path.

The shaman steps from hiding. "Hold up, Son. Why such a hurry?"

The youth stops and looks to the rear as if to flee but decides to stand firm. "I wasn't expecting anyone."

"You were not watching for settlers looking for scalps?"

"No. Whites have left us in peace since the treaty." The youngster shades both eyes with one hand as he inspects the interrupter. "That's a medicine man's kit. Are you one?"

"Yes."

"Mohi is shaman of the lower towns, but I look for another," the youth steps closer. "From Crock. Mother says a great healer named Dideyohvsgi stays there."

"And why seek him?"

"She has the sickness they claim no longer exists."

The man smiles and remembers a time when he was of the same age in search of help.

His mind drift into his memories.

***

A villager points at one open air cabin. Several people live in the dwelling owned by the family matriarch. He runs to the cabin. "Mohi!"

"What do you want?"

"A Kosvkvskini attacks mother. She needs you."

The medicine man grabs a medicine bag. "I know your parents. Lead."

The youth trots out of camp and into the hills.

They retrace the young man's steps. At a run, the two Cherokee eye lightning in the distance. Dark clouds gather over the horizon.

***

The storm clears the memory, and the healer grasps the boy's shoulder. "I am Dideyohvsgi, the one you seek. Take me to help you."

The boy turns and trots on the path.

As the shaman follows, he remembers a similar trek and his memories continue.

***

Without breathing hard, young Enoli sweeps a hand across the sky. "Two spirits, a man and a woman. They came from hiding. Mother sent for you, but as I ran, I looked. The female cast spines which the male made swollen into black sores."

Mohi stops, "The White man's smallpox!"

The boy spins to face the resistance. "Why stop? She's over the next hill."

"We return and bring others to carry the body." The healer turns to retrace steps.

"No!" Enoli rips a knife from belt and brandishes the weapon. "You fear the sickness! Go to mother now!"

The adult stares at the blade and into the boy's eyes. He whips a fist against the youngster's wrist and knocks the knife from the boy's hand.

Lunging to retrieve the blade, his ribs endure the thump of a foot, and he rolls in pain.

***

The memory shocks Dideyohvsgi from night's thoughts.

The youngster spins to face the medicine man. "Why stop? She's over the next hill."

"I am not Mohi, Boy. But if she has the pox, I will treat her my way and your relatives may not agree. Understand?"

"I told you medicine man. Mohi says she has the chicken's pox."

***

Weeks later, in the village, mother fights smallpox on an airy mat within her lodge. Air circulates through open sides around her body.

Son sits and wipes fever sweat from her cheeks, forehead, and arms.

The ugly pustules of the disease dry and heal.

Dideyohvsgi watches. "I believe she's better. You have served her well. And you recover from your variolation. I have done what I am able. I must return to Crock in the morning."

The young fellow looks up at the shaman. "Thank you. There is nothing in my power that repays you. But I promise to forever remember."

Several villagers approach.

"We need to speak." The leader of the group steps forward.

"How may I help you?" The medicine man steps out from the lodge.

"Leave. We follow Dragging Canoe. You are not welcome." The leader's body language reinforces his message.

"My plan is to travel in the morning," Dideyohvsgi studies the trio. "I know your warrior. We fought together. Did he send this word?"

"No. We command you. You come here and spread fear of smallpox. Our leader eliminated its cause. Our people have no pox. You convince this child and infect him with the mother's chicken disease. Take your lies and false promises elsewhere."

"Yes," Dideyohvsgi smiles. "The patient recovers because he found me in time."

The three men crowd closer, and the leader's voice rings icy and hard, "You healed her of children's sickness. For that, stay tonight. But pack your belongings and medicine bag. If we meet you after this night's sleep, we will not be so kind."

Several days later, after Dideyohvsgi's return to Crock, he and Ben walk and talk on an afternoon hunt.

"You vanished for a while," Benjamin watches for game sign.

"I cared for a woman and son. The mother had the pox."

"That end well?" The freedman looks at his partner.

"Yes and no," the shaman chuckles, "Cured the patient, but the family ran me from their town."

"You don't quit? Why did you leave?"

"Big supporters of Dragging Canoe. They believe in the Kosvkvskini lie. Good people who insist no smallpox, that it's chickenpox," the medicine man steps past his friend.

"You are a teacher." Ben follows along the hunting trail.

"Yes, but they weren't interested in truth," the shaman stops.

"Even through their own eyes?"

Dideyohvsgi notices movement in the brush, "Dragging Canoe and Mohi repeat the stories often, and their followers want to believe." He lifts a musket to shoulder and aims.

"A young doe. Take it. We need the meat," Benjamin keeps his voice low not to spook the game.

The medicine man fires, and the target drops to the ground.

As the two hunters clean the prey, the freedman eyes his friend, "You notice Walela and I are… are…?"

"What! Lovers? Committed? Married? Bed partners?"

"No. Good friends, but she wants more." Ben coughs.

"And you?"

"I'm unsure. Not being from her culture, I thought I might ask you." The man clears his throat.

"Which does not sound easy?"

"How does she and her people receive a person like me?"

The shaman chokes with laughter. "Your color? Or ugly? Perhaps unwashed? In her, I mean, our world, nobody cares. The men she meets are clansmen. Cherokee frown on marrying within a clan -- it's a union with your brother! She's lucky you came into her life!"

"That's why you show no interest in her!" Ben claps both hands in delight.

"Was that worrying you?" Dideyohvsgi sits on his haunches in dismay.

"No. But compatiblity does." Ben's eyes enlarge as he looks at his friend.

The healer suppresses amusement and recognizes his friend's seriousness. "Look, I'm a medicine man trained in these things. I can find out."

"Don't embarrass her! Or me!"

"I won't, Ben. It's a ritual her grandmother knows and loves. She'll be for it. Cherokee women have done this for generations." Dideyohvsgi lifts the carcass over a shoulder and stands. "Come. Let's get this deer meat home for dinner."

***

Several days later, Dideyohvsgi carries a traditional clay drinking vessel with two spouts.

The base features a blue and black band around its circumference and matching feathers painted above the pattern.

Each spout repeats the feather design, and an added illustration decorates the handle.

With the vase, he joins Walela as she attends cows.

The woman spots the vessel.

She blushes and twists back to milking. "You are of my clan, Dideyohvsgi. So that must be for someone else?"

"It is for Benjamin."

The milkmaid squeals delight toward the medicine man. "My Ben?"

"That's right. He wants to drink with a person I know," the shaman laughs, glances at Walela's animal's udder and chokes.

191

"Those ulcers are cowpox."

Walela turns. "Yes, this one is new. Traded two old dried-ups for her."

"Have you had the cow's illness?" The healer examines the sores.

"When I was little. Everyone who milks gets it." She watches the medicine man.

"You never had smallpox, right?" He glances at the woman's perfect skin.

"Never. Unetlanvhi protects," Walela smiles. "Plus, It favors those who milk cows."

Dideyohvsgi stands, "Gather your grandmothers. I will help do the drink ceremony. He asked for your consent."

"Benjamin is good, and you are his best supporter. I am honored. Tomorrow night, in my lodge!"

***

The following evening, Ben wears his cleanest clothing and approaches Walela's cabin with an advocate.

"Now remember. I offer the drinking vessel to you and Walela, and it's a test. The clay pot has two spouts, one on each side. Point is, both drink." Dideyohvsgi stresses the occasion's importance. "Her grandmothers judge. The more you spill, the less compatible. Be careful. Don't spill any. The stern woman inside is the wife of Old Tassel. She won't accept a granddaughter's interest in any clumsy clod."

"I'm nervous," Ben trembles. "I'll try not to splash any on the matriarch."

They reach Walela's lodge.

"It is Dideyohvsgi." The healer leans against the entrance.

A sweet voice floats from inside, "You are welcome here."

The medicine man opens the deerskin flap and holds it for his friend.

"Who carries a two-spout drinking jug?" Grandmother Tassel pretends she does not know.

"Benjamin Waters, Honored Matriarch," Dideyohvsgi follows Ben into the lodge. "He is my colleague. We traveled together for many years. We fought enemies and hunted. I vouch for my companion."

"Is he of the Paint Clan?"

"No. Not even Cherokee. But he is a good man with a pure heart and my blood brother."

"Then welcome into our home, Benjamin. Please stand, Walela," Grandmother Tassel presents her granddaughter. "May I introduce the offspring of Old Tassel, the one with skin of soft pelt, of the bright eyes, my families' most precious."

The officiator nudges Ben to step forward, "Offer the jug."

The suitor bows his head and extends the pottery.

His love accepts the gift and turns attention to Dideyohvsgi.

"Spirit thoughts long preserved for our time alive," the shaman intones a chant. "For life, hope, and strength, help this man and woman cope wherever they roam. These ancient words guide them home."

Walela offers one spout to Benjamin, and she drinks from the other.

Nothing spills.

Grandmother Tassel claps with pleasure.

The couple grasp hands and smile as Dideyohvsgi finishes, "Spirit's true, change me and you. Open hearts, protect these two."

CHAPTER TWENTY — Storm

ᎠᏎᏦᎤᎢᏎᎤᎵᏯᎠᏤᏍᏆᏗᎭᎵᏛᎳᏪᏓᎶᎻᏝᏗᎤᎲᏗᎩᏰᏛᏰᏗᎲᏃᏃᏎᏚᎤ

For days after the twin spout ceremony, Dideyohvsgi watches the daily relationship between his friend and Walela acknowledge mutual love and respect.

Pleased, the medicine man continues his pursuit of treatments for smallpox, but as he examines new herbs or mosses, the shaman shakes his head in bewilderment that Benjamin still sleeps in their mutual campsite outside her lodge.

No pox cases call the healer, but he treats and helps several patient families with cowpox in the surrounding woodlands.

In a cluster of three families' cabins near Crock, Dideyohvsgi sits beside an ill child and scrapes a root into powder to lower fever.

The mother watches, "Thank you for coming. We sent word for Mohi but have heard nothing."

"You are welcome." He mixes water with his dust and creates a brown paste. "I live close, and I understand he is with Dragging Canoe. Rumors say White settlers move into our lands in violation of the treaty. They watch for intruders."

"As our war leader, I am sure he does. May I be honest with you, Shaman?" The woman peeks out the entrance to check for listeners.

Dideyohvsgi nods yes as he coaxes the brown paste through his patient's lips.

"My father died fighting the Franklin settlers, and grandfather disappeared as a scout for the British. My oldest son now follows Dragging Canoe, and I fear he will not return." The woman drops the flap closed. "My grandparents told tales of people in lands west of the mountains. They knew distinguished men but never saw a White man. What happened to our communities? We huddle in these lower towns and the settlers still come."

"I believe your child will recover," Dideyohvsgi packs his bag. "My mother spoke of those days. Why did it change? War. Pestilence. We lost many to smallpox."

"No, Shaman. Murderers kill more of us than the pox. Dragging Canoe found the illness's cause and slayed its carriers," the parent kisses her child's forehead. "Now we only have the sickness of chickens and cows.

"May I ask you something?" Dideyohvsgi stands.

The grateful woman nods, "Of course, what is it?"

"You show no scars from smallpox?"

"I never caught it."

"Have you had the cowpox?"

"Yes, when I was young and milked our herd."

"Do you have any animals with disease now?"

"We do. One we raised from a calf."

"May I examine it and take samples from the welts?"

***

In camp with Benjamin at Crock the following evening, the cook fire burns low. The two prepare to sleep.

Dideyohvsgi mixes a small dose of water with dried, ground udder sores, "Look, the powder responds. It resembles fluid from live pox pustules."

Ben leans closer. "It does. As the stuff on Walela's cow, but it's healed."

"Are you and Walela recovered?" The medicine man glances at his friend. "I performed the ritual, but no one appears close to marriage."

Benjamin sits back and peers toward her lodge, "We talked of it."

"And?"

"She wants to. I'm not so sure."

"Why not, Ben?"

"Well, I have reasons. I hear the White settlers move into the edges of our lower towns. I expect John Watts' call soon. I do not want to leave her a widow. There are no more males in her family to care for her."

Dideyohvsgi chuckles, "Believe me. Your milkmaid can provide for herself."

"Not what I meant. In your culture, if a woman loses her husband, her clan takes… no, I guess they adopt her, right?"

"The men that marry into our families merge with their wife's and become of the woman's lineage," the medicine man pours his cowpox slime into a small clay jar.

"But that's not normal to me." Ben's eyes mist as he dreams. "I want her to grow with me. Someday I will have a cotton plantation larger than the one where I lived. Without slaves, of course! Free brothers till my land for a fair wage and share in the good life our work earns. My children, many boys, live beyond me and forge new and surprising things for my grandchildren. Girls with the personality of Walela, I train to lead their people into a wonderful world."

"Not sparse with your dreams, are you, Ben?"

"Dead men have no future. I owe John Watts, and you for being my friends when I had no others. Until we finish our business with the White settlers, wife and kids must wait."

As Benjamin suspects, days later, word arrives that their leader calls for warriors. Dideyohvsgi and his friend break camp in Crock and wish Walela good by with thanks.

The freedman lingers. "I don't know the future. I can't let my blood brother walk alone. When we're finished, I'll come back to you."

They kiss, and Ben trots onto the away trail.

He looks and she waves.

The milkmaid weeps until darkness obscures the path.

***

The men travel for days and approach Turkey Town, the lower town's major settlement, late in the afternoon.

"I believe the new village is over the next ridges," Dideyohvsgi points.

"They tell me Little Turkey moved many of our people here and the place grows," Ben looks ahead.

The medicine man chuckles.

"I hear he's just fleeing the settlers," the freedman smiles.

The two men push forward and soon view the settlement from atop a second ridge.

Below along both sides of the Coosa River, Cherokee cabins and more temporary lodges scatter for over a mile.

People bustle through their lives; smoke rises from campfires and chimneys, and children play without fear.

As Dideyohvsgi and Benjamin walk, the first adult greets their arrival. "Welcome travelers!" A big Scotsman extends a huge hand. "You come from the north. Did you see anyone? I'm waiting for Mohi, Dragging Canoe's shaman." He notices a beaded medical pack. "You a medicine man? Did he send you?"

Surprised to meet a White, the two visitors hold back.

"My name's Daniel Ross." The man's deep voice penetrates the air. "That's my place over there, the trader's cabin."

A late term pregnant Cherokee woman in traditional deerskin steps out.

"And my wife, Mollie. She's running a fever." His loudness shares information with the world.

"Is that why you wait for Mohi?" Dideyohvsgi looks at the pregnancy.

Daniel joins his mate and guides her into the cabin. "Yes. Baby coming soon and fever's not a good sign."

"I am a medicine man if you need me."

"Come into my home. I don't know birthing or fever."

The cabin's interior features two rooms.

The front displays the trader's goods: barrels of corn and native squash, blankets, several muskets, powder, leather straps and other items for sale.

Daniel guides the pregnant woman through his store and into a second space. It serves as living quarters with a fireplace at one end.

The expectant father helps his wife sit on a wood bench and motions for Dideyohvsgi.

"Have you eaten raccoon or pheasant?" The medicine man feels Mollie's forehead, which dampens his hand with sweat.

"No. Nor speckled trout for birthmarks or black walnuts to give my baby an enormous nose," the pregnant woman defends her prenatal care. "I haven't worn a neckerchief, so no umbilical strangulation. Plus, I wash my hands and feet daily and avoid lingering in doorways."

"I will mix something for your fever. A birth comes soon. Do you have female relatives that can help?" Dideyohvsgi digs in his medicine pouch. "Find water, please."

The big Scotsman offers a pottery bowl, and the healer mixes powder into the liquid.

"Daniel, my time comes," Mollie looks to her spouse. "Go, bring mother and grandmother. You fellows wait in the other room."

"First, drink this. I mixed cattail cone and wild cherry bark. It will help your fever and speed delivery."

Daniel's wife swigs the potion and gestures for the men to vanish.

***

A short while later, her husband returns with women relatives who hurry to their loved one's side. One closes the door between the two rooms.

The expectant father looks at Dideyohvsgi. "How long do you think? Is she fine?"

"Soon, I'm sure," the medicine man grips the expectant father's shoulder.

Benjamin sits upon a wooden keg, and the shaman settles against the wall near the entrance.

Ross paces around and through his trading products. He checks the cabin's ceiling as the sound of thunder with evening rain rolls over and patters the roof. "Listen!"

Mollie's mother chants, and her words drift into the men's room. "Here comes an old woman. The horrible one comes, only a short way from us. Quick! Get out of your bed and let us run away. Yu!"

Daniel looks at Dideyohvsgi as thunder sounds louder.

"Kalona Ayeliski (ᎧᎶᎾ ᎠᏰᎵᏍᎩ ka-lo-na a-ye-li-ss-ki, Raven Mockers) come!" The shaman opens the cabin's door and peers out into the darkness.

"What?" The husband's white skin flushes, and his Scottish eyes grow wide.

"Spirits who prey on the souls of the dying." The healer stares at Benjamin. "They torment their victims alive and eat their hearts after death."

"Last time you faced a thing as you speak, I didn't believe you. But why here?" The freedman grabs his musket.

"Why do they come? The baby is the target." Dideyohvsgi pushes a heavy corn barrel against the door. "This child is special. The evil spirits do not welcome this birth! Help me barricade the door!"

Mollie's grandmother chants from the other room. "Here comes an old man. The horrible one comes, only a short way from us. Quick! Get out of your bed and run away. Yu!"

A cabin window explodes open with a gust of wind.

Benjamin leaps to his feet with his musket and points it at the opening.

Outdoors, light flashes, and thunder echoes the flare's disposition.

Rain and water rushes into the trading post, and Daniel shuts the window's storm shutters against the weather.

Dideyohvsgi stares at the Kalona Ayeliski in the middle of the room.

The spirit drips moisture from the outside, and its eyes sparkle lightning as it speaks, "I have come for the Ross baby not yet born. Stand away, medicine man."

The shaman glances at Benjamin and Daniel, who bar the window closed, unaware of the presence in the room.

"Why do you think they want this child?" The freedman twists to his friend.

The Kalona Ayeliski steps to the door between rooms. "Do not interfere! I must kill this infant and eat his heart. If he becomes an adult, the man leads his people into forty years without you or me or any of the beliefs we both hold important."

"What are you saying? We have nothing in common!" The healer recoils from the vision and raises both hands. "By the power of Son of Stone Cloud, I banish you from this birthing place never to prey on this child again!"

Dideyohvsgi's eyes flash, and the Kalona Ayeliski's pupils dim.

"Ignorant Shaman, you birth a most beloved one! He leads your people but destines you and me to die in obscurity." The spirit's voice weakens as its essence dissolves in the air.

From the other room, an infant's cry pierces his father's ears. He turns and laughs, "That is a boy child."

"What do you call him?" The freedman leans his musket against the cabin's wall and smiles.

The new father beams at both guests. "John. That will be the boy's name, John Ross."

Ben looks at his friend's forehead and notices sweat pouring. "I only heard thunder. I believe you saw more."

Dideyohvsgi nods yes in return.

***

The following day, the healer and his freedman friend accept the gratitude of Daniel and prepare to leave Turkey Town.

"Haven't known of anyone with the pox since summer," the White trader shakes hands with Ben, "but your shaman is welcome to stay here with us. We need a medicine man. Mohi rides through with Dragging Canoe and his band, but most of the time, we treat our own."

"No, we must move on," Dideyohvsgi extends his hand. "Take care of that new son. Raise him to be a great Cherokee."

CHAPTER TWENTY-ONE — Promises

ᎠᏲᏓᎶᎢᏍᏙᏌᏯᎠᏎᏫᏈᏆᏘᎦᏚᎤᏪᏓᎬᎹᏅᏠᎢᎯᏝᏳᎤᏫᎬᏁᎭᏃᏴᏅᎤ

Dideyohvsgi and Benjamin travel to John Watts' new headquarters at Willstown, Cherokee Town. The settlement rests near the base of Lookout Mountain and as the men walk in the wilderness, the landmark looms.

"That's much larger than your Cherokee Rock." The freedman stops and admires the landmark.

"In size, yes." Dideyohvsgi gazes at the huge formation. "But not in spirit."

The blood brothers stand and appreciate their view for a moment, catch their breath and continue the journey.

"Dragging Canoe raids the Whites south of the Tennessee River." The shaman leads his friend through the thick brush. "I'm sure Watts is under pressure to join."

"The man handles pressure, but he's forgotten you're tasked to beat the pox," Ben agrees.

"Maybe not? Or perhaps." The medicine man shifts his herbal pack for comfort. "Eliminating smallpox appears impossible. I have investigated the known possibilities. We contain it, but patients never change, so no cure. They refuse proper prevention and treatment."

"Don't abandon the search," Ben's glance reflects concern.

"I was with you at Cherokee Rock. Dragging Canoe's braggart claims damage your credibility."

"That is not on people's minds. The new State of Georgia gives land south of the river to the Tennessee Company." The healer finds an animal path, and the trek opens and becomes less tedious.

"It's not theirs to give." Ben follows.

"Convince the Georgians. Not much we can do. Smallpox and the settlers have killed so many."

"Can Watts gather enough fighters?"

"You and I count as two," Dideyohvsgi chuckles.

"Dragging Canoe's not much stronger," Ben smiles.

"Watts and Dragging Canoe against the United States of America," Dideyohvsgi's voice loses humor. "The Southern District joins soon. Rumor says their new name is Tennessee."

***

The young men follow a ridgeline into Willstown.

The settlement, fifty log cabins built in the Cherokee manner, with an open-sided central lodge, hosts unusual guests.

Three United States Army wagons with teams stand beside the council pavilion.

Troopers hold a remuda of individual mounts while soldiers sit and watch the discussions.

John Watts and a group of Cherokees face an army major with two attachés.

The conference sits in a rough circle.

As Dideyohvsgi and Benjamin approach, John Watts notices, but continues his conversation.

The travelers settle with the Cherokees.

The White soldiers eye Ben, the only man of color.

"I represent William Blount, Governor of the Southwest Territory and superintendent of Indian affairs for the southern district," the army major addresses the leader.

Ben leans close to Dideyohvsgi, "The politician doesn't speak for himself?"

Watts stands straight and proud.

"He believes we should offer the safety and protection power of the United States."

Watts nods understanding, "To keep us safe from what?"

The soldier hesitates with surprise. "Everything, Sir," he sweeps an arm wide.

"Specifically, Major?"

"For a perpetual peace and friendship spirit."

The warrior stares at the officer with expressionless eyes. "That is for, not from."

The major swallows and continues, "We promise to set boundaries between Cherokee homes and settlers."

"We have borders the governor does not honor today."

"Blount agrees to negotiate new ones. He commits to build a road and regulate trade, which offers prosperity to your people."

"And provides more access to our lands for your settlers."

"He guarantees your territory. Citizens cannot settle or hunt on your soil."

Dideyohvsgi nudges Benjamin and nods toward the army soldiers who attend the horses.

The military attendants shuffle among their mounts and reach for muskets as their commander resumes. "The United States offers presents to enable Cherokee to grow food and become independent. Animosities between settlers and your Nation cease."

John Watts considers the emissaries' message. "Major, take this word to the governor. I invite him to come here in peace. Or, if he desires, I travel to him and discuss details."

The major snaps a salute."The Governor hears those words of unity," and turns to the wagons.

Dideyohvsgi and Benjamin watch the soldier escort follow the emissary of the United States of America out of Willstown.

***

That evening, as guests of John Watts for dinner, the two relax in the warmth of his cabin.

The leader offers venison strips, "Much has changed. My thoughts shift from war to peace."

Dideyohvsgi nods, "Becoming your uncle, Old Tassel?"

"The old man was right. White settlers come as locusts, unstoppable. Another treaty is the way forward." The host stares into the light of his fireplace that dances across faces and walls.

"Remember Son of Stone Cloud said treaties with Whites are talking leaves." The shaman accepts and chews a venison strip.

"He was wise," Watts nods. "But now, we are the talkers. And our numbers are few."

"The reason for treaties." Ben chews a strip of meat.

"Old Tassel spoke of real people from the mountains to the prairies." Dideyohvsgi eyes dream as flames reflect off pupils.

"The pox and the White settlers came." Watts checks corn pone that fills the room with aroma. "Now, we clump together in the lower towns, a proud but a pitiful force."

"If you sign a treaty, Dragging Canoe will never honor the terms." Dideyohvsgi swallows.

"That is why I summoned you," John Watts offers the sweet smell of bread.

The medicine man glances at the freedman as he samples the delicacy.

"Put aside the study of smallpox. I have a new mission." The host serves Ben. "You appreciate and understand Dragging Canoe, and I recognize trust and loyalty. Serve as escorts for Blount during these peace talks."

Ben looks at Dideyohvsgi as the medicine man laughs, "Bodyguards! The entire power of the United States guards him."

"His soldiers do not know Dragging Canoe, or Mohi. I do not suspect force but expect deception. Protect the man from Cherokee politics."

"With due respect, I do not predict the Governor accepts such help," the shaman smiles at the leader.

"True." Watts rubs his chin in thought for a moment, "If we cannot ensure Blount's safety, then carry the news of the impending treaty to the Chickamauga and secure the representative from within that group."

"Mohi and Dragging Canoe do not trust me. That distrust stems from childhood." Dideyohvsgi looks from the leader to his friend. "I cannot ask you to go. You have no stake in this fight."

"Won't shed me that easy," Ben smiles. "I go. Know that."

"The shaman is right. You have no interests in this and are not even Cherokee," John Watts grasps the freedman's shoulder. "I promise something significant for your service."

Dideyohvsgi and friend stare into the eyes of the peacemaker who was once a war leader.

"I have listened to your campfire stories," the man grins. "When conflict ends, our nation promises a grant, a part of our land, legal and agreed to by the United States, to grow your cotton field dreams."

The shaman grips his friend's shoulder and smiles agreement and pleasure with the leader's promise.

CHAPTER TWENTY-TWO — Crossroad

ᎪᏢ ᎠᎾᏕᎶᎥᎢᏏᏐᏗᏫᏯᎠᎫᎬᏠᏇᏛᎯᏞᏚᏪᏕᏈᎬᎷᏍᏁᎣᎯᎲᏙᏯᎾᏝᎳᎠᎻᏂᏃᏋᏆᏫ

Days later, camped by a creek for the night, Dideyohvsgi and Ben meet Dragging Canoe and Mohi. The war leader laughs in the darkness. Both suprised friends startle jump.

"What a disappointment!" The Chickamauga warrior rides into the circle of light defined by the two's campfire. "I was expecting White raiders because you were so easy to surprise! But no, I meet John Watts' medicine man and his freedman friend."

Mohi follows atop another mount. "Apprentice of Son of Stone Cloud, do you still chase false hopes to cure the killer pox?"

"No," Dideyohvsgi stands. "We search for you to deliver an invitation."

"Me? Much easier to find you," Dragging Canoe laughs at the young medicine man and poses for his audience. "But I share your dinner and for that, also the message."

The warrior leader and his companion dismount.

The older shaman ties the horses to a tree as the warrior samples cooking meat on an open fire stake. "Squirrel! You skilled hunters should fare better. But the smell reminds me. What happened to the pet that used to follow you, Apprentice?

"It went scouting and never returned." Dideyohvsgi grimaces at the demeaning title.

"Good," Dragging Canoe bites a chunk from the spit. "I thought you ate your pets for lack of game."

Mohi joins the others at the fire. "I'll pass on food. I have venison jerky in my blanket."

"John Watts tasked you with finding a cure for the pox curse. You waste time?" Dragging Canoe stares at the young medicine man. "I fought and killed the Kosvkvskini that brought the death. Everyone knows the sickness fades."

Dideyohvsgi chuckles, "Because you tell them often."

Dragging Canoe's voice steels, "Families need reminders, or they forget."

Mohi looks at Benjamin, "Cherokee need to be told often before any believe."

Ben nods agreement. "No one believes Freedmen. I must carry a paper to prove I am human."

"We should issue a symbol that says they cannot catch the pox?" Mohi glances at Dragging Canoe for a reaction.

"Enough of this. Your message? What does John Watts want?" The leader settles into a comfortable seat near the warmth of the fire.

His follower sits and Dideyohvsgi, with Ben, settle on the fire's opposite side.

"He yearns for peace." The younger shaman looks to Dragging Canoe.

"Without his fighting edge, the man listens to White lies," the warrior laughs with a tint of derision.

"Negotiations for a truce begin with Governor Blount," Dideyohvsgi's words ring soft and strong.

"Does our peace leader realize the new state gave Cherokee land south of the Tennessee River to the Tennessee Company?" Dragging Canoe's tone crackles with contempt.

"Yes. He knows the White settlers are few but represent many that include armed soldiers of the state of Georgia and more from the United States. He knows Cherokee warriors are strong but grow weak in numbers from pox deaths."

"There is no pox!" Mohi leaps to his feet and points. "He killed the Kosvkvskini! The death sickness died!"

Dragging Canoe raises a hand for attention and nods.

The medicine man settles.

"Blount's representative presents generous protection for our lands and people." The younger healer stares into Dragging Canoe's eyes.

The fighter fingers his knife's hilt.

"John Watts and the governor plan to meet and negotiate the last terms for peace." The healer pauses.

In silence, the warrior stands with arms crossed. He leans forward. "Enough. What does the man want of me?"

"He wants you to join in the discussions."

"And if I do not?"

"The least John Watts asks," Dideyohvsgi glances at Ben for reinforcement, "is for you and the Chickamauga to guarantee Governor Blount's safety during and after treaty talks."

"And if I don't?"

"Any raids bring retribution attacks."

Dragging Canoe's back stiffens, "From the peace leader?"

"No." The young shaman shakes his head. "By soldiers in overwhelming force from the United States of America."

Dragging Canoe sits for a long moment, subdued by the argument's reality.

"Tell John Watts that I and my Chickamauga do not join in the negotiations. But we promise not to attack the governor, White settlers, or militia prior to or during his negotiations. The future will reflect the success of failure of this treaty."

"It pleases John Watts that Dragging Canoe adopts a reasonable position on this matter," Dideyohvsgi smiles.

The warrior's expression remains stern.

"Treaties take time." The diplomat watches for facial response. "Our leader wants to know the desires and concerns of the people. He plans a tribal council at Oostanaula, Georgia, soon."

The warrior blinks.

"He requests you represent the Chickamauga Cherokee and Creek allies."

"Tell 'Lesser Tassel,' we attend." Dragging Canoe stands, glances at Benjamin, and jerks a head at Mohi.

The man walks toward his horse, and his medicine man follows.

"Wait," Dideyohvsgi stops Dragging Canoe mid-mount. "We join you."

"To spy for your peacemaker?" Dragging Canoe's eyes focus on the medicine man.

"Yes. But I don't call it spying. I term our presence as official help at the request of John Watts."

The war leader looks at Mohi, "Can the Chickamauga tolerate two shamans?"

His healer chuckles. "One and a half. To me, he is an apprentice."

The warrior laughs and jerks his mount toward the trail, "Pack your things and come spy. If I have a snoop, I want him close and in plain sight. We ride to join our scouting parties. Our camp is on Elm Creek. In a day, we'll be there." Dragging Canoe and Mohi disappear into the brush.

"If I didn't know that man might slice my throat for pure pleasure, I might find him likable," Benjamin gathers goods.

"He is a leader. I understand why so many follow him." Dideyohvsgi rolls his sleeping mat into a cylinder and ties it upon his horse.

"I think Dragging Canoe has Governor Blount's murder in mind. Our protection means little," Ben packs his blanket.

"Agreed." The medicine man looks at the trail where the warrior disappeared, "But, we might warn John Watts."

***

Late in the day, Dideyohvsgi and Benjamin ride along Elm Creek toward Dragging Canoe's encampment.

They move upstream, and the lazy water flows in a meandering, snakelike pattern before them.

Several hills and valleys ahead, smoke rises, too voluminous for campfires.

The medicine man looks at his Freedman friend. They guide their horses away from the creek into the bramble and woodlands.

Both pause and listen.

Upstream, the noise and natural disruption prove the intruders are not indigenous.

Dideyohvsgi dismounts with Benjamin close behind and pulls his mount deeper into a thicket.

From concealment, the two watch a detachment of uniformed Georgia militia move in a ragged column.

Three dozen soldiers led by four settler scouts march downstream in a disorderly formation.

The group passes where the shaman and his friend conceal themselves and soon disappear around a bend.

"Governor Blount promised John Watts protection for our lands and our people." Dideyohvsgi assures himself and reminds his companion.

"I think the settlers didn't get the word." Ben remounts his horse.

The two friends return to easier travel along the creek and trudge upstream.

***

That afternoon before sundown, they arrive at Dragging Canoe's encampment, which crowds a large meadow along Elm Creek. Temporary cabins and lean-tos display charred construction and still smoke without active flames.

Dogs sniff the carcasses of a few women and children.

Dideyohvsgi and Benjamin ride into the remnants of an attack.

As the shaman peers at the scalped skull of an elderly woman in a pool of dried blood by his horse's front hooves, the freedman shades his eyes and views a young boy suspended by one foot from a nearby tree.

"No men dead. These people were unprotected." Ben rides to and cuts the suspended carcass free.

"Dragging Canoe won't tolerate this atrocity." The medicine man slides off his mount. "Watts can't stop retaliation."

216

"And I agree with the warrior this time." the freedman dismounts.

"Today, I do also." The shaman lifts the body of the old woman into his arms. "We must clean up this place and give these people human dignity in death.

***

Midmorning of the following day, Dragging Canoe and a dozen warriors ride into their burned encampment.

Dideyohvsgi sits on a fallen log near a neat line of washed and covered bodies.

Benjamin leans on his musket at the opposite end.

Several fighters slip off their mounts and join a few on foot who walk along the row.

As relatives and close loved ones show death masks when inspectors lift their face coverings, hard men stare at blank eyes for a moment and lower the cloths.

"We got here yesterday, late afternoon. On the way we saw Georgia militia, thirty in uniform and four scouts, no horses," Dideyohvsgi stands.

"Mohi! How long before you can get these people buried?" The war leader looks at his shaman.

"Seven days, or several hours if we ride tonight."

"Watt's Spy, tell your great pacifier Dragging Canoe collects scalps by dusk tomorrow." The warrior kicks dirt at his feet. "If Governor Blount sent these militia demons, his hair bleeds as the bodies here. My warriors and I go to revenge these souls as soon as we bury our families."

"I do not side with Watts tonight. Ben and I have horses. We ride with Dragging Canoe," Dideyohvsgi grimaces at Benjamin, who nods agreement.

The war leader studies the two, then shakes his head with approval.

***

After hard travel in night darkness and throughout the following day, the Chickamauga war party catches the Georgia militia column camped.

A warrior scout meets his commander and announces the discovery. "Thirty soldiers camp just over that hill."

"Watt's Spies, you don't look much of a threat," the leader turns his horse in the center of his fighters. "When we move ahead of these militiamen, let them see the two of you on foot and then run to your horses. They will chase to kill you, maybe ten militia. Draw them away from the primary group, and against lesser odds, I attack. By the time your pursuers return, my warriors scalp most of them and we are free to finish yours. Do you understand?"

Dideyohvsgi nods understanding, swallows, and looks at Benjamin.

The freedman checks the flint in his musket's frizzen.

After Dragging Canoe's men pass the column of militia in stealth, the shaman and his friend wait out of sight to set the ambush.

"I betray John Watts' initiative." The medicine man slides off his horse and joins Ben on the ground.

"Watts did not see the clan massacred. I love peace, but justice more." Benjamin ties both horses' reins to a tree.

"I am not sure the goal is more than blood-lust revenge," Dideyohvsgi strides toward the ridge's crest.

Both men drop to their bellies and crawl to view the valley.

Unaware of danger, a ragged column of Georgia militiamen in their frocks follow mounted officers in a unified but unorganized direction.

The blue coats align and resemble a flock of Canadian geese.

Dideyohvsgi stands silhouetted atop the ridge against the afternoon sky.

None of the militia below notice.

"They don't see me. On your feet. Maybe, someone spots two people."

Both men draw equal attention as undistinguishable tree stumps.

"They would look if we tried to hide," Ben grins at his partner. "Think we should scream or fire?"

"Where are their scouts? I remember four, right?"

"Yes." The freedman scans the surrounding trees. He reflex jerks at the sound of a musket.

Below, a militiaman stands with a smoking weapon pointed at the ridge.

Out of hearing range, a mounted lieutenant turns his horse and points at Dideyohvsgi and his companion.

Eight militiamen follow the bluecoat as he spurs his animal up the hill.

The others continue along the trail as Dragging Canoe predicted.

The decoys scramble to their horses and slip away.

Minutes later, the Georgia officer reaches the ridge with a hand musket primed.

As his force gathers, the lieutenant scans the ground for a track and leads his men in pursuit.

In the distance, muskets echo in the hills as the main column resists attack.

The bluecoat spins his horse, turns, and rushes to support the primary group.

Below, the war leader and his warriors on horseback assault and destroy the militia foot soldiers.

With whoops of victory, Chickamauga fighters slash, shoot, and hatchet White bluecoats, who fall in puddles of blood.

The lieutenant and his eight troopers halfway on the hill recognize Dragging Canoe's superiority and dominance below and stop.

They turn and flee uphill.

Dideyohvsgi and Benjamin wait on the ridge of rocks.

They fire, and a ball impacts the mounted officer, who falls, but his boot catches in his horse's stirrup.

The mount rears and drags the rider, who bounces many times before a concussion with a stone spatters his blood and brains.

The remaining eight militiamen recoil and huddle in a defensive circle behind boulders.

Dragging Canoe's fighters, led by Mohi, see the small last stand attempt and charge up the hill.

Several of the defender's fire. They reload but fall under the hooves and hatchets of their attackers.

The Chickamauga men jump from their mounts and collect scalps.

The blood brothers watch from their perch atop the ridgeline.

Mohi peels the skin off his victim's head, and the White man's dirty long blond hair hangs bloody as the warrior thrusts it high.

Dideyohvsgi watches the fighter whistle for his horse.

The well-trained mount joins its owner at once, and the shaman whips a battle spear from lashings.

He jabs its point through the fresh scalp and shoves the dripping mess above a squirrel's tail lashed on the weapon's hilt.

For adornment, a slash of white fur upon its tip focuses Dideyohvsgi as he remembers. The shaman's eyes fog and thoughts rush forward.

***

Enoli flips a corn kernel near a tree squirrel with a distinctive flash of light color on the underside that sits on hind legs and rubs forepaws together nearby.

The boy studies the animal. "Why do you have five toes and only four fingers?"

The small furry head engulfs the food but takes offense. "Why do you have thumbs, Tsalagi? Don't mock. You think you are the favored people. Not true, I climb trees much better than you."

***

In Enoli's eyes, Saloli's white tail fur stains red from scalp blood.

Dideyohvsgi whips a second musket to his shoulder and spots its barrel sight centered on Mohi's head.

He squeezes the trigger as Benjamin knocks the aim skyward.

Black powder smoke discharges in the air unnoticed in the whooping, shooting, and celebration of the massacre.

Benjamin grabs his friend's shoulders with each of his two hands. "What are you doing? You shoot Mohi and Dragging

Canoe won't be your only enemy. John Watts will desert you. Then your only ally is me!"

"I don't care, Ben!" Dideyohvsgi stares into his blood brother's eyes. "Did you see Saloli's tail on Mohi's spear? I am not at peace anymore!"

CHAPTER TWENTY-THREE — Disavowal

ᎠᎡᏔᏦᎣᎢᏌᎣᏝᏴᎠᏠᎬᏖᏕᏗᎯᏫᏣᏪᏕᏫᎹᎠᏛᎣᏓᎲᏙᏴᎾᏖᎾᏏᎲᏃᏔᎣ

Dideyohvsgi and Benjamin cringe that night as Dragging Canoe's Chickamauga fighters celebrate the victory over Georgia's militia.

The Cherokee and Creek warriors dance and howl around several bonfires of blazing wagons, supplies, and bloody uniforms.

"This raid invites retribution from the White settlements." The medicine man watches the spectacle. "We will meet them with bloodshed."

"Which is just what John Watts needs before the treaty negotiations." Ben stares at the flames.

As the two friends watch, Dragging Canoe guts and cleans a militiaman's body, which hangs from a tree limb and resembles a deer prepared for roasting.

The Chickamauga leader rejoices in the celebration.

His warriors' vengeance lust cheers hate and blood-drawing violence upon the corpses.

Several fighters help the butcher stake the militiaman and suspend the lump of meat.

"This is beyond war," the medicine man swallows as he watches. "But it is what they deserve."

"I heard Dragging Canoe eats his White captives, but I did not accept the stories," Benjamin looks at his friend.

The warrior leader slices a hunk of half-cooked flesh from the militiaman's side and holds the trophy high for his warriors.

As his men whoop and scream, the Chickamauga commander bites a chunk and chews.

Dideyohvsgi looks away from the feast.

Ben gags and spits to free his throat. "I believe now."

"Let's get our horses and report to John Watts. He needs to know what's happening here so he can plan our defense." The medicine man turns and disavows the cannibalism.

With the freedman, Dideyohvsgi slips into darkness.

***

Upon returning to Willstown, the friends find the headquarters in the throes of a smallpox outbreak.

The new peace proponent listens to Dideyohvsgi's and Ben's description of Dragging Canoe's savage and sick treatment of White captives.

Watts nods understanding. "We challenged him at Oostanaula. People know how their war leader treats hostages. Those actions threaten any chance of a favorable agreement with Governor Blount. But, of more major concern is this disease. If smallpox continues, we have no delegates."

"You do not need a conference to fight Blount and his militia." The healer-turned-warrior urges his leader.

"I understand your rage. But anger does not overwhelm superior forces. Georgia's militia is upon our land, but that changes nothing. The governor has the power." Watts lays his hand upon the healer's shoulder. "Become a leader. Suppress your hatred and help me fight by other means, with peaceful negotiation."

"We can treat the pox, Sir," Dideyohvsgi steps closer and subdues his feelings. "In Crock, I discovered how to use cowpox for variolations if the people consent?"

"Mohi claims otherwise. Because of Dragging Canoe, that shaman is influential. The people believe his leader killed the Kosvkvskini. They repeat the lie often. It becomes myth."

"Then change their minds." Ben's friend reaches reason. "No better opportunity arises than the council at Oostanaula," Dideyohvsgi nods affirmative.

"Can you inoculate that many?" Watts peers at the young healer.

"Walela from Crock and Ben can help. Both worked with cowpox."

"Yes, she's Old Tassel's granddaughter and my cousin. Bring her to the meeting."

The freedman smiles at the thought.

"But, before council, I need to stop Dragging Canoe's attacks. Before the Governor retaliates," John Watts rubs his chin and crosses both arms across the chest. "Take me to Chickamauga. We will leave in the morning."

***

Late in the afternoon, days later, Dideyohvsgi and Ben spy rising smoke from a valley as they travel to Dragging Canoe's most recently reported location.

"Look. Too much for campfires," Benjamin twists and points.

"Good chance it's Dragging Canoe." The medicine man turns his horse.

"There's a small settlement over those ridges." Watts rides toward the soot. "That place is Edwards Creek, if I'm correct.

225

Couple dozen farmers and a few slaves, they say. Scouts reported it a year ago."

As the searchers ride closer and their mounts climb the last ridgeline, Ben leans to his friend, "Poor settlers have money to own humans now. Unbelievable. Used to be only rich people."

"A few Cherokees as well. Mostly landowners." Dideyohvsgi follows uphill.

"Slave traders have a market in Parkertown." The freedma watches the rise. "That's where Dragging Canoe should kill Whites."

The three top the ridge and descend toward Edwards Creek.

The small group of cabins burn and smoke.

As the visitors move closer, they watch Chickamauga warriors loot the surroundings of valuables.

Several confiscate horses and oxen while others dress in White man's clothes. A few of Dragging Canoe's fighters dance in female skirts and bonnets.

Dragging Canoe spies John Watts as he approaches and rides his war horse to meet the peace leader. "Welcome! You come to help me rid our lands of vermin?"

"I see you have done that," Watts surveys the Chickamauga mop up Edwards Creek.

Dozens of mutilated and scalped settlers lie around the small cabin-style huts of farmers.

Three slaves stand tied together with rope at their necks, with a five-year-old boy crying at their feet.

"I will soon negotiate a treaty with Governor Blount." The peace leader frowns at the warrior. "You make favorable terms difficult when your people slaughter White women and children."

"We don't kill them all. Only settlers," Dragging Canoe nods to one of his warriors who stands near the slave group.

The designated fighter draws his knife and slits the throat of the nearest.

The body collapses, and its weight pulls the others to their knees.

Dideyohvsgi looks at Benjamin, who stares at the murdered corpse and sees the muscles in his jaw clench.

"But we can, if we wish." Dragging Canoe shakes his chin in satisfaction.

John Watts rides near the slaves, leans from his mount, and lifts the five-year-old slave from the ground. He settles the child before him on his deerskin pillion. "This one, I claim, to be raised Cherokee."

Dragging Canoe nods agreement, "If you wish, Peace Leader. The boy's parents fought well. Do you want their scalps to save for the boy?"

The peacemaker shakes his head.

"They called him Jacob," the warrior laughs. "His mother screamed for him. I cut out her heart."

"We gather in council at Oostanaula, Dragging Canoe. I urge restraint and the end of attacks on Whites," John Watts holds the boy as he turns his mount away from the dead slave and the other terrified laborers. "After they hear of Governor Blount's peace proposal, our Nation's opinion changes. Hold your slaughters until our people have spoken."

"A second council?" The Chicamauguan wipes his blade on a slave's tunic. "Last meeting you chose a weakling most beloved man."

"Little Turkey suffers with the pox," Watts turns his horse toward Dragging Canoe.

"Impossible! I killed the Kosvkvskini," the war leader slams his knife into its sheaf.

The doubting leader looks at Dideyohvsgi and smiles. "He only slayed the spirit of the chicken disease?"

Dragging Canoe kicks the slave's corpse in frustration. "You tweak my anger, Watts!"

"Little Turkey is a qualified, most beloved man." The nephew of Old Tassel's voice steels. "He did not murder White children while I negotiate with Governor Blount."

"We will see who supports you," Dragging Canoe stares. "You and your pacifist friends become fewer. Our enemies increase."

"Yes," Watts nudges his horse away from the slaughter. "Our people shrink and the settlers only grow, no matter how many you kill."

Dideyohvsgi and Ben follow their leader as he rides away from Edwards Creek.

"Did you see any sign of Mohi?" The young medicine man leans toward his friend.

"No. I didn't even smell him."

CHAPTER TWENTY-FOUR — Walela

DRᏠᎤᎢᏚᎣᎵᎩᎠᏨᎬᎤᏘᎠᎻᎦᏣᎳᏧᎦᎢᏣᎷᎦᎹᎠᏍᎣᎲᎷᏚᎩᎣᏤᎤᏏᎠᏅᎯᏃᎦᎤᎥ

Dideyohvsgi, Benjamin, and Walela travel from Crock to Oostanali, near New Echota in the soon-to-be Georgia.

The two men walk and pull a large-wheel hand cart loaded with cowpox inoculation supplies collected at Walela's farm.

"I cannot understand why you volunteered my help to inoculate without asking," the woman looks at Benjamin.

"Say no," the freedman smiles as he drives the wagon.

"No, to John Watts? To the influential uniter of the Nation? How?"

Dideyohvsgi grunts as the wheels bounce over a rock. "Cherokee is a matriarchal society. Assert that traditional authority with a no."

She slaps hands upon hips. "Who had the time? I was too busy gathering pus from sick cows."

"I'm not asking. Our leader talked to my friend."

"My uncle asked him?" She stares. "Not his niece?"

"Yes."

Walela smiles and her eyes twinkle, "I am something to my family, and to Dideyohvsgi's effort, but it's unofficial."

The medicine man laughs and Ben pouts.

***

Several days later, the two men pull their wagon into Oostanali on the Coosawattee River.

Refugees from the Cherokee lower towns in northwestern South Carolina establish the settlement on the flat and lush riverbank.

Dideyohvsgi and party view the location. The sturdy log buildings, corn bins, and livestock pens appear strong and permanent.

Walela's excitement with civilized surroundings stimulates jumps of joy after hard days on the trail. "So much larger than Crock. What a great place."

"Second time, they gathered." Ben looks across the property.

Near the estuary bank, three early arrivals occupy prime near freshwater camping spots.

"Welcome delegates." An Oostanali resident greets the tired travelers.

"Thank you. John Watts sent us. Should we set up somewhere central?" Dideyohvsgi steps forward.

"No, the river front's sites stay reserved for Dragging Canoe's people." The official greeter points across the village far from the stream. "Others camp in that meadow."

Dideyohvsgi looks at the prime spots near the Coosawattee and then at the dry camp spaces. "Who designated the areas?"

"Little Turkey."

"Did he say why?"

"The delegates with Dragging Canoe are warriors, champions, and heroes." The man lifts a triumphant fist. "They earned the honor."

"I need over there," the shaman points at the cabins. "John Watts directs to set up an inoculation location to prevent smallpox."

"Mohi says Dragging Canoe killed the Kosvkvskini. There is no disease around here, only pox from chickens." The organizer's body language stiffens. "Nothing on the river is vacant. Camp in the meadow."

"When was Mohi here?" Dideyohvsgi looks for the man.

"Last full moon, with Little Turkey. The group organized this second council," the greeter stares at Benjamin. "Is this fellow a delegate?"

"No. He's a friend and helps with the treatments."

"Your slave?"

"No, my blood brother."

"Too bad," the official twists back to the medicine man. "A servant exhibits wealth and prestige. I thought you might be someone important. Go, set up camp in the grass."

***

That night, with wagon parked, the new arrivals rest around a campfire under a canvas extended from its hoops on two support poles.

Walela sings while Dideyohvsgi and Ben stare into the fire.

"I dislike Cherokee owning slaves," Benjamin grits his teeth and watches flames dance.

"As do I," the medicine man glances at the freedman.

"Then why tolerate it?" The freedman stares.

"Because I lack the power to correct that status." Dideyohvsgi meets his friend's glare.

"Don't excuse yourself." The freedman shakes his head. "People are individuals. Many choose the White men's ways."

The healer sits in silence for a few moments. "You are right. This council needs to reject slavery before it becomes a new smallpox and destroys our Nation."

"Not practical." The freedman spits into the fire. "Even John Watts owns several slaves."

"But he is a wise man for peace who can make war. He understands and acts."

Benjamin falls silent and watches Walela. "Her choices may foretell the future," the freedman turns back to his friend. "Everyone lives or perishes together."

"That's why our leader proposes a new tribal law against slavery," Dideyohvsgi nods agreement.

***

The following day, the healer mans the wagon as an inoculation station.

Prepared to use cowpox as a vaccine, the medicine man watches delegates, and their families, arrive for council.

Quick to discover river or meadow, they settle into temporary lean-to or conveyance adapted accommodations.

As the arrivals multiply, the shaman gains awareness of which belong to the grassland or to the Dragging Canoe group.

When a person has been in Oostanali enough time to rest and recover, the healer feels free to interrupt.

He chooses a river delegate. "I represent John Watts, who wants Cherokee to be inoculated. My name is Dideyohvsgi, the medicine man of the Paint Clan. May I scratch your arm and apply cowpox?"

The man looks as if the ask makes no sense. "With the death treatment?"

"No!" The shaman shows a small clay container of liquid. "If I rub a spot of this into your skin, the body will be less prone to smallpox."

"Mohi warned of this lie. That pestilence died with the Kosvkvskini. John Watts fears more battles with the settlers. But Dragging Canoe is not afraid. He killed the Kosvkvskini and says cowpox gives the chicken's sickness."

"The treatment may make the arm sore or hot for a day, but that's better than death," Dideyohvsgi grasps the man's elbow.

The patient jerks his joint from the medicine man, "Get away, false shaman!"

As the accuser stalks aside, the man watches the retreat but turns to Benjamin's voice.

"Not going well?" Ben joins his friend.

"That one was a camper on the river," the healer invents an excuse. "Watch this fellow. He's a meadow man."

The fellow approaches.

"Sir?"

The newcomer stops. "Good afternoon. I know you, Dideyohvsgi, Shaman of the Paint Clan and counselor to John Watts."

"Our leader requested me to be here today." The health advocate pauses as his prospect glances at Ben. "And this a freedman friend, Benjamin Waters, who is my associate."

The prospective patient nods and stretches to see Walela, who sits by the wagon.

"John Watts asked us to arrive early at council to protect families from smallpox. I scratch an arm and rub this cowpox into the wound. It protects from dying but you may react."

"Why does our leader want our delegates ill?"

"He doesn't. The White man's illness kills more people than settlers. This is prevention."

"The reaction becomes the disease?"

"I do this for many," Dideyohvsgi nods understanding. "Most sicken but none die."

"No, Shaman. I will not take the risk," the prospective patient declines. "I grow and sell cotton. Life is softer with money, but I must work. Tell John Watts we want a treaty, but I can't risk illness." The fellow turns away.

"Not rudely as the river ones, but the meadow people also say no," Benjamin watches the potential client retreat.

The man stops and returns.

"I spoke too soon." Ben nudges his friend.

"You changed your mind?" Dideyohvsgi greets the returnee.

"No."

"Oh?" The shaman smiles acceptance.

The visitor looks at the freedman. "With my new status in the cotton business, is your boy for sale?"

Ben's hand whips to his knife, but Dideyohvsgi restrains the movement and intercedes. "Cherokee do not buy and sell humans. That's a White man's vice."

"I did not mean offense." The buyer steps away from confrontation. "You must not know of the low country farms. Back home cotton replaces rice as a money crop. Raisers need slaves."

"I suggest move on, sir," Dideyohvsgi pushes the man elsewhere, "before this freedman warrior slits your throat."

A nearby arrival's commotion distracts the three, and the slave buyer wanders away.

With an entourage, Little Turkey arrives by wagon.

Two warriors guide a mule-drawn conveyance and create a path through walkers and loungers. "We suffer the pox of chickens. Make way for our most beloved man."

An appointed camp greeter meets the dignitary and directs the party to a prime site by the river.

Ben raps the medicine man's shoulder with a clenched fist. "A new customer. Your first possible since I didn't gut the slave buyer."

***

That evening Benjamin lies across the campfire from Walela, who sits against a wheel and plays in the coals with a stick.

"That man today wanted to buy you. Am I not right, Benjamin?" She stirs a burst of sparks into the night air.

"He did."

"Someone will always be asking."

"No concern of mine."

Walela stares at the freedman. "That should make you concerned."

Silence settles around the campfire for long moments.

"Benjamin," her voice trembles, "Many things change since our together time in Crock?"

"They have?"

She looks across the fire. "My grandmother approved. But you become distant, not my warm Benjamin of old."

"The Cherokee adapt. Not you or the family, but many like that man today."

"Has Dideyohvsgi changed?"

"No. Only the people. I stay with him because we are friends." Ben stares at his fiancée.

"I hear, Benjamin. But your friend has changed. You do not see it."

"How so, Walela?"

"He was a healer, a teacher, a man of peace. Now he hates with the passions of Dragging Canoe."

"I understand why." The Freedman rises and kneels next to the woman. "He's changed, as I have, and as your people do."

"Things might advance at this second council. But you must understand while the Nation may change, my feelings do not."

The man shuffles and changes posture. "Know we are the same. I want kids someday, our children."

"This I believe," Walela smiles. "But you must promise."

"That's easy." Benjamin grins. "When my obligation to my blood brother ends, we start our own family."

The two stare at each other over the campfire.

They bond in agreement closer than in Crock.

Dideyohvsgi steps into the campfire's circle of light. "Delegates asked me to check Little Turkey. They do not accept truth, but it's smallpox. His entourage refuses my help. The man's going to die soon."

CHAPTER TWENTY-FIVE — Council

ᎠᏓᎶᎢᏍᎣᏏᏯᎠᏤᏇᏢᎯᎦᏣᏫᏛᎡᎬᎹᏤᎤᎯᎲᏛᏯᎧᎡᏁᏗᏃᏊᎤ

The day before the second tribal council, Dideyohvsgi and helpers staff the wagon.

The shaman watches attendees walk in front. Most nod good morning, and with that encouragement, the medicine man continues, "I am here for John Watts to offer variolations with cowpox to prevent smallpox."

He catches his breath.

"Wait. Where are you going? Hear what I said?"

Benjamin leans toward Walela. "Glad we came to help with the crowds. Gives our healer someone who talks in return."

She watches Dideyohvsgi. "Closed minds are difficult. I feel sorry for him."

Thudding hooves into the encampment distract the three, and they turn with most of the council attendees and watch Dragging Canoe, Mohi, and a dozen mounted warriors gallop into Oostanali.

The party rides without interruption or interview to prime campsites on the river.

Other early arrival campers greet the newcomers as they dismount and settle.

***

Later in the morning, the variolation site still waits for its first patient.

Staff observes the calm control of their leader's arrival. John Watts guides a horse-drawn two-wheeler loaded with supplies and trailed by assistants and delegates.

An official greeter points to the campsites in the meadow, and the wagon turns toward his emissaries.

"Don't appear to be busy." The peace proponent greets his followers. "Have we treated everyone?"

"No Sir," the medicine man steps to the dual-wheel wagon. "Come and rest. This has not happened as expected. Little Turkey becomes news."

"And I have new information."

Dideyohvsgi, John Watts, and Benjamin huddle around a clay water pot.

"Dragging Canoe tries to sabotage negotiations with Governor Blount," the leader drinks.

"No surprise," the shaman pats the jug. "Even here, he obstructs our efforts. We camp far from fresh water. Dragging Canoe's followers get the spots near the river."

"His Mohi acts in secret while the boss remains visible to our people." Watts looks across town at the campsites. "The medicine man leads a party that ambushes settlers found in any small groups. They have ventured to the governor's camp on the Tennessee."

"To make you look weak?" Benjamin follows the leader's eyes.

"That and more, to publicize weakness. I do not represent the people. Not even the majority."

The Freedman nods agreement.

"Governor Blount sent an emissary who demands full tribal participation."

"The Governor may regret that wish," Dideyohvsgi smiles.

"And you said news of Little Turkey?" Watts looks at the medicine man.

"He is here as a favored guest of Dragging Canoe. With smallpox. They asked me to diagnose the illness. I did not say chicken pox and their group's unhappy."

"No third council if I cannot sell all of us a treaty negotiation." The peacemaker stares at the campsites on the tributary and in the meadow.

***

The following morning, Dideyohvsgi wakens as the sun rises.

Mists float into camp from moisture condensing above the surface, and the young shaman pulls a blanket tighter over shoulders. He stands and looks over the gathering.

Oostanali rests silent, but a few campsites stir and fires light. From sleep, no one stirs.

Benjamin and Walela, wrapped in pelts, slumber under the wagon.

Dideyohvsgi smiles, lifts a container and slips away for water.

The shaman walks through the village and moves through Dragging Canoe's encampment. He reaches the bank with his pot.

A boy dips a clay bowl near his shoulder. "You are the medicine man who trained under Son of Stone Cloud?" The youngster fills his clay jar.

"Yes."

"He was famous. Mother tells stories of the man."

"He was as good as his father," the shaman stands with a full vessel.

"Then why don't you support the leaders?" The youth sneers. "Dragging Canoe and Mohi say you are a fake."

"What do you think?"

"You resemble my uncle scalped by Whites."

"Sorry. Sounds as if he was a hero."

"No. He was a false warrior."

"Because the man died?"

"No, because he lost."

Dideyohvsgi glances at the boy and lifts the heavy pot to shoulder.

The healer walks away from the lad and returns through Dragging Canoe's encampment.

"Fresh, thank you," Walela accepts the jug and returns the container to the wagon's bed.

Benjamin stows the night's bedding in the wagon. "You appear serious."

"Talked with a boy who shared insight into what we face."

"And what is that?" Ben steps closer.

"False or true may depend on who loses," the medicine man smiles.

***

The second council of the clans convenes that afternoon for a first session.

The delegates meet in a rectangular space between two long open-sided houses. Young sapling posts support roofs twist-thatched with bark over tree-limb support beams.

Attendees sit on blankets, pelts, or an occasional barrel.

Many smoke pipes of strong tobacco, and pungent smells drift with those of fresh cut wood and bramble.

Two shade structures designed to separate factions cover the attendees.

Dragging Canoe's group crowds under one side, those that support John Watts avoid the sun on the other.

The same Oostanali representative that greeted Dideyohvsgi's arrival with directions to the meadow steps forward, raises both hands and waits for the crowd to settle.

"Representatives from seven clans led by most beloved men! Stand as we introduce you."

The crowd cheers.

"From the Anigilohi (ᎠᏂᏳᎦᎯ a-ni-gi-lo-hi, Long Hair) Black Fox!"

Under John Watts' shade, an old man in fine ceremonial robes stands with trusted aids while followers whoop and applaud.

"Representing the Anisahohi (ᎠᏂᏩᎵᎯ a-ni-sa-ho-hi, Blue)…" the Oostanali rep continues through the beloved men of the Aniwaya (ᎠᏂᎦᏯ a-ni-wa-ya, Wolf,) Anigotegewi (ᎠᏂᎪᏖᎨᏫ a-ni-go-te-ge-wi, Wild Potato,) Aniwodi (ᎠᏂᏬᏗ a-ni-wo-di, Paint,) Anitsisqua (ᎠᏂᏥᏍᏆ a-ni-tsi-ss-qua, Bird,) and Aniawi (ᎠᏂᎠᏪ a-ni-a-wa, Deer) clans.

Notables recognized include James Vann, John Watts, Dragging Canoe, Blackfox, Pathkiller, Ganundalegi (later known as Major Ridge) and Charles Hicks.

Many of the younger men present, after the Cherokee wars, rise to prominence, influence, and lead the Nation.

The glaring non-introduction is under neither shade.

The elected beloved brother of the first national council, lies in a wagon, a victim of smallpox.

Benjamin leans close, "Where is Little Turkey?"

The medicine man winks, "Dead, I expect."

The moderator summons, "John Watts requests time."

Near the blood brothers, the peace advocate rises and steps to the center of the rectangle between the shade areas.

After polite applause, he begins, "Delegates, Governor Blount waits in camp on the Tennessee to negotiate a lasting friendship between our communities and the United States of America."

Murmurs ripple through the crowd.

"They demand communication with the seven clans."

Attendees clap and yell approval.

"Yes! But our people must stand together in negotiations."

Dideyohvsgi surveys the delegates.

Their physical language reflects respect but limited enthusiasm.

"Our foes offer peace. Hostilities cease." The speaker waits for talk to calm.

Order returns to the meeting.

"To keep the harmony, their government promises protection from any attack along with support, farm goods, seed, livestock and feed," Watts eyes the opposition under the second shade roof.

Dragging Canoe stands for recognition and raises one fist in symbolic conflict. "To accept these things which sound tempting, our people must give the White settlers more land."

The crowd murmurs discontent.

"Governor Blount proposes the ridge between Little River and the Tennessee as a border."

Several warriors fire muskets in protest.

"They gain more land!"

Attendees shout encouragement.

"My father and his father hunted those hills and roamed where we pleased. I say kill any White man who dares walk here!" One warrior raises a war spear.

The crowd looks to John Watts, "I state the Governor's position. It is open to discussion." He turns and includes both shaded enclaves. "I support the boundaries agreed to with the Hopewell Treaty, but as only one part of our negotiations. Important to this meeting, we must decide what our leader advocates. Little Turkey is not present."

Dragging Canoe leaps to confront the assembly, "He is ill and cannot attend because of that John Watts' appointed shaman. This false healer spreads sickness from chickens and cows, which he claims treats a disease that I vanquished! His treatment murdered our most beloved leader who passed last night of pox."

The council erupts into chaos and disorder.

Dideyohvsgi jumps to his feet. "No! He died of smallpox!" The medicine man's words fall unheard.

***

During that evening's walk to the river, the healer rinses his pot in its water.

The same boy from the morning fills his own.

"Medicine man who trained under Son of Stone Cloud. You spoke truth," the child dips his clay jar.

"I always speak true. So should you."

"Many do not. I saw Little Turkey before he passed. He died of the real smallpox."

"So, now you believe me?" The shaman stands with his full water pot.

"Yes?" The boy stares. "Dragging Canoe calls you a fake, but they lie. I still say you resemble my relative scalped by Whites."

"He should be your hero, not me." Dideyohvsgi lowers his head.

"No. My uncle followed a warrior who lied and so did I, but I trust you."

"Thank you."

"You don't know Mohi plots to kill Governor Blount before we make peace." The boy's eyelid trembles with apprehension. "I heard them talking. They plan to ambush the governor as he travels to the meeting."

Dideyohvsgi stares at the youngster for a moment and drops to his knees. "Tell no one you warned me. They might hurt you. Know those who want peace with the Whites thank you for your honesty."

The boy nods, smiles and, with his water, returns to his campsite.

The healer stands and watches the sun set over the river.

Feeding fish ripple on its surface, and dragonflies swoop for mosquitos.

He turns and totes his container around Dragging Canoe's campsites.

***

The following day, activities in Oostanali quicken.

Benjamin joins his friend, "Come. Mohi incites the delegates."

The two friends walk together to the end of the meadow.

Several dozen groups listen to propaganda delivered from the bed of a wagon. "Today, we gather to pick a new most beloved leader. Little Turkey served well. Now he died from the pox of chickens with red dots over his body." He leans toward the crowd, and they respond with yells and whoops. "We know where that came from!"

"Spreading lies." Ben leans to his friend's ear.

"Who do we choose?" On top of the bed, the healer crosses his arms. "He leads our people to stop settlers and gives his blood in this great battle. This warrior defeated the Kosvkvskini. Governor Blount and the cowards of peace grab more land for the United States. Your champion is Dragging Canoe!"

"Let's move on, Ben," Dideyohvsgi stalks away from the crowd. "This is insane."

That afternoon, the Cherokee vote.

Following boisterous speeches, John Watts nor his opponent wins.

On the fourth ballot, frustrated, the voters choose a compromise candidate, Black Fox.

***

That evening around Watt's campfire, Dideyohvsgi and Ben, with other followers, commiserate their political loss.

"This changes little," their leader gestures. "I must negotiate a treaty with Governor Blount, and I do not speak for everyone.

My words are talking leaves, the ones Son of Stone Cloud predicted blow in the wind."

Dideyohvsgi steps forward, "As our ancestor, I know he wants you to represent us."

John Watts nods. "He was a great medicine man, equal to his father. What was best for his society he supported."

"I fear those who conspire against you," the shaman stares into his leader's eyes. "I hear of plots to murder Governor Blount before he completes the treaty."

"If a Cherokee murders the territorial supervisor, we will never have an agreement," Watts nods.

"A youth informed me of a plot. He overheard Mohi planning with warriors. The youngster said the plan was to assassinate the governor as he travels to your meeting." The medicine man sits, and Benjamin settles next to him.

"A boy? Not very reliable. Rumors sweep Dragging Canoe's camp as they do mine. The kid may only repeat what he hears?"

"Yes, Sir. It's wise to take precautions."

"That do not use many warriors," the leader nods agreement. "I again task you and your Freedman friend to join the governor and be his eyes and ears. Escort him to White's Fort. You don't need support. He will have his own security force."

"We can do this." Dideyohvsgi agrees.

John Watts withdraws a fired bowl of sculpted gray Pipestone with a hand-carved stem of hollow Sassafras from his pack. "This is my finest pipe. Present it to the Governor as my endorsement seal."

CHAPTER TWENTY-SIX — Treaty

DRTᏬᎤᎢᏚᎤᏞᎩAJEᏞᏚᎠᏒᎷᎾᏫᏧᎩᎶᎷGMᎯᏭᎤᏒᎻᏣᎩᎾᎦᏅhᏃᏊᎤᎥ

Days later, Dideyohvsgi and Benjamin, concealed by foliage, rest their mounts.

A United States Army mounted patrol, three dozen armed men, travels along a rocky creek below the pair.

"I don't think we should ride in there." Ben watches the troop's commander, a blue coat lieutenant.

"Good way to get shot." The shaman turns his horse and in the safety of the woods, follows the detachment.

The soldiers stay on the creek's bank and curve with its bed upstream. They eye the rocky ground and the surrounding hills. The riders pick their path with care and suspicion.

"John Watts' pipe won't mean anything to those men." The Freedman remains in trees.

"Maybe to their lieutenant?" Dideyohvsgi leads and keeps the detachment in sight.

Below, the commander raises a hand, and his troops dismount to water their horses.

"We are too threatening mounted." The medicine man pauses, slides to the ground, and hands his reins to his friend. "I'll walk."

The shaman breaks a small branch from a nearby tree and rummages through his pack. He attaches a sun-bleached deer hide and holds the symbol high.

With the banner, the emissary steps out of concealment but stops and returns to get his leader's pipe.

He waves the pelt above his head and descends through the rocks.

A blue coat notices the infiltrator. "Lieutenant, up there!"

The officer spots the flag that swings on its stick. "Hold your fire. He wants to talk."

***

As Dideyohvsgi approaches, the soldiers brandish muskets at the ready.

The commander mounts and motions for two of his men. They ride to meet the intruder.

"Do you speak English?"

"Yes, I bring greetings from John Watts to Governor Blount."

"Sir, this could be an ambush." A soldier stands in his stirrups and surveys the woods.

"No." The healer waves to his concealed friend. "Only one other."

Benjamin leads their horses out of the trees.

"That ain't no Injun." The wary trooper sits in his saddle. "Somebody's slave."

"We are emissaries sent by John Watts to counsel and guide the governor with our language during treaty negotiations."

The soldier cocks his musket.

Dideyohvsgi stares through the commander. "My companion is a Freedman friend."

"Your English is good." The lieutenant watches Ben.

"That warrior coming taught me."

"Why should I believe you?" The blue coat officer turns to the medicine man.

He withdraws Watts' pipe from his belt. "Our leader sends this gift to the supervisor of this territory and future State of Tennessee."

***

That night, the two representatives adopt low profiles.

They huddle and settle under a supply wagon to listen as troops gossip.

Nearby, six soldiers cook venison on a campfire spit and wait for dinner.

"Yo, Johnson! You still glad you joined the army?"

"Had no choice, Cocklebur. Stole a goat. The army's better than jail. On the frontier, never thought that meant escort a Federalist politician."

"The Governor served during the revolution, in the Continental Congress, and at the Constitutional Convention."

"Are you sure, he did? I heard Blount lost his blue britches in land speculation. You be glad the government paying your wage, not him."

The first soldier twists his head to a sound, grabs his musket, and leaps to his feet. "Who goes there! Ride into the light!"

Dideyohvsgi and Ben withdraw into the deep shadows under the wagon.

Mohi, on horseback with his hands empty and raised, knees his mount toward the campfire, and the soldiers surround his horse.

The medicine man withdraws a paper from his belt. He hands it to a soldier.

"Near shot you, Injun!" The non-commissioned officer reads and looks at his companions. "This says we take him to the Governor. It has the gov's seal on it."

The men at the campfire lower weapons and stretch to see. Mohi lowers his hands.

A trooper leads the horse past the supply cart, and its rider cannot see Dideyohvsgi and Benjamin under its bed.

The friends shift to the opposite side of the wagon and watch the intruder and the soldier ride around several campfires of army guards to Governor Blount's tent.

The tent's sides hang open, held by straps, and the two see but cannot hear. "Prime your musket, Ben. If he moves on the Governor, shoot him."

***

Inside, Governor Blount, with long brown sideburns and cropped hair, stands and meets Dragging Canoe's appointed assassin.

They assess each other, both of equal height and age. The White man's features shine pudgy and less chiseled.

"You are Mohi from Dragging Canoe?" The Governor does not offer a handshake.

"Our glorious leader sends greetings," Mohi's English rings hesitant but understandable.

"And upon return, please extend mine. Do you have a message?"

"I do. He will bring warriors to attack Spanish Florida and Louisiana. We promise help to transfer those territories to Great Britain with one condition."

"And that is?"

"Under your seal, give Dragging Canoe a document, a letter, that specifies the arms and supplies you promise for his fight against your nation's White settlers."

"Done. My clerk will execute the paper, and you take it with you. This requires a few moments."

***

From Dideyohvsgi's viewpoint, Mohi sits.

"They appear too friendly," Benjamin squints along the barrel of his musket with its sight on Mohi's head.

"Stay ready. If he touches a weapon, shoot him." The younger medicine man scoots in the dirt under the wagon for a better view.

The two see a clerk bring the governor paperwork.

The emissary accepts his letter, mounts his horse, and rides into the darkness.

Dideyohvsgi turns to his friend, "Dragging Canoe negotiates with Blount. They do not support a treaty. So, the question is why?"

The friends watch troopers regroup around their fire.

Cocklebur continues the earlier conversation. "One goat got me into this army. They say the governor done much worse."

"Who's they?" Johnson lights a pipe with a coal.

"Everyone knows he and his brother bought two million acres out here."

"I knew the old man was wealthy."

"I doubt it!" He preens as he gossips. "The purchase was by credit. The family is in debt. One investor went bankrupt."

"France controls the Mississippi River to occupy Louisiana." Johnson displays awareness of national politics. "This land could be worthless."

"Sure thing." The gossiper agrees. "I figure that's why we're out here in the wilderness."

***

The following morning, Dideyohvsgi and Benjamin travel with Governor Blount's party to White's Fort without further interference or contact with the Dragging Canoe faction.

John Watts meets his emissaries the first evening of their return.

"Mohi met with Blount. They talked as friends and allies. The Governor gave him a letter, and he rode away." Dideyohvsgi sits by the fireplace in the cabin headquarters. He glances at his leader. "Ben and I could not hear the discussion."

"Interesting they even met," Watts puffs a long stem pipe, and tobacco fumes drift into the room. "Dragging Canoe is here, but I understand he offers no support for any treaty."

"And Mohi?" Dideyohvsgi nods at his companion.

"No one has seen him," the leader draws smoke. "Our people say he is not here."

"His adviser stays close," Benjamin scratches an ear. "If he's not here, it's for a reason."

"Which we need to know," John Watts steps to the fireplace and taps his bowl. "I have many allies in Dragging Canoe's camp. We will learn something."

Tobacco embers fall into the flames.

"Governor Blount is not generous with his terms. He demands the rim between the Little River and the Tennessee should form part of the boundary. I want the mouth of the Duck as the Hopewell Treaty read. We insist on a straight line to the Holston at the ridge."

"Both lines decrease our lands." Dideyohvsgi rubs his forehead.

"We do not negotiate from strength," the leader looks at the medicine man.

"That gives the Whites Walela's and Old Tassel's place," Benjamin leans near his shaman friend. "I can't accept that."

John Watts hears the comment, "That property is only part of what we lose. The Governor's demands leave our people with less than we had after Hopewell. Cherokee land retreats west. Our home becomes smaller. Everyone sacrifices."

CHAPTER TWENTY-SEVEN — Holston

DRᏕᏲᎢᏏᏬᏓᏸᏯᎯᏰᏋᏜᏗᏔᏎᏝᏪᏍᏫᎦᏪᎯᏲᎣᏴᎲᏎᎦᎡᎲᎾᏂᏃᏊᎤ

Summer heat warms the Tennessee River's northern flow near White's Fort. A wall of logs planted in the earth surrounds and protects blockhouses and cabins.

The small, fortified town stirs.

Residents, unaware the location will become Knoxville but eager for statehood, prepare for their territorial governor.

William Blount arrives by wagon with an army escort, too many to house within the palisade.

From distant hills above the river, Dideyohvsgi and Benjamin watch the villagers welcome their government to the isolated outpost.

"John Watts comes in the morning."

The pair retreat into the foliage for better concealment.

"And Dragging Canoe?" Ben pats his horse's rump.

"Their group dry camps over that ridge."

"With Mohi?" The Freedman slides upon his mount.

"No sign of him yet." The medicine man shakes his head.

The following day, troopers erect a tent to shade negotiations on the bank of the river near the fortified town.

Dideyohvsgi and Benjamin gather with John Watts and other Cherokee, including several most beloved men.

Dragging Canoe with his contingent arrives.

The fort's entrance swings open and the Governor, by wagon, rides with guards a short distance downriver to the meeting place.

Parties settle in the shade, and Blount stands.

The shaman leans near Ben's ear, "Still no Mohi."

"Representatives of the great Cherokee Nation," the Southwest Territory and the Superintendent of Indian Affairs for the Southern District opens the meeting.

The assembly listens.

"The United States establishes perpetual peace and friendship between our people."

Translators communicate the words. Most attendees do not speak the foreign language.

Polite applause follows.

"Our discussions agree on most points." The governor looks at the crowd.

John Watts stands.

"We acknowledge your protection. We return our prisoners of war." He repeats in excellent English.

Blount nods understanding.

"You regulate trade and guarantee lands under this treaty never to be ceded into the United States. None of your citizens settle here."

The governor waits for the message in his language before clapping.

John Watts' expression firms with resolution. "If they do, you agree the Cherokee may punish those settlers."

Blount expands arms to his audience, "We promise a road for your use." He expects a reaction and receives none. "We will negotiate higher compensation for land ceded to develop this route."

After the words translate, several attendees applaud.

Watts nods agreement, "Citizens that hunt within our lands and anyone that commits a crime must receive punishment."

Blount raises his voice, "Cherokee must give the United States notice of pending attacks by other tribes, and our peoples agree to cease animosities against each other.

"My Nation becomes farmers," John Watts drops his chin to his chest and stares at the earth, "and you supply implements for that aim."

The White politician steps closer, "Let us sit and discuss the border."

***

Six days later, under the same tent on the bank of the river, Dideyohvsgi and Ben watch the Governor, John Watts, Dragging Canoe, and several leaders of individual clans sign their names or marks on the Treaty of the Holston, July 2 of 1791.

After the treaties' formal signing, their negotiator gathers his key supporters. "We did not set up boundaries we wanted. We got a federal road, money for fields of corn and cotton, and an end to our war. But, this agreement our families won't cheer."

"Our people lost territory," Dideyohvsgi nods.

"Yes," the leader smiles. "They might align with Dragging Canoe."

Benjamin stands beside his companion, "We can inform the lower towns around Walela's land."

John Watts nods, "Convince them our treaty is good and lasting. Even if you know better."

"Enduring until bloodshed?" The shaman glances at his friend.

"And still no sigh of Mohi." The Freedman shakes his head.

"He won't be far from Dragging Canoe." Their leader rubs days of negotiation fatigue from his eyelids. "Scout downriver. There are several settler cabins. Make sure they are safe if you can."

***

The next afternoon, Dideyohvsgi and Ben ride into a clearing in the woods.

A small settler's cabin surrounded by vegetable gardens sits in a meadow.

"No chimney smokes." The medicine man reins his horse and watches shuttered windows.

"That farmer in there wants a closer shot." The Freedman separates and guides his mount to a side view. He scans the earth for tracks. "Three riders, yesterday. No iron shoes."

The shaman approaches but slides to the ground. He surveys its door from behind his horse. "Nothing moving."

Ben rides to the front with his musket ready. "Careful."

His companion steps to the wall beside the entrance and listens.

The breeze through the trees rustles, and pigs in a nearby pen grunt.

From the gloomy interior, silence.

Dideyohvsgi pushes with a foot and the doorway swings inward. He waits a moment and enters.

Benjamin holds his breath and fingers his musket's trigger.

The shaman walks out of the cabin and shakes his head. "No one in there. It doesn't appear they deserted the place."

The Freedman uncocks his weapon.

Pigs grunt and root in their pen, and the two investigate.

258

They walk their horses toward the fat, filthy animals that jump away from a feeding trough.

Inside the wooden crib, mixed with corn cobs, half-eaten human body parts lie in dried pools of blood.

The healer gags.

Ben covers his nose against the stench, "At least a couple of adults and a child."

The shaman recovers, "Mohi?"

"Who else?" The Freedman climbs onto his horse.

Dideyohvsgi glares at a child's gnawed forearm, "Our new perpetual peace and prosperity dies by hatred."

***

The two emissaries from John Watts travel to the lower towns.

Time clouds their memory of the cruelty and blood at the cabin. Both build resolve to convince people that the Treaty of Holston beckons a peaceful and prosperous future.

Reality intrudes during their first attempt.

"What are you telling me, Benjamin?" Walela stamps a foot against the clay floor of her home and waves a knife over a venison roast in her fireplace. "You men give the soil that feeds my cows to the Whites for a road?"

Ben sits cross-legged on a deerskin. "John Watts thinks it makes travel easier for you to get your milk to buyers. And they buy the land."

"With money I never see, for a peace that never happens!" Walela cuts a chunk of meat from her spit and serves it to her guest.

Benjamin stands to accept the food from the irritated woman. "You are right. Our leader did the best he could.

259

Governor Blount knew of Dragging Canoe's resistance and used our division against us."

"You delayed bloodshed. Our people still have pride. They will rise against this treaty and ride with Dragging Canoe." Walela sits on a milk pail and stares. "Old Tassel gave me cows and the freedom to care for them. Son of Stone Cloud, my health and the strength to herd. You negotiators give me uncertainty and promises of better days, but I must move from lands that they forced me into with the last agreement. I want my grandfather and his shaman back."

"I hear you, Walela," the Freedman sits beside the woman. "It's only been a few months. Time will show the treaties' wisdom."

She peers into her beloved's eyes. "Benjamin, you and your friend have much to do. Best take care of your business. This is not my land anymore." The frustrated herder looks back and forth between her two male guests. "I must move. May the strength of Son of Stone Cloud help me find fresh pastures for my cows. The question is, can you live with this new treaty?"

Dideyohvsgi steps into the lodge and disrupts the two's first disagreement. "I'm sorry for interrupting. A runner just brought a message from John Watts. He wants us back to camp. We must leave."

"Don't go, Ben," She grasps the young man's hands.

Benjamin looks at his shaman friend, and the medicine man understands the message in his eyes.

Dideyohvsgi steps outside the door.

"I must. One day we settle, but not now." He kisses his soulmate.

***

On the trail to Watt's headquarters, the shaman watches the sky darken and distant lightening flash, "Ben. we better find shelter. Big storm coming."

"You're right. I saw a cavern above that outcrop we just passed."

As the turbulence approaches, the friends double back and settle into a protecting small cave.

"This is a miniature Cherokee Rock." Dideyohvsgi settles on his blanket.

"Don't count on my help if Kosvkvskini come," Ben laughs at the thought. "I'm going to sleep. Wake me when the storm passes."

The medicine man watches the clouds gather darkness on the horizon and billow over ridges into valleys as they draw closer.

Ben's snores become inaudible in claps of thunder.

***

Three dark masses hug the earth more than the others, and as they move, take shape as black horses cantering over the landscape.

Trees bend with the wind of their passage.

Each horse carries a rider, fearsome warriors on mounts bedecked in raven feathers.

The first slides to a halt below the cave's outcrop, and its hooves cleave the earth. "Dideyohvsgi! Cherokee chosen one! Why do you allow your people to become soft?"

The medicine man stands at the entrance. "What do you mean, Warrior?"

The black horse spins in a tight circle. "Chairs! Featherbeds! White man's clothes and plows!"

"I don't control these things." The shaman watches a second dark threat joins the first.

Its spirit challenges, "Grind your corn by hand, not on their gristmills!"

"And that will strengthen my people?" The medicine man extends his palms in supplication.

A third and most violent windstorm arrives at the cave, and Dideyohvsgi's hair whips in the wind.

The apparition delivers its message as thunder, "The mother of your nation cries tears through these clouds! You allow game to be killed for sport, for hides, for White man's amusement! Return to the former ideals of Cherokee Rock!"

"I understand, Great Ones." The shaman looks at the horsemen. *"The ancient ways are good. But I do not control my people's customs."*

The earth shakes, and Dideyohvsgi loses his footing and lands on the outcrop.

"Do as we say, Apprentice of Stone Cloud's Son! Or remember this, the Wabash leads to Hightower!"

"What?"

Tornado winds whip from the four cardinal directions and swoop the black horses and their riders into the clouds.

A last electric bolt flashes across the medicine man's face, and the torrential rain stops in symphony with breaking sun and peaceful sky.

***

Dideyohvsgi sits outside the cave, and warmth dries the raindrops on his cheeks.

"What are you doing out there?" Benjamin stirs.

"Returning to the old ways," his friend struggles to speak.

"In spite of a treaty no one likes?"

"Yes, and earlier. To times before you, the White settlers, or even Stone Cloud."

CHAPTER TWENTY-EIGHT — Wabash

ᎠᏰᏘᏍᎣᎢᏍᏬᎶᏴᎠᎫᎬᏇᏗᎥᎯᎨᎦᏫᎤᏔᎦᎹᎦᏲᎣᎯᎲᏸᏴᎤᎦᎤᏂᎯᏃᎦᎤ

Days later, Dideyohvsgi and Ben meet with John Watts outside his cabin at his temporary headquarters.

The two sit with other trusted confidants and smoke pipes, listen to their leader, and watch the bustle of a surrounding battle encampment.

"Our people dislike our action. The Whites declare it as the Treaty of Holston. Our clans call it 'Watts' Weakness.' Many say I wished for peace, so I gave too much," the speaker surveys his audience. "They are right."

Dideyohvsgi turns his attention to the activities within the camp. "These men prepare for war. You changed your strategy?"

"Because I now believe we can win." Watts stands tall over his seated confidants. "The Creek, Shawnees, Miami, and Lenape in the northwest face an invasion. St. Clair, with a large force of soldiers, invades their lands. President Washington supports the action."

"How many fighters?"

"We are not sure. Dragging Canoe has a letter pledging Spanish financial and supply support from Governor Blount. I have committed men, and he will lead our warriors with the coalition. Little Turtle of the Miami, Blue Jacket of the

Shawnee, and Buckongahelas of the Delaware command the defense."

Dideyohvsgi leans closer to Ben, "That must be the document Blount gave Mohi."

"You know Dragging Canoe and I are not friends. Alignment of our goals is necessary. My old wounds heal but force me to stay here. I ask you, as trusted allies, to support our war."

***

Weeks later, a November wind blows snow through the woods of the Northwest.

Several dozen warriors cluster around campfires in the night. They prepare for battle.

Dideyohvsgi, in charge of a fighting unit, cleans a British-provided musket and munches on a Spanish-financed cornbread ration.

Benjamin sits across the fire and pulls a blanket over his shoulders.

"This is far from home." Ben scoots closer to the warmth. "I believe we fight for the English instead of Dragging Canoe."

"Our groups travel well, with food, and everyone has a musket. Thank the red coats for that," the shaman warrior smiles at his friend.

"I hear there's over fourteen hundred of us, but I'm not sure. I've only seen six or seven parties," Benjamin eyes other warriors that huddle around the fire.

"They are out there. Dragging Canoe expects to attack today. He ordered me to a war council at the crook of the river two hours before dawn. I better leave," Dideyohvsgi stands.

"Why you?"

"I think he wants a John Watts' man there to support his

version of the story." The healer picks up a blanket and swings it onto his shoulders.

"I'm uncomfortable for you to go alone." Ben climbs to his feet. "Mohi will be with Dragging Canoe."

"I'll be fine but won't be too friendly with either."

The morning sun waits beyond the horizon. The shore of the Wabash River sits cold and dark.

The northwest coalition's leaders meet at a fire, which provides the only light in the cloud-covered darkness.

Snow falls on the shoulders of Mihšihkinaahkwa (Little Turtle) and Eepiihkaanita (William Wells) of the Myaamia (Miami.)

Blue Jacket of the Shawnee shivers with Buckongahelas of the Delaware.

Tarhe of the Wyandot and Egushawa of the Ottawa pull blankets tight.

Little Turtle commands in a heavy fur skin coat. A bear claw ring bands his neck as he controls the meeting. "We attack at first light."

The Miami leader picks up a stick and draws a rectangle. "Our scouts inform us of the Mihši-maalhsa (Whiteman) camp on high ground." He points with the branch. "Their women and supply personnel, here. Behind, they have four or five three-pound cannons between them and the river."

Blue Jacket, in a dyed woolen United States Army coat with white trim, steps to the map. "My brothers say those have canister loads. One shot can slay thirty of our warriors."

"Yes," Little Turtle nods agreement, "We have surprise with us, and St. Clair's men, for weeks, built their road to transport that artillery." The leader laughs. "Their commander has fat man's feet. His soldiers carry him on a stretcher between two horses. The fool sent three hundred of his seasoned fighters to protect his supply line. Those left are recruits that never faced a primed musket."

"No surprise." Buckongahelas joins the others. "On the way in, my Delaware exchanged shots with soldiers."

"And did they withdraw at once as I ordered?" Little Turkey's voice steels.

"Yes, but any surprise ambush is impossible."

"The Whites opened fire at our scouts along their new road. Means nothing to them." The leader draws an arc line in front of the rectangle. "We surrounded them on three sides with their back against the river. Seneca and Mohawks man the right flank. Delaware, Shawnee, and Miami occupy the center. Ottawa, Ojibwa, and Potawatomi protect the left. Move your men through the trees and wait for my shot to strike."

The assembled war leaders nod understanding.

"One more challenge," Little Turtle looks at Dideyohvsgi, Mohi, and Dragging Canoe. "Our Cherokee group is small but seasoned by the French and colonial wars. Dragging Canoe, bring your warriors to the right with the Seneca and Mohawks. When we attack, you must silence the cannons."

The warrior smiles and, with one finger, imitates a neck slice across his own throat.

As the darkness of night grays and announces the sun's approach, Dideyohvsgi and Benjamin, with their Cherokee fighters, move behind Dragging Canoe and Mohi through woods with the Mohawks and Senecas led by Egushawa of the Ottawas.

They settle in position and see St. Clair's encampment before the Wabash on a rise.

An added volunteer militia camp bars the path.

Egushawa joins him. "Trees should conceal you. Move your men. Find the cannons."

Dragging Canoe motions for Mohi and the Cherokee party.

Ninety warriors, including the young future leaders Tecumseh and Sequoya, slip through the darkness behind their leader.

Benjamin tugs at his friend's arm. "See the artillery?"

The group arrives at the edge of a tree line.

Beyond, a snow-covered rise extends to a hill with a flat surface.

On the high swell, the Continental's encampment on the top defends three-pounders pointed above the camp toward the center of the arc of concealed attackers.

Between them and the river, a smaller militia group camps with no sentries.

The youthful Sequoya risks the future's Cherokee sylla-bary. He lifts his head above a protective log. "There are the cannons. No one stirs."

"I don't see sentinels," Dideyohvsgi looks at his Freedman friend.

"There's one. By the first canon across the river," Ben squints. "I think he's asleep."

"Now, we listen for Little Turtle's musket shot," Sequoya settles in position to watch the guard and the cannons.

***

The dark grayness of the night becomes lighter as the Cherokee wait to attack.

A few seasoned warriors nap. Their contemporaries nudge them awake when they snore.

Men shiver in the November freeze.

"Something's moving out there," Benjamin nudges his shaman friend, who rolls to his elbows and looks toward the canon.

A shadow, one man across the river, hugs the ground on his stomach and inches to the armament's position.

"What's he doing? He risks alerting the battery!" Dideyohvsgi spits his words.

The form creeps closer as the air tinges orange from first sunlight, and the continental army sentinel stirs.

Little Turtle's musket blast pierces the morning stillness and summons blood-lust screams.

Warriors charge St. Clair's encampment.

"That was Dragging Canoe! He took care of the sentry!" Benjamin jumps but slips in the snow.

His shaman friend pulls Ben to his feet. "Come! We must take those cannons!"

The Cherokee surge forward and sweep into the militia cluster on their side of the river.

As United States Army volunteers waken and struggle for a defense, the warriors shoot, scalp and war-club bludgeon the servicemen in their tents.

St. Clair's regulars form defensive positions and return fire in the European style, standing lines with command ordered volleys.

The delay at the first volunteer's camp allows troops time to man the cannons and discharge canisters.

Dideyohvsgi and Benjamin drop to the ground behind a log at the river's edge.

"Little Turtle said, aim at officers!" Ben extends his musket over the bark.

Both fire their muskets and scramble to reload.

Lead balls from the higher positions joined with canister shrapnel rip the timbers apart twenty feet above the attacker's heads.

"They shoot but look! High! They don't adjust for how low we are!" Dideyohvsgi reloads.

***

The Cherokee, with their allies, swarm across the river. Others from the forests that slipped closer overnight join the assault.

Attackers drop to knees in the snow, fire, and reload while their targets stand in defensive lines.

Army troopers fall by the dozens.

An American officer orders a bayonet assault.

Soldiers hurl themselves forward.

The massed warriors allow the charge, circle the group, end the threat, and slaughter stragglers as they struggle to return to their lines.

With attackers firing behind protection from the woods and lower ground, the troops of the encampment mount futile bayonet charges.

Each effort withdraws, and they compact into less mobile clumps around their women and non-combatants.

Dideyohvsgi and Benjamin, at the sound of muffled drums from the continental's camp, watch movement on the hill above from the safety of trees. "They are retreating! That fat man on the stretcher between the horses must be General Arthur St. Clair," the shaman points. "They're moving freight!"

"They save cannon onto the road," Ben grabs his friend's arm.

Warriors surge out of the forests to prevent the escape. They charge up the hill against little resistance.

A few troopers stand and fire, but most scramble to follow the artillery.

As the Indian coalition's fighters swarm into the encampment, White women scream their terror, and teamsters fall under war clubs.

The rout becomes a massacre as civilians die with army regulars. Scalped prostitutes and wives bleed red on the clean snow.

Dideyohvsgi stops Ben as he bends to scalp a trooper. "Stop. I have no stomach for this."

The medicine man turns and watches Mohi peel long blond hair and a layer of flesh from a soldier's wife's head. He shakes the locks in the air as attached skin drips blood on his face.

"Stuff dirt in their mouths!" The killer drops to his knees, leverages his dead woman's mouth open and forces a handful of snow and earth in the cavity. "This is how you get our land!"

***

Later, Dideyohvsgi and Ben sit below the ravaged encampment along the bank of the Wabash with the exhausted Cherokee contingent as Dragging Canoe rides his mount into the group. "A triumph! I just left Little Turtle. We lost twenty brave warriors and have forty wounded. We killed over one thousand White invaders! Let us celebrate success!" the leader struts his horse before his companions.

Dideyohvsgi leans to Benjamin, "The families of our dead men morn and this gain cannot fill the holes in their hearts."

Ben nods understanding. "But I return to Walela."

The victory speech evolves into a Dragging Canoe led celebration and vindication of his life's devotion to driving Whites from Cherokee land.

With captured whiskey, the party becomes drunken as darkness falls, and the leader dances success around a huge bonfire of St. Clair's tents and wagons.

The young medicine man and his friend watch their commander's frenzied dancing. "I'm exhausted and just want to sit here," Ben's eyes follow Dragging Canoe before the flames. "Look at him."

"My training's worried over how much he sweats," Dideyohvsgi elbows his companion.

Dragging Canoe halts, throws his head backward and gasps for breath. The Cherokee war leader collapses to the snow and dies from a heart attack.

Next morning, the sun rises over the outcome of St. Clair's folly.

A coalition, in defense of their lands, loses their most effective warrior but deliver histories largest defeat of the American army by Native Americans.

This action remains larger and more significant than Custer's massacre eighty years later at Little Bighorn.

CHAPTER TWENTY-NINE — Defeat

ᎠᎡᏘᏐᎣᎢᏐᏆᎥᎩᎠᎫᎫᏌᏪᏞᏗᏞᏡᎳᏪᏍᎡᎦᎻᎿᏲᎣᏱᎲᏝᎩᏎᎰᏪᏔᏄᏐ

The news of Dragging Canoe's death reverberates through the seven clans.

They memorialize him at the Nations' council in Ustanali.

In the same meeting, John Watts assumes the people's position as Red Leader.

The new war commander uses his current influence and power to travel to West Florida and meet with Governor Arturo O'Neill de Tyrone.

Their agreement provides more arms and supplies from the Spanish and bolsters Watt's public stature and his ability to resist White expansion.

Dideyohvsgi and Ben return to John Watts' Chickamauga headquarters with the Cherokee dispatched from the Wabash.

The warriors travel by foot and horse through country, now called Tennessee, led by their dead leader's brother, Little Owl, and his shaman Mohi.

"We won nothing by defeating St. Clair but a long journey home," Sequoya, who walks with Dideyohvsgi and Ben, looks at his companions.

"That so?" Benjamin smiles.

"Yes. We stopped the American army, but they say John Watts met with the Spanish Governor who promises protection from the Whites by Spain." Younger man's eyes flash an interest in politics. "They impose a fifteen percent tax on Mississippi freight to New Orleans. I think we exchange one oppressor for another."

"Maybe?" Dideyohvsgi pats the boy on his back. "But we've followed Watts for years. He does what our communities demand."

"What our families need is not so easy," Sequoya drops his head.

"And what's that?" The healer lifts the young man's chin. "A return to the old ways?"

"No. To be Whiter. To write in our own language."

A musket discharges in the distance. The row stops.

"Hate that sound," Benjamin peers along the men that walk a hunting trail into a tree line.

More muskets fire in quick succession.

"Our scouts ran into something." Dideyohvsgi drops to his knees with most of the other warriors.

Waist-high grass conceals the party. They drop packs and ready weapons.

Little Owl rides toward them alongside the file. "We shot a White farmer on the other side of those trees. They'll bring others, so move up for an ambush!"

Dideyohvsgi and Ben crouch behind shrubs and brush and look across cleared land around four cabins nestled by a palisade called Zeigler's Station.

The dead settler lies in his plowed field near the timber line.

As they wait, the palisade's gate flings open, and a rescue party, five men with muskets, try with caution to collect their deceased.

The rescuers search for movement in the trees, unaware that over eighty warriors threaten. They move within musket range, and the ambushers watch them step across plowed earthen rows.

Mohi leaps to his feet, fires, and the lead settler falls.

The others fire, but only two Whites drop.

The remainders scramble for the palisade's protection with the shaman and six fighters in pursuit.

White men run through the gates as the attackers stop. In response, muskets discharge from firing ports.

Little Owl orders withdrawal, and the warriors slip away through the timbers.

A furious warrior shakes his war club at the relative of Dragging Canoe. "Your brother never left settlers. They will trail and ambush for revenge!"

Dragging Canoe's sibling turns on his horse. "John Watts ordered a return to headquarters. That I plan to do!"

"We have no order to attack Zeigler's Station," Dideyohvsgi confronts the rebel. "We negotiate with Governor Blount soon. He might agree with the Spanish for no more slaughter. Little Owl is right."

An angry Mohi steps closer to his critic, and Ben stands and levels his musket.

Dragging Canoe's shaman stares at the Freedman's weapon, glares into Dideyohvsgi's eyes, and turns to the other warriors, "Our commander slinks, a frightened mouse that hides behind John Watts!"

As the war party argues, across the tree line, settlers from within the palisade collect their dead from the fields and cart the bodies into Zeigler's Station.

"We must leave no one alive to track us! We outnumber these Whites! Who will join?" Dragging Canoe's shaman whips hatred and blood lust into his men. "Attack with me!"

Most of the assembled fighters scream and shake their weapons in the air.

Dideyohvsgi, Ben, Little Owl, Tecumseh, Sequoia, and others hold back and watch the assault.

Mohi's first wave reaches the walls under feeble fire by defenders.

As several attackers fall, Mohi commands timber placement against the wood stakes and sets the fortification ablaze.

The flames eat the defenses.

The palisade's gate flings open and a father with a child in his arms dashes for the trees.

Surprised, fighters chase, but the man makes the woods and disappears into its darkness as the last sunlight fades.

A second settler lunges out of the fort, fires his musket, and kills an attacker.

"You heathens remember Archie Wilson!" The fellow swings his weapon at one warrior. Another clubs him.

With the distraction, Mrs. Zeigler, with a child in her arms, flees the Station and unnoticed, reaches the safety of the woods.

Mohi and his men flood into the open gate. They massacre the defenders, pillage, and pack useful or valuable items.

Dideyohvsgi turns aside from the slaughter. "Come, Ben. We have orders to return to headquarters." With Little Owl, Tecumseh, Sequoia and several others, he leads the group in the darkness from the attack and burning of Zeigler's Station.

***

The news of the incident reaches Blount, who attends the July Chickasaw Conference.

With settlers aroused and aware of St. Clair's defeat plus angry and terrified of potential marauding Cherokee, the governor calls for three hundred militia.

Those troops set up forts and range the woods to protect White farmers.

The Wabash veterans return to their homes.

Dideyohvsgi and Benjamin separate from their companions and join Walela at John Watts' Chicamaugua headquarters.

***

Days later, the war heroes and the woman stand outside her Willstown cabin and watch an arrival from Florida and the Spanish Governor.

The leader rides in front. Mounted warriors and horses laden with supplies follow.

Seven mounts that carry wooden powder kegs and pouches of flints for muskets attract Benjamin's eye, followed by several loaded with knives and hatchets.

Walela watches pack animals that follow with food and living items, including pelts, blankets and decorative beads.

Dideyohvsgi eyes the warriors, experienced fighters with scars as proof, devoted fanatics to their ex-peace leader now converted to militancy.

"With Dragging Canoe gone, our people welcome his successor," the shaman looks at his friend.

Ben nods agreement. "Watts is more popular now that he is more militant."

"They say more war against the Whites comes soon," Walela looks at the Freedman. "And that means you will leave?"

Benjamin slips his arm around her. "No, not this time. I am done with this feud."

Dideyohvsgi chuckles, "That has much to do with the land they gave you?"

"No, my friend. It's her."

"I also tire of spilling blood. But everyone stands behind Watts. The council at Running Water declared war against the United. States. They say our leader plans an assault on the Washington District deep along the Cumberland, even French Lick. I don't believe we can defeat the Whites, but I must support our Nation."

"I am not of your folk, old friend," Ben holds his woman closer. "This time, I stay at home."

"And that you have earned." The shaman pats his friend's shoulder.

***

Days later, at dawn, Watts assembles his forces to attack the fort on land that becomes the Tennessee city of Nashville.

One thousand Cherokee able to continue resistance to White settlement gather with Muscogee and Shawnee allies.

The force is a large group, mounted, armed, and well provisioned.

Dideyohvsgi waits with others for Watts' order to move.

"You think you're going without me?"

The shaman turns to his veteran companion, "Yes, stay here with Walela. We can fight this war without you."

"I couldn't sleep last night. She also told me you cannot leave alone. Remember when we met? Blood brothers don't desert each other."

"We travel to the north, my friend. That is significant. Directions have meanings to my people. At least we do not go west to the black of death. South is white for peace and harmony. East is red for victory and power."

An order commands the shaman and his friend to move out of Willstown.

"And what is north?" Ben shifts his musket to his shoulder.

"Blue for sadness and defeat."

Benjamin stares at his companion. "That makes me thrilled I came."

***

For days, the column moves northwest toward its aim.

Isolated in the wilderness of 1792, sixty settler families live in French Lick (Fort Nashborough, a settlement to become Nashville.)

Travel and communication to the White towns of Knoxville in the East and Natchez, to the south on the Mississippi, prove difficult.

Their security depends on the United States federal government after the area's transfer from North Carolina two years prior.

Both lacked resources and a will to protect the residents.

Dideyohvsgi and Benjamin cook venison and rest from days of travel when mounted warriors return to John Watt's camp.

This mobile force moves in groups, each under the command of a leader.

One returnee reports, "On a creek, there's a picket stockade with a blockhouse at its gate around four cabins."

Watts looks at the ridge. "Yes, the White's call that place Buchanan's Station."

"We cannot leave a fortification behind us. Fort Nashborough is in sight. We must capture this defense, or risk harm from the rear!" the younger James Vann stands before his war leader.

He considers Vann's strategy for a moment. "We attack when the moon is high."

The friends return to their fire and tend to their weapons.

Ben cleans his musket's barrel.

"We are many. They are few. But that doesn't mean Mohi's with us. Have you seen the warrior shaman?" He fills his powder horn from a group wooden keg.

"Not since Dragging Canoe died. I heard he refused to join," the Freedman chuckles. "Too many Watts and smallpox lies. Good thing. I don't have to watch my back."

"He and Governor Blount were too friendly that night. And he shot my Saloli. I will remind him of that someday." The shaman cuts a venison piece off their spit. "Better eat something."

***

The Cherokee force leaves their comfort and move against Buchannan's Station on foot.

The warriors charge the stockade from the woods and meet a pre-warned and prepared, determined resistance.

From portholes in the walls, the White settlers fire their muskets with exchanged weapons.

Fighters gather in mass feet from the wall and hurl their bodies at the gate. Many fall as musket balls rip Cherokee flesh.

Benjamin stands with hands on knees next to the fort. "Climb on my shoulders! Shoot through the port-hole!"

Dideyohvsgi climbs atop his friend and sticks his musket's barrel into the firing opening. He squeezes his trigger and flint falls on frizzen.

A defender inside shoves the weapon from within, and the shaman slips from his perch and lands on his back.

Their commander arrives at the frustrated melee. "Burn the wall!"

Warriors scramble and pile wood against the wall's exterior.

One fighter attempts to light the timber with a torch. His forehead explodes with a musket ball's impact.

Another grabs the flame and stumbles backward, dead from a defender's volley.

John Watts leaps to recover, but a defender ball rips through his leg into his second calf. Dideyohvsgi and Ben surge to their leader's aid, grasp him under his armpits, and pull him away from the stockade and into the safety of the trees.

The shaman examines the wound.

"They were ready! They knew we were coming!" Watts struggles to view Buchannan's Station as the staccato of musket fire continues to reverberate from the attack.

"The ball went through your right, but it's lodged in your left calf!" the healer squints in the darkness. "I need light."

"I'll get a torch," Benjamin leaps to his feet.

"Too much death. They have many long guns and complete protection behind their walls. The flames on the stockade, can you see the fire?" John Watts grabs Ben's ankle.

"Let him," the medicine man sweeps grip away. "I have to cut that lead out."

"Our warriors climb the walls," Ben kicks and runs for a torch.

"Our men! We need them for French Lick!"

"Be still. You kick and you lose more blood," the younger attempts to hold his patient's legs motionless.

"Dideyohvsgi! If I die here, swear on the year's I have known you will avenge this…this…!" John Watts grabs the shaman's knee.

"Betrayal?"

"Yes! One of our people warned them. If you find out who, kill him!" The patient grits his teeth in pain.

Ben returns with a torch. "Someone made the top of the stockade, but they killed him. It doesn't go well. No fire. No withdrawal. Our warriors throw themselves against the wall!"

"And die!" Watts feints from his wound.

Dideyohvsgi sticks his knife into the torch's flame and holds it. "At least the old man's still. I have to get that lead out of him."

Ben stares at his friend. "I didn't tell Watts, but we've lost over half of our men. You told me North is blue for sadness and defeat."

***

That night, twenty defenders slaughtered hundreds of attackers whose goal was not Buchanan's Station but the Cumberland settlements.

Without a loss, the settlers fired from portholes supported by wives and children who reloaded muskets.

John Watts, with the largest assembly of Cherokee warriors, plus Spanish and British support, cannot overwhelm the land now known as Tennessee.

CHAPTER THIRTY — Hightower

DRᏠOⁱꞋᏚᎠꞋYAJEᏘᏡᎬꞀᏏᏔWᏝꞀGMᎻᏒOIHᏃᎩᎾᏘᎾᏁhZᏈOᵛ

Dideyohvsgi and Ben retreat south with John Watts and his surviving warriors.

Their leader, resembling St. Clair in his defeat on the Wabash, rides a makeshift stretcher suspended between two horses.

Other wounded and dying Cherokee suffer over primitive trails on horse-drawn litters.

The force travels as nomads with their women, children, and possessions.

Most of the force's mounts survive Buchannan's Station and provide easier transport for the large settlement on the move.

The vanquished sing as they retreat, "diniyotli - diniyotli - diniyotli – dohitsu – dohitsu. gadosdi hada - gadosdi hada - gadosdi hada - diniyotli - diniyotli."

Ben rides beside his friend. "They sound sad?"

"It is a grieving song. They remember our dead."

"Too many of them. War and the pox destroy your Nation."

Dideyohvsgi continues without looking ahead.

His eyes stare, but his mind focuses on other thoughts. "We are no longer what we were. The Whites leave us nothing."

"That my people share," Benjamin nods.

"We have lost our future." The medicine man stares at his friend. "Where do we find a new one?"

"Mine came with free papers," the Freedman's horse snorts, "but yours lies elsewhere. Many more will die in your search."

"John Watts won't accept this defeat." Dideyohvsgi clenches his fists. "The warrior in his soul blames the traitor that told the Whites we were coming."

"He should blame his Unetlanvhi," Ben points at the sky.

"My people abandon those notions," the medicine man gazes skyward, "and have done so for generations."

"And you?" The Freedman turns to his companion.

"I came from Cherokee Rock and Son of Stone Cloud's enlightenment." Dideyohvsgi breathes the wind and soaks sunlight into his face. "The old ideas take modern meaning, and the good wolf feeds my soul."

The medicine man guides his horse from the trail and the column of defeated fighters.

He directs his path into unexplored land.

Benjamin stares at the warriors in the line before him, shakes his head, and turns his mount to follow his old friend into the future.

***

Unknown to the two friends and to the vanquished war party as they travel homeward, Brigadier General John Sevier and the Southwest Territory Militia invade Ustanali on the Coosawattee River, the traditional seat of Cherokee government.

The colonials arrive in a town deserted, its residents away with John Watts.

Troops destroy the settlement and days later meet scouts from the main returning body of fighters.

Scouting warriors skirmish, and Sevier pursues them southward.

Dideyohvsgi and Benjamin ride through the woods alone.

Musket fire in the distance attracts attention.

"Fighting." The medicine man stops his mount and listens.

"Not enough to be a large group," Ben stares eastward. "Watts released his allies. Only Chickamaugas return this way, and they split up into smaller groups. Could be any of us."

"We better try to help." Dideyohvsgi heels his horse East.

***

The two travel through the woods and stop below the ridge of a hill. They tie their horses to trees and slip up the ascent to the top on their stomachs.

At the base of the rise, bodies lie scattered behind dead logs and under timber.

The smell of black gunpowder hangs in the air, but nothing moves.

"You see any settlers?" Ben looks at his friend.

"No, those are ours. Let's get our horses." Dideyohvsgi stands, and the Freedman follows him to their mounts.

As they ride along the hill into the lower land, the medicine man's hands tremble as he observes a massacre.

Scalped Cherokee women and children ripped from chin to their navels spill intestines across the soil.

Several men, ineffective guards, mutilated, sprawl dead.

From trees, two partially skinned animal carcasses hang.

"These were hunting deer." Dideyohvsgi slides off his horse and examines a United States Army issued bayonet.

He holds the knife for Ben to see. "Has to be militia. Watts is moving south. Think he knows soldiers follow him?"

"They travel in small groups. This one, the militia caught, but they're stragglers." The Freedman studies the blade. "Watts may not know."

"I can't go home. We must warn him," the medicine man takes the army weapon and tucks it away in his pack.

"Stuck with you this long." Benjamin chuckles. "Might as well ride more."

"There's a holy place on the Etowah River, where my ancestors built mounds." Dideyohvsgi stares southward. "Watts moves in that direction. We can join them before they get that far."

***

Days later, the two friends lie at the top of white cliffs on one side of the Etowah with other Watt's warriors, armed with muskets under the command of the war leader Kingfisher.

"Hold your fire until they get in the river. Pass the order along the line." Dideyohvsgi keeps his head low as he looks at Benjamin.

The Freedman relates the directions to the next warrior lying along the cliff's top.

Below on the opposite shore of the Etowah, blue coat troops under the command of General John Sevier of the Southwest Territory United States Militia and Governor Blount prepare to cross.

Too deep to wade, the estuary forms a natural defensive barrier below Watts' assembled scouts and sharpshooters.

Ben watches. "They're pulling canoes and rafts."

"Those white straps will make fine targets." The medicine man steadies his musket on a rock.

Several dozen groups of soldiers pull their transports to river's edge and launch, unaware the Chickamauga's primary defensive group waits in ambush.

Boats slide into the water, and troops call encouragement to one another as they row.

The line moves. Muskets pile together on the hulls. Paddles splash, and most of the force's gunpowder dampens.

As the crossing reaches mid-point, Dideyohvsgi and Ben, with a hundred or more warriors and scouts, open fire.

White powder smoke drifts above the carnage as most of the rowers fall dead or wounded in their canoes or the torrent.

The two friends reload their weapons as the soldiers below turn their crafts in panic to return to shore.

A second volley from above falls many of the retreaters.

"They can't cross!" Ben watches as musket smoke clears.

"These are militia, not settlers. They will try again, I expect." Dideyohvsgi reloads and both wait.

Atop the cliffs, the defending Chickamaugas shift positions for better firing lines and prepare for the next crossing attempt. They settle into rocks and bring logs from the woods.

Nothing moves across the river.

"What do you think they're doing?" Benjamin rolls on his back and faces his friend.

"Massing more soldiers? Maybe moving their rafts upriver?" the medicine man inspects the far bank.

"They have to get dry powder," Ben checks his reload.

Kingfisher's force on the cliffs fortifies their positions and waits as the sun climbs in the sky.

"Aren't there shallows in the river?" Benjamin jerks a thumb southward.

"Yes. Watts left a group there to guard, but our scouts said Seiver's major body is here." Dideyohvsgi looks in the direction of his friend's point.

The defenders wait until distant musket fire interrupts the calm.

Volleys reverberate over the estuary and rise as beacons to the cliffs.

This warning continues, and the warriors on the cliff listen with alarm.

A young warrior moves along the defensive line on the cliff's edge. "Move South! Kingfisher says the militia cross. Hurry!"

The scouts and sharpshooters desert their position above the river and rush southward through the woods to support the shallow crossing's forces.

***

As Dideyohvsgi and Benjamin jog with their fellow fighters, the distant fire decreases to silence.

"No more shooting. You think they overran us?" Ben uses his musket to deflect tree branches and undergrowth.

The warriors smash through the brush as a group and rush to aid their men and protect their families.

"Only thing it could mean is they crossed. The women and children camp near there!" the medicine man follows Benjamin's trail.

A line in the woods ahead explodes white powder smoke, and many runners fall.

The friends drop to their bellies.

Smoke clears.

"Bluecoats!" The shaman spots a white cross against blue.

Kingfisher rallies his men, and they charge the militia with whoops and war clubs.

Another volley from the trees decimates the attackers.

Kingfisher falls with a musket ball in his temple.

"You okay?" Dideyohvsgi crawls on the ground face to face with Ben.

"I am, but Kingfisher's dead." The Freedman hugs the soil as he scrambles through the brush. "Not good."

CHAPTER THIRTY-ONE — Assimilation

ᎠᏣᎢᏐᎣᎢᏍᎤᏉᏆᏯᎠᏤᏫᏇᏈᎠᎵᏐᏪᏍᏑᏣᎷᎶᎪᏪᏊᎠᎯᎭᏓᏯᎦᎬᎠᏍᎻᏃᏬᎤ

Dideyohvsgi and Benjamin, with the remnants of John Watts' force, camp that night without fires or fresh water. The two friends with muskets crouch behind fallen logs in the trees, away from the encampment's perimeter. They watch for signs of pursuit from General Seiver's militia.

"With this clear sky, I see Walela," Ben nudges his fellow guard. "She loves to sit near the cows and stare at the stars."

"I know. I've seen you both gazing," the medicine man peers into the dark forest.

"The woman I love watches without me," Benjamin lowers his face and studies a grasshopper on the log near his chin. "I am sick of this war against the Whites. I'm not even Cherokee and I want to go home."

"Look at that Hackberry out there. Something moved." Dideyohvsgi squints into the darkness. Both men flatten behind the log and peek over muskets.

"Don't see a thing." Ben drops his head and checks his weapon.

"Because you're not looking," the shaman cocks a musket, and his companion returns to a firing position. "A soldier."

"It's not a deer?"

At the end of the tree line, a cluck-cluck sounds.

The Freedman relaxes. "Just a turkey."

Dideyohvsgi cups his hand on mouth and gobbles in return. "No, a scout."

A warrior jogs across the clearing and joins the two sentries.

Dideyohvsgi slaps the young man on his shoulders, "Sequoyah! Good, you are alive."

"I escaped with Tecumseh and a few others," the youngster elbows Ben's back. "They went home, and I was trying to find others. We found a wounded courier from the north. Our men fighting with the Western Confederacy are dead. Mad Anthony Wayne's troops defeated us at a place called Fallen Timbers."

"We cannot defeat the Whites." Dideyohvsgi accepts the news and bows a head.

"Watts camps back there," Ben points.

"Better go tell him." the medicine man pats Sequoyah.

Dideyohvsgi and Benjamin watch the young fellow trot into the darkness to relay the dark message to the war leader.

"We don't need two as sentries. Get some sleep?" Dideyohvsgi nods to his Freedman friend.

"No. Wide awake. You rest. I'll wake you."

The healer settles against the log, "Don't need to tell me twice."

Benjamin sits with a musket propped, barrel out, on the bark.

***

Dideyohvsgi's mind shifts from sentry duty and dream rides a cloud through dark skies and sparkling moonlit time to an earlier vision of his heritage.

Below the sky, in a lush northern wooded landscape, a high mound supports a seven-sided council house.

Representatives of each Cherokee clan occupy a section and speak for large populations far exceeding those in this medicine man's memory.

Officials, Dideyohvsgi identifies as priests and healers by age and ceremonial garb, stand in the center.

A leader in a white vest wears a wide hand-woven cinch below a conch shell chest plate and a light deer skin cloak with moccasins painted with streaks of rust. Over shoulders, he drapes a cape of swan feathers.

Seven clan leaders nearby hold ritual pipes with long wood stems and carved bowls.

The dream cloud deposits its passenger in the center of the council.

"We invoke blessings, remove filth from the polluted and clean for life," the Ookah (ᎤᎧ oo-ka, Greatest High Priest) holds palms up as he addresses the assemblage. "The Spirits work..."

The man drops both arms and turns to face the interruption.

Dideyohvsgi stands alone and deserted.

An assistant and seven holy men, the principal shamans of the clans, stand near with mouths open and minds fixed upon the visitor from the future.

"Who are you?" The Ookah shakes a buck's horn.

"I am Dideyohvsgi, student of Son of Stone Cloud and Shaman of the Paint Clan."

"Of whom?" The inquisitor's eyes widen with fear and suspicion.

"That's a lie!" One medicine man steps forward. "I am the clan's principal healer!"

Dideyohvsgi views an enemy incarnated, but the priest

shows no light of recognition. "By what name are you known?"
The visitor nods respect for this ancestor.

"Mohi!"

"We know of no other Paint Clan healer." The Ookah moves
closer and peers at his visitor. "But the Unetlanvhi (ᎤᏁᏓᏅᎯ
u-ne-tla-nv-hi, Creator God) spoke of a Stone Cloud in our
night talk. He said this hero comes to lead the Tsalagi into the
future."

"He leads nowhere!" Mohi grasps the knife at his belt.

"Hold. Dare you question dreams?" The spiritual leader
points with an antler.

"Not the vision but the interpretation, Most Beloved
Healer."

The Ookah lowers his pointed tip. "This visitor is its fulfill-
ment! The promised Shaman."

The assembled crowd rises and celebrates.

"Dideyohvsgi!"

The exalted object of the crowd's enthusiasm attempts to
quell the fanaticism. "No! Listen! I am not a guide! I am not
Stone Cloud! I am from the future!" The words impact the
fanatics and stoke excess, the opposite of their intent.

The Ookah sucks a deep intake from a ceremonial pipe into
lungs and blows the smoke into Dideyohvsgi's lips.

His knees buckle and eyes roll upward under weak eyelids.

Lead by the beloved leaders of the clans, without Mohi who
steps aside in protest, the crowd lifts a new exalted one above
their heads and sweeps him to a special lodge of long reeds
bent and strapped together with sinew.

The seven representatives undress and bathe the visitor with
hickory root water.

When clean, they dress Dideyohvsgi in a robe of feathers and place a yellow carved wooden staff in his hand. They paint his face white and adorn the head in goose down.

Bearers arrive outside the lodge with a stretcher covered with deer skins.

The seven leaders lift their new religious icon and carry him toward the waiting crowd atop the ceremonial mound.

Propped on soft bales of animal pelts, Dideyohvsgi attempts to focus and concentrate, but his vision remains cloudy and unfocused.

Before and behind the Cherokee-born carrier with its cargo of visitor and yellow walking staff, leaders parade a new Ookah.

They chant in rhythm with steps.

The procession halts atop the ceremonial mound, and an honored warrior hoists, with the help of attendants, Dideyohvsgi onto his back.

He carries the weight to a prepared white elk-hide mat piled with deer skins.

Helpers prop the unresponsive burden on a perch in a seated position.

Dideyohvsgi's eyes try to focus on the first bearer of gifts.

A clan representative lays a fan of fine eagle feathers. Another follows with sacred tobacco and a third with a lit pipe.

Attendants place the smoke on lips and press his abdomen to help him draw.

The leaders also use individual pipes, and fumes hang in the air as the assembly files past and pays homage to a new, most exalted, beloved one.

As they return to their places, each settles into a night of prayer for the Unetlanvhi blessings, lifelong successes, and immense happiness.

As the morning sun glints on the horizon, the new prophet straightens his ceremonial robe and rises.

He looks to the light and spreads arms in welcome.

An elderly attendant turns to the crowd, "I pass to this dream promised Ookah all authority under the commands of the Unetlanvhi and vow obedience."

A standard bearer carries a pole with a carved wooden eagle on top.

Flying from the summit, a deer skin painted with white spots flaps in the morning breeze.

The old man extends arms to the pennant, "Purity adorns his symbol, for unity and prosperity, the Peace Leader!"

Dideyohvsgi's head feels less confused, struggles to open his mouth and move lips. "Ho!" A thought simplifies.

Mohi marches to the ceremonial mound's crest with a second standard.

This features red spots on deer skin.

Into the earth, the warrior plants the pole. "White leader, you may be! But I also had a dream. My banner of war leads into the future. The people follow me on a path of blood!"

Dideyohvsgi wakens from discomfort cramped against a wood log.

He focuses on the face of Benjamin Waters.

"Are you sick? You're sweating and mumbling."

"No, dreaming."

"Not peacefully. Time for your watch." Ben settles against the log.

***

Next day, John Watts gathers the remaining forces in the center of the encampment.

The group includes women, children, wounded and the recovering, along with a spattering of warriors plus Dideyohvsgi and Benjamin.

The leader's voice echoes across the crowd, distinctive, with a subdued tone and sad timbre. "I must take responsibility for these failures. We lost brave men on the Wabash, more at the Etowah. Mad Anthony Wayne defeated our allies of the Western Confederacy, and few warriors returned. The Spanish withdraw support and fight with France. Without supplies, I cannot feed the fighters."

A low, frustrated moan swells from the assembly.

"I do not demand more. A time of few choices approaches. We must accommodate and assimilate with Whites. We lay clubs on the ground and make a truce with Governor Blount. I do this. At peace, build a new life for your families. Thank you for the sacrifices, loyalty, and support. Gratitude is never enough. Go home to loved ones. May Unetlanvhi help you find better lives."

CHAPTER THIRTY-TWO — Indictment

ᎲᎢᎠ·ᎩᏍꭳᏥ·ᏯᎪᏙᏍ·ꮿ·ᎯᎢᎮꮃᎦᏓ·ᎮᎦꭴᎪᎭ·ᎣᎢᎮᏏ·ᎤᎬ·Ꭷ·Ꮎ·ᎮᎾ·ᎿᏃᎤ

Snow falls during the winter of 1798 on the Over-hill settlement, Great Tellico, near Tellico Blockhouse in Tennessee. This three-year-old sixteenth state of a maturing United States of America under President John Adams completes an addendum to the Treaty of Holston.

Wrapped in blankets, Hanging Maw represents the northern clans allied with the defeated Western Confederacy, and John Watts, from the Chicamauguas to the south plus thirty-nine attached leaders and warriors stand, dark totems in the snow.

Momentous events await inside a cabin where commissioners Thomas Butler, George Walton, and agent Silas Dinsmoor, of the United States, prepare a document of truce.

Thomas Butler and George Walton, with a translator, step outside and see the Cherokee representation.

Butler steps forward. "Today we renew a perpetual peace. Our treaties continue in full force. Your lands stay the same except for East Tennessee, which you cede to the United States. For that land, we pay five thousand dollars and one thousand annual dollars. Plus, we grant annual sustenance stipends for a 'reasonable' number." The representative pauses for reaction from the group and receives none. "Both sides execute this treaty in good faith."

The assembly in the snow stares hatred at their enemies.

As the translator finishes, Butler leans to Walton, "They don't react. Do they understand?"

Walton steps forward, "Those who sign, do so inside the cabin."

Hanging Maw and John Watts move to the building's door.

Walton grasps Butler's elbow, "I believe this one's the half-breed they call Watts."

The Cherokee freezes.

Hanging Maw turns to prevent potential trouble.

Instead, the man steels his shoulders, "Yes," in perfect English the leader rejects the insult, "Mr. Walton. My mother was White. I understand the choice of words. Your race is arrogant but victorious."

The assembled Cherokee warriors and leaders follow into the cabin and sign agreement with a powerful new nation that, unknown upon signing, leads into an era of diplomacy, education, and assimilation with their conquerors.

***

Far away from Tellico, Dideyohvsgi studies venison and corn pone.

On a blanket before a fire in Walela's cabin, he shuns dinner with Benjamin's family.

Ben notices the lack of appetite. "What's bothering you?"

The medicine man breaks the reverie and smiles, "Nothing that should concern good folks. Different times approach. You depend upon each other."

Walela serves more corn pone. "Benjamin considers you a brother."

"Brothers by shared blood." Ben studies his friend. "I have news that may perk your interest. Sequoya stopped for provisions this morning when you were searching for herbs in the woods."

"Sorry I missed that."

"He stayed long enough to pick up jerky and pemmican." The Freedman pauses and takes a breath. "But he brought information. John Watts learned Mohi warned the settlers at Zeigler's Station. Governor Blount, his old friend from the parlay, bought that information from the traitor."

"No surprise." Dideyohvsgi shows interest. "Did Watts execute him?"

"No. Sequoyah said Mohi disappeared."

"Off spending the governor's money," the medicine man glances at Walela.

She catches the look. "What?"

"Your love and I shared blood in war, but our paths separate."

The woman looks at the Freedman.

"How so?" Benjamin's brows furrow.

"They granted you that property. Ever since we met, you dreamed of a cotton farm."

"Watts' payment." Ben smiles. "Better than anyone, you know I earned it. Do you resent my reward? You received nothing?"

"No, you are non-Cherokee. Our people own the land together."

"Then why the long face?" The friend sets venison aside to listen.

"Not because of you, family, clan, or race. Training by Son of Stone Cloud as a shaman tells me when the mind is at rest. I support the effort and plan to help you build a life."

Walela beams.

"But this soul searches for a different future. I definitely don't want to become a farmer." Dideyohvsgi's chest vibrates with a chuckle.

The woman smiles.

"No insult intended, but Cherokee Rock, the war, smallpox, the people's leaders, and my ability to talk to animals show me Unetlanvhi guides."

Ben and Walela sit in silence with heartbeats in empathy.

"I plan to go to Cherokee Rock."

"I'll go with you, Brother." The cotton farmer looks to his wife for approval.

Dideyohvsgi smiles. "No. Without you, as before Saloli, this soul searches alone."

***

Months afterward, Spring arrives across the land that surrounds the outcrop, an iconic symbol of a Nation. Warmth and rains burst flowers from the earth to carpet the meadows. Bees pollinate from one bloom to another.

Dideyohvsgi sits in the color and counts the insects.

The medicine man entices a bee to a forefinger. The small flying machine deposits pollen on one fingernail, and after the shaman expresses thanks, it continues to a next perch.

The nectar sparkles on the medicine man's nail as he coexists with nature and collects the elixir with his tongue.

In peace, he returns to Cherokee Rock and sleeps under its massive protection. He rests and prepares for the next day's commune with bees.

Weeks pass before sounds from the night sky disturb the routine.

***

Late in the evening, long after the moon's rise, the healer steps from under the massive outcrop and inspects the heavens.

Among the millions of stars, several move closer and trail sparks, large fireflies that sweep from horizon to moon. They dart in tandem, bird flocks in search of aerial victims.

With a wild rush of wind, one dives toward Dideyohvsgi, and emits a high-pitched raven's cry.

The flier hovers with the sound of a giant hummingbird, its wings beat the air and blow the human's face. Its body resembles an ancient, time-wrinkled bat.

"This is Cherokee Rock, Raven Mocker!" Dideyohvsgi spreads arms and his hair whips from the air flow's force. "I am alone and alive. Why do you visit here? No one is ill."

"You lie, Shaman. This place is the real people's home. They all live here and sicken as your Nation perishes." The ancient one's voice vibrates with a rhythmic beat that reinforces words. "I am old. They replenish my vitals. Pity you live."

"Our numbers are few, and I hear multitudes of you in the air. I know you sucked the blood and ate the hearts of those who perished from the pox or died in battle."

"But more weaken. Look at the sky! My brothers and sisters fly at each other in eagerness. A feast comes."

"Yes, we are weak," the medicine man clenches both fists at the apparition, "but I am the Paint Clan's shaman with the skills of Son of Stone Cloud. I command, let go!"

The mocker cackles, and Cherokee Rock reverberates from the sound. "That old useless healer, champion of a weak and dying race driven from lands by disease and war, is gone! We come! Tonight, your kind nears readiness. Because your teacher's inedible flesh delayed my flight, I warn of our coming."

With a suction the strength of a spring tornado, the Raven Mocker joins other filthy fliers that flash across the moon.

Night's silence falls upon the medicine man's shoulders.

CHAPTER THIRTY-THREE — Resolve

DRᏠᏫᎢᏍᏬᏏᎩᎯᏎᎬᏒᎯᏔᎶᏪᏛᏒᏍᎹᎦᏧᏫᏏᎲᏛᏚᏪᎾᏛᏏᏂᎬᎯᏫ

In the night's peace under starlit skies, Dideyohvsgi listens for more calls. Soft breezes dry fear-sweat from under his eyes, and his senses tune into nature.

Crickets click across Cherokee Rock.

The shaman drops to knees. "Small one of the dark, did you hear those words and see the Raven Mockers?"

"Click, Crick, yes and I warn, be afraid."

"I am, friend. I fear for my people and their future."

The cricket rubs hind legs together, and the sound translates to Dideyohvsgi's talented ear, "Tonight, rest under this protective outcrop, but tomorrow, consult with the animals."

The following morning, Dideyohvsgi leaves the rock's protection. He walks through fresh air to the river that forks nearby.

The seeker drops to knees and cups water to mouth.

A catfish watches, twitches whiskers and poises to dart out of contact.

"Wait! I must speak to you," the shaman drops both hands.

"You want to grab me for supper?" the fish drifts with the current.

"No. But I have eaten your brothers and sisters."

"Then I stay comfortable out of grasp. We miss our siblings but coexist with the Tsalagi. You eat what you take. No as the White man who sells us in markets."

"True," Dideyohvsgi stands. "But how did you know that?"

"Cousins swim in rivers near their cities." The fish's tail moves against the water's flow for stabilization beyond reach. "Fish mongers trade at the river. We watch. The news of the atrocities travels. Why do you exchange words with me?"

"Cricket said consult with animals."

"Consult? That word means to seek guidance or information. Strange. The real people ignored us long ago."

"True, Catfish," the healer nods in agreement. "But we have not forgotten how. So, I talk to you now."

"This is the first consultation in a lifetime. You must want something."

"I do. My race no longer communicates. Times change," the medicine man spreads his arms. "Most died in war or of the White man's diseases. Few remain. Raven Mockers hover and wait for the remaining."

"I know. We enjoyed the nights before without their flights, but our hearts are small, and they have no appetite. Why should we care?"

Dideyohvsgi returns to knees beside the stream. "Simple. If they eat the real humans, the world becomes White."

The catfish ponders for a moment with whiskers stirring bottom sand. "You convince me. Tomorrow morning, gather the animals here. I bring those who speak for the fish. Birds are welcome, but no bears, or any fowls that consume flesh covered by scales." The whiskered one ceases upstream tail action and flows away.

The medicine man turns to the woods.

A doe watches from behind a tree.

"A word, Beautiful Deer," Dideyohvsgi extends open hands and shows no threat. "May I come closer?"

"Leave. I thirst for morning water."

"Let us drink together?" The shaman backs away.

The animal flicks an ear. "You want me to drink with someone that talks to a stream?"

The medicine man chuckles, and the doe reacts backward a step before he chokes the laugh. "I spoke to a catfish on the water's bottom."

"You make me nervous. Are you hunting?"

"I intend no harm. Come."

The deer slips to the bank and lowers a nose into the water.

The shaman sits in the grass, and she lifts a head. "What do you wish to discuss?"

"Wildlife is plentiful, and your lands stretch beyond horizons." Dideyohvsgi watches for reactions. "My people die, and others move into our lodges. Raven Mockers gather to collect the last."

"Without human hearts, the bat creatures starve."

"True, Beautiful Deer."

"At least they don't use your pelts as rugs on floors?"

"Cricket said to consult with wildlife. I meet the fish on the stream's banks in the morning," Dideyohvsgi looks into the doe's eyes. "Could you collect others?"

"Whites stretch our skin as chair covers. The Tsalagi are fewer. I promise to bring my kind." The doe bounds away into the woods.

A Mockingbird watches from a tree nearby. "I watched and listened. You waste effort and appear pitiful. But I am territorial and take offense. Leave this stream at once, and I will also promise to gather the birds."

"On one condition," Dideyohvsgi points at the bird. "None attend that eat catfish."

***

That evening, under protection of Cherokee Rock, the medicine man wakens and listens to the wings of Raven Mockers hover high above the soul of the people.

He turns on his mat and waits for sunlight.

***

Fish swim close during the darkness before the morning's conference.

With first light, Beautiful Deer, a buffalo from the west, a southern armadillo, an elk from the north, and an eastern alligator arrive. They drink water from the stream.

The medicine man joins the assemblage as the birds gather as promised.

"Thank you for attending." The shaman surveys the audience.

"You are a Tsalagi," Wolf notices. "Do you represent humans?"

"No. I speak for my brothers," the healer stands straight and firms his voice. "My people vanish from this earth. Raven Mockers gather to prey upon the remains. I ask you here to plead for aid."

"In times past, we grazed in this land," Buffalo snorts, and samples the grass. "You ambushed our herds with spears and arrows for meat and hides. Why should we listen?"

310

"We only take for use." The shaman nods at the hulk of an animal.

"True," it stomps one hoof. "But we deserted these hills and migrated to the west."

"And how is life there?" Dideyohvsgi crosses arms across chest.

"White men less numerous than you kill with large guns and slice off our skins. They waste our meat, and our bones bleach in the sun. Many groups move further westward."

"They outnumber the bison. You see the hide hunters," the medicine man shakes a head.

The burly beast snorts and stirs the dust.

"Bison cannot defend against weapons. My kind moved west, but even now we die."

Mockingbird flaps low over the group, "You meet in my territory. Come to the point, so this conference ends. What do you want, Shaman?"

"Other White humans invade from the East. Our fighters are brave, but we lose, and the future greets Raven Mockers." Dideyohvsgi looks over the audience. "I propose an alliance between the genuine humans and those of the wild. Our forces kill the invaders. Animals reclaim their kinsmen such as horses captured and trained to serve. Fish avoid for safety. Birds fly west past the buffalo, especially the slaughtered. Deprive the invaders of food and transportation while my people resist. It is the only way to win!"

Beautiful Deer drinks from the river and rises. "I carry a fawn and only wish for peace. But we must decide. Shaman, rest in the shade of Cherokee Rock. Allow time to consider these matters.

***

Hours later, Mockingbird summons Dideyohvsgi.

Buffalo settles to the ground from hooves. "Medicine man, the animals, fish and birds choose me to speak because I am the most displaced. We are not without empathy, but the Whites are many and powerful. You are too few to defend nature as allies. You abandoned and enslaved humans that are not your enemies, or White. For decades, you drift from the ways of Unetlanvhi. Now is too late. We cannot help."

Dideyohvsgi stands in silence for a moment and then turns to Beautiful Deer. "I hear the words. But you speak a death knell for my people?"

The doe steps forward and rubs a nose on the shaman's chest. "You may think so. The animals, birds and fish urge a return to the traditional ways. Listen to Unetlanvhi. Give up the long fight. Reinvent and merge with the Whites. Convert and walk with their march over the earth."

The shaman rubs Beautiful Deer behind an ear. "The real people lost our war. The animals consider us weak and unworthy as allies."

The doe nuzzles closer, "But you talk to animals. You have the Creator God's blessing."

"I have. And a responsibility." Dideyohvsgi gazes across the meadow and the forests at Cherokee Rock. "Alone, I must abandon my war against Whites and lead the clans along ancient paths together, to win the peace."

CHAPTER THIRTY-FOUR — Heritage

DRᏁᏬOᎢiᏕᎠᏈYᎪJEᏫᏁᎪᏂᎱᏓᏯᏍᎱᎢᏀᏀᎷᎯᏋᎣᏆᎯᎲᏃᏪᎾᏃᏋᎯᏝᎾᏁᎲᏃᏀᎤᏔ

Following the winter peace treaty of Tellico Blockhouse in 1798 and Dideyohvsgi's Spring 1799 council with the animals, the warrior leaders of the lower towns, those who fought under Dragging Canoe and John Watts, support tribal stability and dominate affairs.

The medicine man, dejected by nature and conquered by White invasion, attempts solace in the security of Cherokee Rock.

He tosses in sleep.

"Dideyohvsgi!" A voice calls in the shaman's dreams.

"We lost the battle with the White's government." The healer's eyes explore his inner eyelids.

"Take heart."

The shaman's mind searches for the speaker. "Beautiful Deer and Buffalo do not support further resistance. Why do you disturb?"

"Do you trust me, old friend?"

"Who are you?"

"I am a teacher and fellow warrior. Fight the Creator God's battles alone no longer."

The medicine man rolls. "I do not want war, only peace."

"Open your eyes, Enoli."

***

The shaman flutters both eyelids. Silhouetted by moonlight from outside Cherokee Rock, Son of Stone Cloud stands over his sleeping mat.

Dideyohvsgi sits. "I do not fear you," he rubs hands together. "I welcome an ally."

"The people's soul lies under this outcrop as you do. I am more than an ally. I am your home. But I cannot stay."

"Why do you visit, Teacher?"

The vision spreads his arms, "I spoke with Sulu. The people grow corn with White men's tools and ways. Sulu's dying instructions taught her sons how to plant and farm, and she threatens to desert over this change. She promises a tremendous hailstorm upon those who follow the destruction of the earth. Their destiny is death in the ice storm. Your heart seeks a return to the old practices. But the people's faith waivers. Whites spread belief in the Son of their God. They leave Unetlanvhi for the convenience of an iron plow."

"How can I prevent this, Holy One?"

"They convert one believer at a time. Do the same."

"We lack numbers, but in whole are many. Do I have time for such a task?"

"Start with the influential. James Vann fought with us but now gives land to the Moravian Brethren who worship the White's Christ. You can no longer grieve at Cherokee Rock. Waken and travel to Vann's Diamond Hill Plantation where the Christians set up a school for children."

"I wish to fight no more, much less with my own." Dideyohvsgi wraps arms around Son of Stone Cloud. "Help."

The spirit of the great healer pushes the student away. "Your mission is not war, but education. Teach people the old ways. The Whites name their school Spring Place Mission. Resist the black book and invite lives to old callings. Call your invitation the Ghost Dance, and remember what I teach."

Dideyohvsgi rises from his sleeping pallet and stands beside Son of Stone Cloud.

The night visitor slips one arm around the student's shoulder and chants in rhythm with stomping feet. "Like this. This is the Cherokee reel. Move at my side until light comes. Then leave for Spring Place Mission."

The two men's steps echo through the grotto.

The sounds rest with the spirits of ancestors.

As daylight arrives, Son of Stone Cloud retires.

***

Dideyohvsgi travels alone to James Vann's plantation, unaware that Thomas Jefferson, President of the United States, eliminates Cherokee ownership of land within the borders of Georgia.

The State, in return, grants its western part, which will become Arkansas, to the federal government.

Operated by Moravian missionaries John and Anna Rosina Gambold in the northwest corner, Spring Place Mission educates many of the mixed-race elite families' children. These include James Vann, The Ridge, David Watie, and the Hicks.

When Dideyohvsgi arrives, he skips confrontation with the Christians and visits a fellow warrior and the Moravian's benefactor.

"It is good we see each other again." The medicine man smokes a pipe with the younger veteran James Vann. "White's blood stains our hands. I have been recovering from the wars at Cherokee Rock. My soul healed, and I spoke with the ghost of Son of Stone Cloud."

"And through those many days, I live in peace with old enemies. They respect accumulation, which they call wealth. I gather those things they like. The best is whiskey." The host sips from a small Hill and Hill bottle.

"I passed by the school where the White woman, Anna Rosina, trains children to merge with the Whites. Why do you allow that mission on our lands?"

"You fought with Watts as I did." Vann straightens in the chair. "Respect for that war record allows you to challenge my motives."

Dideyohvsgi nods understanding.

"John and our men lost," the host stands. "It's time to learn and understand new ways. Anna Rosina believes in a simple White man's faith, that happiness is a gift from God for salvation, an unintrusive and heart-relationship in fellowship with people. Service to humans is deity worship. Educating children is duty. What is wrong with that?"

"Our lands are for us. Many shed blood and met Raven Mockers for less."

"Please listen, Dideyohvsgi, my friend, student of Son of Stone Cloud, adviser to John Watts and Shaman of the Paint Clan. The president of the United States takes territories in Georgia, private property in return for lands further west. We lost our war, and the Whites won. We must adjust and adapt in peace. Even I accept their salvation from Anna Rosina."

Dideyohvsgi sits in stunned silence for a moment.

His words tremble with the flutter in his soul, "The mother of our clans abandons Tsalagi because we plow the earth with the White man's tools, grind corn in his mills, worship a God of his choice, and join with his women to bear children."

"So? What do you want, Dideyohvsgi?"

"You sit in foreign clothes before a house filled with goods provided by soil furrowed with implements in their way and send your sons and daughters to learn more from their teachers! Return to Son of Stone Cloud's ways. Hunt the hills, keep Whites east, and Unetlanvhi will bless the people."

Vann blows smoke on the ground. "A few still commune, as you describe, mostly the old and hardheaded. Others saw the blood in the snow at the Wabash. We thanked our maker, only to drown and die in the waters of Etowah. I'll never make that mistake again."

Dideyohvsgi rises and looks westward, "At Cherokee Rock, I talked with the buffalo who regret their journey west."

James Vann stands. "I listen and understand your heart. Most do not. But I have a suggestion."

"What?"

"Seek those that think as you. That is what Son of Stone Cloud and John Watts did, and they gained strength."

"The junior leaders do not agree."

Vann studies the ground for a moment, then raises his eyes to meet Dideyohvsgi's gaze. "One does. Find a brave warrior who fought with us on the Etowah, the Shawnee, Tecumseh."

"I remember him well. As you, he influences many."

"Stay the night, Dideyohvsgi. In the morning, many old fighters gather to join livestock with mine for market. Speak to them as you wish, for my heart agrees. But for now, I follow my purse."

***

Overnight, owners and families arrive at the plantation with animals they plan to sell. By full sun, a small crowd gathers around the steps of the main house.

Dideyohvsgi, after a brief introduction from James Vann, stands before his first audience. "I bring greetings from the ghost of Son of Stone Cloud who, under the protection of Cherokee Rock, taught worship. This is his Ghost Dance, I share. It symbolizes change, freedom for the real people, and deliverance from domination. The mother of this Nation abandons us. Why? Because we plow and mill as the White man. Return to the old ways. Hunt the hills. Wear traditional clothing and do not imitate. Abandon material goods and accept the blessings of Unetlanvhi!" The healer stomps and chants the Son of Stone Cloud's foot ritual on the porch.

After a moment, Dideyohvsgi reads his audience. A few nod in rhythm to the chant.

Most watch with expressions of incredulity.

The shaman stops and stares at James Vann.

His host steps forward. "To market! Gather the livestock."

The small crowd cheers and claps in response to the announcement.

***

Days later, after traveling on foot, Dideyohvsgi stands at the base of a hill near a small creek and peers across rows of green cotton that surround a cabin with a chimney that smokes. The medicine man walks forward and drops to haunches.

He examines one of the fresh plants and smiles.

The shaman follows a row of new growth to the log home. Benjamin Waters sits on the porch and enjoys the morning. His old friend saunters around the corner.

"Dideyohvsgi! Walela, it's Dideyohvsgi!"

The two men shake hands. "Blood brothers!" the Freedman slaps his Cherokee ceremonial sibling on the shoulder as the woman bursts out of the home.

"Welcome!" Benjamin's wife glows greeting. "You have been away far too long."

The healer enters.

An enormous fireplace dominates the space, and he eyes Benjamin Water's musket, which rests on pegs, suspended on display above the fire.

"You retired your weapon, I see," the medicine man grins.

"That's right. I am a cotton farmer now. This is a small place. It will grow. The biggest problem is finding labor to work in the fields. I can do only so much."

"Don't look this direction, Ben. I'm willing to help, but not for long. Keep working. You have done well with the land our grateful Nation gave a warrior in thanks."

"I thank the people and John Watts for the gift," Benjamin beckons his friend toward a seat. "Did you hear someone murdered him?"

"Yes. Was it political retribution?" The shaman sits.

"Rumor is Mohi did it. As a hired assassin," Ben reaches for a pipe.

"I don't question that. Anyone who knew that traitor, wouldn't," Dideyohvsgi digs in his pack for tobacco. "But enough talk of death. You need workers. Grow your own. Is Walela with child?"

The wife blushes as she places pemmican before the two men. "No, Shaman of the Paint Clan. We want children but none so far."

"No worry. I promise to pray to Selu," the shaman pats her arm, "and the Corn Goddess will help you produce a harvest to work cotton fields."

"I heard of your activity. Herders came through yesterday. Said an old fellow gave a speech on Vann's front porch a few days ago." Ben blows smoke toward the ceiling. "I figure that must have been you."

"Yes. But they showed little interest."

"Times change. These young fellows never heard of Son of Stone Cloud."

Dideyohvsgi puckers his lips and blows.

The tobacco fumes create rings. "True. That's why I need reinforcements."

Benjamin chuckles and nods his head no. "Not me this time, Blood Brother. This Freedman stays home to create a few field hands. But I will promise something."

"What's that, Ben?"

The husband looks at Walela, "I promised my wife, and swear this. This union's children must grow up to know and respect heritage. Both hers and mine."

CHAPTER THIRTY-FIVE — Wolves

ᎠᎡᏓᏍᎤᎢᏍᎤᏈᏯᎠᏤᏇᎵᎠᏲᎶᏎᏪᏍᎶᎬᎹᎠᏕᎤᎯᎲᏚᏯᎡᏉᎡᏄᎲᏃᏲᎤᎥ

Cherokee Rock, the monolith, stands dedicated to Unetlanvhi (ᎤᏁᏓᏃᎥᎯ u-ne-tla-nv-hi, Creator God). Its origins shroud in the history and traditions of a Nation.

The mass symbolizes a Tsalagi floating island in a sea hung by cords from the four directions. The rock begins when a water beetle descends from the sky to discover what is below. It dives to the water's bottom and returns with soft mud that expands in every direction and becomes earth.

Other animals wish to come. A Buzzard swoops to prepare for more life but avoids the soft ground. When the bird tires, its wings dip into the muck, and the action makes mountains and valleys.

Earth dries and more wildlife comes, but darkness reigns.

The sun sets itself on a sky track. Too low, it scorches the crayfish red.

Life changes the orb's elevation. During adjustment, they must stay awake for seven nights.

Only the owl and panther do. They receive night sight and can prey upon the others.

A few trees such as the Pine remain alert, but sleep forces the rest to drop leaves in the winter.

***

Dideyohvsgi stands in a valley before Cherokee Rock.

He thinks of the first people, a brother and sister. The male hits his sibling with a fish and tells her to multiply. She gives life to a child every seven days.

Much too soon, the new world has population. Women change this forever and prepare for birth in nine months.

The huge outcrop called Cherokee Rock looms above as the shaman thinks of his own mother's story. *"Your father's father said that two wolves battle for the soul. One is bad, angry, envious, jealous, filled with sorrow, regret, and greed. It feeds on arrogance, self-pity and guilt, resentment."*

She looks at the son to assure attention, "plus inferiority, lies, false pride, superiority, and ego."

"Evil eats wrong things. Am I as those?" Enoli stares into the mother's eyes.

"No. The other wolf is good. I pray to Unetlanvhi you become that. Its cubs are joy, peace, love, hope, serenity, humility, and kindness. They feed on benevolence, generosity, empathy, truth, compassion and faith."

Enoli thinks of this for a minute. "Which wins?"

Mother looks at the boy, "The one you feed."

***

That night Dideyohvsgi sleeps under the protecting outcrop.

Predator wild dogs hunt because they stayed awake for the seven days with the owl and the panther. With bellies full, they search for high places and howl at the moon.

Cherokee Rock stands higher than any other and attracts two black wolves who choose to sing from its heights.

The sound wakens Dideyohvsgi.

The medicine man loads venison into a basket. He climbs to the top of the outcrop. "Your songs disturb," the shaman steps forward.

"That is close enough," the wolf bares fangs.

"I mean no harm. Mother told of good and bad wolves. Which are you?"

"She didn't tell you?" the brother animal sniffs at the medicine man.

A second animal growls nearby, "Our song is of these hills and valleys. You are the first real person here in years."

First wolf relaxes, lips low over white teeth that flash in the moonlight.

"As cubs, our mother ordered us to hide from your smell," Second wolf recoils from Dideyohvsgi's scent.

"Don't hold back, listen." The medicine man sits cross-legged. "A spirit from Cherokee Rock advises that the real people fade, and our only hope is to return to the old ways. I teach that to the Nation, but they do not pay attention. I am a single shaman and insignificant when clans ignore healer powers."

"Mother feared you." First Wolf rubs its nose with a paw.

Dideyohvsgi extracts a piece of venison from the basket and pitches the meat near the wolf. He sniffs.

"My favor is not for sale," the doubter pulls away.

"She was right. We carry muskets and before that, bows with arrows and blow tube reeds that dispense death."

First Wolf gulps the tasty morsel, "Did you kill this deer?"

"Yes but asked permission. The doe could have no fawns, so she allowed me to harvest her."

The animal swallows a mouthful. "Wolves don't ask. We just take."

"You should act as the genuine people." Dideyohvsgi pitches another piece.

"Yes. There is much to learn from humans," First Wolf shares venison with his brother. Second smells before he bites.

"Travel with me. Help attract my people's attention. With two magnificent black wolves, they will listen."

Second's eyes narrow with suspicion. "Remember your mother's story, the opposing forces. Do you know which you ask?"

"She said the good wolves are the ones you feed."

"Wise woman." Second Wolf swallows his venison. "We hear the animals voted to not support you."

"That is true."

First Wolf steps close and rubs fur against the medicine man. "We suffer. Unetlanvhi whispers when we sleep with dreams of you."

Second Wolf paces to the shaman's side, "Yes, we are for you. He told us change was coming."

***

Weeks later, far from the rock, north of Spring Creek near the Georgia Road, built after the Treaty of Tellico over the middle of an ancient trading path, the people of a settlement stand in awe.

Dideyohvsgi and his two black wolves parade into their lives.

The shaman walks with his head held high and chin in the air. He wears a swan-feather cloak, chest length in front that sweeps low to his knees behind. On light moccasins in a white deerskin breechcloth and matching leggings, the shaman chants the Ghost Dance and shakes a rattle. In his other hand, the man carries an ornate beaded medicine bag.

First Wolf struts and snarls at his right knee, and Second Wolf hugs his left, both large, ferocious animals with black fur, in contrast to Dideyohvsgi's feathers and garb.

As they pass, a mother from the village gathers her two children for protection. "Here walks a great prophet with spirit escorts. Don't block his path."

A crowd follows the spectacle to the town's center and a modest ceremonial circle covered by a bark shingle roof.

The village's most beloved woman steps forward. "Medicine man, who are you and why do you visit us?"

The healer strides into the middle of the council house's shade, and the two wolves sit upon their haunches beside him. He raises a hand for silence.

The audience calms and eyes the impressive animals.

"You are our Nation. I am Dideyohvsgi of the Paint Clan. I come to you from Cherokee Rock, where I have walked with your ancestors. They tell me the Corn Goddess Selu abandons you because you farm in the White man's way with their tools. She predicts your crops fail. Your children grow hungry. Return to the old ways and desert the Son of their White God. Their mission school teaches you to become as they are, followers of those dunked in water."

The village's most beloved woman steps into the circle. "We use their plow to till our earth and his mill to grind our grain. He gives both for land that we signed away without our consent. He feeds the children and tells them stories from his black book. They do not starve and enjoy the tales."

"Selu refuses to grow life planted with iron tools. Unetlanvhi does not change. The ghost of Son of Stone Cloud appeared to me. They promise a massive hailstorm on the night of the full moon. The thunder ice destroys believers in the White God and their corn. I gather the faithful to the protection of Cherokee Rock! Come! Follow me and the absolute spirit to safety!"

The crowd bursts into cheers and many hurry to their lodges and cabins and collect belongings for travel.

***

Dideyohvsgi and his animals march from village to village, spread his message and recruit converts to their pilgrimage.

Two days before the new moon, the assemblage camps under the massive protection of Cherokee Rock.

For security, the black wolves guard the trail that climbs the mountain and tucks beneath the spiritual mecca.

Under the enormous outcrop, Dideyohvsgi organizes a Ghost Dance. Workers build a square elevated platform in the center of the camp. Each flat side faces a cardinal direction and rests on a ring mound from times before memory.

Keepers who nursed their flame from its original place stoke logs to embers in a pit. Smoke hangs low under the outcrop, and from the dimness, four warriors emerge.

"Red, Blue, Black and Yellow," Dideyohvsgi presents each man a straight stick, "you are strong, good and true. You walk with Unetlanvhi and have the honor. Stir the ash of the sacred fire."

As the sun sets, he fills his pipe with tobacco and steps to the ceremonial flames. The shaman lights his bowl and drags fumes seven times.

Other medicine men step forward, led by the wolf band, and puff once for each clan before passing the smoke.

"Elders of our clans!" Dideyohvsgi welcomes attendees. "A hailstorm comes with the new moon. Lead our dance as Selu spares us!"

The participants, including most beloved women and shell shakers with turtle shells filled with small rocks, shuffle and stomp around the circle.

Their rhythmic accompaniment sets the cadence for the chanting worshipers.

The dancers continue that night and throughout the day preceding the full moon.

Males and females dance at a tepid pace, dampened by exhaustion.

But, under Cherokee Rock, in the sacred smoke from the ceremonial fire, their minds reel, and they join hypnotic foot stamps of a self-induced trance.

The campsite under the outcrop darkens as the sun sets and thunderstorms gather.

Dideyohvsgi watches the sky outside as he dances. The medicine man smiles as Unetlanvhi gathers the power to grant Selu's prediction.

***

As the hours stomp by and the circle dance extends into the evening, Selu, the Spirit of the Corn, captures the clouds and summons her sons. "Lightening, throw your spears. Thunder, clap your hands! Non-believers cover our lands. Let your mighty and terrifying roar bring hail upon them!"

Her offspring spread across the turbulence and to the horizons in each cardinal direction of the ceremonial fire.

Thunder's claps echo over rocky outcrops and rolling hills as lightening's blasts split massive, decades-old trees.

The awesome display of Selu and Unetlanvhi power and might force the genuine humans under Cherokee Rock to abandon their Ghost Dance and huddle together.

They expect last of their people's status and tremble from fear of the storm and its predicted damage.

The night quiets the thunderstorm, and the group becomes restless as a new moon completes its path across the sky.

Black Wolf and his partner prowl the perimeter of Cherokee Rock crouched on four paws as stealth sentinels, and the crowd complains, "Dideyohvsgi, the darkness wanes and hail has not come! Call off your guards so we may return home!"

* * *

As the morning sun crests the horizon's tree line and the last clouds disappear, the medicine man's credibility collapses, and in front of his followers he calls his wolves, "To me, Wolves. Let my people go."

When the clans desert Cherokee Rock, the soul and symbol of their heritage, the animals confront Dideyohvsgi.

First Wolf threatens the shaman's security. "You lied, Shaman! No one can lie to a black spirit."

"As cubs, our mother said to hide if we ever smelled you," Second recoils from his brother's aggression. "She was right!"

"We knew better than to champion your cause. Wildlife decided not to help you, but no, we thought we understood, so we followed you."

Dideyohvsgi drops to his knees before the two. "You were not wrong, nor were my people. We must return and listen to Unetlanvhi."

First Wolf bares his fangs. "There was no hail!"

A calm breeze vibrates whiskers as freshness sweeps under Cherokee Rock. The huge black animal sits on its haunches and sniffs the air.

***

Corn stalks break the earth in the distance resembling porcupine spines and pop out of the soil.

The carpet spreads toward Dideyohvsgi, and the wolves watch with amazement as yellow cobs adorn the plants. They grow to a height above the shaman and the animals and encompass their space.

A Cherokee woman in a soft deerskin robe swings through the crop.

She carries a glorious belt of sun-bleached gulf water seaweed adorned by hand-polished shells and beads.

Her voice resonates with sweetness and nourishment. "Dideyohvsgi does not lie. I, Selu, Goddess of the Corn, promised hail. The shaman gathered true believers in this sacred place for their protection. He did well."

"There was no hail." First Wolf cowers before the power.

"The ultimate one visited me and commanded no deaths."

"Why, Selu? With no ice, my faithful abandoned me." Dideyohvsgi spreads his arms in supplication.

"Unetlanvhi wants humans free to choose." She sweeps closer to the shaman. "Those that deserted us today follow another path. They join the non-followers. The nature of faith is personal, one follower at a time. You, Healer, still believe, and I pass this heritage belt into your keeping." Selu rests the sacred object upon his outstretched arms.

The animals rest their heads on front paws.

"The belt tells of your people. Guard the story well. They choose not to follow Unetlanvhi. This teaches what they have forgotten."

***

The black wolves lick Dideyohvsgi's moccasins in friendship and pad away through the corn into the woods.

CHAPTER THIRTY-SIX — Dance

Alone, dejected, depressed and discouraged, Dideyohvsgi sulks at Cherokee Rock.

The days creep one after another, longer than the nights, but more peaceful.

Dark haunts the shaman's mind with sleep, and he tosses and turns on his mat. Dreams turn to the previous meeting with James Vann.

The mixed blood stands. "I listen to words and understand the heart. Most will not, but I have advice."

"What recommendation?" The medicine man opens his perspectives.

"Seek those that agree. That is what Son of Stone Cloud and John Watts did, and they gained strength."

"The younger leaders of the people do not walk with me."

Vann studies the ground for a moment, then raises his eyes to meet Dideyohvsgi's gaze. "One does. Find the brave warrior who fought on the Etowah, the Shawnee, Tecumseh."

***

The following midmorning, the dejected medicine man with provisions packed upon his back watches the horizon's snow clouds.

His moccasins tread a frozen Cherokee hunting trail northward.

Unaware a few years earlier Buckongahelas died of smallpox and that his supporters believe the death a result of witchcraft, the discredited shaman travels into a maelstrom of religious witch-hunt turmoil.

Although the prominent leader of the Lenape stood for accommodating the White settler invasion of the northeast, Tecumseh's brother Tenskwatawa leads factions of the fervor in a native revival modeled after Dideyohvsgi's Ghost Dance from the south.

After contact with the Shawnee, Dideyohvsgi, escorted by two warriors, with his hands bound behind his back, arrives in the lodge of a younger sibling at Tippecanoe (Prophetstown) near the Wabash's and Tippecanoe's confluence.

"You are the Shaman of the Paint Clan?" The brother of Tecumseh stands. "The warrior who fought years ago against St. Clair and Blount?"

"Yes."

"Cut this man free. He is a friend," the Shawnee orders and dusts snow off the prisoner's shoulders. "Tecumseh does not lead this revival. I do. We have found and eliminated most of the witches who murdered Buckongahelas. While we search, the people reject the ways of the Whites and return to the paths of the ancestors."

"Good news." Dideyohvsgi rubs his wrists.

"But one more witch I want the most."

"Who is that?"

"His name is Mohi."

"The same man who betrayed John Watts?"

"Yes. He is powerful." The brother of Tecumseh nods. "Nothing is important to him except the White man's silver."

"I experienced his greed."

"My brother remembers and could identify him. But Tecumseh travels with Blue Jacket and Joseph Brant of the Mohawks," Tenskwatawa watches Dideyohvsgi rub the bindery whelps. "They recruit warriors who believe land is owned by the tribes and not for sale."

"I endorse common ownership. Treaties with the Whites surrendered that birthright," the Paint Clan's medicine man nods yes.

"I heard of your Ghost Dance at Cherokee Rock."

"Where my following died. Selu promised hail, but Unetlanvhi intervened."

"I question Unetlanvhi's wisdom. He did not protect the Shawnee under that sacred roof." Tenskwatawa lifts a pipe and loads the bowl with tobacco. "Your Cherokee Reel inspired my hunt for the witches who murdered Buckongahelas."

The brother draws smoke and studies Dideyohvsgi. He passes the long smoker to the older man.

"How did traitors and assassins become sorcerers?" The Shaman of the Paint Clan sucks nicotine into lungs. "

"They drink liquor, wear White man's style clothing, and lust for firearms. Most cooperate with the Whites and sign treaties that give away land," Tenskwatawa retrieves the pipe. "Enchanters, they are."

"Why do you want Mohi?"

Tecumseh's brother draws and expels fumes. "He is a wisp that drifts from the White man's lips. The witch betrays Unetlanvhi. For silver, he brought pox in settler's blankets into the clans, and the traitor's eyes served Governor Blount while he swore blood loyalty to Dragging Canoe. He warned the Whites and defeated John Watts. Then he came north and joined the plot against Buckongahelas. The same old tactics infected the noble warrior."

Dideyohvsgi stares into the brother's eyes. "He killed my mother, shot and cut the tail off my companion squirrel, and I witnessed what you claim."

"Then join my hunt for witches?"

"I yearn for a return to the old ways and teach the Ghost Dance from Cherokee Rock."

"But without the spirit hounds?"

"Both stayed there."

"Then I, Tenskwatawa, become the new dance's wolves. Two dark visions visited me in a dream. They told of a wraith reel and instructed all warriors to wear green, hill-bamboo vests. The shields protect from White guns."

"Cane against cannon?" Dideyohvsgi shudders and remembers the battle against St. Clair.

Tenskwatawa reads the guest's expression, "The journey through the winter tired you. Rest here. Wait for my brother and the warmth of spring."

***

The Cherokee new arrival settles into a temporary home in Tippecanoe.

Others gathered by the witch hunt and anti-White, pro-the-old-ways tirades of Tenskwatawa swell the village's population with a curious mixture of tribes, cultures, histories, and customs.

The Paint Clan medicine man, when weather allows, sits outside his small cabin, smokes a pipe, and observes daily newcomers.

Shawnee, Canadian Iroquois, Meskwaki, Miami, Mingo, Ojibwe, Ottawa, Kickapoo, Delaware (Lenape), Mascouten, Potawatomi, Sauk, and Wyandot mix with freedmen, slaves, British traders, and occasional Chickamauga Cherokees.

This morning, a warrior parades before Dideyohvsgi's seat with a mule and a two-wheel wagon loaded with trade goods and provisions. A person trails, roped to the rear by a collar.

The animal limps and its master slaps across haunches. The beast stops, and the Delaware whacks its neck and ears with a walking stick.

"Beating the animal won't pull that cart," Dideyohvsgi stands.

"Did I ask?" The mule's owner points the rod.

"No, but how much for that mule?"

The Delaware's personality changes to selling, "Fine animal and for sale." The man yanks the rope attached to the follower's neck. "My slave can pull the wagon."

"I'll buy her as well."

The seller's eyes widen with greed. "A no name. This is her kid." The seller lifts a bundle from the cart and holds the infant high for display. "A boy. Make a good cotton hand."

"Cut her loose. Woman, take your child inside before it freezes out here."

The slave stares at Dideyohvsgi.

"She only speaks the White man's language. I got her off a slaver on the trail," the Delaware points to the entrance as he hands the mother the baby. "You have a new family!" The seller laughs as she scurries into the warmth of the log building. He turns to the buyer. "Field workers are not cheap."

***

As days pass, a parent and child intrude into the shaman's life.

Accustomed to living alone, he jerks away from an inventory of his medicine bag when the slave stands nearby.

She holds his short stem bowl and her eyes question. "Pipe?"

He shakes no at the pronunciation in Cherokee, "No, pipe!"

The woman drops to knees and touches her lips. She sucks in air and points.

"Understand. Yes. Thank you." The medicine man stuffs the bowl with tobacco and steps to the fireplace.

She watches him light and draw.

He exhales smoke that drifts around the baby, who lies cuddled in a blanket on a mat near the fire.

Dideyohvsgi indicates the child, "Name?"

The mother panics, crawls on her hands and knees to the infant, and sweeps him into arms. She draws away and curls in a corner.

***

The following day, the medicine man buys tobacco from a British trader who visits Tippecanoe.

The merchant shows a sheaf of leaves, "From the South. You people are from Georgia. This is the best. Carolina grown."

"You know from the Carolinas?" The buyer inspects the product.

"I served under Tarleton but deserted after Cowpens and went west. Also lived in the Indiana Territory with a Potawatomi wife until William Henry Harrison became governor. Her people sold the land along the Wabash north of Vincennes. The big politico signed the Treaty of Fort Wayne with the Kickapoo, so I left and started this trading business."

"Heard of that agreement. It forced Tenskwatawa's ghost dancers into war." Dideyohvsgi selects and pays for a tobacco stash with a silver coin.

"His brother has a cooler head." The salesman wraps the remaining product.

"Tecumseh may be calmer, but he believes treaties are no longer good. I agree with that. Native lands are owned by the tribes, not individually." The medicine man eyes the merchant.

"That's why I'm traveling. Wife's a Kickapoo but a ghost dancer with a club won't ask. There's three thousand people in Tippecanoe. That could be a big war party. Even though I am British, this coward seeks shelter."

***

Dideyohvsgi reenters the cabin with tobacco under one arm.

Inside, the slave woman stands over and admires his Cherokee Rock beaded heritage belt.

"What are you doing?" The shaman rushes to her side, and she spins in defense. "That is sacred!"

The woman's expression changes from startled fear to rapt appreciation.

She spreads hands above the garment as if palms touch the beads.

Her face smiles and eyes dance with pleasure. "This is your God?"

"Not is, but from."

"Scared?"

"No, sacred."

The slave nods a chin. "As Jesus?"

Dideyohvsgi understands and realizes he owns a Christian.

With one eye following the woman, he packs the historical testimonial and freshly bought tobacco in a backpack beside a sleeping mat.

He shudders with the thought, "If I can't convert believers, might as well buy them."

CHAPTER THIRTY-SEVEN — Tippecanoe

DRᎦᏫᎣᎢᏕᏫᏏᎩᎯᎫᎬᏒᎮᎯᎴᎲᎳᏫᏍᎡᏪᎹᎯᏓᎣᏆᎲᏋᎩᏏᏫᎢᏁᏢᎯᏫᎤ

November snow coats Tippecanoe as Dideyohvsgi finishes construction of a miniature stone and log shelter under an outcrop outside the town.

He stands, admires his efforts, and satisfied the location remains secret; the shaman returns to the cabin.

The slave woman waits and smiles at her owner's return. She prepares a morning meal at the fireplace as the medicine man plays peek-a-boo with her child.

After breakfast, Dideyohvsgi withdraws the Cherokee Rock sacred heritage belt from its pack and turns to his human, "This object is the history of my people. Tenskwatawa's scouts say an army of Whites moves on the Wabash. Protect this. Understand?"

The woman's blank expression answers.

He steps to the fireplace and grasps the cool end of a branch with a charcoal tip. With the implement, the medicine man draws a depiction on the cabin's wall. "These are White soldiers." He sketches stick figures with guns pointed at the artifact. "Troopers attack Tippecanoe, so we must hide history." The shaman shows a hut over the item.

The woman's eyes brighten with understanding.

He motions to follow. "Someone other than me must know where it hides. Come." He replaces the sacred item into his pack and shifts the weight to a shoulder.

The woman lifts the baby from beside the fireplace, wraps him in a blanket, and follows her owner out of the cabin.

***

Bright morning sunlight sparkles ice crystals in the snow and, for a moment, distracts Dideyohvsgi from the bustle of activity.

A few people load wagons, packs, and horses for flight, but many more clump in groups and spread rumors.

Others sharpen war axes and paint faces for war.

He stops a passerby, "What's going on?"

"Six hundred White soldiers come!"

A few steps further, a messenger from Tenskwatawa jogs to Dideyohvsgi. "Tenskwatawa meets Harrison and needs you. Come now."

The older man grasps the youngster's shoulders. "Calm, Son. Tell me details."

The boy steadies. "Governor Harrison marches one thousand men from Vincennes along the Wabash. Tenskwatawa says they camp and call for a parley. He wants you to attend."

"On the way." Dideyohvsgi pats the boy's back and the young messenger jogs away.

The shaman grasps the slave's elbow. "But not now. Come."

Both hurry through the snow from the village and into the surrounding woods.

At the temporary makeshift hut, the medicine man removes his pack and places it in the shelter.

He stands and spreads hands wide above his head.

"Unetlanvhi, hear me now. Sacred history rests far from Cherokee Rock as war sweeps over the people. Guard this belt. If I don't return, help this woman deliver it to a shaman of the Paint Clan. This I ask for my people."

The slave woman cuddles the boy baby and stands silent in the snow.

"Our heritage lays here. I know you don't understand but when it is time, He will guide you."

***

In Tippecanoe, Tenskwatawa councils with warrior Red Leaders.

They meet in a larger cabin with a fireplace at each end, the council house.

As Dideyohvsgi settles into a place, Tippecanoe's spiritual Ghost Dance leader slips into a vest. "Scouts estimate we outnumber the Whites three to one. We blessed these cane shields, and they repel the White man's musket balls and cannon iron. I hear the Red Leader's call to attack. But Governor Harrison sends word he wishes to talk. That message arrives by a snake that crawls on its belly. Bring in the messenger."

Two warriors drag a beaten and bloody native dressed in a soldier's tunic, tattered and ripped Anglo-civilian pants, and a dirty black wide brim hat that dislodges as he drags across the floor.

Tenskwatawa turns to Dideyohvsgi as the man struggles to his feet. "This snake says his name is Mohi of the Cherokee Paint Clan. True?"

Unsure, the healer walks close for a better look.

Mohi's eyes sparkle as the snow outside, but not from sunlight, but hatred. "Enoli, son of Ahyoka, friend of squirrels, ghost dancer of the rock, do whatever, but the people abandon you. They fall to the mercy of Governor William Henry Harrison and the United States of America."

He spits, and spittle dribbles on Dideyohvsgi's face.

The true Shaman of the Paint Clan steels both shoulders and wipes with a sleeve. "Mohi, I protect the heritage belt of the Cherokee, and that reality will once again spread among the brothers and sisters."

"Ghost Dancer?" Tenskwatawa returns Dideyohvsgi to attentiveness.

"Yes, he is Mohi."

"I have searched for this snake," Tenskwatawa stands. "Governor Harrison presents him as a gift. The enemy delivers him with our surrender terms."

The assembled warriors laugh and whoop at the absurdity.

"Harrison does not know the British delivered one hundred horses loaded with guns and ammunition. Tecumseh rallies the tribes to drive the soldiers eastward but has not arrived. We are strong, but wise. Release this snake with word that Tenskwatawa agrees to meet at dawn below Tippecanoe on the third curve of the Wabash."

As Mohi departs with the message, Dideyohvsgi watches his enemy leave.

Tenskwatawa steps close. "I may regret freeing that man and suspect treachery. Five hundred warriors will stand watch tonight between Harrison's camp and Tippecanoe."

"That is good. You cannot trust Mohi to deliver your words to the Governor."

"Come to my talk with Harrison." Tenskwatawa's eyes value his Cherokee adviser. "And if he spreads lies, you will know."

***

After midnight, Dideyohvsgi rides with Tenskwatawa and the Red Leaders through the woods and approaches their scout positions.

Musket fire shatters the frosty night air, and the brother of Tecumseh stops to listen.

Volleys reverberate through the trees.

The Ghost Dance Shawnee turns to a warrior. "The Whites betray us. Call up the men before surprise overwhelms our scouts! Go!"

As a rider pounds away for reinforcements, Tenskwatawa signals the others to follow.

They crash through the woods and underbrush toward the river. The party bursts into a clearing.

Black powder smoke hangs low over the snow and several fighters lie dead or bleeding.

Life splatters and stains White ice crystals.

Empathetic warriors stand over their own men.

The Red Leaders leap from mounts to help the wounded. Many cane vests display musket holes blown through the armor.

A fighter turns to Tenskwatawa and points at a fallen comrade. "You lied! That is blood spurting. Through the sacred vest!"

"Gather our forces! Attack before the Whites overrun!" The brother of Tecumseh spins his horse as he shouts commands.

Warriors on horseback and foot stare at the Ghost Dance leader for a moment and then step backward.

One by one, they abandon the deceit of the spiritual revival and disappear into the trees.

Dideyohvsgi looks at Tenskwatawa for orders.

"Evacuate!"

The larger force retreats before Harrison's advance.

A volley from a tree line falls several of the Red Leaders, and confusion reigns.

A musket ball smashes into Dideyohvsgi's shoulder and knocks him from his horse.

On the ground, he struggles out of his cane vest and crawls into the underbrush.

On elbows and in pain, the medicine man scoots for concealment. He rolls over an embankment into a stream bed.

"They run! Kill everyone you catch!" A Kentucky rifleman screams from nearby.

Dideyohvsgi, with his good arm, drags snow and winter debris over his body.

He lies still and listens to Harrison's soldiers and volunteer militia press the attack. Stillness slips into unconsciousness.

***

The wounded medicine man regains awareness as morning light warms the creek's channel. No sounds alert, other than wakening birds who rustle in nearby trees.

In pain, the survivor tears at leggings and straps, the cloth he wraps around his shoulder wound.

He struggles to feet and faces a fellow dead warrior that sits upright against a tree. The corpse wears a cane breast plate. Two ugly holes in the protection fester near the heart.

Dideyohvsgi stumbles from the creek into the woods and steps over several more casualties.

Hours later, the medicine man limps into Tippecanoe.

The village's cabins and other structures burn, and black smoke billows skyward, a symbol of defeat silhouetted against snow-covered hills.

Dead and desecrated old men and women from different tribes of the alliance lie scattered in the snow as he approaches his cabin and searches for life.

Dideyohvsgi shields his face from the fumes and flames and attempts to discover life. No sign shows of the mother or the child.

The medicine man drags his worn, wounded, and exhausted body out of town and into the woods.

At the makeshift shrine, the wound hurts more than the slave woman's dead stare. At the end of a blood trail in the snow, she lies in a fetal position around the small shrine.

Dideyohvsgi drops to one knee and slips the mother's deer coat collar off the face.

He touches her cheek, and his tears spot her dark frozen skin.

"Whaa!" A baby's cry breaks the silence from within the hut.

He reaches and cuddles the infant against his body for warmth, and the boy settles.

The shaman pulls the pack with the sacred heritage belt from its enclosure and grimaces as he shifts it to his shoulder.

With a baby slave boy and the documented history of the Cherokee race, the Paint Clan's healer stumbles away.

Tippecanoe, the last major Native American effort to oust White invaders from the lands that serve as western doors for United States expansion, Dideyohvsgi abandons.

CHAPTER THIRTY-EIGHT — Legacy

ᎠᎡᏔᏐᎣᎢᏏᏐᏲᏴᎠᏎᎬᏇᏢᎯᏛᎭᏫᏛᏟᎬᎷᏅᏴᎣᎲᎦᏕᎩᏇᏜᎬᎮᏂᏃᏐᎤ

Dideyohvsgi wakens on a sleeping mat in a warm lodge under blankets and deer hides. He moves, and pain shoots across his back and shoulder. Medicinal herbs and tree moss pad the musket ball's hole with a light wrap.

The wounded healer relaxes as a youngster Cherokee drops to knees.

"You stir, Dideyohvsgi. This is good. How is the wound?" The young man pulls a blanket over the patient's shoulders.

"Where am I? Do I know you?"

"Rest," the warrior sits back on heels. "No, but I remember you. Our people rescued the wounded before Harrison's killers finished the massacre."

"The baby and my pack?"

"The infant is with my wife. Your things are over there. We dug the musket ball out of that shoulder. You passed out on the trail away from Tippecanoe."

"And the White troops?"

"Up the Wabash toward Vincennes." The young man offers a slice of venison. "Tenskwatawa and most of the others retreat northward. Not us. This abandoned cabin is safe for the winter, then I'll take the wife home to Cherokee lands."

Dideyohvsgi accepts the meat and bites a chunk. "You took risks. I thank and owe you."

"No, I am the person indebted. My mother was forever grateful. You saved the family from the pox in Ustanali years ago. She taught the family to remember."

The medicine man props on an elbow, "There were dozens ill then."

"Every day, she thanked Unetlanvhi for your skill."

"What clan are you?"

"The Anikawi (ᎠᏂᎧᏫ a-ni-ka-wi, Deer.)"

"Please, my pack?"

The grateful youth retrieves the item, and Dideyohvsgi withdraws the heritage belt. He spreads the treasure flat.

"This is a holy relic from Cherokee Rock." The medicine man's voice reflects the importance and significance of the icon. "It records the people's beliefs and stories."

The youthful representative of the Deer Clan strokes the belt's bead work with fingertips, "Fine craftmanship. Mother loved color."

"It is old, before known time. Seaweed from the great waters in the south binds those sewn beads, and each group tells a different fable." Dideyohvsgi hands his knife to the boy. "Cut it into seven equal pieces."

The youngster recoils, "What!"

"There are fewer real people than ever in our people's history. Whites such as Harrison, St. Clair, and Blount defeat our warriors, burn towns, and destroy culture. The belt is no longer safe in the keeping of a single person. You keep one and I another. The rest, I plan to search for and find responsible homes."

The youngster warrior accepts a seventh of the heritage belt, "You honor me, Great Medicine Man."

"Take care to protect that forever."

"Yes." The younger pauses and considers his words. "You are not a youth, Sir, and have a baby. The wife and I wish to have a family. We talked about the child but do not believe we can care for him. Can you provide for the baby?"

"The boy is mine. His mother was a slave who died, but I cannot stomach owning anyone in the future. But I have a friend with land where I can take the boy."

"Not on the James Vann plantation?" The younger recognizes possible offense and qualifies his comment. "He is an outstanding leader but mistreats slaves."

"No, not there. To a Freedman who fought alongside during the days of Dragging Canoe."

***

Winter passes the secluded cabin in the woods, and Dideyohvsgi recovers from his shoulder wound.

Spring winds fan his face and the wraps of a back cradle board as he strides along a hill beside a creek. He gazes across rows of small plants that peek through the earth.

The plow-created furrows stretch to a wooden cabin with a chimney that smokes, an invitation to a tobacco pipe.

The traveler hoists his load, walks, and admires cotton. At the house he lays the burden against a front porch post and hefts the toddler and cradle board. He leans the child against the wall as Walela burst out the door.

"Dideyohvsgi!" She hugs the medicine man.

"Good to see that perfect skin!" The traveler smiles in return, "It has been too long."

"Benjamin went to Dahlonega for supplies. We were not aware you were coming. Rumors said they wounded you when Tecumseh and the Ghost Dancers fought Harrison at Tippecanoe. I'm so glad you are safe!"

"Safe but old man's pain twists my shoulder when it's going to rain," Dideyohvsgi laughs.

"You must be hungry and thirsty. Come in," Walela turns to open the cabin's door but spies the cradle board. "Goodness!" She drops to knees before the toddler. "So cute! What's his name?"

The healer's forehead wrinkles. "Doesn't have one. The birth mother was a slave. I purchased both in Tippecanoe, but Harrison's troops killed her when they burned the village."

"You bought a person!" Walela lifts the baby. "Not something I expect. Benjamin says both of you detest owning any human."

"Yes. But it's a long story."

"Shorten it for an old friend, Medicine Man."

"They suffered under a cruel owner," Dideyohvsgi follows into the cabin.

"Understand."

The healer searches for conversation. "This plantation grows fine cotton."

"Ben struggles. There is only so much he can do." The wife leans the cradle board against the cabin's wall and makes food for the guest. "He plants only the cotton seed he prepares and uses only a small part of the land."

"No children play, Walela. None grow to work someday?"

"Not that we don't try," the woman smiles and turns to the

shaman. "Selu does not bless. Can a shaman change that? Do you have influence with the Corn Goddess?"

***

The following day, Dideyohvsgi sits on the cabin's porch with his back against a post. He smokes a pipe and watches Benjamin drive a wagon along the road and cotton.

"I wondered who smokes in my shade!" The landowner jumps from the bed and lunges toward a blood brother. "Good to see you!"

"Ben! It has been far too long."

"Let's look at you." The Freedman holds the friend at arm's length. "Heard you got involved in the Shawnee Ghost Dance revival up north, then joined Tecumseh. Someone said you died in that battle. Others tell stories that Mohi murdered you!"

"I saw the traitor."

"Slit his throat, I hope.

"Didn't get the chance."

"I should have been there to help."

"No. You're settled now. Days for slitting gullets died. For me as well. I took a musket ball in my shoulder, and it's hard to raise this arm."

"Yes, old friend." Ben captures the medicine man and pulls him toward the cabin's door. "Times have changed. I've been in Dahlonega and got a small loan to buy cotton seed. Never considered Whites had cash for a Freedman."

"Surprised the place is big enough for a bank," Dideyohvsgi bumps the door frame and grunts with pain as he enters the cabin.

Benjamin kisses Walela, "Mmm, that's good. Glad to be home."

"You borrowed money?" The wife looks concerned.

"Yes and pledged land for collateral."

She turns to the healer. "What do you know of borrowing?"

"Fine when it works. If not, it's just another way for the Whites to grab property."

The landowner laughs, "Friend, want to prosper? Work with bankers."

"That may be," Dideyohvsgi rubs a chin. "But they are White. Our people must develop banks, manufacture plows, become educated in White ways and win at their game."

"Remember Sequoyah from the Little Turkey battle?"

"Yes."

"The kid invented written symbols for your language." Ben settles into a chair. "Now he travels and teaches reading and writing. The Cherokee are eager to adopt his syllabary and communicate with the ease of the favored ones."

"That boy did well then, but the rest lost. Sounds more promising than banking."

The cotton grower laughs, "Someone who learned the secrets of Son of Stone Cloud is not too interested in becoming a banker."

"I've been fighting Whites too long, Benjamin. I am tired."

"Stay here forever if you wish, Brother," the Freedman grasps his friend's shoulder.

"There is more." Dideyohvsgi looks deep into the Freedman's eyes. "The child. I cannot care for him as a wandering bachelor. I own the kid, but you are aware of how I can't stand that. You need workers to make this dream plantation. I can stay for a while and help with the crop? But I ask Walela to take the infant."

"A slave, I don't want. Thought we agreed on that."

The medicine man thinks for a moment. "I'll sign the boy over because you respect humans. I cannot offer the child a place to develop and become an adult. You can."

"And I will always treat him like I would you."

The two friends shake hands.

"I'll raise him, treat the kid as my own, and when he is of age, free papers," Ben nods agreement. "What is his name?"

"The mother never chose one."

"I'll call him Ezra. That sounds perfect." Benjamin smiles at his blood brother, "I swear to support Ezra Waters."

"That is good. You need workers. But grow your own children to pass your legacy on someday.

"Walela and I want kids. Just no luck yet."

"I'll work up a Selu corn potion. It's guaranteed to help."

CHAPTER THIRTY-NINE — Government

ᎠᏣᏙᎠᎢᏌᎣᏟᏴᏯᎠᏤᎲᎯᏋᎯᎦᏒᎥᏌᎦᏒᏃᎠᏋᏲᎣᎮᎯᏍᏴᏁᏳᏎᏁᏟᏂᎤᏏ

Years later, Dideyohvsgi still smokes a pipe on the porch as the sun sets and peace permeates Benjamin Waters' small cotton plantation.

This evening, Walela plays hop stone with Ezra, who walks.

Ben sits with back against a post, his year-old daughter bundled in loving arms, and watches the light vanish.

"I couldn't have grown this farm without you, Dideyohvsgi. You have worked as hard as I have. I want you as a partner."

The medicine man draws deep smoke and blows circles into the evening's air. "No Ben. You're holding your new owner. Thanks, but I have no wish for any part of cotton. Too much work."

The baby girl in Ben's arms cries.

"Everything is okay," the father swings and quiets the child.

"Ella Waters," the medicine man savors the infant's name. "Selu worked a miracle with her potion. But you have captured your father's heart."

The Freedman smiles, "And we imprison you on our farm."

"I'm not a prisoner."

"I thought you might volunteer to fight the Red Sticks with Andrew Jackson. But you stayed here," Benjamin watches his blood brother's expression. "You don't want to raise cotton?"

"The Creeks have been enemies. It was tempting," the shaman drags fresh smoke. "Andy won, as the Whites always do. It cost native lands in Florida, even though the English and Spanish didn't agree. Old Hickory showed the redcoats. But his volunteers got less land and more dead brothers."

"Your new council President, that fellow named John Ross, was Jackson's adjutant for the Cherokee regiment. His trading post on the Tennessee is most successful. Hear he added a ferry. Great choice of location near Chattanooga Creek. South is the Nation. North is the United States."

"The council is mixed bloods, Ben. They don't even understand what the Rock's heritage belt teaches."

"You found a home for five belts?"

Dideyohvsgi nods. "The last one I gave to a beloved woman of the Wolf Clan."

"So that task's finished?" The Freedman stands and stretches. "I hear the wife singing sleep time to Ezra. Think I'll join the family."

As Ben enters the cabin, the shaman stares at the stars in the sky.

A shooting star blazes across the horizon.

His mind says, "I see you. One task completed for now, but the reason's not forgotten."

***

Later in the summer, Benjamin, Walela, and Dideyohvsgi harvest cotton. The three pick the white fluff bolls and drop their product into long bags. The weights drag along the rows. Heat adds discomfort to the strenuous effort.

"Good crop, Ben." The picker shaman wipes sweat from forehead. "We'll finish soon."

"Two full wagons, I expect." The Freedman straightens to rest his back. "You and I can cart the loads to the landing late this week. This time of year, buyers pay top dollar."

"I remember John Ross as a baby," Dideyohvsgi stares northward. "From Turkey Town. His father was a big Scotsman named Daniel. The son's done well."

"They elected him head of the Council. Good thing," Benjamin looks in the general direction of the landing. "The man's against those 1802 Articles of Agreement and Cession."

"That compact extinguishes land titles in Georgia. Andrew Jackson supports it. The politician betrays those warriors that helped him win the Creek Wars." Dideyohvsgi rubs his back. "Think you might lose the farm some day?"

"No. You forget I'm not Cherokee. I registered my land deed in Dahlonega." The Freedman shakes his head, "But many folks around here could."

"People can't let that happen. It's just more land grabbing."

"Get to work, Men." Walela laughs. "I don't plan to pick this entire crop."

***

Days later, Dideyohvsgi and Benjamin creak into the market at the reins of laden mule-powered wagons that drop cotton seeds and lint alongside the winding dirt road.

The avenue twists through a wooded valley between a massive rock outcrop mountain and the Appalachians.

The Tennessee River curves before them, and a few log cabins, one the trading center, cluster at the Cherokee side of a John Ross-owned ferry.

A flatboat on the opposite shore deposits freight and passengers in the United States of America.

Dideyohvsgi and Ben pull their wagons to the post's front.

A mid-thirties man with piercing brown eyes and dark hair parted in the White man's manner steps out of the log cabin, "Benjamin! Great to see you. Your cotton harvest looks good."

"Yes, Mr. Ross. Hope you have buyers."

"Two bidders. Prices are high."

Ben indicates his blood brother. "Meet an old friend of mine, Dideyohvsgi."

The older medicine man drops to the ground from the wagon's seat. "I knew your father and you as a baby."

"No need for an introduction, Sir," John Ross extends a handshake. "My parents spoke of you often. Paw said I was a difficult birth, and you were there for mother."

"Unetlanvhi helped." The healer laughs and accepts the greeting. "I held your father's hand."

"You and Ben fought for Dragging Canoe and John Watts. The school for shamans and home of Son of Stone Cloud at Cherokee Rock is a legend. Some call it a myth, but not me," the elected leader of the Nation nods. "Yes, Sir. My pleasure to meet you."

The three enter the trading post. A gentleman sits at a table and scrutinizes the entry.

"This is my brother-in-law, Return J. Miegs," the owner sweeps a hand toward the White man. "Sit, gentlemen. Make yourselfs comfortable. I will send a runner to the buyers."

The relative watches Ben but speaks at Dideyohvsgi, "We don't drink with slaves, Sir."

John Ross intercedes, "More hospitality, please. This is Benjamin Waters, a war hero and cotton producer near Dahlonega. He has papers, and John Watts honored his service with a property grant."

The offender leans backward in his chair. "My apologies. More and more people have servants. I presumed that was the case here."

The Freedman stares at the brother-in-law. "We are guests here, and I choose to take no offense. But careful, sometimes presumptions offend."

The proprietor serves the men tankards of ale. "These warriors know. Come, talk of more pleasant matters."

"Such as what you do for the people?" Benjamin turns his attention to John Ross.

"Have you seen 'The Phoenix'?" Ross offers a folded periodical.

"What's that?" Dideyohvsgi reaches for his ale.

"A newspaper. Since Sequoyah's travels taught many to read, it's published in our language and English by Elias Boudinot in New Town." Their host lifts his drink for a toast. "To Sequoyah."

The four men honor the inventor of written words.

Their host sits a mug on the table. "A missionary, Samuel Worcester, cast the metal type for the Cherokee syllabary. Good thing. Now, we even construct a government, bicameral as in the United States."

"What's wrong with the old ways?" Dideyohvsgi shrugs.

"Justice." Ross licks ale from lips. "Blood for blood. Courts and jurisprudence are more important."

"Agreed." The medicine man nods.

"They elected me as President."

"Sounds important."

"I proposed a Senate and National Council similar to the House of Representatives."

"That makes it just?" Dideyohvsgi pushes his mug toward the table's center.

"We divide the land into eight judicial districts, each with a judge, a marshal, and a local group." Ross leans forward. "We only have a couple qualified, so they travel. For safety, with a company of Light Horse."

"Means taxes?" Benjamin switches the subject.

"Only a poll tax, fifty cents per male under sixty."

"So, I have annual levies to pay as I age?" Dideyohvsgi grimaces.

"More than that," Ross's tone becomes serious. "The people know you well and that you represent traditions. You should be in this modern government. Run for the National Council. I think you would win, but election is not certain."

Dideyohvsgi's eyes sparkle with interest. "I will give it thought, but that means I have to pay the poll tax."

***

Months later, the Cherokee choose representatives, and Dideyohvsgi attends a meeting in New Town as an elected delegate.

The government house bustles with excitement, and others mill in the yard with many in political discussion on a porch.

The two-story log cabin with four windows on each side, three on each floor, features a fireplace at one end opposite the entrance.

On a sturdy stonework foundation, its open window shutters help illuminate the interior.

Another building stands nearby, the print shop for the Cherokee Phoenix, and many of the delegates read and share the latest edition.

An attendee thrusts the newspaper in front of Dideyohvsgi. "The United States Secretary of War is coming to negotiate! Do we want a treaty?"

"Let me see that." The healer-turned-politician reaches for the paper.

"President Monroe and the cabinet sides with Georgia!" The delegate waves the news in the air. "I say no more land concessions!"

Another jumps for attention, "Not one foot of Cherokee ground!"

Three men exit the national governing building onto the front portico.

John Ross, who presides over the council, raps a cane on the porch rail.

The elected turn to the noise.

"Delegates, I stand here with two witnesses," he indicates those with him and utters their names, "Charles Hicks, second leader, and Alexander McCoy, clerk, who with me refused a contemptuous bribe of twelve thousand dollars offered by William MacIntosh, Leader of the Creeks and emissary from the United States' commissioners!"

The crowd applauds the action and defames bribery.

"We meet this day," Ross points to the cabin's interior, "and reject the old Treaty of Hopewell, which made us tenants on our own lands, and abrogate the Georgia Compact of 1802!"

With cheers, the Cherokee delegates, including Dideyohvsgi, crowd into the cabin to vote and express collective indignation.

CHAPTER FORTY — Death

ᎠᏆᏍᎣᎢᏍᎤᏝᏴᎠᏂᎬᏪᏗᏞᎦᏟᎾᏝᎪᎳᏍᎦᎹᎾᏕᎣᎲᏐᏯᏯᏓᏔᏁᏂᎭᏃᎤᎢ

Winter blows its unkind breath through the leafless trees of Georgia, and Benjamin Waters' cotton fields lie fallow.

The farm's activities, other than daily maintenance, lessen and the family protects themselves in the warmth of the main cabin.

Dideyohvsgi smokes his pipe at the table while Walela, pregnant with a second child, prepares an evening meal.

"I understand why the Bowl and his Arkansas followers left for Texas." He looks at his friend. "They are wise. I would do the same without this farm." The Freedman nods.

"Don't believe I could be comfortable under Spanish rule." The shaman lights his long smoker.

Ben plays with Ella as Ezra sits with the medicine man and watches him smoke.

"I want a pipe." Ezra blows into the cloud above the shaman's head. With one hand, he shapes the fumes.

"Never," Walela smiles, "It's an old-fashioned Cherokee passion that smells of White men."

"How do I smell?" The boy's innocence shines in his eyes.

"Of cotton, today." The woman moves cornbread off the fire. "We live in the fields."

"I want to grow up as Dideyohvsgi." The boy looks at his hero. "Sit around, smoke, go to New Echota for meetings, and read the news."

Benjamin glances at the child. "Takes an education. When Ella's older, you both must go to the Presbyterian mission. When Dideyohvsgi was a boy, no schools existed."

"I thought you went to a Cherokee Rock school," the youngster stands and smells the floating smoke.

"I did, Ezra, but that was different. It was not a formal place."

"Can't I go there?"

"No classes, not anymore. Times have changed. No one wants that type of training these days. They want to learn the White man's ways."

"And his religion," Walela chuckles.

The word attracts Dideyohvsgi's attention.

"Yes. You must listen to Jesus' stories in class, or the Presbyterians won't teach."

"Honey, you usually say Baptists," Benjamin, on the floor, rolls closer.

"Same thing but different flavors." The woman wipes her hands on her apron. "Remember we raise these kids to know Unetlanvhi and Dideyohvsgi's fables."

The cabin's occupants turn toward an unusual knock on the cabin's door.

Ben lifts his musket from wooden pegs above the fireplace.

Walela gathers Ella and Ezra into a corner.

Dideyohvsgi steps to the entrance and opens the wood doorway a sliver.

A Cherokee warrior stares in return.

The man carries a musket and displays a hand loader in his belt. Wrapped in a deerskin coat and leggings in the traditional manner, he wears a White man's floppy brim hat, and his horse stomps ground off the porch.

"What do you want?" The shaman blocks the door's swing with his foot.

"I am Dull Knife with the Light Horse." The warrior does not threaten. "We escort a land agent from Return J. Meigs. He wishes to speak to Benjamin Waters."

Dideyohvsgi opens the door and steps out.

The final rim of a setting sun silhouettes the official and three mounted riders.

The medicine man shades his eyes.

"You are not Waters," a familiar voice emerges from the glare.

"But I am." Ben steps outside with his musket primed. "And you're not a land agent for Return J. Meigs. John Ross does not allow scum to serve the Cherokee Nation."

Atop his mount, Mohi chuckles. "Meigs takes bribes for favors, just as our political leaders, except the president. I bought the job, but you people out here don't get 'The Phoenix' regular. They elected me to the national council, equal to your fake medicine man."

"Then I suggest you ride back to the assembly." Ben's finger tightens on his trigger. "Before I put a musket ball in your stomach for John Watts."

"And others," Dideyohvsgi recognizes the rider.

Mohi pulls papers from his saddle's bag. "You claim Watts gave you this land. It wasn't his to give. Georgia owns the property, and as their agent, I will sell it."

"To whom?" The landowner steps forward to look at the document.

"Well, I thought I might want a prosperous cotton farm."

Benjamin whips his musket to his shoulder with its barrel pointed at Mohi's head.

The agent's Light Horse escorts point their weapons.

"Hold men!" The shaman steps to the center of the confrontation. "My name is Dideyohvsgi. You may have heard of me. I am a member of the national council. This is a mistake. Benjamin Waters and I rode with Dragging Canoe, fought with John Watts, and I at the battle of Tippecanoe. We are veterans."

The Light Horse on foot looks at his companions. "This is true. My father spoke of this man. I met him as a boy. This feels wrong."

"It is. Ride back to New Echota." Dideyohvsgi spreads his palms with no threat.

The mounted men look at Mohi.

"Arrest these liars!"

"Check with your headquarters. We are not going anywhere." The medicine man drops hands to his sides.

The Light Horse on foot mounts, "If an error, we apologize for disturbing your evening. If not, we will be back." He turns his mount and grasps Mohi's reins.

Dideyohvsgi and Benjamin watch them plod away from the porch.

"I can shoot him in the head." Ben glances at his blood brother.

"Don't," the medicine man squints at the departing riders. "It might cost your farm."

***

Weeks later, the National Council meets at New Echota.

The Freedman, with his deed in hand, stands with Dideyohvsgi outside the entrance.

Aware of the long history of bribery in the Cherokee Nation, the assembly passes a declaration against graft.

This day, Alexander McCoy, clerk, steps out of the cabin and reads the decree, "The principal leaders and their administrators of our nation shall not hold treaties or dispose property without council approval."

The crowd murmurs discontent.

"This judiciary," the official pounds a gavel, "determines those exchanges legal and final only in conformity with the laws of our nation."

Dideyohvsgi slaps Ben on the back, "That means, my friend, Mohi can't take your land unless approved by a Cherokee court!"

***

Traveling Judge John Martin, an eighth mixed blood, blond and blue-eyed signer of the new Constitution, is the first appointed on the Tribal Circuit Court. Without a legal education, the judge's reputation proceeds as a man of reason, common sense, and good judgment.

Accompanied by a company of Light Horse security weeks later, Martin hears Benjamin's property case brought by land agent Mohi and his influential employer Return J. Miegs, brother-in-law to John Ross.

The impromptu court hosts men and women. Mixed race and Whites gather, attracted by the controversial nature of the proceedings.

One Cherokee leans toward his wife. "The Old Chiefs had no right to make treaties for our land. It is owned by everyone."

At an open-air desk under a cottonwood tree and protected by armed Light Horse, the judge listens to arguments from Mohi and Miegs.

Benjamin presents his documentation and speaks of his war service with John Watts.

Dideyohvsgi testifies in confirmation and support of his blood brother.

Both face cat-call interruptions and derision from Whites in the crowd.

One White farmer stomps a foot in anger, "Treaties awarded those lands to Georgia!"

As the hearing concludes, Judge John Martin summons the parties to hear his judgment. "Gentlemen, I look more a citizen of the United States than of the Nation. My blue eyes and blond hair show I support the rationale presented by those who argue against tribal ownership of Indian lands."

Mohi and Miegs shake hands and clap each other's backs.

"But do not predetermine me. This case does not concern native land," the judiciary looks at Dideyohvsgi.

The shaman nudges his Freedman friend.

"Benjamin Waters," the official nods, "holds title to his farm, registered with the United States of America."

Return J. Miegs jumps to his feet, "Sir! Stolen from our Nation!"

"It is my understanding that our Nation awarded this property to him for extraordinary service during the Cherokee American wars?"

Miegs shakes a fist in the air. "He did no more than any warrior during those times. Mohi and Dideyohvsgi fought in those conflicts and received no land!"

Mohi joins his boss. "This person isn't even our blood! He was a friend of John Watts. I was there. Waters did nothing we didn't do. He just had different colored skin."

"Watts died in 1802. He cannot testify here." Judge Martin clasps his hands. "But this outstanding leader in our tribal heritage and history, we cannot ignore. Any gift of land he gave a Freedman, or to an enemy of our people, even President Andrew Jackson, my duty must honor."

Mohi shakes and lathers the corners of his mouth as the Judge speaks.

"I declare Benjamin Waters legal owner of his farm under our and the law of the United States of America."

The crowd observes Mohi's physical issues and draws closer.

Mohi extends both arms into the air and heaves for breath.

His hands shake and his knees buckle.

A red, blood-pressure-bloated face falls and impacts the ground.

The traitor lies dead from a violent heart attack.

CHAPTER FORTY-ONE — Resurrection

DRTᎦOꞌiՏᎣⱵYAJEⱷꝚᎪⱣᏜᏔᏛᏒGMᎯᏧOIHᏘᎩ⍵ᏛᎾᏁhZꝬOᵛ

The following day, Ben and Dideyohvsgi load their horses' packs to return to Ben's farm.

The Freedman tightens his saddle.

"Important thing was the judge made the right decision." The shaman looks at his blood brother over his mount's back.

"Thought scalping was Mohi's destiny." Benjamin's eyes flash over years of memories.

"I had an easy shot the day he wore Saloli's tail."

"Should have taken it. I remember the little one."

***

Later their mounts move through a small village. "They are burying the traitor this morning near here. I expect a large crowd of fans." Benjamin guides his horse. "People always saw that traitor differently. Let's stop and watch? Curiosity, not respect.

"Sounds good. We can remember him covered in rocks." Dideyohvsgi turns into trees.

The trail leads upward past an outcrop where a large group of people watch Mohi's funerary wrapped form.

Several place stones on the grave and a younger boy carries the first rock for over the feet.

Dideyohvsgi and Ben stop but do not join the entourage.

Murmurs ripple through the assembly as someone notices movement.

Rocks roll from the body as Mohi sits erect.

Gawkers recoil and jump away in fear.

The buried man rips at his funerary wraps, extends both arms palms skyward and moans.

A watcher's voice trembles, "He's alive!"

Another boy falls to his knees. "Mohi lives!"

The risen corpse tears binderies from his mouth. "Be not afraid. You are my people! I am your father!"

The crowd kneels and lowers their heads.

"I return to you from the spirit world under Cherokee Rock. Your mothers and fathers and the Creator gave me a message. Listen to my words!"

Many in the assembly tremble.

"Adopt the ways and laws of the Whites!"

Someone's voice in the crowd voice trembles, "Believe because Mohi rises!"

A woman's hysterical cry floats above the gathering, "He was dead a full night and day. The spirits of our ancestors speak through his lips!"

Dideyohvsgi shakes his chin no and looks at Benjamin. He turns to the crowd. "This man slept because he took a compound known to medicine men! Don't believe this! He is a fraud!"

Mohi realizes onlookers watch and leaps to his feet. "Silence! You revile Unetlanvhi and reject the people!"

With the words, someone hurls a stone.

The projectile bounces off Dideyohvsgi's skull, and his mount bucks and twists.

Several others grab rocks as Benjamin grabs his friend's reins, steadies him in his saddle, and pulls away from the confrontation.

Mohi continues preaching, "The old ways brought only blood and poverty to the people. Unetlanvhi sees the pain. Our future lies with the Whites. We must become as they, grow crops, wear store-bought clothes, attend churches, and model our law and government on theirs!"

The crowd claps and cheers every inflection.

"Mohi speaks for the White's God!"

As Benjamin supports his reeling friend, both retreat from the encounter.

***

A year later, Dideyohvsgi, an elected delegate to the National Assembly, attends a session in New Echota.

Delegates mill around the official meeting's cabin and talk in excited groups.

The shaman leans against its wall and reads an article in"The Phoenix" on its recent but passed constitution.

The preamble, he voices aloud, "We, the representatives of the people of the Cherokee Nation to establish justice, tranquility, to promote common welfare, and secure ourselves and our posterity the blessings of liberty: acknowledging with humility and gratitude the goodness of the sovereign ruler of the universe, in offering an opportunity so favorable to the design, and imploring his aid and direction in its accomplishment, ordain and offer this constitution for our government."

A passerby stops, "Reading that article about our new constitution?"

"Yes."

"Governor Forsyth read it as well. Sent a copy from Georgia to Adams in Washington."

Dideyohvsgi turns attention to the fellow representative, "The president?"

The delegate looks to assure no one listens, "The state legislators protest. They want removal from compliance to the Compact of 1802."

"You are aware of everything."

"Adams sent Colonel Montgomery to negotiate."

The healer nods understanding.

"As some old philosopher said, more talking leaves."

"I knew the man," Dideyohvsgi's eyes tear. "His name was Son of Stone Cloud."

"Sun what? Adams doesn't have enough time. Jackson's a sure bet in the next election, and he hates our kind. Who you going to vote for as principal chief?"

"John Ross."

"I like him too. He's our only hope with Andy Jackson. But I support Mohi as well. He stands for progress." The passerby stops talking long enough to consider the listener. "Aren't you that medicine man who leads the protest movement?"

"The name is Dideyohvsgi. I believe in the traditional ways and am against acculturation. We plan a rally at Cherokee Rock during the next full moon."

"Too far from New Echota for me. You are out of step, friend. I stand with Mohi and most of the National Council."

***

That same evening, the shaman attends a political gathering, invited by the primary candidate for Principal Chief of the Nation.

The medicine man enters a smoke-filled cabin crammed with attendees.

Attired in the clothing of a southern planter, in boots and a black wide-brimmed hat, John Ross spots the anti-acculturation advocate and works his way across the room.

Dark-haired full bloods and Anglo-appearing mixed blood Cherokees stop the nominee at every step to hob nob and slap his back.

The candidate focuses steady blue eyes on the medicine man and extends a hand. "Wish this meeting was at my landing over a peaceful tankard of ale."

Dideyohvsgi chuckles and grasps the extended handshake.

"How is my friend Benjamin Waters?" The charismatic leader leans closer.

"Has children now, daughters, Ella and Bella and Lisa. Doing well in the cotton business. I'm sure you know since you sell his crops."

"He purchased a few slaves?"

"Yes, had to, although the man barely tolerates owning any human. His fields demand workers." The healer shrugs. "And he can't free paper. They serve as collateral for loans to buy seed."

"Good to know of Ben," John Ross steps closer, "but I asked you to come tonight for a different reason. I want you to call off the rally at Cherokee Rock."

Dideyohvsgi shakes his head, "Mohi stokes the people's fear, and most believe he rose from the dead. The fellow becomes a faith leader, claims to speak for Unetlanvhi. The spiritual home of our people is at the outcrop. There, the Creator's desires surface."

John Ross, the mixed-race politician, steels his blue eyes. "As a Nation, we must hold together in Georgia. Dishonor or betrayal, we cannot tolerate. Mohi must compromise. We need to unite, or Whites take our lands. They urge immigration west, and intimidate, arrest, or imprison those unwilling. We have to adopt the American slogan, 'United we stand and divided we fall'."

Dideyohvsgi stares into the man's eyes, "I am sorry, Sir. As much as I understand and respect your point of view, my soul listens to Unetlanvhi. Supporters and I form a council that will circle a fire under Cherokee Rock."

John Ross takes no offense and claps the medicine man on his shoulders. "That is what I expected. The blood in these veins appreciates why you say it. In good conscience, I cannot attend, and Mohi's followers align with my politics."

***

During the following weeks, the anti-acculturation traditionalist movement's upcoming council attracts hundreds of supporters, and Dideyohvsgi basks in the sweet aroma of success.

Under the massive outcrop, members of the clans build an imposing woodpile in a square pit. Men and women debate attire, faith, history, and current politics.

The shaman sits in a small group and presses his point of view. "Yes, John Ross urges unification and stands against Georgia and President Jackson. We support that. As the Whites want land, our duty is not to surrender a belief in Unetlanvhi to ensure public safety!" The medicine man surveys the audience. They focus on his words, "Ross is a mixed-blood, rich planter who educates his children at a mission school. It is good that he is successful, for him and our people. But the poor fellow who struggles in the backwoods and scratches a living from a corn crop feels abandoned."

One woman turns from the speech. Her eyes widen with astonishment. Others twist in that direction and Dideyohvsgi looks.

With an animal hulk at both sides, in a beaded buckskin jacket and leggings, with his entire face painted red and head shaven except for a single row of long hair from forehead to shoulders, a new prophet stands with black wolves, silhouetted by the sunlight.

"I am Mohi, who returns from the dead with a message. Unetlanvhi speaks through this mouth to the people, 'You desecrate these grounds with petty desires to be as your ancestors. The Creator God who presides over and created the earth adopts humans into him.'"

Many in the gathering fall to knees and stomachs before the sight between two wolves.

"These are his words, 'Adopt and adapt to the White man so that people unite. Leave the animals in peace and eat food grown or raised on your land. Merge and build a future together that benefits everyone!'"

Dideyohvsgi steps forward, "Unetlanvhi can talk for him/ herself!"

Black Wolf One haunches its back at the sight of its past owner and curls lips above fangs, "Unetlanvhi told us that change comes. You lied!"

"Hail did not come," The shaman falls to knees, "but my words were true."

"Our new prophet does not speak untruths!" Second animal rubs a shoulder against the medicine man's finest beads and buckskin. "He claims the heart of the people at Cherokee Rock. You heretics trespass on this holy land."

CHAPTER FORTY-TWO — Hospice

ᎠᎡᏔᏍᎣᎢᏚᏍᎣᏈᎩᎪᏤᏫᎦᏝᏈᎶᎨᎵᎦᏫᏍᎡᎬᎹᎭᏍᎤᎰᎲᏚᎩᎾᏈᎲᏂᏃᏊᎤ

Benjamin and Walela nurture a hard working but spiritu-
ally wounded shaman on their small cotton plantation tucked
in the hills of Georgia. Far from the cultural and spiritual
heart of the Cherokee Nation, for years, the farm offers peace,
prosperity and belonging to a broken soul.

The Waters girls, Ella, Bella, and Lisa, watch with intriguing
curiosity of their short youthful memories. They welcome their
grandfather figure into youthful lives.

Dideyohvsgi sits on the cabin's hearth and stares into flames
within the stone-framed pit at one end of the room. He attempts
to stuff tobacco in a pipe's bowl, but fingers tremor and most
leaves drift to the floor.

"Why do your hands shake?" Ella's big, brown, eight-
year-old eyes watch the shaman's movements.

"Because I smoke too much."

"Daddies' don't. Why not quit?"

"I have. Hundreds of times. Your father did as well."

Ella scoots closer and focuses on this man so different from
her parent. "How do you know that?"

Dideyohvsgi reaches and lifts an ember from the fireplace
pinched between tongs strapped together at one end with a strip
of beads.

He pulls the hot coal to his pipe's bowl but loses control, and it falls to the hewn plank floor. The smoker stamps the spot black under a moccasin.

"I knew your father long before your mother," the medicine man rubs the small smear clean.

"Even before I was born?"

"Yes," the shaman chuckles. "When you came, you cried, but they rejoiced."

"Mama says you and my daddy were not there. You were at war."

"But I was with your paw when he first saw you." Dideyohvsgi runs fingers into Ella's hair and shakes. "He was proud and happy."

"Were you?"

"Yes. I want you to live life so that when you die, the world cries and you rejoice."

"Will people cry for you?"

"Don't think so." The healer attempts to snare another hot ash.

Walela steps to the smoker's side, takes the wood tongs, and with steady hands, uses the tool to grasp an ember and holds it on Dideyohvsgi's pipe's bowl.

He draws air and the tobacco lights, "Thank you."

"The world may not cry, Shaman," she replaces the tong. "But my husband and I will. Finish the tobacco, then time for supper."

The cabin features a wooden hand-hewn table of split logs secured by deerhide sinew.

Similar benches extend along each side of the construction's length.

The fireplace functions for cooking.

A few objects not made by human hands include iron pans and kettles. Several cook pork and cornbread.

Benjamin Waters swings the cabin door open. He closes the entry and shakes off the remnants of a fall temperature plummet.

"Sorry Walela, if I'm late." The husband lifts a musket and rests the weapon on pegs above the fireplace.

"Any deer sign?" Dideyohvsgi tamps his pipe empty into the fire.

"Saw tracks," Ben turns to the blood brother, "but no luck today. Scarce as the buffalo used to be. Think both moved west. But I talked to a Baptist minister named Johnson."

Walela, with a pad, transfers cornbread to the table. "Did he have any news?"

"Remember President Jackson's first message to Congress?"

"Yes, he promised a bill to remove Cherokee with the bison."

"Well, the preacher says Georgia's legislature passed a group of new laws. All native land transfers to the state."

The healer listens.

"And it prohibits further meetings or other assemblies. Allows militia to arrest anyone who rejects immigration."

Dideyohvsgi straightens and tucks the pipe into a vest, "That does not sound good."

"But that's not everything," Ben looks to Walela.

"Men, come eat." She wipes hands on an apron. "Talk politics after the girls get fed."

Benjamin turns and sweeps the child into arms. "And how are my Cherokee aquetsi (ᎠᏩᏟ a-que-tsi, offspring?) Glad Daddy's home?"

After supper, the adults rest and stare into the fireplace.

"The girls settle?" Walela looks to the loft platform above the couple's bed.

"Yes," The Freedman touches a finger to lips, "Speak low. Lisa's different from the other two. She falls asleep but wants to stay awake."

"You said the preacher had more news." She settles and pulls a blanket around shoulders.

"Nothing good." Ben looks at Dideyohvsgi. "The Georgia legislature declared contracts between Indians and Whites void unless sworn to by two Anglos. And now Cherokee testimony against a White in court is illegal."

"This is outrageous!" The shaman spits into the fire.

Benjamin glances at his wife and stares at the friend, "Jackson pushed a bill through the United States Congress called the Indian Removal Act. Self-explanatory."

***

The following morning greets the healer with frosty breath as he mounts a horse.

"Ride Northwest to Little Creek, then follow the flow to an old hunting trail. The place lays to the west over three ridges." Ben hands his friend a musket. "Should get there by supper."

"Preacher Johnson said they asked for me by name?" He slides the weapon into a deerhide sheath.

"Yes. Thought their kid might have smallpox." The landowner steps onto the porch. "They knew of you."

"Haven't heard of pox in years." The medicine man turns the mount away from the cabin. "I better ride."

"Got your medicine bag?"

Dideyohvsgi pats a saddlebag. "In here. Thanks for asking.

I'm getting to the age when you need to watch."

"If you're not back in two days, I'll come look."

The shaman pulls a worn Spanish-provided wool campaign coat tight against the wind and kicks the horse northwest.

Through the woods, the rider moves with the ease of an experienced traveler.

The mount travels north-westward and by midmorning drinks from Little Creek. Later it turns on an ancient hunting trail.

Dideyohvsgi's mind floats to memories of his youth in similar hills.

***

The surroundings fade from the brain of a young Enoli as he runs through the brush and scouts for White colonists on behalf of the British.

The leafless winter terrain that he travels changes in summer heat to a parched green.

His mother walks nearby, spots berries and stoops to gather the delicacies into a woven reed basket. "I am of the Unetlanvhi, Ho! I am of the Unetlanvhi, Ho! Ho! It is so. It is so. Ho! It is so, it is so."

With a head full of recent fireside stories where Cherokee warriors battle White settlement encroachment onto native lands, Enoli imagines the British and Indian allies staged against colonials and settlers.

He scouts for a detachment of soldiers and scans the surroundings for blue coats and brass buttons.

The boy ranges before the column and looks back.

Ahyoka hums a tune and adds more fruit to a basket.

He hears movement in the brush and stops to peek forward

along the trail.

Farmers, colonialists with muskets, approach on horseback between trees.

***

Dideyohvsgi clears the head and focuses on the path ahead.

Two riders carry weapons with butts on thighs and barrels in the air. One pulls a sloppy wide-brimmed headgear lower over eyes and the other chews a wad of tobacco that puffs a cheek resembling a blowfish.

Beyond the men, a distant column of smoke rises from the woods a distance from the horizon.

The two rein mounts to a stop and inspect the trail's obstacle. "Why you out here, Injun?" Floppy Hat lowers a musket to chest high.

"I ask the same question," Dideyohvsgi eyes the interrupters. "This is Cherokee land."

Tobacco Cheek spats brown juice and chokes a laugh. "You ain't got no property anymore, Chief. Land belongs to the state."

The shaman looks past. "There's a fire burning up ahead. I suspect you had something to do with it."

"Georgia militia took possession of a farm. Didn't need the cabin, so we burned it." Tobacco Cheek smiles and brown slime dribbles from a chin. "Nobody can trespass there anymore."

The healer reaches for a musket but freezes as six other riders show themselves from the woods.

One pulls a sick boy, two girls, a woman, and a stumbling bloody father by a rope attached to loops around their necks.

The Cherokee mother trips and falls to knees. "Dideyohvsgi! Help! My child has the pox."

"What did she call him?" Floppy Hat nudges a mount close. "Must mean medicine man in their talk."

"Your son is sick, but not smallpox," the shaman speaks in their shared language. "The actual problem is these horse patties."

"What you saying?" The closer militiaman grabs and unsheathes the shaman's weapon.

"I said you should free these poor folks." He switches to English. "You have the land."

"These people are under arrest. We head for jail, and you're impeding an officer of the law!" The guardsman slams the butt of the musket into Dideyohvsgi's neck and chin and propels him off the horse to the ground.

The medicine man struggles to regain feet. "My name is Dideyohvsgi. I am an elected delegate to the Cherokee National Congress! I will report what's done here!"

Floppy Hat heels a mount forward and knocks his target backward, "Ain't no such thing anymore."

In the dirt, the healer struggles away from the horseman.

"Tell Governor Forsyth, Mr. Legislator, the militia arrests you for no witnesses!"

Dideyohvsgi lunges for the assailant's musket, but Tobacco Cheeks clubs his skull.

The two Georgia guardsmen laugh and force their mounts over the defenseless shaman's body.

The injured medicine man lies on the ground with arms crossed over his chest.

***

His eyes blur upon Son of Stone Cloud, John Watts, and Benjamin Waters, who stand stern-faced and painted with fire ash. They stare at their friend.

Ahyoka, in her finest beaded deerskin, huddles on knees and sings his name with a hypnotic rhythm.

The older shaman bends and attempts to comfort the grieving woman, but her wails deny his effort.

Dideyohvsgi's eyes roll backward and his body floats above the ground.

He looks below at those who grieve and others that laugh, but the sound of wind rushing about his ears distracts.

A giant apparition sweeps him into the clouds.

"Want to eat my heart, Raven Mocker?"

The prey and death seeker, with huge swashes of wings, glides with little effort over the Georgia woods, "Not yet. Unetlanvhi wishes to show you something first."

Below, a river forks around a massive outcrop. The flier swoons downward in a tight spiral toward Cherokee Rock.

At a bonfire, a host of followers bow and grovel before Mohi, who sits with each arm resting on a black wolf.

The bitter enemy looks up and spies the aerial circles.

The wolves' bare fangs and snarl, and their owner urges the crowd to shake fists at the apparition in the sky.

"Leave me here, Raven Mocker."

"No."

"Please, let me fight for my people."

"No, Dideyohvsgi. First, I'll start a fire and camp before we freeze," Benjamin Waters, on horseback holds his blood brother close.

***

Later, wrapped in blankets, the medicine man opens his eyes under a wind break. A flame roasts a rabbit on a spit near his feet.

Ben crouches and stirs a cooking pot of concocted medical roots. "You going to live?"

Dideyohvsgi groans and props upon one elbow, "Yes. Feels as if a horse ran over me." He examines a primitive splint on his leg.

"That's broken." The Freedman pours a concoction into a small clay vessel. "Here, drink this."

"What is it?"

"Don't know. I found your mount and cooked this up from the medicine bag. You give the stuff to other people, figured it's not harmful. From the surrounding sign where I found you, looks as if several men did this."

"My fault. A company of Georgia militia ran poor folks off their property." The medicine man shifts for more comfort. "I stumbled into the mess."

"Sorry for them."

"You need to be worried. The same scum could pick your farm."

"Don't think so. The Removal Act only applies to Cherokee."

Dideyohvsgi considers the idea for a moment. "When I heal, I'm leaving the farm."

Ben looks at his patient. "You have been much more than a friend, or a blood brother, and earned half my cotton plantation. You don't want to go anywhere."

"Can't accept that."

"Why not?" The Freedman retrieves the medicine bowl and returns the pottery to the fire.

"Ella got the whys from you. It's simple. If I owned any of the property, the militia could remove you."

"Then why leave?" The man cuts a hunk of roasted rabbit and hands the food to his injured companion.

"I dreamed. There's unfinished business at Cherokee Rock."

"Mohi?"

"Yes."

"You cannot win without my help, Dideyohvsgi, but I can't do more killing. This cotton planter with a wife and three kids doesn't have the stomach for it."

"It's more than that. My good and bad wolves battle."

Ben's eyes blink, "What?"

"I must decide which wolf wins."

CHAPTER FORTY-THREE — Survival

ᎠᎡᎢᎣᎤᎥᎦᎧᎨᎩᎪᎫᎬᎭᎮᎯᎰᎱᎲᎳᎴᎵᎶᎷᎸᎹᎺᎻᎼᎽᎾᎿᏀᏁᏂᏃᏄᏅ

Months after the physical crisis, Dideyohvsgi's agitated soul demands a return to the well head of his culture.

Scents from flowers drift above the woods of Georgia, and hummingbirds dart from nectar to blossom with relish for the red flowers.

In the distance, Cherokee Rock looms and marks the river's fork.

The shaman's mount picks its way along a hill over and around the remnants of winter logs and slippery spots.

In the trough between hills, a stream trickles, the last memory of snow melts.

The medicine man slides off his horse, drops to his knees, and scoops fresh water to his mouth with one hand. The drink clears his eyes, and something glints from the creek bed.

With two fingers, the shaman picks a small gold nugget next to a larger piece of quartz.

Dideyohvsgi stands and examines the shiny rock. He smiles and tucks it into his knife's sheath.

"You trespass, Heretic. Why should I allow you to live?"

The medicine man spins to face the fangs of Black Wolf One.

His horse snorts at the smell of the animal and prances and strains against the length of its reins.

The rider's musket flaps against the mount's ribs, out of reach.

"The one you knew long ago is dead. You talk to a shell left by land invaders."

The beast drops to its haunches. "We are much the same. Then, I hunted from the eastern mountains to the great river. Now I roam the woods around Cherokee Rock. You remember the freedom of buffalo hunts but now hide in my forests abandoned by the majority of your pack."

Dideyohvsgi withdraws the small nugget from his knife sheath and extends it toward the animal. "Do you see this?"

"Yes. It's the yellow stone."

The medicine man steps closer. "Whites call this gold. To them, it is of immense value and importance."

"Those rocks lie over the ground and in the streams of my hunting territory," Black Wolf licks its lower lip. "Do you have any pemmican?"

"Mohi does not share his food?"

The animal glances away. "He shares nothing and does not follow the Cherokee way. Unlike a real person, his skin is a clansman, but the soul smells of a Raven Mocker."

"I have some in my saddlebag." Dideyohvsgi tucks the nugget in his knife sheath. "I must warn you. When the White invaders discover gold, they will swarm these woods with picks, pans, and shovels."

"I believe you know what is good and bad for wolves. More than that. You want us to roam the land as we once did."

"I do, but I am no longer a warrior. Or a shaman. Except for a few, my people run from me to the Whites' religion."

The animal scratches its side with a paw. "I tire of Mohi. He and his followers adopt that faith."

Dideyohvsgi pulls a piece of pemmican from his saddle bag and pitches it to the ground in front of the beast.

Black One sniffs the food, then enjoys the treat.

"I cannot fight him, his followers, plus the land and gold grabbers alone."

"Considering my history with you, may I join with you?" The wolf swallows.

The shaman chuckles. "Of course. Thank you. I don't wish to destroy your self-esteem, but you only make two of us against everyone."

The animal licks its paw, then rises, "Wolves have no individuality. We know packs. Community is much more important."

"You and your brother are different. Why is that?"

"We are of the time before man. As the birds and the fishes, we connect to Unetlanvhi," Black Wolf pads away. "You call it gohiyudi (ᎪᎯᏳᏗ go-hi-yu-di, faith.) Mohi calls it dinvdadistodi (ᏗᏅᏓᏗᏍᏙᏗ di-nv-da-di-ss-to-di, memories.) Come with me."

Dideyohvsgi mounts and follows the lead. They climb through the woods to the top of the hill. The wild one stops. "Rest with me."

The shaman and the wildness of nature sit together beneath a spring sky with white fluff clouds.

A slight breeze drifts through the tree leaves which rustle as they rub each other.

A beetle crawls across the medicine man's moccasin and ambles under a stick nearby.

Dideyohvsgi watches a spider weave its web between two branches.

Afternoon light turns golden and tickles the ornate pattern as a small insect lights upon the entrapment. The bug struggles for freedom encased in sticky ropes as the predator inches toward its supper.

Soft air stirs the trees, and the sound becomes words, *"Why?"*

Dideyohvsgi looks around, but the beast remains still. The question repeats louder, *"Why are you here, Wolf?"*

Animal licks his lips, "I sniff the wind."

Leaves respond to another breath of breeze. *"Does this Tsalagi search with you?"*

Wolf's fur at its neck ruffles, "Yes."

"For what do you seek?"

The animal's nose twitches. "For a future."

The air stops for a few moments. Fresh stirs. *"For you or for your kind?"*

Animal looks at Dideyohvsgi, who opens his arms palms up to include them both. The wild soul in the dog swells to his mind, "For our packs."

Leaves rustle, *"Prepare to speak of the future. Another demands the same, the medicine man Mohi. He has counselors. Others consult with him. Therefore, you need help. I will send aid."*

After a moment, Dideyohvsgi looks up into the timbers at a "Chit, Cheeit" sound.

A small furry, animal stares and fluffs a white splash across its tail.

"Saloli!" Enoli recognizes his childhood friend. "Come here."

The furry appendage wags. "You think I have a death wish? That's a hungry dog beast with you."

***

Unseen through the woods, Mohi stands atop Cherokee Rock with an uncommon evening sunset backlighting his defiant stance, his feet spread and his hands upon hips.

Black Wolf Two sits beside the man.

The traitor looks upward.

A distant Raven Mocker circles the outcrop halfway to the emerging stars.

The false shaman shudders, then stares across the forests that surround. "Our enemy, a nonbeliever, is out there. He comes for a revelation. Gather men of the collar, learned in the Christian religion, and bring them to Cherokee Rock."

The heart-devouring, bat-like presence beats its wings above and swoops toward the earth upon its quest.

***

That night, Dideyohvsgi and Saloli camp beside a tributary, now known as Ward's Creek, a stream to the Chestatee River.

Their fire crackles near the fresh water's embankment, and the medicine man sits, warms his feet with his furry counselor on his shoulder, and stares at the fire's reflections.

"Mohi shot you years ago and cut off your tail."

"Yes. But tonight, I am with you. Not sure why, for I am of the spirit world."

"See the sparkle rocks in the stream?" Dideyohvsgi changes to a more pleasant topic as a wolf's howl echoes over the woods.

"What's the matter with that animal? He's been calling out there since it got dark." Saloli twitches its nose hair.

"The wolf grieves the loss of his brother. They choose different paths."

"Fine," its whiskers vibrate faster. "Grieving's one thing, but does he have to sound so lonely?"

"He fears White men come for the glitter stones in this creek." Dideyohvsgi pulls a blanket around his shoulders. Saloli cuddles to his back side, and both listen to wolf's songs.

***

Next morning, the shaman shakes himself awake as his cheeks warm with a new day's light. He opens his eyes and focuses on Black Wolf One, who stares at the sleepy older man who wakens after dawn.

"My brother found me last night. Mohi sent him to bring men of the cloth to Cherokee Rock." The animal drops to rest on his belly with paws extended. "He delivered a message for you to meet and settle your differences with his master atop the outcrop on the day of the new moon."

Dideyohvsgi rubs sleep from his eyes. "Was your sibling upset you changed sides?"

"Yes, but not enough to join us. He believes the dribble that spews from Mohi's mouth. I told him the man is a false prophet, but his mind considers you worse."

The healer props on an elbow. "Your brother may be right."

"The animals don't believe so. They gave up on you years ago, but things have transformed them." The wild eyes look to the hills. "Or I should say you did."

Dideyohvsgi sits and feels Saloli stir. "Changed? What do you mean?"

"You wanted to lead people when you consulted with them," the animal turns his attention to the shaman. "Now, your kind no longer want you."

He stands and folds a blanket. "Only because they lost their way."

Wolf pushes to his feet. "Perhaps. The animals last night told me to ask you for a meeting today. They gather where this creek flows into the Chestatee to accommodate the fish."

***

Saloli rides Dideyohvsgi's shoulder as the Black wolf leads along the trail to the midday gathering.

"Your horse doesn't spook from that beast?" The furry bundle shifts on his shoulder.

"She did at first, but she's not afraid anymore." The shaman brushes the animal's tail away from his nose.

"Wolf does not bother me as well. Is that because it's a spirit mount?"

Dideyohvsgi laughs, "No, I ride her. Am I also an apparition?"

The black wolf leads the travelers to the meeting spot, and as the human representative rides out of the trees, a doe stops his progress, "Do you remember me?"

"No. I am sorry." The rider holds the mounts reins steady.

"It has been years, and I am old. You called me 'Beautiful Deer'."

"How could I not recognize you! You've not changed."

The animal falls in step with the horse. "You are kind."

The healer leans and rubs her ear. "And you are an old friend."

Buffalo from the west, Armadillo from the south, Elk from the north, and Alligator from the East wait and watch the real human's representative's approach.

Mockingbird darts above the assemblage with other birds. None eat fish in deference to the Catfish.

Dideyohvsgi dismounts and stands before the animals.

Beautiful Deer looks at her colleagues and steps forward. "When we last spoke, you and your kind failed at war, but vowed to win the peace."

The healer observes his audience, "Yes, and Buffalo with others moved west and became unsatisfied." Few in the audience react. "Now the Whites push everyone westward and we are not happy."

Bison stomps for attention. "Does that mean you lost both peace and war?"

"Yes."

Mockingbird swoops and lands on Buffalo's hump, "You came years ago wanting our help to defeat the White man. We refused. Big mistake. You both kill our kind without asking, and our population decreases. Real people are fewer with less land as the Whites sweep everyone from our earth forever!"

Buffalo shakes its massive head. "What can you do about it?"

"The clans no longer follow me as they did when we met. They want to become as our conquerors. I and a few others cling to the old ways, but we are alone."

Black Wolf One pads to a place beside Dideyohvsgi, "Do you see the squirrel on this holy man's shoulder?"

Many shuffle spaces for a better view.

Birds dive closer, and fish jump from the water.

They shake their heads no together.

The speaker sits upon its haunches. "I do, and the shaman does."

Wildlife listens in awe.

"Squirrel is a spirit given to us on a hill near Cherokee Rock. This medicine man speaks for the old ways. He soon presents our cause at a revelation with the new moon. Nature's spirit presides, but a human named Mohi with my brother wolf and experts in the White man's beliefs argue for a different way."

Wildlife sits in awed silence.

After a few moments from Buffalo's back, Mockingbird flaps its wings. "This meeting is unnecessary. The Allocator directs us as well. We have no say in this matter."

Beautiful Deer steps forward, "We may have little input, but unlike the time when we met with Dideyohvsgi, our survival lies in his hands."

The animals bow with respect to the last true Cherokee.

CHAPTER FORTY-FOUR — Unetlanvhi

ᎠᏕᎸᏐᎢᏐᎯᏴᎠᎫᎬᏇᏔᎯᎦᏌᏪᏍᎬᎹᎠᏎᎣᎢᎲᏑᏴᎣᏖᎠᏁᎲᏃᏊᎤ

In fresh air and the clouds, sustained by woods and waters, nourished by millions of Native Americans who walked its hunting paths, the massive granite of Cherokee Rock welcomes its creator.

The Unetlanvhi (ᎤᏁᏢᎤᎯ u-ne-tla-nv-hi, Creator God) who presides over things and created the Earth, who is the Cherokee's and the White man's God, descends to earth.

The breeze stirs but settles into ultimate peace and order.

A freshness sweeps the forests around the spiritual center of Tsalagi life.

Leaves rub words that drift over everything, *"Who calls for this revelation."*

Below, two oracles attend, first with a ghost squirrel as counsel and the other supported by historical theology devotees.

Dideyohvsgi, with Black Wolf One at his elbow and his mentor on his shoulder, stands before a round, slight elevation.

Mohi, his beast, and several incarnations of White clergy, including a Moravian missionary, a Baptist fire-breather, and a Presbyterian pacifist, stand primed on the opposite side.

The wind atop Cherokee Rock subsides, and the traitor Mohi steps into the circle. "The Lord says, 'Have you seen this, son of man? Is it a trivial matter for the house of Judah to do detestable things here?'"

Saloli, at his friend's ear, rubs a nose against an earlobe. "Quote from the White man's black book, their Old Testament. I think he claims we're Judah's clansmen."

"Must they fill the land with violence and provoke me to anger?" Mohi points at Dideyohvsgi.

The furry mentor wriggles and switches shoulder sides for self-protection.

"I will not pity or spare them." The speaker shakes his fists in the air, "Although they shout in my ears, I do not listen."

"Open minded, isn't he?" The fuzzy little animal rubs his nose behind Dideyohvsgi's second ear.

Black Wolf Two at Mohi's side growls and ruffles its fur.

His leader pitches a strip of venison, and it calms.

Mohi beckons for the Moravian incarnation.

A slim gentleman in sandals and a ground-length robe removes his large brim hat and fingers a cross that hangs from his neck. "I am of the New Brethren. Our brotherhood brings education and Christianity to the Cherokee from our missions at Spring Place and New Echota. We welcome converts, but standards are high. Forty-five souls have accepted our beliefs since we arrived decades ago. They now live and prosper as civilized members."

"Two per year," Dideyohvsgi's adviser looks at Black Wolf One, "not as many as in a litter of pups. Mohi feeds more deer to your brother."

The animal growls and sits on its haunches, "Better than squirrel."

The mentor wags its white stripe tail, "And who speaks for us?"

"I do."

The gathering turns to the voice.

An elder warrior, revered by the seven clans, steps from a dust devil and extends his walking stick with both hands above his head. "Old Tassle resents the New Brethren and their education and religious indoctrination. The people knew me as a man of peace, who strove to unite those with differences. The unification I preached was a joining, not a doctrine. I refute the Moravian way. It disjoints any potential union."

The dust spins around the visitor, and he blurs to vanish in the whirl.

Mohi points at another chosen accuser.

The Baptist follows the missionary and rolls his eyes to the heavens. "You sinners deny Christ and stand as an obstacle as civilization sweeps these lands. From East to west, we move in trust with God to expand our nation. We offer life, liberty, and the pursuit of happiness! Accept our generosity and grow our country to the western ocean!"

Saloli twists behind Dideyohvsgi's neck and chit-chits.

A single small thunder cloud dumps prolific rainfall in the center of the circle between the adversaries.

From within the storm, a younger warrior emerges.

"Yes, I stood in opposition to White advancement." John Watts withdraws his war club from a waist belt. "The settlers expanded, trusting their God, but ignored the pestilence that ravished my culture. When I accepted their inevitable victory, treaties lied to enable a march westward. Then I resisted, but we were few and weak." The famous leader returns into the deluge.

Black Wolf's brother snarls at Mohi, and the traitor summons his pacifist.

The Presbyterian grasps the Baptist's arm and pulls him away from confrontation.

The minister places his palms together and nods, "The American Board of Commissioners of Foreign Missions provides learned men and women to serve our Cherokee faithful, and we plan an Indian Presbytery."

He extends his arms in welcome. "We build peace and prosperity for our children with cooperation and mutual respect. Walk with us now into that future."

Black Wolf Two howls celebration.

Saloli recoils from the meat eater and hides behind Dideyohvsgi at the belt. Clinging to the waist, the little furry mentor spits at the Watts thunderstorm and rain becomes hail.

With a deer pelt stretched above his head, Son of Stone Cloud protects himself from the storm.

The legendary shaman smiles at the Presbyterian. "Your Presbyteries, boards, and committees do not absolve you, Sir. I reject your invitation to the trail you choose for our destiny. Pander to us no more. Search your heart for what is right and fair. Only then, do not impose but lead yourselves to a better path."

The only child of his illustrious father bows and retreats into the miniature hailstorm.

The ice fall ceases, but dark clouds spread to the horizons.

Mohi pitches his last strip of meat to Black Wolf Two, which the animal devours.

The convert to Christianity raises both hands in the air. "Tsalagi! Abandon our pagan ways. Accept the new religion and blend our culture into theirs for a better tomorrow!"

****

Dideyohvsgi steps into the center of the circle.

He stands for a moment as the breeze stirs his hair and the sun soaks his skin.

The medicine man looks at Black Wolf One and shifts Saloli from the top of his head to a shoulder. "Moravians, Baptists, Presbyterians, the real people and Unetlanvhi – I plead with you, listen to my words. Yes, we desert the old ways and meld with the new. I and a few have not. Am I a pagan?"

Dideyohvsgi pulls a pemmican chunk from his beaded breast plate and feeds his protector. "Pagans worship procedure instead of the Creator, the Allocator. A heathen stands ignorant of the highest. My kind adores and worships no images, remembered men, evil spirits, or luminaries. We bury our dead before the sun sets, if possible."

He turns toward his accuser. "You argue we are primitive, emotive supporters of tradition. We protect our land, the people, and a belief in a most high deity! We bow to no man nor kiss any idol!"

Mohi grips the war club that hangs from his waist.

The boy Enoli's emotions surge into his adult soul. "This is my catharsis! Unetlanvhi is pantheistic. The physical expresses the spiritual. Life is sacred, and too many died."

The grown man falls to his knees.

"There is no 'Sky-Father' or 'Earth-Mother' but only a supreme, a Creator God, who is omnipresent, omnipotent, and omniscient!"

Black Wolf Two attacks as Mohi rips his war club from his belt and charges.

With a howl of blood lust, Dideyohvsgi's protector meets his brother and the assassin.

The crash of impact reverberates above Cherokee Rock.

Momentum and the force of an animalistic charge drives enemies to the edge and off the outcrop.

The shaman steadies his beast at the precipice, but Mohi screams as he plummets earthward.

A traitorous soul turns from human to that of a mocker.

"Upward, Tsalagi." Saloli scratches his medicine man's neck.

Above, from far away, as a buzzard circling, it descends.

The rim of Cherokee Rock dusts from the blast of wind. A Raven Mocker's wings sweep around prey.

Black Wolf One pants with its tongue lapping outside its mouth as the three peer off the outcrop's edge at the ground.

On the rocks below, his brother lies motionless with a broken back, and the predator's beak slashes into the traitor's lifeless chest alongside and eats its heart.

Saloli's whiskers vibrate. "Tsalagi, time for me to go. Mohi's Christian advocates melted away when his morality turned to murder, and so must I. But I hear a voice in the wind with a message to you."

Dideyohvsgi and Black Wolf One step back from the precipice, and Saloli jumps from the outcrop to the top of a towering tree.

"Beast, Unetlanvhi requires you to protect Cherokee Rock." The furry one's white slash tail whips back and forth. "It was your home first, but now becomes the perpetual lodge of the Tsalagi, and you must guard its gates."

The spiritual mentor turns its nose to Dideyohvsgi. "Enoli, Unetlanvhi finds no victor here. It gives humans the freedom to choose, and the wolf that wins is the one you feed."

As peace settles, the squirrel disappears into the foliage.

Its voice floats above the leaves. "Goodbye, my friend. Nourish yourself and face your future."

***

Weeks later, exhausted by stress and travel, the medicine man stands in chest-high cotton and watches Benjamin's log cabin.

Walela hangs wash from a line spread between two poles as Ella, Bella and Lisa laugh and play chase nearby.

New small cabins cluster behind the principal residence and in the rows, several slaves bend their backs and remove weeds from rows by hand.

Dideyohvsgi shifts his pack onto his shoulder and watches the labor.

"You've returned," Ben's voice interrupts the reverie.

The shaman turns. On horseback, with a teenage boy of color straddled before him, they sit their mount in the hot afternoon sun.

"That child one of your slaves?" The healer nods toward the teenager.

The Freedman slips off his horse. "This is Ezra. He grew since your last visit."

"But I see others." The medicine man shrugs to the workers in the fields.

"I don't accept it any more than you. But times change, and I can't take care of this place by myself."

"I remember when you scalped anyone who even used the word slave."

"I've grown old, as you. No scalps anymore." The landowner smiles and extends a hand to his blood brother. "Come on to the house. Walela will be excited to see you, and she fixes supper."

"It's been a while since I ate a proper meal." Dideyohvsgi grasps his friend's handshake.

"Stay with us." The life friend puts his arm around the medicine man's shoulder. "This is your place and can be your home."

"It is a tedious story, but I am never home. A vicious black wolf guards the only lodge that I know."

"Then visit when you wish. It's a new time. Cotton prices climb and…"

Dideyohvsgi looks at his blood brother, "… and what?"

"They discovered gold in Ward's Creek and the Chestatee River's tributaries. Miners flood the state. They call them 'Twenty-Niners'."

"I think we're accustomed to Whites taking our land."

"Maybe, but this bunch is rougher."

"No, you're older." Dideyohvsgi laughs.

Benjamin climbs upon his horse and Ezra jumps behind him. "Come in and see Walela."

"With you." He watches them plod toward the cabin.

***

The slaves across the field stare at the visitor as he passes.

After a moment, he slips the small nugget from his knife sheath and fingers it for a time.

The late afternoon sun glints off the gold.

The medicine man slings the dolomite quartz, sprinkled valuable with precious metal, as far as his strength can hurl the rock.

– END –

ACKNOWLEDGEMENTS

DRT☼Ọ'iᏚᏠᏏᎩᎪᎫᎬᏛᏢᎩᎻᏥᏔᏍᎱᏀᎷᎠᏥᎤᎯᎲᎫᎩᎾ┇ᎾᏒᏂᏃᎯᎤ

The author acknowledges the following contributors to this book:

My wife, who enabled endless hours of research and writing time.

Ella Waters, my paternal grandmother and Dawes Roll signee, who inspired my interest in all things Cherokee - even though we never met.

Ed Fields and Mary Rae, who teach the Cherokee online language classes from the Cherokee Nation. And their language department for expanding my interest in our culture, syllabary and speech. The author reccommends their book, *Journeying Into Cherokee*, for help and encouragement learning the Cherokee Language.

The author, Grace Steel Woodward, who introduced me to Cherokee history through her book, *The Cherokees* published by University of Oklahoma Press, Norman.

ᎠᎡᎢᎦᎣᎢᏍᏉᎢᏚᎤᏯᎠᎫᎬᏋᏈᏗᎯᏈᎳᏬᎭᏛᎦᎮᎹᏣᏋᎣᎯᎲᏚᏯᏇᏓᎧᏄᎯᏃᏊᎤ

ABOUT THE AUTHOR

ᏙᎳᏈ ᏂᏍᏗ

Thank you for reading *Cherokee Rock*. I hope you enjoyed the book and ask you to recommend it to your friends.

That recommendation is important to spread Cherokee culture, history, and language awareness.

I am a citizen of the Cherokee Nation and work daily to learn our Class IV language and our history's nuances.

Married for over fifty years with two children and four grandchildren, I live in Grapevine, Texas. Other than writing, my interests include painting in oils and watercolors, making short films, plus anything that makes my grandchildren happy.

ᎤᎹ (Wa-do Thank you.)

James A. Humphrey

ALSO BY JAMES A. HUMPHREY

ᎠᎡᎢᎣᎤᎥᎦᎧᎨᎩᎪᎫᎬᎭᎮᎯᎰᎱᎲᎳᎴᎵᎶᎷᎸᎹᎺᎻᎼᎽᎾᎿᏀᏁᏂᏃᏄᏅ

This historical novel, *Cherokee Rock,* is book one of the Cherokee Trilogy, the story of the extended Waters family from 1779 through Civil War Reconstruction.

The other two are:

Cherokee Rose, the second book, tells the epic story of Benjamin Waters's half-Cherokee daughter, Ella, who after his death battles pestilence, bigotry, alcoholism, starvation, and a record cold 1838 winter during a forced removal led by white profiteers and her father's murderer to Indian Territory. On the trek, she earns her people's respect and adoration as the Cherokee Rose, then illegally jumps her land allotment and faces a white jury in a trial that sets national precedents for Native American rights.

Cherokee Reel, the trilogy's concluding book, follows Lisa, the frivolous daughter of freedman Benjamin Waters and his wife Walela, who strives to imitate her white socialite philanthropist friend. Cultural conflict, the civil war, her sister's murder, and the death of a beloved husband compels a basic "Who am I?" confrontation with a Confederate demigod's racist immorality that avenges her loved one's deaths and molds her individual and indigenous identity.

All three historical novels are available for purchase at www.cherokeetrilogy.com or from Tsalagi Books, tsalagibooks.com

ᏩᏙ (Wa-do) Thank you.

415